Spirit of the

To. Beryl.
Enjoy the read.
Susan Pope

Susan Pope

This edition includes the folk tale *The Legend of the Jaguar* written as a precursor to this novel

 New Generation Publishing

Susan Pope

Lives in Kent and has been writing since 1990. Spirit of the Jaguar is the second novel she has written as a time-slip historical story. Susan says she loves the research necessary to place her characters within their true historical setting and to enable readers to enter their lives and times. Susan leads a women's writing group called Medway Mermaids in Gillingham and was an inaugural member of The Write Idea writing group for all, which currently meets in Leybourne.

Other works by Susan Pope
Lighter Than Air
Bedtime Stories for Grown-Ups
Available from Amazon in paperback and Amazon Kindle

Books edited by Susan Pope
Murder at Chatham Grande by R H Taylor
Available from Amazon in paperback and Amazon Kindle

Edited by Susan Pope in association with others
Mermaid Tales – an anthology from Medway Mermaids
A Wealth of Words – an anthology from The Write Idea
Available from FeedaRead.com self-publishing website.

Contents

This book is dedicated to the members, past and present of Kent Writing Groups: Medway Mermaids and The Write Idea. Without your encouragement and support none of my books would ever have been written. Thank you all.

Prologue

Mount Yaguar, Peru, 1931

I cannot imagine how we will find an entrance. It is four hundred years since Tlalli came to this mountain. Earthquakes since then could have closed all her entrances. Perhaps they never existed, and the whole thing is a fable, a story that has taken on a life of its own.

I can see him scanning all the ridges and crevices looking for a way up. I shade my eyes and look up also. On the highest slope to my right I see a movement. Is it a bird stretching its wings? I squint and steady my gaze. It is the briefest glimpse but I freeze. A cat, I'm sure it was a cat, the shape and colour of…a jaguar?

I bite my tongue not to call out. It is gone now and I look to him. Did he see it also? He is grinning at me, a look of triumph. He points to the exact spot. 'That is the way we must go,' he says.

My spirits drop, perhaps a thousand feet, and I wish I was anywhere on earth except where I am. He takes one of the saddlebags. Inside he puts food, our water bottles and two electric torches with spare batteries, and loops it across his shoulders.

I feel a hollow void inside me, and am sure history is now repeating itself; only our identities are changed. He comes to me and takes hold of my hand, leading me in the climb, and I do not resist. It is as if I have to do this although there is no sane reason why I should. I am not a prisoner, but there is nowhere I can flee to, and I feel invisible ropes pulling at me from the past.

1

Christina

April 1930, London, England.
Today should be the highlight of my year. Now, as our car moves at a snail's pace in this long procession up The Mall, my stomach churns. Outside, I can hear a busker playing ragtime on his trumpet. People press forward on the pavement, laughing and singing in holiday mood, and there's a carnival atmosphere of expectation and excitement. I lock my door, afraid someone will pull it open, exposing me in my finery as if I'm on public display in a zoo.

Grace's eyes are watching me, hawk-like. 'Christina, my dear,' she says in her coaxing voice, 'you look as if you're going to the tower, not to be presented to the King and Queen of England. Please relax, and try to smile.'

Her perception brings me up short, but a smile fails to appear. She has coached me to portray the refined young lady, but I feel as if a cage is closing round, hemming me in, and I want to kick and rage against it. Far from coming out, it feels more like caving in, to their expectations. Is this what I want? What is the point of me being a debutante?

'Here,' says Daddy, pulling out his hip-flask, 'have a sip.'

'No, Hubert.' Grace puts out her hand. 'She can't greet the Queen reeking of brandy.'

Daddy laughs. 'Not brandy, Grace, vodka laced with orange. It'll steady her nerves.'

Grace tuts. 'Well, tip some in this,' she says, removing a small crystal glass from the little wooden cabinet set into the partition of her chauffeur-driven Rolls.

The trumpeter is now accompanied by a chorus of rowdy singers. As my medicine is measured, I look from my father to Grace. I know it's not nerves though my mind is in turmoil. I had been looking forward to this day for months, but for some reason I cannot fathom, I find my resolve is slipping away; everything is changing.

I can't admit it, not to either of them. Daddy has been my only family since Mamma and Tom died, and I have missed him since I came to stay with Grace in London. Lady Grace Drummond Hay, once my mother's closest friend, is now mine. Guiding me in the social graces, she has become more the sister I never had. How can I let them down after everything they've done?

I sip the vodka and it burns my throat, making me gag. Grace laughs, and lights a cigarette in her long ivory holder. Looking through the window I raise a smile at last, but it's with relief for we have reached Queen Victoria's Memorial. All the cars swing round and point towards the palace gates, like ants in a line.

Free of the gapers, my thoughts turn inwards once more. There is no way to explain my sudden reticence over their plans to launch me into London high society when I don't really understand it myself. I touch the white silk gown falling in folds at my feet. It's a design by Reville of Hanover Square; the matching diamante shoes wink, half-hidden in the foot-well. This outfit alone has cost Daddy over one hundred guineas and is meant to make me look the part. I've a further six gowns with matching accessories closeted in my wardrobe at Grace's Mayfair apartment, to wear to all the balls and parties I'm expected to attend, including my own, tomorrow.

I refused to have my long hair cut in a modern bob, so my pale blonde locks have been scraped back into a chignon. The three absurd white ostrich feathers sit heavily on the back of my head. This is to honour the Prince of Wales, though I doubt Prince Edward will even be there now his name is linked with dubious lovers and ladies of the night, as was his grandfather's before him. I feel I have more in common with these royal rebels against polite society than I have the courage to show.

Our car passes through the gates of Buckingham Palace. I breathe slowly, knowing I must steel myself to get through the next few hours. One thing is certain: I have no intention of hooking a financially eligible husband, which is apparently the whole reason for this extravagant year of pomp and pageantry.

At last we stop under the portico. The door is opened by a royal footman and I'm escorted into the great entrance hall. We walk through corridors ablaze with enormous chandeliers and up the grand staircase towards the ballroom where the presentations will take place. Grace, ever elegant, is wearing her latest Victor Stiebel creation: a long green patterned gown with matching turban hat, while Daddy, always debonair, is in full morning dress, carrying his grey top hat. Now we are separated, as they will apparently view the proceedings from the far end of the huge ballroom. Slightly bewildered, I follow other debs-in-waiting and we are lined up on little gilt chairs to await entry to the royal presence. I don't know any of these girls, so I fix my eyes on the magnificent royal portraits displayed on the walls.

'Hello,' says a voice close beside me. Startled, I find myself looking at a face which reflects my own uncertainty. 'My name's Anne,' she says. 'What's your name?'

'Hello, Anne,' I reply. 'I'm Christina.' Anne is a rather plain, dumpy girl but she has a friendly face and hasn't dangled a title with her name which is rather refreshing. I am immediately comforted by her presence and her kindness in speaking to me, so I say, 'Are you looking forward to meeting Queen Mary and King George?'

She looks abashed. 'To be honest, no.' Her voice drops to a whisper. 'I have been dreading this day since I was ten. Mother said I would have to come out at seventeen, as there was no other way for me to find a husband, because I was so ugly.' She gives an embarrassed giggle.

She's certainly no beauty, but I catch my breath thinking this a dreadful thing for a mother to say. 'Oh, I hope you prove her wrong. Your friendly smile is more endearing than the haughty expressions on some of the so-called beauties here today. If you want to catch a husband I'm sure you'll have no trouble.'

She positively beams. 'As second daughter, I don't have much option, but thank you for your kind words.' She grips my arm. 'You won't have such problems. You're the most beautiful girl here today, and believe me I've seen a lot of debs.'

Now I'm the one embarrassed, so I just smile and tell her not to speak too loudly or we might both have our eyes scratched out. At this point we are moved near the head of the queue and given our instructions to watch the girls in front of us. Anne is before me and I follow her short, plump figure making her entrance. She gives me courage, and I think I must get to know her better.

As I enter the ballroom I blink against the glare of flashing lights. Thousands of diamonds and gem stones flicker like fire flies, as jewellery worn by royalty and guests is caught in reflected beams from the room's vast illuminations. I fix my smile and walk as Grace has shown me, placing my feet as if they are following a single line, head up looking straight towards Her Majesty.

My title and name are boomed out by a court official: 'The Honourable Christina Victoria Freeman, daughter of Lord Freeman of Madeley.' It stings that my mother's name is not mentioned, for had she lived, I know this day would have made her very proud.

I manage to perform the deep curtsey and keep my eyes on Queen Mary. Her wrinkled face smiles weakly and she looks rather bored. As I take the required three steps sideways to be in front of His Majesty the King, I have a weird sense of having been here before, or at least having been in a royal court before. An image of being dressed in a long white gown and paying homage to a King or a great Lord flits across my mind. When I make my curtsey to the King I sense, more than remember, I must not look at the royal persons; that is forbidden on pain of death. I shake away this macabre shadow, and as I follow in Anne's wake, out through the opposite door, she turns and smiles again. It is then I realise I have crossed paths with this friendly soul before. When or where I have no inkling, but the emotions I feel about her seem strangely linked to a past I cannot catch, as the fleeting images slip away like silent moths in the night.

2

Tlalli

1532 Willkapampa, Tawantinsuyu (The Inca Empire)
Tlalli stood on the very edge of the precipice. Her dark eyes stared, hypnotised by the charging white foam as it churned through the narrow gorge far below. Dizzy, she put out her hands, kneeling on the flat granite ledge, jutting over the vast emptiness. With eyes closed, she listened to the river's great voice roaring through the canyon, muting out every other sound.

Ispaca leaned close, looking over her shoulder. 'What you dreaming about, little sister?' The presence of his bronzed body wrapped in a single loin cloth was comforting, but her disturbing dream from the previous night clouded the scene.

She shivered. 'Strange men came to our village. They frightened me.' She looked into her brother's eyes. 'They scared you too.'

With predictable boyish bravado he pulled a face. She felt a sharp jab in her lower back and struggling to keep her balance on the narrow ledge she gasped, grabbing at his arm. He dodged away, singing out loud and clear. 'Monkey got y' tail!' He skipped along the granite path worn flat by a thousand years of footfalls, laughing like their pet macaw.

Tlalli's momentary shock at nearly tumbling into the gorge turned to fury and a strong urge to kick her mischievous brother. She ran after him, her long black hair flying, her voice shrieking the only bad words she knew.

'Smelly-boy!' she screamed. 'Issy is a smelly-boy!' She kicked her leg out into thin air for Ispaca had already disappeared. She followed, clad only in her thin tunic, bare arms and legs shining and bronzed like her brother's. The path snaked away into the dense forest in the clouds. As she followed the twists and turns of the trail she slowed, listening as the roar from the river, thousands of feet below, receded. Ispaca's teasing over her dream faded as she tuned into a different world.

Thick foliage enveloped her and a fine mist rose from the dripping flora. Leaves rustled overhead. Through gaps in the green canopy, she saw the steep escarpments of snow-capped mountains glistening far above. Damp ferns brushed her skin and she paused. The forest floor, thick with leaf mould, buzzed and clicked with insects, some whirring round her head. Swooping birds shrieked, while hidden monkeys howled. Now, which one was Ispaca?

The distinctive call of the blue and red macaw, roosting high in the tree tops, sounded right over her head. She looked up and there he was, swinging from a branch on the cupuaca tree. He picked off one of the brown fuzzy-skinned fruits and hurled it at her. Tlalli was too quick and the over-ripe fruit splattered on the ground.

'Smelly-boy, Issy!' she shouted, stamping her foot with renewed temper. He answered with the deep throaty boom of a howler monkey.

She shouted louder, 'Monkey will be in a whole load of trouble if we don't fill our baskets and get home soon!' Younger, but wiser than Ispaca, she knew better than to cross their mother's orders.

The growl of a forest bear sounded behind her, so real her skin tingled. She looked around, half expecting to see the quizzical brown face of the bear, its eyes ringed with pale circles. Ispaca's laugh rang out from the treetop. She shook her fist in a feigned adult gesture, aping her mother. He grabbed more of the cupuaca fruit and dropped them into the basket on his back. Shinning down the tree trunk he landed at her feet.

'My basket's half-full already,' he said, and laughing again he ran off barefoot, deeper into the forest.

'That's not fair,' she said, but she ran on, her sandals flapping as the llama hide soles hit the ground; her feet not yet hardened like her brother's. She panted up to him, resigned to her status as younger sister. 'I can't climb the big trees.'

He stopped and took some of the fruit from his basket tossing them into hers. 'Best I teach you then, Dreamy Head.'

'We're supposed to gather sarsaparilla today,' she reminded him, ignoring his sarcasm.

'I know where there are lots of those bushes,' he said, 'deeper in the forest. Come on, Tilly.' He ran off again, leaving her to trail after him along the narrow winding pathways made by animals and people, all looking for food.

Mother would turn the sarsaparilla into a healing balm. Another day they might collect the red berries of the molle-tree for making drink. Most valued were the coca leaves. Father would trade these with the Inca people who lived over the mountains and beyond the rivers. Like father, the Incas chewed the leaves, but Tlalli didn't know why this was special, only that father always came back with sacks of corn or salt, foods their tribe did not have.

She stumbled along to keep up with Ispaca. At eleven years of age her brother sometimes acted as if he was already grown up. At other times, like now, he played the fool. Tlalli would soon be ten, and secretly she thought Ispaca very clever. He could mimic all the animals and birds of the forests and mountains, even throwing his voice from tree to tree or across the canyons, answering his own calls.

Their father, Kusi, had told Ispaca, 'Your talent is a gift from the gods. You will be a great hunter when you grow to be a man.' To Tlalli he had said, 'Your dreams bring messages from the gods, so this means you are also a special child.' Ispaca said she made it all up to get father's attention. She tried not to care, and hoped her father would always think of her as special.

She ran as fast as she could to keep up with her brother. The fruits made her basket heavy but she wouldn't grumble for Ispaca had shared his spoils with her. When she caught up with him she called out, 'Where are the sarsaparilla bushes?'

'Shush up, bird-brain,' he whispered, wagging his finger. 'When you're this deep in the forest you have to keep very quiet.' He unhooked the basket from his back and dropped it to the ground. 'First, I'll teach you to climb up high. If bear or jaguar come along you need to disappear.' He pointed up at a tree. 'That's the safest place, though they can climb too, but it's safer than the ground.'

Tlalli felt a chill and moved closer to Ispaca. She looked up at the tree; an enormous old nut tree, its crown disappearing into the high canopy. She couldn't see how anyone could climb this tree for it had no low branches. Next to it, a dead tree's spindly trunk leaned over like a drunken man. Ispaca grasped the dead tree trunk and dragged it closer to the great nut tree. He pushed and shoved until he'd wedged the trunk against the nut tree's huge girth. Swift as a monkey, Ispaca climbed up, wedging it further onto the trunk. It made a steep incline against the bigger tree; a perfect nursery slope for her to learn the skill of climbing high into the forest canopy.

Ispaca made a sudden and very rapid descent, almost falling. 'Hurry, Tilly, now's the time for you to learn to climb, double quick!'

She didn't question her brother's command and dropped her basket. Ispaca stood behind her, helping her stretch her arms and legs to find the notches in the trunk. He guided her as high up as they could climb. She felt Ispaca's arms curl around her, securing her hold on the tree. He pointed down to a thin animal trail on the forest floor, only visible from above.

She couldn't see anything but she heard, first mewling, like a baby crying and then a deep low roar. The sound echoed around the tree and her heart thumped like a drum. It seemed so loud she was afraid she would give their hiding place away. On the trail a little way off was the distinctive spotted coat of a jaguar. The animal was engrossed, pulling a carcass towards a clearing further on. There was the source of the mewling: two tiny cubs nervously awaiting the arrival of their mother and their dinner.

This was the first time Tlalli had seen a jaguar and she stared, afraid to even blink. She knew jaguars were fierce and would attack, especially if they had cubs. She tried not to move, watching the mother cat pull her catch over to her kits. They gave little squeals of delight, barely waiting for their mother to rip open the belly of her quarry. Tlalli thought it looked like a monkey.

She remembered the campfire stories of the jaguar god Toquri and his goddess Izella. The storytellers retold the history from ancient times and always said these gods originated in this part of their land. Jaguars normally lived in the river jungles far below. If seen in the cloud forest near the mountains, they must be descended from the gods. She wondered if this family could be the sacred animals.

Her legs ached and she began to wobble, but Ispaca tightened his arms round her. They sat entwined, straddled on the tree trunk, their rivalry forgotten. Together, they watched the jaguar family until the cats had their fill from the carcass. The mother dragged the remains under a tree and buried it in the thick leaf mould that smelt of the forest. She led the family away, deeper into the undergrowth and eventually out of the children's sight.

The following day Tlalli watched the Incas travelling on the road high up on the steep hillside. Her family lived in one of the stone houses perched on the lower, sheltered slopes. Nearby on the narrow terraces, cut like wide sweeping steps going up and down the hillside, the tribe grew food.

Her eyes swept over the jungle-like vegetation of the forest, to where the road had been carved into the rock-face and paved with stone by the Inca road-builders. This formed the boundary of her life. Other than going into the forest, or down to the hot humid gorge below, she had never ventured further than this hillside and didn't know what lay beyond.

The Incas weren't enemies of the children's tribe but rulers of the region. She sensed mistrust around her, and suspicion when strangers entered the tribe's territory, even Incas. While Tlalli and all the children and women of the foraging groups hid, their men appeared from the bushes. They materialised like ghosts, carrying their bows and arrows, slings and maces. Among them she could see her father, Kusi Manari, the tribe's curaca (chief).

Tlalli hid in the bushes close to her brother and watched their father group his men behind him, waiting in full view of the Incas on the road. As she jostled with Ispaca to keep out of sight, the long full skirt she wore today snagged on the spiky brambles, dragging in the dirt. She wanted to see the scene unfolding on the hillside and she gathered up the precious skirt, woven by her mother from alpaca fleece, a privilege for the curaca's daughter. Her fingers twisted nervously around her long black braids which fell almost to her waist.

Ispaca stood still as a rock on his strong bare legs, daring his sister to move. He ran his hands down the sleeved jerkin covering his body; wiry dark hair fell loose on his shoulders. Tlalli's chest swelled with pride for her big brother, so like their father, a true jungle Indian. She had the same big oval eyes and heart-shaped face as her brother, but she also resembled her mother who carried their mountain Indian heritage.

Through gaps in the bushes, she could make out Inca soldiers carrying weapons. Also porters, and llamas used as pack animals, heavily laden. At the front of the group the banner of the Sapa Inca, Atahualpa, fluttered in the breeze. She couldn't see any sign of the royal litter, which meant he wasn't there. A silence descended on both groups as they viewed one another. All she could hear were buzzing insects, bird calls and the distant roar from the river far below. Tlalli felt a tightness in the air from the veiled hostility between the tribe and the Incas.

The banner up on the high road began to wave from side to side. Ispaca whispered, 'The Incas want to talk.'

'What about?' said Tlalli, perhaps a little too loudly.

'Shush up, silly girl.' He gripped her wrist until she winced. The Incas made no move to descend into the tribe's territory. Tlalli was stiff from standing still but scared to move. She tried holding her breath but her heart began thumping so loudly she had to let it out again. Her brother glared at her.

More of the tribe had arrived from their hunting and farming tasks. Now about fifty men grouped behind their father. He signalled them to go forward up the hill. Tlalli peered from her hiding place, relieved to see her father surrounded and protected by his armed warriors as they walked to within shouting distance.

'Hail, Manari!' called the leading Inca, using the language of the people. 'We bring news from Cajamarca and would speak with you.' His voice echoed against the granite rock-face and down into the valley. When Incas came they usually wanted to collect tribute (taxes), sometimes to trade, or to seek safe passage, repaid with goods and favours. But today, Tlalli felt things seemed different and her father, who could be a very patient man, waited. Eventually the leading Inca left the road, and with a group of his armed soldiers, he walked towards Kusi.

She could just see through the bushes to where her father spoke with the Inca. After a lot of pointing and discussion between the two leaders, they seemed to come to an agreement. Father led the Incas down one of the trails into the forest. Behind them the porters guided all the loaded pack animals.

'Where are they going?' Tlalli asked her brother.

He shook his head. 'I don't know, but that trail leads to the old goldmine in the Yaguar Mountain.'

She had heard lots of stories about the Yaguar Mountain, for it was not very far from their village. 'Is there gold there?' she asked.

'No, not now,' Ispaca replied. 'I've been there with Father. It's very old but the tunnels and shafts remain and animals use it for shelter.'

'Perhaps the mother cat is there,' said Tlalli.

'Maybe,' said her brother.

Tlalli thought about this. She hoped that if the jaguar family from the forest had gone to live in the mountain they would not be caught.

3

London

May 1930, London, England.
London wakes early, and although the windows are shut tight, sounds seep round the frames. The noisy Mayfair motor traffic mixes with the steady clip-clop of horse-drawn drays and carts. Trams hum on the conductor rails and news vendors shout out the early morning headlines. A wave of nostalgia peeks my thoughts. Life in London doesn't compare with galloping across the North Downs in the early morning on Delilah, trying to catch up with Daddy on his bay hunter. Although I suppose it does have a certain charm of its own, and is how every morning now starts for me in Grace's swish apartment.

It's been refurbished Art Deco by an American stylist and has every modern facility: central heating; en suite bathrooms; a fitted kitchen and the latest luxury sofas and soft furnishings, and of course, modern art displayed on every wall and table. In comparison, Madeley Hall seems a draughty old-world mansion, but I did love my life there; all my memories of childhood with little Tom, dragging his gammy leg, as he followed me everywhere. He was only eight when he and Mamma died from influenza. They caught it when Mamma insisted on visiting the holy shrine at Lourdes.

The events around this time are etched irrevocably in my mind. They went into the pool together, which Mamma prayed would provide a cure for Tom's lame leg. I thought the waters grey and foul and had refused to go in. This was at the end of a wonderful family holiday in the south of France. We'd visited the Camargue where I had been entranced to see the white horses running wild. To my young, impressionable-self, they seemed magical and I begged and cajoled Daddy through the rest of the holiday and after we returned home, to have a white pony of my own, thinking only of myself.

But it wasn't to be. At least not then. Mamma and Tom were the first to succumb to the illness, then we all caught it. But Tom was already weak, and he and Mamma died in the infirmary. I don't think Daddy ever fully recovered from the effects of the illness, or losing Mamma and his brave little boy. After that, I had my pony, and everything I wanted. I was much indulged, but I never regained my previous innocent trust in god to know what is best for me.

As I lie in bed, still half asleep, I reach back into the night recalling my dream. This is the second night I've had the same dream: I see a girl running, her dark hair flying behind her like a horse's mane. I feel the soft caress of sandy soil on my feet and I sense this child is me. I'm running, wild and free, laughing with another. A strange, but familiar feeling tightens in my chest. If she isn't me – then who is she?

When Daddy arrived in London last week, it was with the sad news of my Uncle Peter's death. Sir Peter Bosworth was actually my Great Uncle, and Daddy revealed that I was the sole heir to his estate; a fact I had never known. It had all been arranged during his visit to us, the year after Mamma and Tom's passing, when I was twelve. No one would understand how keenly I felt this news for I only met him that one time. He had lived in Peru for many years, indulging in the life of an amateur explorer. Since then he has corresponded with me about his amazing life in South America and I have longed to go there and visit him.

He gave me a precious gold pendant. I remember Uncle Peter's excited face; his full set of whiskers wagging up and down as he spoke; his blue eyes shining like a magician about to produce a rabbit from his hat. I recall holding the pendant while he explained it represented a jaguar, probably a god, worshipped by ancient people. As I was only twelve, it had to be locked away in our safe. Daddy insisted it was too valuable for me to wear and I remember my disappointment at not being allowed to keep it. I suppose I forgot about it until Daddy brought this piece of ancient jewellery with him to London. Apparently I can now look after it myself and wear it. When I put it on I had the strangest sensation; a sadness for all the years it had been locked in the dark and a curiosity to know who owned it in the past.

Daddy and Grace took me to see Uncle Peter's solicitor here in London. My head reeled with the long list of uncle's assets. There are bonds and investments totalling over fifty thousand pounds; his house in Berkshire, which has been put up for sale; and his home and vast collection of antiquities in Perú. Daddy wanted the solicitor to arrange for these to be sold also, but I spoke up and said no. Everyone was surprised by the strength of my feelings. I am only seventeen but I'm determined to have my own way over this. If I'm old enough to consider a husband, then I'm old enough to make such decisions, and in the end Daddy agreed. I have asked for a detailed inventory to be drawn up, and for photographs of the house and contents to be sent to me. If there is any way I can travel to Perú to see them before they are disposed of, I will go, whatever Daddy or Grace might think.

After breakfast this morning, Daddy gives me an item of post from home. He had held this back until my palace ordeal was over. It is Uncle Peter's final letter to me, posted before his death. Just holding it unread, opens up a well of sadness, so I go to my room.

He had always written to me about his explorations of ancient sites and the artefacts he had found. The letter says he is unable to travel owing to a decline in his health. He speaks of a new project, some translation work that occupies his time while he is unwell. The original documents, written in old Spanish, date from the sixteenth century, and were the work of a Spanish chronicler. This man had written down stories told by some indigenous Peruvians about events during the conquest.

In his letter uncle also says, the one he has just begun to translate into English, might be of interest to me, as it talks about a gold talisman shaped like a jaguar. I hear my own sharp intake of breath and my fingers touch the pendant at my neck. Coincidence? Perhaps, but I wonder if Uncle Peter finished this translation before he died and where I might see it. I must tell the solicitor that nothing in the house is to be touched. I am so grieved that he has gone; I have lost an understanding heart.

Now the London Season has officially begun, I must turn my thoughts to the present. Daddy hopes I make the most of this opportunity even if I don't find love or a husband. Tonight, my debs' ball is the first of the season. By 7.0.pm I'm sitting in Grace's car trying not to crush the new couture gown of palest blue, chosen to match my eyes.

I'm full of apprehension over tonight. Grace is fussing for me to hold my head up to keep Mamma's diamond tiara in perfect place. As we arrive at Grosvenor house there is a buzz of activity on the pavement. Press photographers' flash-bulbs pop and glare. Men in black evening dress and young debs in silk, satin and diamonds giggle and chatter on the forecourt. As the hosts for this event we are ushered through first, to greet the waiting guests. Daddy is laughing and hands me a glass of champagne. While a pianist plays jazz I feel like the queen bee, standing at the door of the ballroom to welcome the excited debs and the hopeful young men. Grace has also hired a dance band. Maybe it will be worth going through this ridiculous pantomime just to enjoy the dancing.

'Hello again,' says a familiar voice. It is Anne, my friend from the palace. 'Christina, this is my older sister, Isabelle.' I'm introduced to a taller version of Anne, who seems to have the same friendly disposition as her sister, so I hope they are both lucky in finding a suitor tonight.

'Look out, 'laughs Isabelle. 'Here comes David.' She steps aside and Sir Michael Lewis's son, David, is the first male guest I greet. He displays charming manners, kissing Grace's hand and then mine. But when he speaks he sounds rather dreary, and full of his own self-importance. And so the arrival of guests and introductions continue for around thirty minutes, until I feel I could scream and long to sit down.

Most of the girls have Marcel-waved, short hair. To me they all look the same while I now stand apart. The young men queue in line with the debs to be received. They are all like the first, speaking only of their own lives and achievements, which don't amount to much. Else they are shy and tongue-tied, with spotty, adolescent faces, making me feel acutely embarrassed on their behalf. Grace is nudging me to acknowledge a new arrival. He bows to us and kisses our hands, just as all the others have done.

'Good evening, ladies. I'm Sam Watson, eldest son of the Earl of Langley. I'm very pleased to meet you.' He looks at me with soft brown eyes and I wonder if he is different from the rest. 'How are you enjoying your time in London, Miss Freeman?'

I am right, for he is the first to ask me anything. I also know he must carry the same title as myself, but he hasn't mentioned this. I find I'm tongue-tied but manage to say, 'My hostess is taking great care to see I have a wonderful time.' I feel the colour in my cheeks creep up.

'Please may I request the pleasure of the first dance with you, Miss Freeman? Although,' he adds, 'I have to admit to not being a very good dancer.' He laughs as he says this which sets me giggling like an embarrassed schoolgirl. He is so very handsome and I struggle to give him a coherent answer. Now I cannot wait for the dancing to begin and to ask him to call me Christina.

When I eventually fall into bed around 2.00am, it is the first time in this long week I don't immediately think of the girl who seemed to have lived a long time ago and now resides in my strange dreams. I'm remembering Sam; his smiling face, his rather clumsy dancing, the way he made me laugh and feel embarrassed and happy, all at the same time. My hand automatically touches my pendant making me wonder about what my future can possibly hold.

Is this talisman my oracle? My head is still full of champagne bubbles and the jazzy tunes we danced to. It is hard to reconcile that now I seem to be living in two separate worlds of night and day. In spite of these puzzles, I fall asleep, and my mind opens to every possibility.

4

The Legend

1532 Willkapampa, Tawantinsuyu (The Inca Empire)
When the sun disappeared behind the mountains, darkness swept the Andean valley. At the tribe's village on the edge of the forest, Tlalli crept from her bed. She should have been at home asleep but she lay, shivering in the damp grasses, listening to the men grouped round the campfire, where her father conversed with his brothers and the tribe's elders.

She had been taught the tribal history by her father: how his grandfather had been the curaca of this Manari tribe when they had lived in the jungle on the far side of the mountains. In Great Grandfather's day the Inca ruler, Tupac Inca, had expanded the Inca Empire into the jungle called the Antisuyo and made the people who lived there his subjects. Great Grandfather had been forced to move his tribe to this part of the region called the Willkapampa. In return, they were given homes, clothes, food and livestock to begin a new life with the mountain Indians already living there.

Her mother, Neneti had laughed when she told Tlalli and Ispaca how the jungle Manari people grudgingly adapted to the more mountainous region and learnt new skills from her tribe, the Q'ero: farming on terraces; keeping llamas and alpacas for their valuable fleeces; spinning and weaving. Eventually they accepted this new way of life and Neneti and Kusi had married. But the tribe still retained many of the old jungle ways, like the nightly campfire, with its story-telling and traditional music whilst following the spiritual beliefs of both tribes. Tlalli crept close to the warmth of the fire to hear what her father said to the men gathered around.

'Strange invaders have come from the sea,' she heard. 'There are only a few of them, but they ride on giant animals, appearing like beasts with two heads. Their faces are pale with long hair on their chins and they dress like gods.' She could see her father stirring the fire with a long stick. Sparks flew, crackling up into the night sky. He spoke with a fierce anger. 'They have already attacked other tribes and killed many people.'

Tlalli almost stopped breathing. She had seen these strange beings in her dreams, exactly as father had just told the elders. She wriggled closer, to hear her father's words better.

'The Sapa Inca has been taken prisoner and the strangers have demanded a huge ransom in gold and silver for Atahualpa's life.' Kusi spoke slowly, controlling his anger. The men grouped round the fire remained silent. Tlalli had been taught silence was important, giving time

16

for thought, and a mark of respect to the speaker. Her father stood, wrapping his red and black wool cloak round his shoulders. She felt she would burst with love and pride as she watched him silhouetted by the firelight, wearing his woven and feathered headpiece, which marked him out as the curaca.

Father began speaking again. 'All the temples and Inca palaces in the cities and towns are being stripped of their gold. They are even robbing the graves of the ancestors, such is the greed of these invaders for gold.' He paused, spitting into the flames as a sign of his contempt. 'We have been asked by these Incas from Cuzco to protect the treasures from the Sun Temple and to hide them.'

Tlalli sensed the men grouped around the fire seemed uneasy.

'What do we gain in return for this favour, for it surely puts us in danger from these hostile intruders?' said father's brother, Uncle Tutsi.

Her father turned to him. 'The Incas have agreed to protect us from the strangers provided we continue to give allegiance to the Sapa Inca.' He lowered his voice and only Tlalli's sharp young ears enabled her to hear what was meant only for the tribal elders. 'In this gold hoard are some of the Inca's sacred treasures, including the great Punchao. It would be punishable by death to touch these, yet they have given me these assurances and twenty sacks of corn and fifty of salt, so I think it was a fair trade.' Her father dipped his bowl in the cooking pot and all the other men then followed.

She thought about the strangers who'd appeared in her dream. She tried to picture the animals ridden by the invaders. In her dream she had thought they were fearsome, magical beasts, not like any animal she had ever seen. They were much bigger than llamas but not cats like jaguars. She wondered about the jaguar family and the Inca's golden treasures now hidden in the old mine. She made a vow: I will go back to the forest and find the jaguars again, with or without Ispaca.

Her eyes grew heavy, but a lone piper was playing softly by the campfire, entrancing her with haunting notes. She knew the piper was Paullu, a rather handsome boy and a friend of Ispaca. Every day Paullu and his father took the tribe's llamas and alpacas up to the high pastures above the Inca road, where the grazing was good. The fleece of the alpacas were softer than the feathers of the humming birds. Like all herdsmen, Paullu played a quena flute and sometimes panpipes. He made all these instruments himself, out of bone and bamboo, just as his father had taught him. She liked Paullu and when he and Ispaca went off together Tlalli tried to follow them. Ispaca would be cross with her, but Paullu always laughed and his smile filled her with joy; so did his beautiful music.

The notes sounded so sweet and soft, she stayed where she was, lying in the grasses, to listen just a little longer. Then the storyteller took

Paullu's place by the fire. His name was Egecati and he began the enchanting tale of two brothers' journey to seek their fortunes. Tlalli loved this story, called The Legend of the Jaguar, more than any other. As she listened to the familiar words that had been passed by mouth from one generation to the next, she thought again about the Yaguar Mountain, now with its hidden treasure.

She became wide awake listening with sharp ears as the storyteller told how the greedy brother, who was also called Egecati, gave his first-born baby daughter to the jaguar god in exchange for gold. Although she always fretted that the baby had been given to the jaguar, she remembered the little girl had been called Tlalli, which means Earth. The god Toquri turned her into a beautiful jaguar goddess and named her Izella.

Tlalli wondered what it would be like to be able to change her shape from human to animal and back again. Since the day she and Ispaca had seen the jaguar family in the cloud forest, she had been convinced these were the sacred cats, descended from the gods. As she listened to the story once more it took on a deeper, more magical meaning. Would she ever learn the goddess's secret and have the power to change her shape into a golden jaguar? She drew her feet up under her skirt, hugging her knees for warmth.

She tried to imagine what she would do if she had this magical power. Could she use it to do good? Would she be able to help her family by becoming a jaguar? She couldn't think how that might help them. Then she remembered Father's words had revealed these strange men were enemies to all their people. Could a jaguar frighten them away?

The storyteller raised his voice and clapped his hands bringing her out of her reverie. He was mimicking the sound of thunder caused by the jaguar god's anger with the greedy brother. Her eyes grew heavy and soon she fell asleep.

Tlalli felt herself being lifted up. She opened her eyes and looked into her father's face as he carried her home. 'Would you have given me away in exchange for gold?' she asked him.

She heard his deep throaty voice. 'Of course I would. A girl child is of little use, not like a son.'

She gasped and fought back tears blurring her vision. Then she saw a big smile cross his face and he hugged her tighter, chuckling softly.

'Perhaps not you, my daughter, for you are a special child.'

Yes, she thought, I have dreams and visions. My father knows what these mean and uses the knowledge to keep us safe.

As father carried her home, Tlalli could hear the storyteller imitating the greedy brother's howls and cries. Because of his greed he couldn't return to his family. He had lost everything and so, as the story went, Egecati began to roam the mountains, hills and forests.

Tlalli knew the end of the story, how he became a shaman, which means a wise man, and how he would urge everyone he met to listen to the words of the gods and obey them. He would tell how Toquri commanded an earthquake to seal the mountain called Yaguar, to keep away all gold-seekers. Any person who tried to take gold from this mountain, would be cursed, and lose everything they possessed. For the Yaguar Mountain is protected by the Spirit of the Jaguar: the god Toquri, his goddess Izella, and all their descendants forever.

The storyteller would also tell the children that Egecati still roamed their land. When they asked if he was the shaman, he would laugh and say, 'Perhaps I am; perhaps I'm not.' Tlalli liked to think he was, and that he also knew the secrets of the Yaguar Mountain.

5

Sam

When Grace wakes she sends the maid out to buy the first editions. We breakfast in her bedroom and giggle over the society pages, but it is usually only the flamboyant celebrities caught doing something outrageous, that make it into the papers. Grace scans through them and reads out snippets she think will interest me. Nothing I hear seems to equal the quality of Grace's own features published in the American press. She is a freelance journalist but works mainly for Hearst Newspapers of New York. Since her husband Robert died she has rejoined the world of journalism. She writes travel features but never contributes to the society pages. I admire Grace for she is on an equal footing with male journalists and highly thought of by William Randolph Hearst, owner of that newspaper group. She is someone to aspire to.

'Are you seeing Sam again today, Christina?' she asks me.

'Oh, yes.' I begin to blush. 'I think he's planning something special.'

'Like a proposal, perhaps?' She laughs.

'Oh Grace, no! We've only known each other three months and dated less than that.' I sigh, thinking about Sam. He is so very good looking and he has escorted me to all the society venues. We've visited Ranelagh gardens to enjoy alfresco tea on the terrace and to view the flower show. Then he took me to The Theatre Royal, Drury Lane where we saw Noel Coward's musical *Bitter Sweet,* now in its second year. He's contrived to be at every ball I've attended during the season. Of course, when other hopeful suitors request a dance my card is always full. Grace is rather keen on him and frequently invites him for morning coffee or afternoon tea.

'Half the debs in London would give their eye-teeth to be in your shoes.' She folds the papers and prepares to go for her bath. 'I've seen how he looks at you with those big, brown puppy-dog eyes.' She smiles and then puts on her serious face. 'I promised your mother that when the time was right I would find you a good husband. I can't think of a more eligible candidate than The Honourable Samuel Watson.'

I am embarrassed again but need to speak my mind. 'Truth is, Grace, I'm not sure I want to settle down yet. Marriage is such a big step. I would like to travel more first and enjoy being single; I certainly don't need to marry for money.' In spite of my attraction to Sam, my secret night-time vigil with the girl in my dreams pulls me in her direction. Besides, I now own a tiny part of her homeland and this provides a more solid bridge between us.

Grace laughs at my reluctance and goes to have her bath. I use my en suite bathroom to prepare for my day out. Grace has shown me how to apply make-up to enhance my features; the pale and interesting look is all the rage. Accentuating the eyes with black pencil and mascara, a little rouge and lipstick and dusting the face with pale powder certainly changes my country-fresh appearance. As I look critically into the mirror, in spite of myself, my head is full of Sam; his chestnut brown hair smoothed back on top and cut short at the sides like the film stars and the giddy sensation in my tummy whenever we meet.

Grace is right about the other debs. Girlfriends say he is a real dish and I know they are envious since we started dating regularly. But apart from all the flirting and flattery I really find Sam very interesting. When we met at my party he asked me: 'Do you like to travel, Christina?' This was so refreshing after talking to so many young men who thought only about themselves.

I remember hanging on his every word. 'Yes,' I stammered. 'I've just returned from Paris. Before that I went to Venice with Lady Grace.' It wasn't like me to be so bowled over by a boy; although Sam is more man than boy.

He wanted to know what we had seen and what I liked most. 'I've recently been to Egypt,' he said, 'visiting the Nile and the Pyramids.' He told me all about them and said, 'You would love it, Christina,' as if he wanted to take me there.

I shiver thinking about his manly, athletic physique and have to distract myself by recalling his jokes and cheeky humour. His family are very wealthy but he is a real gentleman and I feel comfortable with him. As for love, I meant what I said to Grace. I'm not ready to settle down and I definitely want to travel, especially to Peru. Even so, if I'm destined to fall in love, Sam could be a possible candidate. Of course the initiative has to come from him. Much as I like my own way it wouldn't do to be forward.

Sam arrives punctually at ten o'clock. He looks quite dashing in a check sports jacket with light coloured trousers. Although it's a very warm day, he insists I take a coat. I can't guess where he is taking me and he won't say.

'It's a surprise, Christina, in fact I have several surprises for you today.' He smiles secretively, apparently savouring my participation in his plan. 'And the first is right outside.' When we go down to the street there is an adorable little red sports car with an open top parked outside. He opens the passenger door for me, with a flourish and a bow as if he is my chauffeur.

'I didn't know you had one of these, Sam.' I snuggle into the low seat, tingling with excitement. He stretches his long legs into the driver's position. 'I only got her yesterday. I'm glad you like it.' The engine starts without having to use a handle. 'It's got a three-speed gearbox', he says raising his voice over the motor's deep, throaty roar. Now he shouts: 'Oh, and listen to the exhaust!' The noise is deafening, far louder than one would expect from such a little car; like a kitten pretending to be a lion. We take off at speed and Sam zooms through the London traffic as if we are on a race track. I grip the side of the car as we swing from left to right and I'm thrilled. My spirit of adventure is released after a whole year striving to be a perfect young lady.

London's crowds and smuts are soon behind us and Sam drives even faster now on the country roads. Conversation is impossible over the noise of the engine. I take off my new cream cloche hat and let the wind stream through my long hair. Sam grins, seeming delighted to see me like this and I feel as I do when I ride across the downs, laughing out loud with the joy of just being alive.

We eventually pass through the grand gates of a picturesque estate in the beautiful Berkshire countryside. Sam drives onto an airfield right in the middle of this majestic park. He stops the sports car and we sit watching planes take off and land.

'This whole estate belongs to my friend, Charlie de Havilland's family,' he says, 'and although it's private I've got their permission to come here.' He flashes me that covert smile again. The scene is mesmerising and I think today quite perfect.

'I've brought a little picnic,' he says and points to a huge wicker hamper in the space behind our seats. 'But before we eat I have another surprise.' He leans across to open my door and his face brushes close to mine. I feel his lips touch my cheek and he whispers in my ear. 'You are gorgeous, Christina.' I remember Grace's advice to act cool and sophisticated, so I flutter my eyelids and blush to acknowledge his compliment.

He chuckles and walks round the car to help me out then guides me over to one of the planes parked at this end of the runway. Sam holds my hand. 'Christina, this is my very own Sopwith Strutter.' He pats the big nosecone affectionately as if it is a horse. 'Isn't she a darling?'

'Oh, Sam, she is!' I am more delighted than I thought possible and he walks me right round the biplane.

'I got her for a song in a sale of surplus equipment from the Royal Flying Corps.' His arm slides round my waist and I feel a shimmer of electricity from the physical contact between us. 'Would you like to go up for a spin?'

I leap inside at the very thought of flying. 'Do you mean now? Oh, gosh yes, Sam, I would!' He holds out his other hand and helps me climb up onto the lower wing and into the open cockpit. I am showing a lot of leg as I clamber into the plane in my short summer dress but I am so delighted I really don't care. Then he runs back to the car and brings my coat.

He is laughing again. 'I said you might need it,' and he helps me slip it on, giving me a pair of goggles to wear. A man in overalls comes over and as Sam sits in the pilot's seat, checking the controls and also donning a pair of goggles and a leather helmet, the man winds the propeller to start the engine.

The biplane looks freshly painted light blue and in a few moments the engine starts. Sam drives the plane out onto the grass runway. He is waved on by men with flags and we gather speed, bumping along in quite an alarming way. We seem to go right across the field like this and I can't imagine how we will get into the air before we reach the trees at the end of the airfield. Suddenly the bumps stop and we leave the ground, soaring up into the sky and over the trees. My breath is swept away as the ground recedes and my head reels with the sensation of being airborne. I look down, aware that the world has taken on an entirely different perspective now I am viewing it from above. The countryside looks like a flat game board, with model houses, farms and fields, where we are the only piece that is moving, sailing above the world.

This is my very first taste of flying and I love the exhilarating sensation. We soar through the clouds and I adore being piloted by this dashing young man, who seems to have chosen me from all the eligible young ladies in London.

Eventually, our flight comes to an end and Sam brings us back onto the field with its bumps and jolts. I am so elated I quite forget my earlier resolve to play hard to get. As he lifts me down from the cockpit I fall so naturally into his arms. We kiss spontaneously, ignoring the grinning mechanic who is waiting to take the Strutter back to the hangar.

Silent now, we digest the subtle shift in our relationship. Sam drives us to a secluded spot on a hill overlooking the airfield and we open the picnic hamper. I lay out the cloth and enjoy setting out the lovely lunch he has so thoughtfully provided. I forget all thought of not becoming emotionally involved with anyone, for now I am in over my head. At this moment I feel I could stay with Sam forever, he has made me quite delirious with happiness.

I'm tongue-tied and so, I think, is he. He tucks in hungrily to the lovely sandwiches while I nibble, really too excited to eat. Sam opens a bottle of champagne and the cork pops loudly, flying over the picnic cloth and vanishing in the bushes.

'Oh, dear,' he says, 'we'll have to drink it all now,' and I giggle as the bubbles go to my head.

'What are we celebrating?' I ask.

'Us, I hope,' he replies and then he takes me by surprise yet again, but the words I hear are not quite what I expect.

'I'm going abroad soon, Christina. It's something I've been planning for some time.' He is lounging on the grass, barely a foot away from where I am sitting with my knees resting to one side. He turns to look directly into my eyes. 'Since the day we met I have been in a quandary, and now I don't know whether to go or not. Will you help me to decide?'

'Do you mean for a holiday?' I really can't follow his thoughts.

'Oh, no, it might be for good. I'm going to Brazil to start up a charter flight business.'

I am instantly jolted out of my euphoria and feel my fragile new happiness begin to drain away. 'Why Brazil?' I ask trying not to think how far away that is.

'There's money to be made out there,' he says, and I think this seems rather at odds with his social position.

'I thought you were already rich.'

He screws up his face and scratches his head. 'Correction: my father, the Earl of Langley, he is already rich as you put it.'

'I didn't mean to be personal,' I say, fearing I am treading on private matters.

'No, no, Christina, you're quite right to question the reasons behind this venture. You see Father is a very shrewd businessman. Dear old Great Britain is in a bit of a pickle, financially that is. But dad is riding the crest of the wave, so to speak. He has a lot of investments in South America: coffee, cotton, tin and copper to name just a few. Financially, he's coining it in.'

'And you?' I ask, trying to follow his drift.

'I will inherit, of course, but my father is adamant I make my own money and not just from investments. He wants me to work for it with my own business. He knows how passionate I am about flying and from his own visits to Brazil he's identified a new business potential with charter flights.'

I try to look composed and interested but every word he utters knocks me with an ominous thud.

'The whole continent is vast, Christina, and it's mostly virgin territory: mountains, pampas and rain forest. The roads are bad and railways are subject to constant flooding, even earthquakes.' His speech continues bursting with enthusiasm. 'With the coming of the aeroplane the whole region is opening up; development of the continent is racing ahead.

Charter flight companies are springing up round all the major ports. Dad wants me to go out to Rio and grab a slice of the business.'

I can tell Sam is already passionate about the prospect of this venture.

'Dad's going to invest fifty thousand pounds to start me in business, but he wants to see a profit and double his money; he's given me five years to do it.'

I try to think about this from Sam's point of view. The business potential sounds very credible. 'If I were a boy I think my father would agree with yours and want me to make my own money too.' But in my head I am praying this won't happen. He looks at me with what Grace calls his puppy-dog eyes.

'Since we met, Christina, all these plans for me to go and live in Brazil have turned sour.' He comes close and takes my hand. He takes a deep breath as if summoning his courage and then it all comes out in a few simple words. 'Fact is, my dear Christina, I love you.' He is silent now, searching my features, waiting for me to speak.

But I am speechless. I'm sure I love him too but the words won't come; it is all too much too soon. Then he compounds my impotence even more. 'Christina, darling Christina, will you marry me and come to Brazil with me?'

My hand flies to my head and I close my eyes in an instinctive defence against so many conflicting emotions. I turn away from him, hugging my knees which have turned to jelly.

He is distraught. 'Oh, my dear, please don't be upset.'

Tears prick in my eyes and I blink them away. 'No, Sam, I'm not upset, just completely overwhelmed, and a little bit confused. This is all too much for me to absorb.'

He laughs at this and squeezes my shoulders. I feel the tension of the last few minutes slipping away.

'I'm sorry,' he says very tenderly. 'I shouldn't have said all that at once but I've been bursting to tell you for weeks.'

More at ease now I feel I can think clearer. 'Well I'm sure about one thing, Sam and that is, I do love you.' I'm sure it's true, and I feel it's right to say so.

He lets out a deep sigh and a look of pure joy fills his handsome face. We are both kneeling now, facing each other. We hug and then kiss again and the feeling is one of utter contentment. I temporarily push thoughts of Brazil away; I have never experienced this kind of happiness before and wonder if this is real love.

In this quiet moment, my foggy brain suddenly clears, and I see the map of Perú in my head; the border crosses into Brazil. Thoughts speed up and project impossible scenarios. I have to tell Sam about Perú for it seems this was, after all, meant to happen. 'You're not going to believe this, Sam, but I own a house in Perú. It's in Cuzco and belonged to my Great Uncle Peter.'

'Perú?' He says as though he has never heard of the country.

'Yes, Perú, it's next to Brazil on the map.'

He nods his head. 'Yes, but it's a very long way from Rio.'

'Well, I only recently inherited the house but I've already made up my mind to go there and see it before it is sold.'

'Then you shall, my darling. It would be a long flight from Rio but with the right plane I'm sure I would be able to sort it out.' It seems my own reason to go to South America has given him new hope. 'Does that mean you'll come with me?'

Now I find my thoughts confused again. I want to say yes right away but caution checks me. 'Give me time, please Sam. I really need to think about this and consult with my father.' The thought I might at last go to Perú is clouding the real issue of marriage to Sam and going to live with him in Rio. That's a decision I can't make lightly.

Sam seems to understand. 'But you do love me.' It's a statement and a question.

'Oh, yes, Sam. I think I love you very much.' We kiss again, a long and very passionate kiss. I want to stay in this wonderful moment. He said he loves me, so I put all thought of the future away.

6

Celebrations

1533, Willkapampa, Tawantinsuyu (The Inca Empire)
As the farming year came to an end Tlalli's excitement grew. The time for the festival of Inti Raymi, when the whole tribe gave thanks to the sun god Inti for the successful gathering of the harvest, would start tomorrow. Today was the celebration for Ispaca's coming of age and also for Tlalli's birthday.

Before the feasting began their father spoke to them. 'Ispaca, you are now entering the years leading to manhood. You must learn the skills needed to prove your worth as a leader and be ready for the day you will be the curaca of our people.' Father turned to Tlalli, 'For now you will work alongside your Mother to learn the crafts of womanhood. But you have been promised to the Sapa Inca since you were born, to go to the Sun Temple and serve him as a holy Aclla.'

Tlalli shuddered at her father's words. She should have felt privileged, to be honoured as a chosen one, but she could not hide her fear at the thought of leaving her family and the only life she had ever known. 'Do I have to go, Father? My dreams tell me I will never see my home again.' Life as a holy Aclla was very strict, and the girls were kept shut away from the outside world, some for the remainder of their lives.

Her father answered her gently. 'Your dreams speak to you, making you wise beyond your years, my daughter. You know better than many that the invaders will bring much trouble to our world. You may perhaps be safer in the Temple than here in the village. Besides you are promised as part of our tribe's tribute. You will have to go, even though it grieves me.' Her father clasped her by the shoulders. 'I respect the visions you see in your dreams and the messages you receive, for I also have these gifts. But a word of caution, daughter. When you go to Cuzco do not speak of these.'

'What do you mean, Father?' She could see both love and fear in his eyes.

'You are an innocent child but there are those who would perhaps misread your messages. Soothsayers are not always respected. If people do not like what you tell them, you could be branded a witch or a demon.' Kusi sighed deeply. 'This is one of the reasons I am reluctant to fulfil my obligation to send you. I have to find a way to protect you.'

Tlalli had always known living in the Sun Temple would be her fate and that she would have to bear it for the honour of her tribe. Now she had a further burden for she understood her father's warning. Her gift of prophecy, the messages she had always shared so eagerly with her trusted family, would have to be kept secret, hidden away in her heart.

As the sun began to wane Tlalli went out on the hillside with her father, mother, Ispaca and all their younger brothers and sisters, for tonight the tribe would feast and celebrate the curaca's son's coming of age.

Earlier that day news from around the empire had been brought by the chaski. These were relays of runners, who ran across the vast road system, delivering news and commands from the capital to the curacas in towns and villages. The news Kusi had received today he would now pass on to his people. As he stood on a high rock to address the tribe gathered around, Tlalli could sense her father's heart was heavy. He raised his voice to the waiting crowd.

'The Sapa Inca, Atahualpa, leader of the Inca Empire, has been killed by the evil invaders. Even though they were given huge quantities of gold as ransom for his life, they still executed him!'

'No!' 'Murderers!' 'They will kill us all!' shouted the tribe. Tlalli, Ispaca and everyone in the village had heard about the ruthless strangers who had arrived from the sea, crossed the deserts and entered their mountainous region. The stories had spread as the invaders travelled through the land.

A few days ago, a travelling shaman had come to their village and told them, 'These strangers say they come from a place called Spain. Their king is a god and they all bow down to him. They said everything we own will be taken and given to their King. If we didn't surrender our gold and wealth they would kill all our people with their huge swords and lances, or with fire balls propelled from strange sticks held in their hands.' The shaman had left the town where this happened and taken to the road to warn others.

Chaski had brought more news to the village, saying, 'The Spaniards have robbed the roadside tambos of supplies needed by the local people and travellers.' Tlalli shuddered when they said, 'They kidnap women and young girls and take them away from their homes to be slaves and servants.' As Kusi spoke to the tribe he raised his hand to stay the people's angry response.

'I am not always in agreement with our Inca masters but we must work with them against these new enemies. The strangers are moving down from the north, passing through our territory. They are bound for Cuzco and one way or another will try to wrest control of the Empire from the Incas there. They have shown how ruthless they are by executing the Sapa Inca, but they have also revealed how treacherous they are; they can never be trusted.' A silence had fallen around the campfire. Tlalli held her breath, waiting on her father's words.

Kusi turned to the men, his warriors. 'My brothers, we must be ready to fight! You must keep your bows and arrows, clubs and maces ready for my word.' Tlalli's father raised a clenched fist, and she listened as the tribe shouted their support with loud howls. The women banged metal pots; their sign to frighten enemies, human or animal. Her father held up his hand for silence.

'These evil men are demanding we give up our sacred religious worship. They shout out strange words in the name of their own god, calling us pagans and heathens.'

'Our gods are sacred to us.' 'We are not heathens!' shouted the angry crowd. Tlalli knew her father's mind so well. He would be determined to continue with their ancient traditions and celebrations. Even so, she had seen him place more look-outs to watch the Inca road above their settlement. She bit her lip, fearful of what would happen if these men came to their village.

Father lifted his arms up high and the shouting stopped. 'Today my friends, I believe we are safe. What say you? Do we continue with our planned celebrations or do we hide like frightened children and hope the Spaniards will pass us by?'

Uncle Tutsi spoke first. 'I say we follow our own gods and celebrate as we always have.' He shook the spear he held in the air. 'Damn the invaders, they will not stop us!' Everyone shouted their agreement and the ground shook as the whole tribe stamped their feet on the hard earth and howled their war cries.

Tlalli felt very small and afraid until she saw her father's face break into a broad grin and he laughed out loud. When the noise subsided he spoke again. 'Friends, we are here to celebrate my son Ispaca's coming of age, and his sister Tlalli's birthday also.' Father hustled them forward in full view of the tribe. 'Pipers play!' he commanded and the panpipes and flutes of the mountains played with the drums of the jungle. Tlalli breathed easy again as the tribe began dancing and chanting. For now they could revel in their joyous celebration as the music broke the tribe's angry mood.

Father presented Ispaca with his new headdress. Tlalli had helped her mother weave the pointed cap, in traditional colours and design, from fine alpaca yarn. The long tail feathers from the brightly coloured birds of the jungle adorned the crown. Long earmuffs would keep out the cold winds that blew on the high mountain passes. Behind the earmuffs, his long black hair fell in braids. She knew more feathers would be added as he learned the lessons of manhood. One day he would have a full feather headdress, like the one their father wore for these special celebrations. Her heart quickened thinking Ispaca would also wear it if he went into battle.

Tlalli put aside her own fears of the invaders and her future life in the Sun Temple as she joined in the celebrations for Ispaca. Excitement grew among the young people as the evening wore on. The hot fat from the roasting guinea pigs scalded Tlalli's fingers as she helped serve the feast, piling the roasted potatoes and corn cobs into the carved gourds used for eating. Chicha, made from fermented maize and berries, ran down her arms as she lifted the heavy flagons to fill the men's drinking vessels of pottery or silver. She sipped a little of the strong drink but found herself light-headed and wanting to laugh too much.

Tlalli joined in the dancing as the musicians played their panpipes and flutes, and rhythmic beats were drummed out on animal skins stretched over hollowed wood. The music filled the whole valley, bouncing off the granite escarpments of the surrounding mountains, echoing back to the celebrating villagers, who danced in a mix of jungle and mountain costumes to the haunting melodies. Something stirred inside her; a feeling that life should always be like this and the invaders must never be allowed to change the lives of her people. But her dreams had already shown her this would not be the outcome. Tonight she wished she did not have the gift of prophecy and tried hard to forget about the future. She wanted to hold on to this moment forever.

Ispaca's friend Paullu played his quena flute. He laughed at Ispaca's attempts at drumming to his trilling pipes. As Tlalli watched their easy friendship Paullu smiled and winked at her and she danced to his merry tunes. He put his flute into the bag slung on his back and took out the panpipes. Tlalli thought how she would like to know him better, with his smiling eyes, and the notes of his panpipes making her melt inside.

Kusi came over to where the three young people talked and laughed together. He put his arms around the shoulders of his son and daughter, leading them away from the feasting villagers. 'Ispaca my son,' said their father, 'we will soon be called to fight again in support of a new Inca leader, of this I am sure.' Tlalli had seen recently that Ispaca had become a quieter, more serious boy.

'But I thought the civil war with Huascar was over, Father,' he said.

Their father shook his head. 'The war continues but the threat now is from these Spaniards. It is said they support young Prince Manco and want him to be the new Sapa Inca.' Father's mood had become dark and serious again. 'We are bound to give allegiance to whoever is chosen as ruler, but I do not trust these foreigners. I have to tell you, the more I hear from the chaski about their double dealing with the Incas in Cusco, the more I want to give you and your sister the means to protect yourselves against the inevitable consequences of misrule.'

Ispaca was puzzled. 'What do you mean, father?'

Kusi sighed and led the two children further away from the festivities, and he called Neneti his wife to go with them. 'I have tried to give you both a grounding in your tribal history, but only from my own history, the Manari side. You are descended from two tribes and the time has come to forge the link with your other heritage. When the Manari people arrived here from the jungle regions under enforced Inca resettlement, I was just a boy, like you Ispaca. I raged against this new life. We were warriors not farmers; then I fell in love with your mother.'

Tlalli smiled to see her father take her mother's hand and draw her close to him. 'I'm ashamed to say the identity of our mountain hosts was eclipsed by my more aggressive, vocal tribe. Your mother's people were part of the bigger tribe of Q'ero people, and had lived on these mountain slopes for generations.' He smiled again at Neneti. 'Now I see myself as a jungle hot-head, while your mother and her people were clever and resourceful, not only in the way they farmed this difficult land but in their use and knowledge of textiles, and the preservation of their myths and legends.'

'Do you mean the Legend of the Jaguar?' said Tlalli, impatient to know everything.

Neneti answered her. 'That is one of our stories, but there is so much more. The Yaguar Mountain was always the source of my tribe's power. My ancestors defended themselves with the aid of the mountain's deities. They worshipped the Jaguar as god of the mountain. The mountain spirits provided gold and silver, and the ancient people were skilled in the forging of precious metals. Trading these ornaments kept the tribe prosperous, and our remote mountain home kept us safe from enemies.

'But the gold mine is worked out now,' said Ispaca, 'there's no more gold in Mount Yaguar'.

Neneti and Kusi both laughed. 'Well, the Inca's temple treasures are hidden in the mountain now and perhaps there is more,' said their mother.

The children looked excited and impatient. 'More gold?' said Ispaca.

'More treasures?' asked Tlalli.

'Perhaps, but you will have to wait.' said Kusi.

They both opened their mouths full of questions, but Father raised his hand and they fell silent. 'We will all go to the mountain tomorrow and then perhaps your questions will be answered.'

7

Secrets of the Mountain

Daylight could not come too soon for Tlalli. She had tossed and turned in her cot impatient to learn what her father had meant.

Yaguar Mountain was the highest in a range of mountains dominating the landscape surrounding her home. In The Legend of the Jaguar, the storyteller told how Viracocha had created the world and made his son Inti, god of the Sun and his daughter Mama Quilla, goddess of the moon. Their children all became gods and leaders of all the tribes of their world. Toquri the Jaguar god was one of these, and he was the god of the golden mountain called Yaguar.

When the two brothers came to seek their fortunes and begged for gold from his mountain, Toquri set them a challenge. They were to bring him their first born children and he would give them each half the gold in the mountain. The good brother would not hand over his child and the Jaguar god sent him on his way with blessings, so he and his wife lived poor but happy. The greedy brother, called Egecati, gave his little baby daughter called Tlalli, to the Jaguar and he was allowed to mine half the gold in the mountain. But it didn't make him happy. His wife was distraught at the loss of her child and she remained barren. Without a family, all the riches in the world did not bring happiness.

Tlalli remembered how this sad tale continued. Egecati returned to the mountain and asked for his child back. Toquri showed him his daughter. She was now a beautiful golden jaguar goddess called Izella, with two cubs of her own and could not be returned to him. She had the power to shapeshift from human to feline just as Toquri had.

Toquri was not a vengeful god and told Egecati to give all his riches and gold away and live in poverty like his brother, then his wife would give him another child. Egecati reluctantly did this to see if the prophesy would come true. Sure enough the following spring his wife gave him a son and later that year, another daughter. Egecati grew restless with being poor and having to work to provide for his growing family. He waited until his wife had another baby, a girl they named Necahual which means survivor, and he spirited her away, back to the mountain. When he asked Toquri for the other half of the gold in the mountain, in exchange for this baby, the Jaguar god was very angry. He roared and howled saying, the man had not learned his lesson and still coveted riches over the life of his child. Egecati agreed, and then asked if he could have the gold and keep his child.

Toquri went into such a rage he told the man to place the baby on his throne in the heart of the mountain. The jaguar god stormed, with thunder and lightning and eruptions of fire. Egecati covered his head in fear. When the storm abated, the jaguar god and his family had all disappeared, so had all the gold in the mountain. Egecati peeled back the blanket wrapped around his precious daughter. She was perfect in every detail but she was made of pure gold.

Too late, greedy Egecati realised he had lost everything he held dear. He couldn't return to his family with a golden baby … he couldn't have her melted down into the riches he craved. His greed had robbed him of everything in his life and he realised too late that he really loved them.

Tlalli couldn't imagine her father would give away any of his children for gold. The bright yellow metal was only used for decoration; it was too soft to be made into tools. But the greedy brother had thought gold would bring him a life of ease and riches. Tlalli thought how readily some men deceived themselves. The message in the legend was clear: a man who put riches above the life of a child would never know love, and would be doomed to wander alone forever. Then Tlalli remembered another important message from the storyteller: 'You may see him still, for he is the guardian of the sacred site called Mount Yaguar. He will tell travellers he is anything but wise, and entreats all people to listen to the voices of their gods and follow their commandments. He will say that after Viracocha the creator and Inti the sun god, the wisest god is Toquri and that he takes the form of a jaguar.'

Tlalli had be wrestling all night with this knowledge, and the revelations from her mother and father about her mountain heritage. When daylight at last seeped through the doorway she rose and dressed and prepared the cornbread and maize for the family's first meal. She hoped her father had not changed his mind about taking them to the mountain.

They walked in single file, taking the trail Tlalli had seen her father lead the Incas down with the llamas loaded with treasure. Ispaca knew the way and went ahead and Tlalli had to run to keep up with him. It was a long way and the mountain didn't seem to get any closer even after the sun had moved up to the top of the sky. Tlalli thought they would have to climb up the mountain, but instead they went to an entrance low down; a track that had been carved right into the bowels of the earth. She felt as if they were burrowing into the roots of an enormous tree. At first the track was open to the sky but then they came to where it went beneath the rock. They stopped and Ispaca was instructed to make a fire as he had been taught. From this they lit torches which were stacked at the entrance.

As they passed through the darkening passageway, Tlalli's torch cast its light onto the rock with eerie shadows that moved strangely, making weird shapes appear and disappear like leaping wild animals, as they turned and twisted further into the mountain.

Kusi stopped and they grouped round him. 'The Inca's treasures have been taken up into the mine's high passages where they will be safe from flooding and thieves. But we brought you here to help us find a much older treasure.'

Neneti spoke. 'When I was a child my grandfather brought us to the mountain to hide the tribe's treasured heirlooms. They had been handed down through generations of the Q'ero, long before the time of the Incas. Grandfather knew there was great uncertainty about our future. We were expecting the arrival of your father's people, the Manari. We were very afraid, for we knew the jungle Indians were more warlike than our own tribe. These precious heirlooms had been forged by the goldsmiths of old and blessed by the mountain spirits. My grandfather hid them here, in this sacred mountain, and here they have remained.'

Kusi spoke now. 'Your mother's grandfather was right to be cautious. My people were very aggressive when we first arrived. In fact I don't know how they tolerated us. But once we learned that the Q'ero people knew how to survive on the mountains, we had to listen to their wisdom, or else we would have perished.'

'Now your father and I think it is time for you to receive the heritage that is yours by right,' said Neneti. 'You are the future for our people and you deserve the protection of the old gods.' Neneti moved forward again. 'I have not been back to this sacred place since the day my grandfather buried the heirlooms. It will be a miracle if I can find them again.'

Tlalli felt frightened and excited together. 'Why did you leave them here so long?' she asked.

Kusi answered, 'Mother told me of their existence when we married, but we decided to leave them where they were safe. Now is the right time for them to be revealed once more.'

'But what are they, Father?' asked Ispaca, always the impatient one.

Kusi laughed and scratched his head. 'Well, if your dear mother can't remember where they are we shall never know.'

Both children rounded on their mother. 'Are they buried in the ground?' asked Ispaca.

'Or hidden in the rocks?' queried Tlalli.

'I thought I knew exactly where to look, but somehow the tunnel is different, not as I remember it.'

Neneti sounded puzzled and Tlalli sensed her mother's unease. 'We must be quiet and let Mother think.' So they all sat down on the cold rock of the passageway in silence, holding their torches up high. But it was not silent. Winds blew through the mountain, whipping up sound through every crack and tunnel. Tlalli felt the ancient spirits of the mountain spoke with the howls of jaguars and pumas, pacing their territory as of old. She didn't know why, but she felt compelled to continue down the passage. She pulled at her mother's hand to follow her. Some instinct led her further down, then off to the right, where they reached a dead end. Within this cul-de-sac was a shrine. Dozens of flat granite stones placed on top of each other, replicating the shrines on their hillsides where they often went to pay homage.

Neneti gasped. 'Of course! I had forgotten about the shrine.' By now Kusi and Ispaca had followed them. They carefully removed the stones one by one and near the bottom they uncovered an old blackened silver casket. Neneti lifted it out with shaking hands and passed it to Kusi.

'Before we open the casket we must replace the stones of the shrine and give thanks,' said Kusi.

When that was done Ispaca said, 'Open it, Father, please open the casket.'

Kusi laughed and said, 'No, we will take it back home and prepare a ceremony for you to receive your heritage.'

Tlalli felt she had already received her heritage. The spirit of the mountain had spoken to her and led her to find the treasures, and she walked back home as if on air.

When they returned to the village, the preparations for today's Inti Raymi festival had begun. This was the most important event in the tribe's calendar. Now Ispaca and Tlalli could also look forward to receiving the treasures from great-grandfather's ancestors.

Father went off with Uncle Tutsi and mother joined with the other women of the tribe preparing the feast. This was the second feast in as many days but Tlalli knew they would not eat so well again until the following year. As on the previous day, the food was cooked in holes dug underground or roasted over the campfire.

Celebrations began mid-afternoon with feasting, music, chanting and dancing. The tribe performed their Inti Raymi ceremony. Kusi was conveyed on a curaca's litter to their central point, where they had their campfire. He held a mask of polished silver before his face to represent the sacred Punchao, and all the tribe bowed down to him. This caused great merriment among the tribe for they knew Kusi was their curaca, and was not actually the sun god. Kusi performed the blessing on the harvest which everyone had worked so hard to bring in.

Then Father held up his hand for silence. 'My people! We have lived here together for three generations; the jungle Manari and the Q'ero mountain people. The older members of our tribe will remember things were not easy in the beginning, but I'm glad to say we live well together and are now truly one tribe.' There was laughter and cheers and mock fighting among the men, while the children all looked on bewildered.

'Now, I want to pay a long-overdue homage to the people who welcomed my tribe to their home so long ago. We were not always patient of your own rituals and religions but I think we have learned to accept one another's ways. The Q'ero people believe in the spirits of the mountain. Overlooked as we are by the great Mount Yaguar, we jungle Indians have come to accept your deities as our own. The ancient Jaguar god Toquri and his goddess Izella have long entertained us with their legend. We must remember these were once real gods in the eyes of our ancestors. When the mountain produced gold and silver the gods were worshipped and revered by the people. Somehow, we have forgotten these deities and they have lost the power to guide us. That is our fault, not theirs.

'I want to right these wrongs and resurrect the power of the ancient gods, for I feel a time will soon be at hand when we will need all the protection the gods will lend us. We are fortunate, living in this remote mountain stronghold, and hopefully safe from the long noses of our Spanish enemies.

'Today, I took my family to Yaguar Mountain. We went hoping to recover treasures buried by my wife's grandfather before we Manari came here. We found the precious heirlooms we sought, and now I want to pass these on to my own children, for they are the future of our tribe. These talismans represent the old jaguar gods, and I hope they will protect my children and this tribe as we go forward into a very uncertain future.'

He held up two almost identical gold pieces. They were square and flat, each one shaped and engraved with the face of the wild cat that roamed their forests; the jaguar. The face of one showed fierce bulging eyes, the mouth open with fang-like teeth. The face on the other looked serene, the mouth closed, the eyes oval and hooded.

Kusi took the fierce jaguar piece that represented the Jaguar god Toquri and attached a strip of hide through a protruding bar behind the jaguar head, and he tied the hide into a long thong. He placed it over Ispaca's head. The jaguar sat on Ispaca's chest like an avenging bodyguard. Then father did the same with the benevolent jaguar, representing Izella, and placed it over Tlalli's head. She looked down, carefully tilting the face towards her. She was immediately calm and for once, silent. One of the tribe elders, who was of Q'ero descent, raised his hand, chanting an ancient incantation. Others joined in and soon the whole tribe were chanting mystic words that made Tlalli feel something very special had been gifted to her.

When the ceremony ended everyone began to drift back to the feast and Kusi again spoke to his son and daughter. 'You must wear these talismans under your clothing and not display them. There are those who would rob you just for the gold they contain. But they have a far greater value in their spiritual power.' He put his hands out and touched his two children. 'I have protected you through your childhood but now you are both about to go out into a world that can be harsh and cruel. I hope the spirits of these old gods still have the power to protect you.' Tlalli and Ispaca thanked their father and pushed the talismans under their clothing. Ispaca bowed as a sign of his respect and then they all returned to the feast and the music.

Tlalli wandered away from the throng. She could feel the jaguar next to her skin, heavy on her chest, her head once again full of the image of the jaguar family in the forest, and of the legend. It seemed as if she drew strength and courage through the talisman; a spirit speaking to her with a sacred voice. She needed to be alone and as darkness fell she drifted away to the edge of the settlement and sat on the hillside hugging her knees.

She looked up to the tops of the mountains above, back to the Yaguar Mountain. The sun still illuminated the caps of the snow-laden peaks with a golden light, while above them, the darkening sky hung like a deep blue curtain. Stars appeared. The brightest shone first, and one by one, all the stars took their places in the night sky. Later the moon goddess, Mama Quilla, would rise.

Each of the stars had a spiritual meaning for Tlalli's people. The seasons moved with the constellations, some stars only visible at certain times of the year. They guided the lives of the tribe, telling them when to plough, sow and reap. She could not bear to think of a life where she would be unable to see their beauty.

Her move to Cuzco had not yet been decided and that made her very happy. Yet, in her head she could see visions telling her Prince Manco would become the new Sapa Inca. With a hollow pang she remembered her destiny lay in the Sun temple serving the Inca as a holy Aclla. Her mood clouded over as if the sun god Inti had spoken, reminding her of her father's obligation. She loved him dearly and knew, come what might, she would have to obey him.

8

Madeley Hall

1930, Madeley Hall, Sussex, England.

I'm home again at last. Oh, the joy of feeling Delilah's strong muscles under my body and her rough coat under my hand. I gallop on, to catch up with Daddy at the top of the rise. He reins to and waits for us.

I turn to look down on Madeley Hall and see a granite and stone miniature of this great house. The familiar buildings and cottages belonging to the estate shrink into the green landscape like tiny dots joined together by the tracks and paths that snake around the house. We are twenty miles from the coast but I can smell the sea brought on the sharp east wind.

We've come home as Daddy didn't want to travel to London again for my engagement to Sam. London was beginning to stifle me also, so it's a relief the celebrations will be held here. We take one last ride across the top of the downs and then head for home. Grace is waiting by the kitchen door when we come in from the stables. I'm sure she feels personally responsible for our match-making, so she is organising the party for Sunday. She has hired extra staff as we have not employed full staff for this house since our housekeeper, dear old Mrs Pearson died four years ago. I excuse myself from Grace and Daddy's company on the grounds of going for a bath, but I hurry with this for there are things of my own I'm anxious to do. London-life was such a whirl of activity I want to enjoy my solitude for just a few more days.

I'm sure there is a link here with the second life I'm now living through my dreams. There are times I'm overwhelmed by this secret life blossoming within my own, and I can't think about anything else. The young girl's thoughts and her days fill my nights in random visions and I struggle to understand what is happening in her life and how this can possibly reflect on my own for we are two very different people.

In my room are several boxes which I filled with childhood memorabilia before I went to London. I changed my mind about disposing of them; now I wonder if I had a premonition I might want them again. Instinct leads me to the third box down in the pile, and I hump the others out of the way, lifting the lid to find my journals.

I started keeping a journal when I was ten and I pull out the very first and settle on the floor to read. I smile at my childlike spidery handwriting. Here, days in the schoolroom under the tutor I shared with Tom spring from the past. Life was difficult for my little brother. He had to drag his leg with the iron calliper, which was supposed to support him and stop the leg from being completely useless. His eyesight was poor and he couldn't see anything without his glasses. I could weep now remembering I wasn't always kind or patient with him. He loved me so much and followed me everywhere like a puppy. I loved him too and we enjoyed happy times together, but his constant company sometimes became a burden, and half-way through the year I was sent to boarding school. I think my sharp temper had enraged Mother once too often. I read the entries for when I was there. I hated it, didn't make any friends, and even missed Tom's clinging attentions. I recall I raged and stormed like the spoiled brat I was, not to be sent back. After I had been there one year, Mamma relented, and I remained at home until the summer of 1924.

These entries don't tell me anything remotely connected with my dreams, but I don't really know what I'm looking for. The later entries might help. We went on a family holiday to France, our first since the end of the Great War. The next entry reminds me it was in the Camargue that I first saw the wild white horses:

Journal entry -17th August 1924
I saw them plunging through forest pools, sending up sprays of water with their hooves, shaking their proud heads, their thick white manes cascading showers of water droplets that shone like stars in the sunlight. They are so graceful I want to gallop with them.

I remember how I plagued poor Daddy for the rest of our holiday to buy me a white pony to keep at home. I wish now I had thought more about Tom. The next entry reminds me of an incident I had forgotten. It concerned someone Tom and I met on the steamboat from Boulogne to Folkestone. I had instigated escape from the adults, up onto the deck where this dandy of a man was smoking at the rail:

Journal entry - 10th September 1924
The Spanish man was called Don Roberto Chavez. I think Don means he is of high birth or a nobleman, although he said he was a student at Oxford. He was rather handsome and I think he liked me. His clothes were brightly coloured and very fashionable, but I think he was younger than he looked. Roberto was kind to me and Tom, yet somehow I think he could be a devil also. But I doubt I will ever see him again now we are nearly home.

I remember now, this man's image stayed with me for a long time. His face crept into my adolescent teenage fantasies after the horrible events that followed our holiday. I think I drew some comfort from remembering how he had smiled and bowed to me, sweeping off his hat like a Spanish

Lord. Of course, I later realised he was making fun of me because I had told him Tom and I were 'Honourables'. None of this helps me over the dreams…and yet, there is something niggling at the back of my mind for his image has reformed in my head; at least I think it's his image.

With a hollow, empty feeling I pass over the next few entries. They were written around the time of our sickness and Tom and Mamma's deaths. After that, came the terrible time when Daddy was so full of grief even I could not comfort him; at times I felt he had forgotten all about me.

I think I plagued him more, because soon after he bought me Flossie, my first white pony, and he also bought Sampson, his Hunter. Riding out most days brought both of us back to health and sanity and closer together. The following year Uncle Peter arrived unexpectedly on our doorstep. His visit was the beginning of my regular correspondence with him and deepened my interest in the history of Peru. I find the bundle of letters from him tied together. A rather blurred photograph of a big cat drops out of the bundle. I remember Uncle Peter gave it to me when he visited. A man who took him into the jungle took the photograph after they waited all day by the river; it is of a jaguar. I trace my finger over the image with fond remembrance. I wish I'd been allowed to keep the pendant then, but I have it now and can appreciate its beauty and, I'm sure – its power.

I feel like Mr Stevenson's split personalities, Jekyll and Hyde, although not in a wicked sense. My Miss Jekyll has to be the sparkling debutante, dazzling society and in love with my dashing fiancé, Sam. I have to make a good impression on his parents today, The Earl and Countess of Langley. I really don't know what they will make of me. Will they think me flighty and shallow? I've never been good at polite conversation, but for Sam's sake, and Daddy's, I will try my best.

Miss Hyde is perhaps a misleading comparison, for she is certainly not evil. She over-takes my personality at night in my dreams, and is in my thoughts every day. She is very different from me. I have everything I want and am now an heiress and wealthy in my own right from Uncle Peter's estate. The girl, although she is a chief's daughter, is poor and lives a harsh life. But she is rich in spirit and believes she has a special role, able to see the future for her people. I just want to know everything about her and her life. I feel so close to her spirit. I'm sure she was a real person and not a figment of my imagination, and that perhaps I was her in that life. The thought is mystifying; could it possibly be?

I jump, perhaps guiltily, when Grace comes into my room to help me get ready. I have to tear myself away from my musings and be ready for my guests.

She takes the pale green gown from the closet which I'd agreed to wear today. 'Now Christina, let's not have another argument about jewellery.'

40

She bustles about the room. 'Your mother's pearls are very suitable for daywear and it would please your father to see you in them today.'

I want to protest, but hold my tongue. In my last dream the girl was given a pendant like mine, also her brother received a similar heirloom. The children were told to hide the golden talismans under their clothing. That is not an option for me as this dress has a low neckline. I'll have to think quickly not to be thwarted.

'Perhaps a formal gown is not the right choice for a Sunday lunch party, Grace,' I say. 'I could wear my heather tweed skirt with the lilac twinset. In fact I'm sure that would be much more suitable, especially if we walk the Earl and Countess round the gardens.'

Grace momentarily pouts, then she smiles and I think I have won the point. 'You could still wear the pearls. They would sit well on the lilac. Yes, perhaps that would be better.'

I sigh with relief. 'Excellent,' I say trying not to sound triumphant. 'You go back to the kitchen, Grace, I can manage perfectly well now that's settled.'

She laughs, 'Yes, milady. Will there be anything else, milady?'

I laugh too, thankful for her endless good humour and also that now I can secrete my jaguar under my clothes, just as my alter-ego did.

9

Jaguar Girl

1533, Willkapampa, Tawantinsuyu (The Inca Empire)
Following the ceremonies and Ispaca's coming of age, Tlalli saw little of him. The rainy season began and she filled her days perfecting the crafts taught by her mother; dyeing, spinning and weaving the soft alpaca yarns into traditional textiles. She hardly saw Paullu either, for every day he went with his precious flocks up to the high pastures, where it was always cold and wet.

At last the rains passed and Tlalli joined with a group of youngsters to once more gather berries and leaves in the forest. She waited her opportunity and slipped away unnoticed, deeper into the vast tracts of trees, vines and creepers. Her sharp young eyes picked out the winding animal trails weaving through the dense undergrowth and round the enormous trees. Above her, the high branches, thick with leaves, formed a canopy blotting out the sunlight.

She crept on in this damp, twilit world, listening to the sounds of the cloud forest. She searched the ground for animal tracks and found where a fox had brushed its belly under a low branch, leaving footprints in the soft loamy soil. Then she saw the small hoof marks and coarse hairs of peccaries; probably a day old. Ispaca had taught her how to read all these signs and to listen to the language of bird and animal calls. How she missed being with her brother every day. She looked most carefully but didn't find any of the signs a jaguar would leave: five-toed paw prints, scats, or perhaps golden hairs rubbed against tree bark.

Thinking back to the day she and Ispaca had seen the mother with her two cubs she knew this had been something very special. Now she had her jaguar talisman she truly believed the message told in the legend. If jaguars came to the mountains they were descended from the gods Toquri and Izella: sacred animals.

Her legs began to grow heavy as she went up a steep incline where the trees grew stunted and the canopy thinned. She had reached the foothills leading to the great mountain of Yaguar. She remembered the darkness inside the mine when she found the hidden talismans. She wouldn't go back there but knew she was close. Looking up through the trees she saw the rocky outline of the mountain peak.

Soon she came to a clearing where the sun reached down to the forest floor. Tlalli paused and listened, fixing her gaze on the sheer granite slopes above, which appeared impossible to climb. A movement on a high ridge caught her eye, a golden silhouette against the blue of the sky. She squinted, shading her eyes against the glare of sunlight. Yes, she could see it now. The outline of a cat, perfectly still, as if it watched her. A movement alongside seemed to metamorphose from rock into a smaller cat shape.

Tlalli felt a stir of pleasure. She had longed to see this: the jaguars on the mountain. But there had been two cubs. Her eyes scanned across the ridge and she frowned, very aware not all young animals survived the perils of this territory. The cats had gone from her view and the sun moved behind the mountain. It was time for her to turn for home.

She retraced her steps back through the forest, sure she would remember the way, but found herself on a different trail. The vegetation grew thicker and the vines so tangled she didn't know which way to go and then she became quite lost. The little knife she carried could not cut through the web of undergrowth that barred her way and she kept a watchful eye for the snakes and spiders that could bite and could kill her. If she died here no one would ever find her.

Panic overwhelmed her futile attempts to find the right path. As she stopped to regain her breath and look for the trail again a sound reached her ears: the pitiful cry of an animal in distress. She moved as quietly as possible and stopped near a thicket below the tree from where the cry seemed to come. Looking up, she saw a rope made of twisted vines had been slung over a bough of the tree, high above her head, and stretched down to the ground.

A trap! It must be a trap, with an animal caught in its snare, still alive and probably injured, so she must act quickly. The crying stopped and she could see the rope stretched taut, entangled in the thicket. The silence became more menacing than the animal's cry. She gripped hold of her knife, well aware that an injured animal would be terrified, and could be vicious; an agouti perhaps or a deer. She picked up a stout stick and used it to prise away the tangled branches. She tried to work gently and quietly, and voiced soft, soothing sounds, as she would to a crying baby at home.

'There, there, little one, I won't hurt you. I want to help you.' She could see part of the animal, the flanks moving up and down rapidly in an uneven rhythm. A little daylight still remained and as she continued to pull the branches away she could see the animal clearly – the missing jaguar cub.

A loop from the end of the rope was caught around one hind leg. It would have pulled the animal off the ground but had snagged in the thicket saving the poor creature from instant death. Her little knife would not cut through the thick rope vine. So how could she free the tethered leg?

She breathed deeply, summoning all her courage. Touching her jaguar talisman Tlalli closed her eyes and in desperation she called out loud:

'Izella, help me!' The raised jaguar image under her fingers tingled, growing warm. A strange sensation moved within her, from hand to head to feet. She could hear her heart thumping in her head as the blood pounded through her veins, strengthening and empowering her fragile human body. She felt very strange but sure the goddess had answered her call and now she must act.

She scraped frantically at the thicket. As she looked down at her hands it was as if they had become huge paws, stripping away the branches with sharp claws. The little cub lay in a fitful sleep, held fast where the hunter's rope cut savagely into the leg. With her teeth Tlalli gnawed gently at the thick vine rope encasing the injured leg. Deep in her consciousness, she believed she had become the medium for Izella's spirit, aroused from sleep by the call of her kind. With her tongue she washed away the dried blood, cleaning, comforting and healing. She purred, singing the jaguar's song of love until the little cub's breathing became controlled in a natural sleep.

She sensed the energy seeping away, but she truly believed Izella had worked through her to help the jaguar goddess's own feline kind. Was the talisman the key to unlock this special power? As Tlalli looked down she saw her own hands and feet and wondered, did I really change into a jaguar to rescue the cub? She couldn't answer these questions, but she did know she had undergone a startling change. She was no longer a frightened child, but filled with hope, courage and the Spirit of the Jaguar. She felt surrounded by an aura of calm and peace, ready to take control of this or any situation. Older and wiser, far beyond her years, could she now use Izella's spiritual power to help her own people? It was beyond her to think how this could be done. Her trust had to be in the spirit to guide her.

She must go home. Yet to others she would still be just a child. Even her family would not understand what had happened to her today, for she hardly understood herself. It would perhaps be unwise to tell anyone, even her brother. What happened in the forest would for now remain her secret.

She stared down at the young jaguar cub, knowing her work here was not finished. To do that she must use her human abilities. In her pocket Tlalli carried a little knob of the healing balm made by her mother, wrapped in a piece of cloth. She spread the greasy substance thickly around the cub's wound, working it in with her fingers, while the little kit continued to sleep.

It would be best if she could move the cub away from this wretched place. She managed to get her arms under the sleeping animal and pull herself up onto her feet. Now she had been filled with the jaguar god's spirit, Tlalli felt much stronger and able to accomplish greater tasks. She would bear her parents' wrath and take the cub home to nurse it back to full health.

As she walked steadily, the cub seemed no heavier than the baby llamas and alpacas she carried in the fields. Its coat brushed warm and soft against her chest. She knew it was a female and the young jaguar had now been blessed by the goddess Izella, but so had she. At the edge of the gloomy forest the damp dusk deepened as twilight twisted through the trees. Birds swooped away to find their roosts, jostling in the high branches; flashes of blue and red as the parrots called out to their kind. As she trudged on, the moon rose, red and round filtering luminescent light through the climbing canopy, and the moon goddess, Mama Quilla guided her home.

She saw Ispaca waiting on the trail for it was now very late. 'Tilly!' he called. 'I felt you needed my help. What have you got there?' He stared at the bundle in her arms then shook his head laughing. 'You're going to be in a whole lot of trouble now, Tilly.'

'I don't care. She's so badly hurt; I couldn't leave her to die.' Tlalli's new-found confidence wavered, thinking of her parents' wrath.

Ispaca touched the cub. 'Show me.' He gently examined the injured leg. 'Oh, that is bad isn't it, but I don't know what Mother will say about you bringing a jaguar home.'

Mother said a lot. 'You might have been eaten alive by its mother! You foolish child.' By the next morning the little jaguar showed signs of recovery. She opened her eyes and began to cry, softly at first and then louder like a hungry baby. Curious children came to see what the curaca's daughter had brought home. Faces peeked in the doorway and Neneti shooed them away. 'That animal must go back to the forest today or I will cook it for supper!'

Tlalli appealed to her father but he shook his head. 'You have done all you can, my child; she needs to go back to her mother.'

Her father was right, and she had to be content that the animal seemed so much better. The cub scrambled to her feet, took a few steps then collapsed to the ground. She tried again, slower this time, managing to hobble on three legs. Eventually the little kit grew stronger and more accustomed to the disability in the injured leg.

'I think I am ready to take her home.'

'I am pleased by your actions, Tlalli. Perhaps the old jaguar gods are waking up,' said her father. She beamed at his praise. He called to Ispaca. 'Go with your sister and make sure she is safe.'

Ispaca looped a sheath of arrows over his shoulder and carried his bow. Tlalli held the little cub close to her chest. It seemed to look deep into her eyes and she felt a strong spiritual connection stir in her heart.

A group of children followed them to the edge of the village. 'We will call you Jaguar Girl now, Tilly.' They cried out, 'Jaguar Girl! Jaguar Girl!'

Tlalli led the way she had taken the previous day. She showed Ispaca the rope trap. 'The hunter probably meant to snare a deer,' he said. 'This little jaguar was just unlucky.'

'Well, she's lucky now, because I found her. I shall name her Izella, after the jaguar goddess.'

He smiled. 'I felt you were in trouble, Tilly. I almost thought my talisman was speaking to me.'

'Did you, Izzy? Well I'm sure mine spoke to me and showed me where to find the cub.' She wanted to share her amazing experience with Ispaca.

But then he spoiled everything. 'Na, that's rubbish. The talismans are old and beautiful, but I don't believe they have any power now.'

She was speechless. How could Izzy not believe? She found her voice. 'You have to believe, Izzy. If you don't believe the jaguar gods can't help us.'

But he laughed at her, making fun the way he always did when she was serious. She gritted her teeth, more determined than ever to keep everything to herself.

They reached the part of the forest where Tlalli had found the cub. She heard a deep roar that stilled her feet and she held her breath. A little way ahead, through the trees, she saw the mother jaguar. The big cat walked stealthily towards Tlalli and Ispaca, rapidly closing the space between them. They kept perfectly still and the jaguar also stopped, watching them.

Whether the cub heard the mother's call, or whether some other instinct registered with the animal, she began to squirm in Tlalli's arms, mewing softly. She laid the cub down. It sat up on its haunches and Tlalli gave her one last stroke, and in that moment she felt a strong bond between herself and the cub that could not be broken and she knew they would meet again.

The children walked away very slowly. The cub began crying loudly, calling to the mother cat. When they had moved far enough away not to be a threat, the mother jaguar bounded over to her cub. Tlalli felt sure now that she was protected by the jaguar goddess; so perhaps was Ispaca, whether he knew it or not.

They watched from a safe distance. The mother licked and nuzzled the cub with her head, trying to coax it to stand, but it was too weak. Tlalli remembered the feel of the cub's fur under her tongue, reminding her of her magical experience. Eventually the mother picked up her kit in her mouth and carried her away; the second cub scampered behind them. Tlalli and Ispaca watched the cats until they had completely disappeared, swallowed up by the forest.

10

The Spaniard

1534 Willkapampa, Tawantinsuyu (The Inca Empire)

Time had passed since Tlalli found the cub in the forest and reunited the jaguar family. She had not forgotten the joy of that moment, or her strange experience when she was filled with the spirit of the jaguar working within her, to save the life of the cub. It had been a gift from the gods, as special to her as her gift of prophecy.

Wisely, she remembered her father's words of caution; not everyone would understand her gifts, so she must continue to hide her special abilities. Although her father had delayed her move to Cuzco, she sensed her days with the tribe and her family were numbered. Today when she saw her father go up on the hillside to meet with the chaski she hurried to hear the news.

As the villagers gathered round their curaca he told them, 'The Spanish invaders are offering to share control of the country with the last remaining royal family. As I predicted, Prince Manco, Atahualpa's younger brother, has been chosen by them to be the ruling Sapa Inca and his coronation has already been held in Cuzco.' He continued relaying the news from the chaski. 'I find it hard to believe Manco is collaborating with the Spanish chief, Francisco Pizarro. Their armies have helped the Inca to win more battles in our civil war, but I can't help thinking they are playing a double game. The new Inca, Manco, is young and naïve. I fear he is being played for a fool and we will all live to regret his trust in them.' Tlalli could see her father's troubled look but she realised, in spite of his misgivings, the tribe would now have to support Manco as Sapa Inca and pay tribute to him.

She felt even more despondent when her father told them, 'Manco is now occupying the palaces and temples in Cuzco, including the Temple of the Sun.' She read the unspoken message in her father's eyes. The Sun Temple, called Qoricancha, was where the holy Acllas were schooled. There seemed no escaping that as the chief's daughter she would soon have to go there. For Tlalli, it would be like being imprisoned.

The Acllas lived in the palace attached to the Sun Temple. Tlalli would have to join other girls specially chosen to live there and be trained by the mamaconas to prepare special food, weave beautiful cloth, and generally serve the Inca and his royal household. Some girls would eventually be given as wives or mistresses to favoured nobles. Now that would mean to the Spanish lords and nobles also. As Tlalli grew taller and her long black hair fell down to her waist, her father often told her she became more beautiful every day as she moved towards womanhood. This made her even more afraid.

On her twelfth birthday the rejoicing for the curaca's daughter began. The music, dancing and feasting started at midday. The sweet tones of the panpipes filled the air as the village celebrated Tlalli's special day. Her spirits lifted when she saw Paullu come down from the high pastures to join in the festivities. Thunder had been rolling round the valley all week. Lightning flashed, bouncing around the tops of the high mountains. Underneath her happiness, she felt uneasy, thinking the dark clouds forecast more than just a summer storm.

As always, before the feast her father addressed the tribe. He spoke openly of his deep mistrust of the Spaniards, now living at the Inca's court, justifying his delay in sending Tlalli to serve there. He warned his people about what he had learned from the chaski.

'These foreigners are bringing their Spanish priests with them, strange looking men in dark gowns, their heads shaved on top. They carry black boxes which open up revealing thin white sheets covered with tiny black marks. They hold up crosses and pray to them. These priests remain at the villages and make our people build what they call churches, to their god. They force the people to do this and burn any evidence of native worship to our own gods. Those who refuse are flogged or murdered.'

The tribe cried out with their jungle howls and banged their pots, but Tlalli followed the direction of her father's eyes as he looked up the hillside. She spotted movement there as he called for silence. Two lookouts ran from the high road down into the settlement. They pointed back up the hill but it was too late.

Tlalli watched with everyone else in fearful silence, as a group of Spanish soldiers moved towards them. They were led down from the road by Inca warriors. They didn't wait for the normal courtesy of asking permission to enter the curaca's territory. Tlalli looked around, frightened that one of the strange priests might be with them.

As the group's leader rode towards them on a big black horse, she swallowed the terror rising in her, telling her to flee. She stood her ground and tried to follow her father's dignified stance, even though he had no choice other than to allow them entry into the village. There had been no time for the women and children to hide. Tlalli moved closer to her father. As curaca, he had to speak to this strange man.

'Well, Manari,' said the Spaniard, speaking through an interpreter, 'I have been told you have in your possession gold taken from the Sun Temple in Cuzco.'

Her father did not answer him. Tlalli remembered that when the treasure had been hidden two years before, Father had been sworn to secrecy by the Inca's emissary. She peeked out from behind her father. His silence seemed to anger the strange man, who remained seated on his horse.

The man shouted at her father, 'I am Gonzalo Pizarro, brother to the great Francisco Pizarro who has conquered all this land.' He swept his arm in a circle and his voice boomed out, 'All the gold in this country now belongs to His Majesty the King of Spain. I demand you hand it over to me!'

Tlalli gripped tight hold of her father's tunic as she saw the man's eyes blaze with anger. His soldiers began helping themselves to the food prepared for the feast, drinking the chicha, and spilling it on the ground.

The horse stamped its hooves and the Spaniard rode up and down scattering the frightened villagers. She stayed hidden behind her father fearing she might be trampled by the enormous beast. Somehow, these men had discovered that the Inca's golden treasures had been hidden by the tribe and they had come to collect it.

The man calling himself Gonzalo came right up to them. Tlalli felt the heat of the animal's breath as it snorted and neighed. She peered out from behind the bulk form of her father. The white-faced bearded man looked straight at her and she could see evil in his eyes. She didn't know how she could defend herself against such a powerful man who seemed to possess unearthly magic. He would take whatever he wanted and she didn't think even her father could stop him.

The Spaniard laughed at her feeble attempt to hide. He drew out his long steel sword from its scabbard, and pointing it at her father, he drew the horse closer to them. Her father did not flinch and the man flicked the tip of his sword round Kusi and hooked Tlalli by her skirt. He jerked her clear away from her father's protection and she fell to the ground, almost under the horse's hooves.

The Spaniard shouted, 'If you will not produce the gold, Manari, I will have this girl instead,' and he leaned down from the saddle to take hold of her by her skirt.

Her father leapt forward and pulled Tlalli clear. 'No! Spaniard, you will not have her; she is my daughter.' Ispaca and Paullu also came up either side of her, as if to form a guard.

Gonzalo Pizarro laughed even more although he could not now reach Tlalli. 'All the better,' he said, his voice booming loudly. 'A chief's daughter will make a fine mistress for me.'

Tlalli clung to her brother's arm, terrified that the strangers from her dreams had actually come to their village. She clutched her talisman, praying for help from her jaguar goddess. But she had no idea how Izella could help them or if she would.

Gonzalo turned his attention back to Kusi and held the point of the sword to his throat. 'Which is it to be, Manari, the gold or your daughter?' He looked around at the bewildered crowd. 'I could take all these women and girls. They will make excellent servants and mistresses for my soldiers.'

The villagers heard these words through the interpreter. Uncle Tutsi spoke up. 'Give him the gold, brother. We have no need of it but the women are our family.'

Her father held up his hand and spoke to the man. 'We have no quarrel with you, Spaniard. We serve the Inca and the gold belongs to him. Will you return the treasures to the temple at Cuzco?'

The Spaniard laughed at Kusi again. 'Of course, Manari, the Inca will be the first to see what I have retrieved from his thieving subjects.' Tlalli despaired that this man had called her father a thief. She flinched as he threw back his head and his booming laugh rang out, displaying his contempt for the Inca and her father.

But her father didn't answer the accusation. 'We will take you to where the gold is hidden,' he said and he summoned men to go with him. He whispered to Tlalli, 'Go home and tell the women to stay in their houses until the strangers have gone away.'

She ran off with Paullu towards the group of stone houses and viewed the men from a safe distance. From there she could see her father with some of his best warriors, including her brother Ispaca, lead the group of Spaniards down the trail which led to the old mine shafts in the big mountain.

Paullu said, 'Go home, Tlalli. I must return to my herds for my father is alone up on the hillside.'

'Goodbye, Paullu,' she said. 'I wish I could go with you to the safety of the high pastures.' As she watched him hurry away, she again touched her talisman, praying the goddess Izella would protect the jaguars who lived in the mountain; Paullu and the herds on the high pastures; and all her family. She hoped Izella could work her magic for Tlalli could do nothing.

11

Izella Awakes

Her father, his men, and the Spaniards had disappeared from view, swallowed up by the thick vegetation and trees. Tlalli began to walk up the terraces, planted with maize and potatoes, back towards her home. As she watched Paullu trudging up the steep hillside she thought about how he had stepped forward to protect her alongside her brother. She wished again she had not been promised to be a holy Aclla.

In the heat of the afternoon sun, perspiration ran down her neck and arms. Lightning still flashed back and forth around the mountains. She hardly noticed, her mind entirely preoccupied with the events she had just witnessed. Something welled up inside her she didn't recognise, a deep resentment and growing hatred for the invaders. They were now changing everything and everyone she loved.

As if to accentuate her feelings, a deep rumble filled the air and the ground began to shake. The earth trembled so violently her feet slipped from under her and she fell to the ground. Shock knocked the breath from her lungs. Villagers in the stone houses ran out into the open shrieking and yelling. Mothers clung to their babies and children wailed, pitifully clutching at skirts and hands. It was as if an angry giant stamped his foot and the whole world shook. Almost as suddenly as it had begun, the tremors ceased.

Tlalli had witnessed earthquakes before and they were always a terrifying experience. She scrambled to her feet, running home, frightened for her family. Some of the stone walls of the houses in the village had crumbled, but no one was badly hurt, just very frightened and bewildered, children left crying. She ran the last few paces to her house and was relieved to find her mother shaken but unharmed. She set about helping to calm her younger brothers and sisters and putting their home back in order. Plates and bowls had crashed to the ground from their ingle-nook shelves, smashing on the earthen floor. Pitchers of chicha and pots of maize had shattered leaving mess and muddle everywhere.

Mother began to weep over the spoiled food. 'Never mind,' said Tlalli, 'we are all safe so what does it matter?'

Her mother spoke fearfully, 'We are, but what about your father and brother, they took the Spaniards to the mine!' Tlalli's heart jumped, realising that the men could have been inside the old tunnels when the tremors struck. She rushed outside and ran like a deer, back across the terraces and down the old forest trail. She was joined by others who had also realised their men could be crushed in the mine. Had her plea to Izella been answered? Making an earthquake seemed a strange way to stop the Spaniards.

She cried with relief when she saw their men coming back up the trail, led by her father, with her brother beside him. Only then, did she remember her father's order to stay hidden and she ran for cover behind the trees.

The Spaniard, Gonzalo Pizarro, now led the big black horse he had been riding when they arrived, for the horse was limping. 'A curse on this wretched country!' he shouted. 'We will be back, Manari,' he snarled at her father. 'The gold may be sealed in the mountain for now, but I expect your men to dig it out for us. We will return to collect the treasure in ten days.' He waved his sword in her father's face as if the curaca had caused the earthquake and the loss of the gold. 'You will hand over every last piece to me. Should you fail, every woman in your tribe will be taken!'

The Spaniard and his men continued up the valley back onto the Inca road to Cuzco. From her hiding place, Tlalli saw her father with his hand on Ispaca's shoulder watching them go. Her growing hatred of this particular Spaniard churned inside her and she marvelled that her father seemed to remain so controlled.

During the days that followed Tlalli wondered if Izella had helped her or the tribe. It was true she had not been taken by the Spaniard, and that the treasure remained safe in Mount Yaguar, but now the tribe were under threat of a worse fate.

Her father sent more and more men to try to open up the collapsed mine shaft and gain entry to the area where the gold had been hidden two years previously, but the task seemed impossible. A very long length of tunnel had completely collapsed apparently burying the gold in the mountain. Her father called a council with the tribe's elders. Tlalli went with him and Ispaca. She had been told to serve the elders with the chicha, but she also listened to discover how her father intended to deal with the tribe's problem.

Kusi told the elders, 'I do not think the gold can ever be retrieved. I am sure that when Pizarro comes again he will think we have tricked him and will take reprisals against the tribe as he threatened.'

'A plague on these wretched invaders!' said Tlalli's Uncle Tutsi. 'If we have to defend our homes and families we will fight them.'

'Bravely said, my brother,' answered her father, 'but our tribe alone cannot hope to win against these men. They will keep sending more soldiers until we are defeated.' Tlalli's father walked among the trusted elders. He went up to the campfire and stared into the flames.

'If I go to Cuzco and speak with Manco Inca, he may offer the tribe some protection.' He looked to his brother Tutsi. 'I leave you in command and charge you with continuing the search for the gold. It is the only way to stop the Spaniards from taking all the women.'

Tlalli had heard her father's words and she shuddered thinking of his mission. Why had Izella not heeded her call for help? What could she do to help father?

That night Tlalli fell asleep thinking about the problems brought on the tribe by the Spaniards. Her mind moved on to remember the jaguars she had seen up on the ridge at Mount Yaguar. As the images appeared through her dream, a huge jaguar materialised before her, not as a solid form, but translucent, its golden coat shimmering like the wings of a dragonfly.

'I am Izella, goddess of the mountain,' said the jaguar. 'For thousands of years we have been forgotten and our powers have grown weak. Only human prayers can make us strong again. You have called and awakened me. It is you who must fulfil my work to keep the land of our fathers sacred and free.'

Tlalli stared at this apparition, not really understanding the words. 'I am only a child. Tell me what it is I must do.'

The jaguar lifted its huge head and gave a mighty roar. 'You must follow the Legend and remember the lesson learned, then you will know what to do.'

Tlalli could see the image of the goddess was fading. 'Please, Izella, how can I help my people? How can I help the jaguars living in the mountain?'

She felt frantic to know the answers as the image receded before her eyes.

Izella's voice began to fade. 'I will protect the jaguars and they will guard the treasure. You must fight for the rights of your own people. You will see these things are all the same; we are both guardians of our heritage, of the past and of the future.' The image of the jaguar disappeared and Tlalli slept on the wings of the dream.

Before sunrise, she awoke with a plan in her head, for now she understood the message in her dream. She hurried to speak with Ispaca before he joined the men working at the mine shaft. She knew exactly what she must say to him.

'Issy, last night I dreamed the earthquake was a sign from our jaguar gods.'

Ispaca began to laugh, for he had always considered her talk of dreams just childish prattle. This time she held up her hand demanding he listen.

'Don't you see, brother? The treasure cannot be taken by these wicked men, or anyone else, for it is under the protection of the jaguar gods.'

Ispaca drew his eyebrows close together. 'But that makes a big problem for us, Tilly,' he scowled. 'Now the Spaniard will persecute the tribe just as he threatened.'

Tlalli would not be silenced. 'I understand what you say, but we can overcome them.'

'You heard what father said, how can we when they are so strong?' Ispaca looked as if he would walk away from her pleadings, so Tlalli tried again to make him understand.

'Issy, don't you see, the treasure represents everything we stand for. The invaders have already taken so much gold and silver, now they will rob us of our homes and land. This treasure is the last symbol of our heritage as the rightful people of this land. If these Spaniards are allowed to take it they will crush our people as well, and everything we love. It is just as told in the Legend of the Jaguar.'

'I don't understand. What are you saying we must we do?' Ispaca was no longer mocking, seeming to wait on her words.

'You and I must make a vow, Issy, and promise to follow it forever.'

He still didn't seem convinced. 'Tell me first,' he said.

She held up her hands to the sky as they did when they worshipped. 'We must promise to fight against those who try to crush our way of life and our beliefs. We must keep the secrets of our ancestors safe and hide our sacred treasures from thieves – even to the point of death. We must do this in the name of Inti the Sun God, and the jaguar gods Toquri and Izella, for you and I are under their protection.'

She turned to her brother and took hold of his hands. 'Will you take this promise with me, Issy?'

He still seemed perplexed, not quite understanding her. 'But you are a girl, a child. How can you talk of fighting such a fearsome enemy?'

Tlalli shook her head. 'No, I cannot fight with weapons but I can still be a warrior. You are a skilled jungle hunter. You must use the cunning tricks you know to hunt this enemy down and you must teach me also.' She shook his arm. 'We can do this, Issy, and we must.'

Ispaca's eyes revealed his understanding. 'Ah! Now I see what you are saying,' he said, 'We can harass them on their journeys, set false trails, sabotage their camps, steal their horses and hide what they try to steal from us. There are many ways we can hinder them. I like that idea.'

'Yes, yes!' said Tlalli. 'We can ask trusted friends to join us. The jaguars have shown us what we must do and their spirit will guide us.'

Ispaca caught her enthusiasm. 'I am with you, Tilly. I will take this vow with you.'

'I knew you would, dear Issy. But we must keep this a secret. Tell only those we trust completely, or our lives will be at risk.' Then she thought about her father going to see the Inca and putting his life at risk to save the women of the tribe. She felt sure that her prayers to Izella would offer him protection and this was, perhaps the best gift she could give him.

She held hands with Ispaca and they repeated the vows once more, just as the rising sun cast a halo of light around Mount Yaguar. Tlalli felt Izella's spirit glowing within her. She had persuaded Ispaca to be by her side she was not afraid any more.

12

Germany

April 1931, Friedrichshafen, Germany.

I open my eyes and look out of the carriage window. The rhythmic movement of the train as it devours the miles from Stuttgart, south to Friedrichshafen and Lake Constance, has lulled me into dozing and I am only vaguely aware of the countryside flashing past. Half in my subconscious, I am back in my dream world with Tlalli, her homeland of mountains and forests, the challenge she has set herself to fight the Spanish invaders. Her name came to me in a dream, and I know she spoke directly into my mind. She is so brave; I constantly wonder what happened to her and if I will ever know.

Grace's voice breaks my reverie. 'I'm going for a cigarette, Christina.' Still half asleep I nod to acknowledge her. As she pulls open the sliding door to the corridor I am jolted wide awake as a blast of track noise enters the carriage. It is immediately shut off again as the door closes once more.

I watch Grace through the inner carriage window. I like viewing her discreetly; she is such a sophisticated lady. She attaches a Black Cat cigarette to one of her many holders and sparks a flame with her jewelled gold lighter. I learnt long ago that Grace has never been content to sit idle and live on her husband's money, not even when he was alive. Travel is her passion, especially by airship. With her title, Lady Grace, she is more a celebrity than just a journalist, particularly with the Americans, who treat her like royalty. So now I have two women in my life whom I admire.

I'm impatient for our trip to South America on the German passenger airship *Graf Zeppelin* to begin, which is why we are going to Friedrichshafen, the starting point for the flight. Our destination is Brazil, to meet up with Sam. It seems such a long time ago we became officially engaged and then last September he left the country. I have to admit that I find the idea of being a married woman quite daunting. Sometimes I long to see him again and feel the warmth of his love. Then I imagine living permanently in Brazil and being so far away from home. The image of his face seems to fade and I can't recall his features. This vacillating of my emotions is very disconcerting and I try to think only about seeing him again; surely that will help me to decide. Do I love him enough to marry him after all?

I have been at a loss since dear Daddy passed away last winter. His health had been very poor this last year. Now I miss him and his wise counsel and wish I had been a better daughter. Grace is now my official guardian until I come of age. So far she has been just the same dear friend as before and we discuss everything together. I'm sure she won't ask me to do anything unless we both agree the details first.

When Sam and I became engaged Daddy was very happy for me. He told me: 'Money will always ensure you have a good and comfortable life, Christina, but only sharing that life with someone you love will make you truly happy.' He shook Sam's hand warmly and kissed me but when we were alone again he said: 'Wherever you go in the world to make your home, don't sell Madeley Hall, then you will always have a home in this country to return to.' I wonder now, did he think if I went to live in Brazil I might discover it was not just a big step, but a step too far?

I stand up to smooth out the creases in my skirt and I catch my reflection in the wide speckled mirror over the seats. For this trip I've finally had my long blonde hair cut short: shingled at the back, but with the sides longer, level with my chin. It does look very chic; now I wonder if Sam will like my new look.

Grace returns to our carriage. She has arranged this trip to help me make my decision. She knows all the German airship people and I'm only just beginning to think about the journey which will start in a few hours' time. 'What's it like travelling in the airship, Grace? Does it rock like a ship?'

Her face betrays a childlike anticipation. 'You are in for a rare treat, my dear. I really can't explain how wonderful the sensation is when you travel in the *Graf.* It's certainly not like being on board a ship, and won't make you feel sick. And it's not like an aeroplane, which sometimes is noisy and turbulent.' She smiles at me encouragingly. 'Besides, when you meet Commander Eckener you will know you are in very safe hands.'

Uppermost in my mind is the prospect of travelling on to Perú from Rio. I must ensure this is part of our itinerary so I steer the conversation to this. 'I've studied the inventory of Uncle Peter's house in Cuzco, and all the photographs, Grace. It's just as I imagined it to be.' I had received these from the solicitor only days before we departed for Germany and was pleased to discover the photographer was the friend who took Uncle Peter to the river and photographed the jaguar. I tell Grace he has invited us to visit him when we reach Cuzco.

'Oh,' says Grace, 'what is his name?'

'Martin Chambi, he has a studio in Cuzco and he sends me his condolences. He also said he would be happy to be our guide during our visit.'

'Hmm, well, we'll have to see about that, if we ever get to Perú,' says Grace.

I worry I still might not have the last word on that subject, but distract myself by looking out of the carriage window. The train seems to be slowing down and I guess we are nearing the end of the journey.

'Are you looking forward to seeing Sam again?' Grace asks and she takes a gold compact from her handbag, looking at her reflection critically.

'Oh, yes,' I reply, 'I'm longing to see him and the hacienda he has bought. He tells me there are lots of paddocks and pastures and I can have as many horses as I like.' She dabs her nose with the puff as I prattle on. 'Do you think he will still agree to take me to Perú? It has been in my mind for so long.'

'Longer than your commitment to marry Sam?' says Grace and I realise she knows what I am thinking.

I hesitate. 'Oh, yes, well, I have known about Uncle Peter's house in Perú since I was a child. But seeing Sam again is more important.' I hope I have allayed any fears she may have about my commitment to marry Sam. I can't even tell Grace about the affinity I feel to Perú and my own connection to it through my dreams, so I change the subject. 'Sam has said he will teach me to fly!'

'That all sounds marvellous, Christina, but before you finally decide to marry Sam you need to be very sure you really love him.' She snaps the compact shut and drops it back into the bag. 'Believe me,' she continues, 'I know what it's like to be trapped in a loveless marriage.' I realise now I misread her concern. It is for me, not my promise to Sam, and I love her all the more for that.

We go to bed very early and I'm glad sleep overtakes me quickly. We are woken at the unearthly hour of 2.00am and I realise I have just experienced another dream about Tlalli. She was upset by something. The Spanish soldiers came to her village. There is one who is in charge and she is very afraid of this man. I can see his face and it seemed familiar to me. Why should that be? Perhaps I have lived through these times, and my own subconscious memory is stirring as these dream images flash through my head. It is a puzzle and I have no answers. I promise myself I will record this in my journal later, but now I hurry to dress and be ready for our epic journey.

It's still dark when we leave The Kurtgarten Hotel on the shores of Lake Constance setting off at 3.00am and travelling with other ticket holders by taxis to the airfield. Along the dark and narrow road, little huddles of pedestrians are momentarily illuminated in the head-lamp beams from the line of cars and bicycles; then they are left behind in pools of darkness.

Even inside the taxi, I can sense the aura of excitement in the night air. Grace says no one wants to miss the dawn lift-off of the great airship. As we approach the airship shed this huge structure rises up out of the night and towers over a hundred feet into the sky, so long the opposite end disappears, lost in the night shadows.

At the gate our taxi is surrounded by a crush of people. The driver sounds his horn and revs the engine with impatience. We are waved through the gate by the guard and we drive right up to the entrance. The two huge doors are wide open, ready for the airship's departure. We climb out, each holding one bag of luggage. Our heavy cases were taken when we arrived yesterday and placed on board the airship.

The *Graf Zeppelin* almost fills the vast interior of the shed; I have never seen anything so enormous. Grace tells me: 'It's over seven hundred feet long and higher than a ten storey building.' The nose looms over our heads, facing the entrance and the night sky.

The gondola, containing the passenger car, is right under the hull resting on wooden trestles and the whole airship seems balanced precariously on the back of the gondola. It shimmers and glints under the lights like a giant mythological being.

There are hundreds of people in the shed and such a babble of noise. So great is the size of the *Graf Zeppelin* I can't believe that we are about to travel to the other side of the world inside this huge craft, or that Grace has already done so several times, including a flight right round the world.

'I said you would not believe your eyes,' says Grace, and I see she is brimming with pride and pleasure at my amazement. I catch hold of her arm and together we begin the long walk down the shed to embark on this incredible journey.

13

Graf Zeppelin

I am fascinated watching dozens of men hurry about their tasks. Handling lines splay out from the airship's hull like the mooring ropes of an ocean liner, then split into many ropes each held by two or three men. It is manmade but so majestic in its size, shape and elegance, my thoughts return once more to the gods of mythology. I am sure they would have demanded to be transported to the sun, the moon and the stars in the glorious *Graf Zeppelin*.

As we near the entrance to the hundred foot long gondola which is the centre of activity, a buzz of voices breaks into my thoughts, bringing me back to earth. Multiple accents reach my ears: French, Spanish, Russian and English. Replies from the uniformed officers by the airship doorway are in German, some repeated in English, and everyone seems to understand one another. As ticket holders we are asked to wait while the last of the preparations are made to receive us.

The front end of the gondola is the control car. It is curved like a giant horseshoe with large open windows. Airship officers lean out shouting orders to the ground crew. Grace clasps my arm tighter and gestures towards one of these men. 'Look, that's Commander Eckener,' she says. 'He is always in command, even when the flight is under another captain.' She steers me towards the gangway; she knows the procedure precisely and that it is time for us to board.

A voice speaking English with a heavy German accent booms out. 'Lady Grace Drummond Hay and Miss Christina Freeman, please board the airship.' We are the only lady passengers and are accorded privilege over the men.

Once on board I am introduced to some of the crew. Like naval officers, they are all resplendent in their airship company uniforms. All except Herr Kubis, the chief steward, who wears a dinner jacket with bow tie which looks a little out of place at four a.m. We follow him to the accommodation. He is a big man, and seems to bulge under his civilian clothes. Perhaps he conceals a woolly jumper and long-johns under his smart attire. The thought makes me smile but I wonder if I will be warm enough in what I have brought with me.

Kubis cossets Grace like a long lost daughter and they reminisce over the round-the-world-flight in 1929. She told me that's what propelled her to world-wide celebrity status; her and the *Graf*. She telegraphed her reports to the Hearst newspapers in New York and then they were sent around the world. It seems that today this is the only way to travel around the globe. It's certainly much faster than the ocean-going steamers so perhaps soon we will be travelling into space, like Buck Rogers or my mythological gods.

'These are your cabins, ladies,' says Herr Kubis, 'side by side.'

'We were quite prepared to share,' says Grace.

'Not necessary, my Lady,' says Kubis. 'There are only twelve guests on this flight, we have cabins to spare.'

Graces smiles and nods as Herr Kubis makes his excuses to go and attend to the other passengers although he calls them guests. And that's what we are, privileged guests in a luxury floating hotel.

Grace is hanging some of her gowns into the narrow wardrobe space in her cabin. She puts on an extra coat over her jacket. 'Now, go and unpack your warm coat,' she says to me. 'You will need the extra layer once we are up in the clouds.'

I check my cabin and am glad to find it has a porthole where I can look out on the world. Once I have put on my wool coat, Grace leads us back to the main part of the accommodation. She calls it the drawing room, although it is to be our dining area and communal lounge. It spans the entire width of the gondola with a large window in each corner. We find the seats we want by one of these view-points.

'Ah, my dear Lady Grace, how wonderful to see you again.' A uniformed officer holds out his hands as he moves towards her.

'Commander Eckener!' Grace clasps his hands and he lifts hers to his lips. 'You know you can't keep me away for long,' she enthuses. 'I keep finding excuses to travel across the Atlantic just to see you again.'

He is a great bear of a man with thoughtful eyes, a goatee beard and short-cut greying hair; a pair of binoculars swings from around his neck, slung from a worn leather strap. 'I think your love affair is with the *Graf,* not me,' he says chuckling.

Grace turns and pulls me into their rather personal space. 'Commander, may I present my friend, Miss Christina Freeman. We are going to Brazil on a holiday. Commander Eckener, whom Kubis called Doctor, stretches out his hand and shakes mine, very firmly.

'Delighted to welcome you, my dear; you could not have a wiser or lovelier travelling companion.' Another officer is trying to attract his attention, calling out his name from the floor of the shed via the open doorway. 'You will have to excuse me for there is much to do before we can lift off.'

'Of course, Commander, we understand,' says Grace and we let him go.

A steward is immediately before us with a tray, laden with flutes of sparkling golden champagne. I am tempted to take one but Grace waves him away. 'Champagne before breakfast?' She shakes her head. 'Please bring some hot tea.' The steward disappears to do her bidding.

We sit down again at the window seats. Outside I can see dozens of men now assembling in groups, grasping hold of the rope lines. More passengers have joined us in this room. It is very richly decorated, with flocked wallpaper, deep red drapes and carpets. The chairs are all lightweight, upholstered in matching dark red brocade. Dining tables are laid with white damask linen, bone china and silver cutlery, monogrammed with the company emblem. The only absence from the tables is ash-trays; smoking is strictly forbidden anywhere on the airship.

As we sip our tea Grace takes a folded sheet of paper from her handbag and sitting close to me she opens it. 'This is a list of the passengers,' she whispers. I must look surprised. 'I am a journalist first,' she says. 'I make it my business to know these things.'

From the list she points out the men she already knows. There is Max Geisenheyner, a German reporter and editor of the magazine *Frankfurter Zeitung*. Another journalist, a young Frenchman, who is a reporter for *Le Matin* and an American financier, who she says lives in Switzerland, She also says that she will avoid him as he is always complaining because he can't smoke.

Another American is Bill Leeds, who is a multi-millionaire and heir to a tin-plate fortune. She knows a lot about these society people and tells me he is recently divorced from his wife Xenia, who is a Russian Princess. He has plenty of money of his own as his family also builds ships. Grace had already told me about his antics on the 1929 flight, constantly playing his wind-up gramophone, which infuriated Commander Eckener. On the list are four other names, people she says she has never met: a Frenchman, a Spaniard and two Brazilians.

One of the airship officers closes the main door and announces our departure is about to commence. I'm glad that Grace made sure we had a window seat, as several men are gathering behind us for a glimpse of this historic event. Perhaps one day it will be thought quite ordinary to travel like this. Or perhaps, as Sam once told me, big aeroplanes will be built to carry passengers more quickly even than airships and this delightful mode of travel will then be obsolete. But for now, I savour the moment and feel I am truly part of history.

The order is shouted from the control car. 'Luftschiff Marsch!' Airship March!

The handling ropes are pulled taut by the groups of men hauling on each line and the *Graf* is now balanced on the giant wheels beneath the gondola and the tail fin. The famous 'walking out of the shed' begins. We are moving slowly, and everyone in the shed is walking with us. The men set a steady pace and metre by metre we move out towards the open doors.

As we emerge, I am surprised to see the dawn has broken and the sky is shot through with ribbons of pink and blue dressed with lacy white clouds and a hazy golden sun. The new day has the innocence of a child's painted nursery and we are the new and exciting toy. Once the airship is well clear of the sheds we stop.

The voice of our captain, whom for this trip is Captain von Schiller, is heard, announcing from the adjacent control car. 'Luftschiff Hoch!' Airship up! This command is repeated, as the instruction is passed to all the crew, even by some of the passengers.

Through the window I can see the heads of the men below us. They stand side by side clinging on to the rail which is mounted right round the bottom edge of the gondola. As the water ballast is released the men stretch their arms up above their heads as they attempt to hold the airship down against the lift of the hydrogen gas.

Then they let us go. In fact they seem to throw the airship up in the air and we rise very quickly leaving the ground behind. Straight up we fly to join the clouds and lose ourselves in the pink and blue sky. Everything below is shrinking smaller and smaller, until the waving ground crew and onlookers are like tiny ants and we are the eye of the giant lumbering above them.

The passengers, including us, applaud the lift off and more champagne is drunk. Now we are airborne, the men soon leave their window views and turn their attention to the business of ingratiating themselves with each other.

Grace raises her eyebrows. 'Business will be done on board and deals will be struck as if they are all still within the hallowed halls of banks, boardrooms and men's clubs throughout the world.' I am not sure if she considers this good or bad, but it seems that we will be excluded from this male preserve. 'I keep my ears open and my mouth shut,' she adds with a chuckle. 'It's amazing what comes out of the mouths of men when they think you don't understand them.'

I smile. Recently, I have tried to be more assertive but now I feel quite naïve, and I am very glad Grace is my mentor and friend. It is also obvious that as the only ladies on board we will attract a lot of attention. The American, Bill Leeds, comes over and I am introduced to him. He is with another man. 'May I introduce Don Diego Alvarez, Grace?' says Leeds.

Grace shakes the man's outstretched hand and introduces me. 'Are you going to Brazil on business, Don Alvarez?' she asks.

'I live there, Lady Grace,' he says in English but with an accent. I am not sure if he is Spanish or Brazilian. He continues, 'I have business interests in various parts of South America.'

Grace does not pursue her questioning and he smiles at her and then at me. His eyes are dark and beguiling like glittering black jet; I shiver involuntarily and feel uneasy. Don Alvarez is very suave and is immaculately dressed in a dark green suit, sporting a bright yellow silk tie. His small black moustaches make him look a little menacing, although he smiles constantly.

The American seems to want Grace to know the other man's business. He speaks with an American drawl. 'Don Alvarez owns gold and silver mines on the continent. He is looking for investors to fund new mining opportunities.'

'Well, I'm sure there will be plenty of takers on board,' says Grace, looking round. She turns to me. 'Shall we go and make ourselves respectable for breakfast, Christina?' She takes my arm to lead the way back to our cabins.

The two men let us pass. 'Two more respectable ladies will surely not be found for hundreds of miles,' says the American. They laugh at Bill Leeds's silly joke as we retreat out of the drawing room.

As we reach our cabins Grace says, 'Why must men always treat women like empty-headed china dolls? I do not answer her, for I am replaying the conversation in my head. I find myself gripped by a feeling of déjà-vu for which there is no reasonable explanation, since I have never met either of these men before.

14

The Flight

The Graf Zeppelin, over Europe.
Because we have all been up half the night, breakfast is served at 6am. Now Grace wants to finish her first newspaper report so I sit by the window in my cabin and gaze down on the world as we drift over Europe.

The *Graf* follows a route along the Rhine. Below us the river winds a silver-grey ribbon through the German countryside. Our first landmark is the falls at Schaffhausen on the Swiss border. Where the river hits the rapids it erupts and cascades in a mass of charging white foam leaping up towards us. I have never seen such a landscape before yet something scratches deep inside me as though it is grating at my memory.

The airship doesn't fly very high and now the countryside is rather flat. A patchwork of fields and hedges divides the land unchanged since feudal times. I can see farm labourers ploughing with yoked oxen or standing with horses and carts in the lanes. They look up and wave their caps or clasp tight to the horses' bridles as the animals take fright at our fearful and noisy passing in their quiet rural patch of sky. We are as alien as spacemen to this rustic community.

I am in awe of Grace's journalistic skills and not to be outdone, I rummage in my suitcase for my new journal notebook purchased for this trip. I had written a little on the train at the start of our journey from England; now I add the detail of our time in Friedrichshafen and the wonders of the *Graf.*

As I write, I think about Sam and the new life I am contemplating. Perhaps this visit will help me finally decide to settle in South America with him. My stomach tightens, and I realise making that decision will not be as easy as perhaps it should.

Now I have brought my journal up to date I go to see if Grace is finished. She is, and we go to the control car wearing our hats and fur coats, as she says it is always chilly in there. Commander Eckener is looking out of an open window but he turns and greets us again. His face is beaming. 'Ah, my dear Lady Grace I must tell you about my forthcoming trip to the North Pole.'

Grace gasps with surprise. 'Oh, how wonderful! You told me you wanted to make the trip when we flew round the world. So when are you going?'

'Sometime later this year, I hope. It will be such a coup for the company and further proof of the capability of my airships to the world. Will you write about it in your newspaper?'

'Of course, of course, dear Commander, it will be such an achievement for you.'

He smiles and nods his head. 'We will take Arctic scientists with us and when we hover over the ice they will climb down rope-ladders to perform their experiments. Then they will climb back on board.' He laughs heartily. 'No trekking hundreds of miles with dogs and sleighs for them, or sleeping in the bitter cold under canvas.'

Grace laughs also. 'Oh, it sounds so exciting. You must let me know when you are going. I might even ask to join you!'

'You are always welcome aboard my airships, dear lady, always.'

He goes back to where the crew are steering the airship and I'm introduced to Captain Hans von Schiller and the other officers of the watch who explain how the airship works. I find this all so fascinating and watch the wheelman turn the rudder-wheel holding our course and the elevator man at another wheel maintaining the trim and taking the airship up and down. Then we see the navigators who plot our course on detailed charts.

We can hear the wireless operator giving a constant stream of information on the weather and this is overlaid on the navigation chart. All will define the weather through which the *Graf* must fly as it travels south-west across the globe. The captain explains these men are all experienced sailors who have trained at the Helmsman's School of Navigation in Hamburg.

He smiles and tells us, 'When Commander Eckener is on board he always has the last word in all the airship's manoeuvres, for he has kept the *Graf* and her passengers safe these last three years.'

Grace asks his permission to send her copy to the newspaper in New York via the ship's telegraph. The Captain is delighted to assist and we go to that section of the car. We wait while the operator taps out her words via the tele-printer. We thank the operator and return to the drawing room for morning coffee.

Several of the men are engaged in lively conversation. They all look smart and smell of cologne, which probably masks the fact that none of us are allowed more than one jug of water to wash. Bill Leeds is again with Diego Alvarez. They are talking to Joseph Viner, the American financier, also to Eduardo Moreno, a Brazilian, who is, I believe, a banker.

Coffee is served by Herr Kubis and the young cabin boy Fritz. Grace has her 1930 South American Handbook and is now busy reading. I sit opposite her by a window but cannot help listening to the men's conversation which is mostly in English. We have left the French coast and, skirting the North West tip of Spain, are now crossing the Bay of Biscay.

Alvarez is speaking of surveys just completed on two of his mines. 'In Mexico,' he says, 'the mines at Veta Madre were thought exhausted by 1890 after 400 years of working by hand. The mine El Verde, which has belonged to my family since the time of the conquistadors, has been re-surveyed by a specialist company selling new drilling equipment.' His black eyes dart around the faces surrounding him. 'They consider there are many seams which will show good yields of gold and silver deeper in the rocks than hand-working could ever have found.' Alvarez seems to have captured everyone's attention.

'I've seen the surveys, gentlemen,' says Bill Leeds. He claps Diego on the shoulder. 'Tell them about the Perúvian site, Alvarez,' he enthuses and says to the listening audience, 'You must hear about this.' The mention of Perú sharpens my interest.

Diego Alvarez tells of another mine in a remote part of the Vilcabamba, north of Cuzco. 'This mine has also revealed hidden deposits of gold and silver but my survey also found evidence of diamonds and emeralds.'

I am very familiar with this area; at least I am on paper. It is on the maps and photographs I have received with the ones of Uncle Peter's home in Cuzco, and of course, this is the landscape in my dreams. As he talks I am imagining the scene.

Alvarez then says, 'I own four other mines on the continent, which could also be re-opened. However, I need more funds to continue surveying them for new seams.'

I am intrigued by this connection, but also I am again struck by the feeling I had when I first saw him, that there is something familiar in his manner and voice. In looks, I do not know him, and of course he is a stranger, but the feeling persists and I find it curious as if I am being drawn into a mystery.

The conversation progresses to talk of issuing bonds and raising capital for a new mining venture. Alvarez maintains he is a novice in such things but the Brazilian banker is offering to act on his behalf, for a percentage of the profit. The American, Joseph Viner, wants to see the surveys and to make some enquiries. Tentatively, he says he may put up some capital.

'God knows,' says Viner, 'we have all taken a hammering since the Wall Street crash. It would be good to put money into gold mining. I like you, Alvarez, and I trust Leeds's judgement.'

Leeds is cock-a-hoop and calls for drinks all rounds, setting Kubis off to collect the orders. Leeds turns to us. 'Please order what you like ladies, the drinks are on me.' It is nearly lunchtime so Grace orders sherry for us. She whispers to me that a deal is on the table so we may as well celebrate with the men.

I pick at the lunch, still preoccupied with thoughts of a gold mine in Perú. There is a parallel in this with my dreams but I can't seem to grasp the thread. Bill Leeds and Diego Alvarez sit opposite us. I feel the Spaniard's eyes and when I look up he is smiling at me. Why does his face seem familiar? After lunch I am thankful we retire to our cabins. Grace wants to sleep but I sit by the window once more intending to write in my journal.

Dream images float before my eyes. Tlalli went to a mountain to find the jaguars. Her mountain had once been a gold mine. Is that the connection I was looking for? There was no gold left in her mountain, even then. Is that right? I'm not sure. These dreams don't follow any chronology, so I am always confused; confused but fascinated. Am I really seeing my own past life?

15

Mount Yaguar

1534, Willkapampa, Tawantinsuyu (The Inca Empire)

Tlalli stared up at the high road her eyes searching for movement. What if the Spaniard had taken Father prisoner? What if the Inca couldn't help him? She felt Ispaca's hand on her shoulder. It had been many days since their father went to Cuzco to fulfil his quest, seeking the Inca's protection from the Spaniard's vengeance.

'Let's go home, Tilly. Perhaps he will come tomorrow.'

Tlalli was reluctant to give up her watch. As she turned round for one last look she spied something moving up on the road. Shading her eyes she waited. 'Issy! It's him. I know it is. He has come home!' They shouted out a greeting and hurried to meet him.

Father looked tired and dusty from the journey, but after he had refreshed himself and eaten with his family, he told them what had happened in Cuzco. 'I waited three days for an audience with Manco Inca. When at last I came before him, I told how the earthquake had sealed his treasures inside the mountain.'

Father said, 'At the Inca's court, Gonzalo Pizarro grudgingly agreed to leave our tribe to continue the search without further harassment.' Their father had made a promise to the Inca: if the treasures could be retrieved from the mountain, he would return them to their rightful place in the Sun Temple. Tlalli knew their father would keep his word, but he told them, 'I doubt the Spaniard will keep to his side of the bargain.' Tlalli watched her father set more lookouts on all the trails leading to their settlement, showing he would never trust these treacherous foreigners.

Later, Ispaca came to find her. 'Little sister, I have thought long and hard about our vow,' he said. 'I want to start doing the things we talked of.' He looked very serious. 'You are still very young and only a girl.'

She wanted to argue with him but he didn't give her the chance. 'I am going to talk to Father. You must, for now, leave this with me. Our missions will be very dangerous but I promise it will begin.'

'But without me?' Her eyes pleaded with him.

'Only for the present, Tlalli. I cannot begin on this work with you. I need the strength of other men and permission from our father, for he is our leader, and must be consulted. It is my duty as his son.'

Tlalli knew Ispaca spoke the truth, but she looked away fighting back tears. She couldn't bear to think she had no part to play.

'Have faith, little sister,' he said. 'Your time will come. This is still your mission, and I will keep our vow.' He laughed as she scowled at him. 'Besides, you are the Jaguar Girl, the one who receives the messages from the gods. What can we do without you?'

She still didn't know how much Ispaca believed or if he was just teasing her. 'Very well, Ispaca, I hear you, but one day you will see me in a different light. When I am grown big and strong like you.' She walked away to hide her tears from him, determined she would still play her part. Her heart told her she had been born to fulfil this mission.

Although the immediate threat of reprisals against the tribe had been stayed, Tlalli's prophetic dreams still filled her nights with messages from the jaguar goddess Izella. In one of these dreams she had been set a task of her own to complete: Izella had told her she must journey to the dark side of the mountain.

A few days after her father's return she left home at first light and went into the forest. She didn't even tell Ispaca. His words had stung her deeply, so she went alone. She followed the trail into the forest trying to remember where she had found the cub, but that had been moons ago and the scenery constantly changed. She listened to all the sounds of the forest but she didn't see any signs a jaguar might leave.

She followed a little-used trail which led over the next pass and across country, using her instincts to try and reach the far side of Mount Yaguar. Cut paving blocks showed here and there, marking out an old Inca trail which wound through the foothills. She had been walking for hours when she looked up, aware that the high peak of Mount Yaguar had blotted out the sun. She had come a very long way from home, to the dark side of the mountain.

She heard rumbling. The ground trembled and her skin pricked with fear. Was this another earthquake? As she turned round she saw a group of men coming towards her; Indians running and Spaniards on horses coming from the direction of Cuzco. The animal's hooves thundered on the ground. This empty back road left her completely exposed with nowhere to hide. One Spaniard, riding a big black horse, shouted to the Indians and pointed at Tlalli.

'Ha! It is the Manari Curaca's daughter!' he shouted, and broke away from the other men. The huge black animal charged towards Tlalli. The man and the horse became as one beast and her feet seemed frozen to the ground. As they came closer she saw the rider clearly: the terrible Gonzalo Pizarro, who had tried to kidnap her before.

He laughed at her and the beast snorted and stamped while she stood still, stunned with fear. They circled round her and the animal's head pushed her forward, forcing her to stumble along the trail. She tried to recall the fine words she had spoken when taking her vow with Ispaca.

Faced with the reality of certain attack by this hated enemy, she knew that Ispaca had been right. The Spaniard would kill her and she didn't have the strength or courage to repel him. She touched her jaguar talisman mouthing a prayer to Izella.

'Qori!' shouted the man. 'Gold!' The beast's head pushed her forward once more, to make her keep walking. Her legs trembled so much she could barely stand and the path seemed to wash away as she fought back the tears filling her eyes.

Why does he say gold? Does he think I can lead him to the Incas' treasure? This evil man appeared set on a plan of his own to find the riches trapped by the earthquake. Tlalli desperately tried to recall her vow and the words of the jaguar in her dreams; she must not help him – she must stop his plan, and somehow, she must evade capture. Perhaps if she tried to climb up higher the beast would not be able to follow her. She stumbled on and soon they had left the other men far behind. The horse's head came so close she could feel its hot breath snorting down her neck. She trembled. Why had Izella told her to come to this place?

The sun did not penetrate the dark side of the mountain and she shivered as the trail turned and twisted leading higher up the mountain. Looking up, she saw snow on the mountain peak and looking down the forest had melted away. Now there were only grey rocks and boulders along the sides of the steep trail as the ground rose higher. Rigid with terror Tlalli lost her footing, and fell on her knees unable to go on.

Gonzalo kept laughing at her in a loud booming voice. She scrambled to her feet and turned round to face him. The Spaniard threw back his head and laughed all the more, his black eyes pierced right through her. The animal shook its huge head and the black mane flew out rippling in the cold wind. It neighed, as if laughing with the man.

She opened her mouth and screamed. Her voice echoed round the mountains. The man and horse seemed to laugh even louder and their voices echoed round and round the granite peaks, chasing her voice. Her eyes searched this way and that, trying to find a place to escape. Desperation gave way to anger, and that gave her courage. He must not capture me – I will escape!

As she looked up, the mountainside rose steeply: a wall of solid granite. Above that, she could see a shelf of overhanging rock, jutting out with a small crevice underneath. This was her only chance, and she scrambled away from the path, leaping up onto the rocks and squeezing into the crevice. He could not follow her through this narrow entrance, but she heard him bellow angry words she did not understand.

Tlalli squeezed her body through the tiny gap and pushed into a narrow passage through the rock-face. The rough, hard stone bruised her bones and scraped her flesh but her frantic efforts put distance between them. The passage seemed long, dark and cold. She could no longer see him but she could still hear the Spaniard's harsh angry voice echoing up from below.

The passage seemed to take a vertical climb and her sandaled feet slipped beneath her. She pushed further on, still climbing upwards, elated by her escape but so cold. The wind howled through the rocks and seemed to suck her breath away. A tiny shaft of daylight filtered down from the sky guiding her. The crevice narrowed and she had to shuffle sideways. She seemed to be right inside the mountain.

The tunnel came to an abrupt end with a big boulder barring the way. Trapped between the rocks, her hopes of escape died and she sank to her knees running her hands over the surface of the boulder. Low to the ground her fingers found a space between the rocks. Her heartbeat echoed in her ears and her chest heaved with the effort of breathing. She lowered her body flat and inched her way into the space. She could see nothing and had to feel the way forward with her hands, afraid the ground beyond might drop into an abyss. Her breath came in short rasps and she gasped as she crawled into the darkness.

There was a strange smell coming from the other side of the opening and when she had crawled through the length of her own body, she sensed the coolness of open space, and the terror within her began to subside. She sat up and stretched out her arms.

Very slowly she stood up and thought, this must be the jaguar's cave, for the smell was much stronger. One small shaft of light came dimly from the low entrance. As her eyes adjusted to the poor light, she tried to make out her surroundings. A low roar echoed round the cave paralysing her and she stared into a huge pair of amber coloured eyes! Not an apparition, but a real, live wild animal.

Tlalli crouched down then flung herself on the floor of the cave; she acted instinctively, and those same instincts told her the eyes belonged to a jaguar. Her best hope was to submit as a juvenile would to its parent. She kept her eyes tightly shut and clutched the talisman at her neck praying to her goddess. The cat did not attack, and from exhaustion and relief, eventually she fell asleep.

She awoke to total darkness. No light came seeping under the low entrance, for night had come. The smell of the jaguar still filled her nostrils but the cat didn't seem to be there. With joy she realised her prayers had been answered and she had made a friend. Perhaps now she could truly call herself Jaguar Girl, for Izella had protected her.

Tlalli stayed near the entrance to the cave for she couldn't find her way back down the mountain in the dark. She wondered if the Spaniard still searched for her and if she would be able to evade him and return home the next day. She felt a small sense of achievement. She had escaped from him

72

and stopped his attempt to make her lead him to the treasure. But whatever happened next, in this man she knew she had made an enemy.

16

Atlantic Crossing

April 1931, The Graf Zeppelin, Mid-Atlantic Ocean.
As I float thousands of feet above the earth I see a glorious sunset. It makes me feel close in spirit to Tlalli for her people worshipped the sun as a god. My joy of being on top of the world has surpassed all expectation. I watch the sun sink, leaving a trace of radiant colours across the sky. Tlalli's people thought everything in the natural world and the universe was sacred. How can it be wrong to worship the sun, the moon and the stars? Without them life on earth would not exist.

Uncle Peter passed this wisdom and philosophy on to me in his letters. Only now can I truly understand his words. I think he hoped I would benefit from his teaching and use it for good when I inherited his life's work. As I draw closer to his world and Tlalli's world I hope I can understand them both better and perhaps use the knowledge for a good purpose. What that could be I don't yet know.

The sun has disappeared from view and the colours fade, washed away in the dusk. The lights come on in the drawing room and the windows darken to reveal banks of slate-grey clouds through which we fly. Everyone is in party mood and to compensate for the fact that smoking is forbidden, Bill Leeds winds up his gramophone and treats us to some jazz numbers. He fools around doing Charleston steps and tries to persuade Grace and me to dance with him.

'I know what these lovely ladies would enjoy,' says Diego, 'something much more romantic than this clown dance.' He disappears towards the accommodation.

Bill Leeds smirks. 'Oh ladies, watch out for our romantic Spanish gentleman. He will try to steal your hearts.' I wonder what he will do. This man is beginning to dominate my thoughts. Diego returns, a gramophone record in his hands.

'I purchased this when I was last in Buenos Aires.' He places the disc on the turntable and Leeds insists on lowering the needle. The music, slightly distorted through the speaker, is very arresting. The rhythm is tango but with a strong Gypsy style influence. I do not think I have ever heard anything like it.

'Ah, a tango,' says Grace.

'An Argentine tango, milady,' says Diego and his feet are tapping to the staccato beat.

'Show us the steps,' calls Bill.

Diego looks despondent. 'Unfortunately, this is a romantic dance for two people and the steps are very complicated. Clown capers will not suffice for this passionate pas-de-deux.'

'He is right, Bill,' says Grace. 'I saw it performed in New York. The closeness of the dancers would make you blush.'

I feel a little overwhelmed by all this sophisticated chatter and decide to say nothing, but Bill seems used to having his own way. 'Then I must see this exotic spectacle, and perhaps learn to dance this tango myself.'

'I will take you to Buenos Aires, Bill.' Diego stretches his hand in a circle encompassing everyone listening. 'I will take you all to see this wonderful example of Spanish Latin American dancing.' The record comes to an end and Bill puts it on again.

The music seems to have lent the Spaniard courage and he stands up holding out his hand to Grace. 'Please, milady Grace, as you have seen it performed we may be able to give a taster to this interested audience.'

I am surprised that Grace agrees, allowing Diego to hold her close in a tango embrace. She looks so elegant in a black knee-length silk dress, embroidered with tiny pearls, wearing high-heeled court shoes. He propels her with a twisting movement and Grace's feet tangle round his legs. They laugh and try the move again. This time Grace lifts her feet, swinging her legs from her knees and apparently makes a reasonable effort to place them correctly around his feet.

'Bravo, milady!' he says, 'that is very good.' But it's his graceful movements which capture my attention. Grace protests that she can't dance anymore and Diego takes her back to her seat. He turns to me. 'Would you like to try, Miss Freeman?' he asks.

I realise I'm dying to try this dance. I hesitate, conscious it's against my better judgement.

Grace says, 'Go on, Christina, you will be better than me, I'm sure.'

I stand up, feeling flattered but also rather nervous. My dress is straight and knee-length. I am used to dancing in my cream leather, high-heeled shoes. Although I know the basic steps of modern ballroom dances, I don't know any Latin American dances, which are quite provocative.

Diego holds me as he did Grace and he counts the beats in my ear. I feel his hand on my back through the thin material of my dress. He twists my body using his grip on my other hand to twist me to the right, and then to the left, back into contact with his body. My hands shake and the pale coral pink silk seems to ripple. I feel the heat from his chest and the masterly grip of his hold on me. Our closeness both shocks and thrills me.

'Good,' he says, 'now this time we will walk, but lift your feet from the knees as you twist around me.' I tremble then stumble, treading on his feet as the music finishes.

'Oh, I'm sorry,' I say, giggling and blushing. The record is started again by Bill. Diego seems not discouraged and continues my lesson in the Argentine Tango. After three attempts I manage the moves without tripping over his feet again.

'That is very good,' he says. 'I will turn you into an expert dancer like the ladies of Argentina. Will you come to Buenos Aires with me to see them?' He is still holding me in the dance pose and his eyes seem to suggest more intimate invitations. My fleeting courage deserts me, and I stand back embarrassed, aware that all the eyes in the room are upon us.

'Grace and I are staying in Brazil,' I say a little flustered. 'We will have a better idea of our itinerary when we land at Recife. Then we are travelling to Rio with our host.'

Diego says, 'How will you go?'

'By plane,' I answer. 'It is all arranged.'

'There are many new air charter companies near the airship terminal,' says Diego.

'Yes, my fiancé owns one of them.' I feel compelled to say this to temper his advances.

'Oh, your fiancé!' he repeats, and then he hangs his head like a marionette. 'So you are spoken for, Miss Freeman. Oh, now I am very sad. I thought I might win your heart with my dancing.' He looks sad but his eyes flash with amusement. I know I am blushing and Grace comes to my rescue.

'Christina is engaged to Mr Samuel Watson, The Honourable Samuel Watson,' she says. 'He is also the owner of the British South American Air Taxi Line.'

'Sam!' says Diego, 'I know him well. I have used his services many times, but I didn't know he had an English rose for a fiancée.' Diego turns to Bill. 'It was Sam who flew me to Mexico.

'Well I'm damned,' says Bill. 'What a small world.'

'And with more air travel,' says Diego, 'it gets smaller and smaller.' Everyone laughs at this and he escorts me back to my seat. He bows with a flourish and although he is smiling I feel I am the subject of the joke. Once again my memory stirs with a strange recollection which I cannot place.

So ends our first day on the *Graf*. The Bay of Biscay and the islands of Madeira are well behind us now and there is nothing below us but the ocean and the darkness of the night. We say goodnight to the men in the drawing room and I go with Grace to retire to our cabins.

I am troubled by Diego and sleep is a long time coming. I feel drawn to him and yet, afraid of him, for his personality is magnetic and mysterious. The memory of being in his arms feels etched into my skin and the thought of his warm body makes me shiver. Eventually I fall into a restless, dream-fuelled sleep.

I move in a line with others. We are dressed in white and form a procession as we dance to strange music, deep melodious pipes and the slow beat of drums. It is a ceremony and we move past ancient kings dressed in jewelled robes. As we dance before them my skin crawls in fear. I feel they are staring at me and I look up. Their eye-sockets are empty and their faces decayed. Yellow teeth rattle in bone white skulls – these kings are all dead!

17

Mysteries

I awake to daylight streaming in through my little porthole. Last night's dream has left me feeling unsettled, as if I had not slept at all. I am sure there is a reason why I have these dreams, a message I am meant to understand.

Now I sit by the window in the drawing room mesmerised by the endless ocean, hoping it will help me think more clearly. From up here I can see shoals of grey sharks basking on the surface enjoying the sunshine. I see a lone blue whale blowing water through its spout, and now there is a big shoal of smaller fish. They skim over the surface of the ocean as if they are racing one another.

'They are flying fish,' says Diego. He startles me for I hadn't realised he was there. 'Miss Freeman, forgive me,' he says, 'but I have been thinking about what you said last evening, about being engaged to Sam Watson.'

I begin to regret telling him. He makes me feel nervous and I am afraid he can almost read my mind.

'I cannot imagine that Sam will want to leave his flourishing business and return to England,' he continues, 'so does that mean you intend to make your home in Brazil?'

'This is the reason for my visit,' I say, mustering as much calm in my voice as I can. 'Sam has much to show me and marriage is still a long way off.' It's all I can think to say to keep my composure and I wonder if he too was stirred by our close encounter last evening. He is obviously curious about my intentions but so am I about his. I ask, 'Whereabouts in Brazil do you live, Don Alvarez?'

'Oh, please, call me Diego,' he says, sitting in the chair next to me. 'I live wherever I need to be,' he answers. 'My mining interests are all over this huge continent. Since I arrived two years ago, I have reclaimed four mines, all in different countries. I am arranging geological surveys to assess their potential and reopen some of them.

'So I live in hotels, with friends or I rent properties.' He smiles and I detect a slight condescension towards me. 'I have stayed with Sam at his hacienda outside Rio. He is an excellent host and gives wonderful parties, but of course this time I will stay at one of Rio's many hotels. I would not want to intrude on your reunion.'

I am left truly speechless and go to my cabin to unravel my thoughts. Diego says he knows Sam quite well and therefore knows things about his life. But he didn't know about me, or my impending visit. Sam has never mentioned Diego Alvarez in any of his letters or said anything about giving parties, so he must have made new friends in Rio. I wonder why he hasn't written to me about them.

As for Diego, the mystery surrounding this man seems to deepen, and my instincts tell me he is more playboy than businessman, so why would Sam befriend him? But in spite of this I feel my resolve to control my feelings is slipping away, for I cannot help thinking about Diego more and more.

This afternoon we fly over the Cape Verde Islands; it is a relief to see them after the endless blue-grey sea. They seem stranded in the middle of nowhere, but we soon pass over this group of islands, then there is only the Atlantic Ocean once more filling the four points of the compass.

After dinner we leave the men playing poker in the drawing room and retire to the privacy of Grace's cabin. She tells me: 'I'm thinking of investing in Alvarez' mining company.'

'Oh, Grace, is that wise?' I say. 'We hardly know the man.'

She scoffs at me. 'Christina, investments are not judged solely on the company's proprietor, known or not. Investments are made on the prospect of a good return. If Alvarez' figures are based on sound advice from professional people and backed by reliable financiers, I'm willing to take a chance with a small sum.' As she says this she begins removing her jewellery.

'I was particularly interested,' she says, 'when he mentioned diamonds and emeralds at one of his sites.' She lays the jewellery in a small leather case which is secured with a lock and key.

I also have jewellery at home, inherited from mother, but I rarely wear it. Sam has promised to buy me an engagement ring during my visit. I know Grace adores her jewellery, but other than perhaps as an investment, owning precious stones doesn't interest me.

'Daddy always told me to invest in gilt-edged securities,' I say. I feel a pang of grief at the loss of my dear father, who was always so wise in matters of finance.

'Well since the crash even they have tumbled,' says Grace, 'and goodness knows when we shall see a return on our money in government bonds or securities again. We do have to be prepared to look at other investments, even if they may seem a little risky,'

I don't know what to think. My own fortune is tied up in the Madeley Hall estate. There are other investments, including Uncle Peter's. My income from these has dropped but I have enough for my needs. I wouldn't dream of arguing with Grace, but although I feel attracted to Diego, my instincts tell me he is not altogether trustworthy. 'Perhaps we should wait and consult with Sam,' I say, 'as they apparently already know each other.'

Grace agrees to this and we go to bed, for this our second night on the airship, and my head is full of many conflicting thoughts. I will have a very different life if I stay in South America with Sam. My home has always been Madeley Hall, but if I remain there I face a lonely future. And Diego Alvarez? Yes, I do have to consider him, for he has cast a strange spell over me, even though I said to Grace that we hardly know him.

I search my mind and my conscience once more why this should be and why I feel so drawn to him. And then it comes to me, quite suddenly, as a fully formed picture. A young man is leaning on the rail of a ferry steamer, smoking and waving to me. I am just a child, but the picture is clear and what I felt then, the turbulent emotions of emerging adolescence, I recall now.

But then again, I realise this cannot be the same man, although there are similarities in his manner, characteristics and voice, but the other man had a different name, which for the moment escapes me, and as I fall asleep I tussle with this puzzle.

Today, I'm glad I wake early for we are due to cross the equator at 7 am. I go to wake Grace, but she is up already.

'We mustn't miss this, Christina,' she says. 'It's proof that the Germans do have a sense of humour.' We make our way to the drawing room where most of the passengers are assembled for the ceremony. The airship crew have invented their own version of the crossing the equator ritual. Instead of King Neptune, our captain is confronted by Aeolus, God of the Winds. He looks remarkably like the officer called Fleming wearing a long white robe and a wig of long stringy hair. He requests a payment of one hundred Reich marks before granting Von Schiller permission to fly the ship across the line. This causes great hilarity among the officers and the passengers, with Von Schiller vowing to win his money back. So he and Fleming set a wager on the time of our arrival at Recife de Pernambuco. It's also another excuse to drink champagne, of which there seems to be an endless supply.

My eyes seek out Diego, even though my head tells me I should not do this. By tonight our journey will be over and I may never get to speak to him on the matter which is troubling me. He is with Bill Leeds again, joking with Fleming over the wager and his Aeolus costume, which is so comical. Fleming reckons we will arrive at 14.00 hours but Von Schiller says he will land at 12 noon. Grace goes back to her cabin to finish her final article for the paper and for once I am glad she leaves me alone.

My eyes fall on Diego. Eventually, I catch his eye and he saunters towards me.

'Good morning, Christina,' he says with a little bow of his head.

I invite him to sit down beside me and he calls for coffee. 'Can I ask you something, Diego?' I may not have much time and feel I need to be direct.

He looks at me questioningly. 'Of course, what do you want to know?'

I waver. I was only a child, so why would he remember me? So I ask a different question. 'Have you ever been to England?'

He takes his coffee from the tray placed on the table by the steward. 'Why yes,' he replies, 'I studied at Oxford, as did my cousin and other young men in our family.' He sips his coffee then puts the cup down turning his attention to me. 'Why do you ask?'

Encouraged by his reply, I decide to jump in now or I will never know. 'I think we may have met once before,' I say, ignoring the fact his name was unfamiliar when we were introduced two days ago. He is looking at me with that flirtatious glint in his eyes, but he seems genuinely surprised.

'Really, what makes you say that? I'm sure I would have remembered meeting someone as lovely as you, Christina.'

I blush at this and nearly lose my composure, but now I have gone this far I need to know the answer, even if he is flirting with me. 'Oh, I doubt you would remember me as I was only a child, but the occasion was on a cross-channel ferry steamer, from Boulogne to Folkestone, in September 1924.' The date is not forgotten as it was just before Tom and Mamma died.

I watch for his reaction and he hesitates, just for a second. There is a flicker of something in his face: realisation or perhaps recollection? I cannot tell and then he shakes his head and picks up the coffee once more.

'So long ago, and you were just a child?' He says this as though mystified by the thought. 'But it would not have been me, I never travelled that route. I used to go from Bilbao all the way to Southampton by boat.' He is smiling again and I sense his curiosity is aroused. 'What made you think it was me?'

I am beginning to wish I hadn't asked. There is some physical resemblance, particularly in his eyes and voice, but to admit to this would declare more than a vaguely remembered incident. 'Well, I think he told me his name,' I say, 'but I honestly don't remember what it was.' I laugh to cover my embarrassment. 'Oh, it's not important for he obviously wasn't you, but the man I met was Spanish and you do resemble him.'

He throws his head back and laughs quite loudly. 'Perhaps Spaniards are like Chinese. To others, we all look the same.' He laughs again and it is like finishing a jigsaw puzzle. I know I am not mistaken, it is him.

18

The Chaco

1534 Willkapampa, Tawantinsuyu (The Inca Empire)
Tlalli lifted her head from her spinning task and listened. Conch horns echoed through the valleys and up and down the forested mountains heralding the chaski who ran down the mountainside into the village settlement. She watched as her father met with the native runner and she ran with other villagers to find out what the messenger had said.

Her father called everyone round him. 'Friends, the runner tells me Manco Inca's soldiers, backed by Pizarro's Spanish army, have driven our old enemy in the Inca's own wars from our land. 'I am encouraged to know our civil war is over, but I still do not trust these Spaniards, these vipers in our nest!'

Father looked towards his brother, Tutsi, and to Ispaca. Tlalli had seen that sometimes these three disappeared with other warriors for days and nights together. There had been reports of traps being laid on the roads, pits dug and ambushes in the passes. Spaniards had been killed in their sleep and horses stampeded from their tethers in the night. No one had been caught for the raiders always melted away into the cloud forest. During the time they were gone, she prayed very hard to Izella and she was comforted knowing Ispaca wore his jaguar talisman and was protected. She couldn't be a part of this work and had to be content that the mission had begun.

Tlalli had not been allowed to leave the village since she returned from her night on the mountain. Her father and mother feared then they had lost her. When she told them of her escape from Gonzalo Pizarro, her father said he wouldn't send her to live at the temple in Cuzco, for this man had marked her, and the Spaniards had too much influence in the Inca's court. Tlalli knew her father risked the Inca's displeasure over this decision but she felt only relief. Now she wanted to stay and help Ispaca with the mission he had begun to oust the Spaniards from their land.

Father continued telling the news. 'Manco Inca has decreed there will be a celebration of this triumphant victory. It will begin with a Royal Hunt for his new allies, the Spaniards, followed by many days of feasting and drinking.'

Tlalli feared this was very bad news. She wrung her hands, fretting over what she could do to help the animals. That night she spoke with Ispaca and Paullu when they came to sit round the campfire.

Paullu remembered a previous hunt, and he told them, 'It's called a Chaco, and the wild animals will be hunted over a vast area of the land.'

He said, 'The Chaco means thousands of beaters will encircle the animals. Over several days every animal in the vicinity will be herded towards one place in preparation for the final slaughter.'

Ispaca told her, 'There will be no hiding place for any wild animals, Tlalli. Llamas, vicunas, guanacos and roe-deer. Bears, monkeys, mountain foxes, hares, agouti and even jaguars will be surrounded by a thick wall of men.'

'I will have to bring all our herds down and contain them in the village paddocks, or we will lose them to the Chaco,' said Paullu.

But the boys also told her the Chaco usually caused great excitement to everyone who lived in the valley. Not only would the Inca and his entire royal household have their fill of meat from the hunt, the chiefs and villagers from every settlement would also stock their nearby tambos with dried meat from the kill. Tlalli knew that apart from the little guinea pigs that ran about the houses and often finished up in the cooking pots, they rarely ate meat.

Father later told them, 'I don't welcome Manco's friendship with the Spaniards; no good will come of this alliance.' Tlalli felt very confused. The Chaco meant the tribe would have food for the winter, but slaughtering all the animals at once seemed cruel and barbarous.

Paullu said, 'The Chaco will pass right through our territory and all of us will be expected to act as beaters with thousands of other natives from all the tribes and settlements within the area.' She listened to all this talk but she had only one thought – the threat to the jaguars living in the mountain.

While everyone prepared for the great hunt, she slipped away into the forest. It would be a difficult journey but this time she went prepared, taking food and the means to light the cave if needed. She would have given anything to protect all the animals from the beaters and the slaughter that would follow. She couldn't stop it, but she could try to find the cave again and perhaps do something to protect the jaguars.

She took the path to the mine along the well-trodden trail used by the men who toiled daily to clear the tunnel. They worked hard trying to cut through solid granite and shore up the tunnel with stone slabs and ashlars, trying to prop up the entire mountain. But today the mine had fallen silent. The men had left to travel to where the hunt would begin, for they would act as beaters for the Inca's Chaco.

Tlalli examined the tunnel. She could see they still had a long way to go to reach the chamber. It was much deeper in the heart of the mountain than where they had found the tribes heirlooms. Father had said the treasures had also been taken up to a higher level, to protect them against flooding. When she emerged back into the sunlight, she heard sounds in the distance; drumming and chanting, accompanied by a loud swishing noise, like a great wind. Her heart hammered for it was the noise from the thousands of beaters – the Chaco!

She couldn't use the back trail where she had been caught by the Spaniard, so she began to climb this side of the mountain, trying to get up higher, and hoping she could work her way round to the far side. She wanted to find the entrance she had found by chance that fateful day when she had escaped from Gonzalo Pizarro. The sack holding her provisions bumped on her back, hampering her movements. Climbing as best she could, she eventually reached the steeper terrain. The sound of the beaters seemed louder up here. She wondered just how far away they were.

Tlalli looked down and the ground seemed alive; the very bushes and grasses were rippling with movement as a herd of roe-deer took flight, streaking across the land followed by other animals. She clung to the rocks and thought about her jaguars. She prayed, 'Please Izella, let the animals of the Willkapampa find sanctuary. Save them from the Chaco!'

She gasped for breath, but still had to complete her climb. Scrambling to find hand and foot holds, she moved her position inch by inch round the mountainside. The shadow from the mountain's peak fell across her, blotting out the sun. Once again she had reached the dark side of Mount Yaguar.

Below, she could see the Inca trail on the back road. Scanning the mountainside she recognised the crevice in the granite rock-face and saw the opening that led into the mountain cave, this time looking down from above. She gasped with surprise; there on the rocks, overhanging the entrance, stood a jaguar. For one moment it looked like a statue, a figurehead guarding its lair. Then the animal, a young female, moved. Tlalli saw that she favoured one leg, bracing her strong lithe muscles, ready to spring down to where she could gain access to the cave. The jaguar jumped and seemed to disappear.

Tlalli had to get out of the wind and cold before she was blown off the rocks, but would the jaguar attack her if she tried to enter the cave? Could this be the cub she had rescued in the forest, now fully grown? It had been a long time ago. At least she knew up here this jaguar was safe, but what about all the other animals, would they find hiding places? She hoped some would and escape from the fearful round-up.

She climbed down to where the jaguar had disappeared and eased her body into the crevice. This led to the passage in the rocks giving access to the jaguar's cave. Having come so far she didn't want to turn back, not now, while the Chaco was in progress. The passage didn't seem as long as when she was being chased by the Spaniard and eventually she summoned up the courage to enter the cave. She squeezed herself into the low, shallow entrance, pulling her sack behind her. Once on the other side she lost the light. As before, she could smell the strong odour of the jaguar and she waited, keeping perfectly still, near to the entrance. Her eyes gradually adjusted to the low light provided by the small shaft.

She could see more clearly today than she did the first time, making out the size and shape of the rocks. There didn't seem to be any sign of the cat except for the strong smell. Moving as little as possible, she pulled the sack close and put her hand inside. She drew out the maize bread she had brought to eat. She thought that jaguars only ate meat but perhaps they would eat bread if they were really hungry; it was all she had to offer so she left some near the entrance.

She reached into the sack again and brought out her fire-making tools. Every Manari child learned how to make fire as soon as they were old enough to acquire the skill and strong enough to work the sticks. Tlalli didn't want to make a big fire but she did need a torch to light the cave. She laid out her Indian bow drill, the small bundle of kindling from lama wool and pieces of dried bark, and two stout lengths of branch the length of her arm and about the thickness of her wrist. These had been frayed at one end and soaked in tallow made from animal fat.

On the flat ledge inside the entrance she began to work the bow drill. She set the spindle into the notched bow, holding it steady with her foot. With the cord wrapped around the spindle, she began to move the bow drill back and forth. The spindle spun round creating the heat to make a spark. Soon there was enough friction to create a glow. Smoke rose up and then a spark dropped onto the bark and wool. She blew gently and the kindling flared, illuminating the darkness. She laid one end of the torch wood into the glowing kindling, adding more to hold the fire until the wood caught the flame. As it did, it spat and hissed and then the specially treated wood burned with bright yellow flames.

The torch would not last long, so, taking the second branch to light when this one burnt down, she started off to explore her surroundings. The jaguar had entered the cave before her and disappeared, so this cave must lead somewhere else.

Now she could see that the cave went back a long way. Under her feet, solid granite formed a floor. What looked like the back of the cave turned, leading to a passage with worn steps sloping down into the mountain. She went down the steps, feeling the grit and stones from rock falls under her feet, running her hand along the damp rough sides to keep her balance. She felt half afraid but also excited as the further she travelled the steeper the steps became. They turned and twisted in passages she thought must have been made long ago by ancient tribes mining for gold. The jaguar did not show itself, but Tlalli sensed its presence.

She turned another corner and an unexpected beam of daylight filtered from above. High up over her head a piece of sky seemed to hover at the top of an open shaft and she felt fresh air on her face. The restless movement of bats roosting in cracks and crevices caught her eye. She thought this shaft must have been for ventilation in those long ago times when the mountain had been a gold mine. Or perhaps, just as in the legend, this was the chasm that opened into the mountain.

The sides looked very steep with no footholds to climb up to the top, but she thought perhaps a jaguar could probably climb up and down. She could hear water trickling through the rocks. Following the sound, she found a spring flowing straight from the rocks into a pool, carved by the flow of clear water over the passage of time. Ah, she thought, so water attracts the jaguars into this part of the mountain. Water would be like gold to them in this arid place.

The Chaco beaters would be right below the mountain now. She quickly scooped water and drank from her palm. It was pure, straight from a mountain spring. Her first torch was nearly finished so she lit the second branch from the first and continued on through the passageway, leaving the open shaft behind her. As she turned the next bend, she heard the sound which she had both longed to hear and also to dread: the distinctive low roar of the jaguar.

Her feet wanted to turn and flee back up the passage but she forced herself to go on, and entered another chamber, wide and deep like the first cave. She held her torch up high, illuminating the shadowy granite rocks. The cat sat on her haunches on the far side of the cave, hissing through bared teeth. Then the jaguar lifted her head and roared again. The sound echoed round the hollow cave but the cat did not move. Tlalli sank to her knees, murmuring calming words in a small soft voice, full of human fear, but relieved this animal had not attacked her and for now seemed safe from the Chaco. If this was the young female she saved from the trap, perhaps she sensed Tlalli did not pose a threat.

In the light from her torch she could make out sack-covered goods in all different shapes and sizes. Some were partly open and the bright flames caught the shining reflection of pure gold. She said a silent prayer of thanks to the gods for she had found the Incas' treasure. Items taken from the Sun temple in Cuzco and hidden by her tribe before the Inca befriended the Spanish. They had not been crushed in the earthquake.

She had called the cub Izella, after the jaguar goddess. If this animal was a descendant from that blood line it would confirm everything she believed. The sacred jaguar protecting the golden treasure, the fight she was determined to continue, protecting the heritage of her people through the Spirit of the Jaguar! Then she remembered the whispered words exchanged between her father and the elders around the tribe's campfire all that time ago. Somewhere in this cave lay the sacred *Punchao,* the Incas' glorious shining image of the sun god, Inti.

19

The Inca's Court

Manco Inca's Court, Cuzco, The Inca Empire.
When the sun rose the following day, Tlalli eventually plucked up courage to leave the cave and the treasure behind. She looked down the steep mountainside, awed by the tremendous height she had scaled, and the sheer drop below should she slip. Step by step she managed to reach the ground and safety.

She would be in more trouble when she returned home, but consoled herself remembering the brave jaguar in the cave, and knowing it had not been captured in the Chaco. Tlalli felt certain this was the cub she had rescued from the hunter's trap, now a full-grown adult female. She had another secret, for she had discovered the Inca's lost treasure being guarded by the jaguar just as told in the legend. Her head became filled with dreams of saving her people from the Spanish invaders and the role the jaguars would play in her mission.

The sun beamed down, now high in the sky. The day grew hot and she lingered in the cool forest, reluctant to face her mother's anger at home. She planned to plead that she had lost her way and took shelter when it became dark. She decided not to tell anyone about finding the Inca's gold, as it would put the jaguars at risk.

Eventually she reached the trail leading back to the mine entrance. She heard the sound of hoof beats only seconds before two horsemen came in sight, leaving her no time to hide. Crouching fearfully on the ground she held her breath, hoping they wouldn't see her. The Spanish horses filled her with dread. These enormous animals, together with their riders dressed in rich colourful garments, armed with swords and lances, made a fearful sight, like one huge animal with two heads. That image had haunted her dreams since the day she had been chased by Pizarro.

The leading Spaniard, mounted on a black horse, pointed at her and shouted. She knew him, her enemy, Gonzalo Pizarro. Both men laughed as they moved their horses closer to Tlalli. She looked around frantically for an opening to escape and run back into the shelter of the forest, but the horses had come too close, and they snorted and neighed as their heads were reined in tight by the riders.

As she turned to run away, Gonzalo charged towards her. He scooped her up off the ground. She screamed, her arms and legs flailing as he threw her across the giant horse's neck, knocking the breath from her body. Sick with fear, all she could hear was the thunder of hooves and the laughter of the Spanish riders as they took her further away from the trail leading to her home.

As they drew nearer to the golden city of Cuzco, Tlalli was very fearful of her fate. She saw the mountains and hills with the city built in a tight valley between them. She saw the mighty walls, built long ago, surrounding the great palaces and temples of the Incas. It was a beautiful city and its majesty filled her with awe, but her heart filled with dread, for she knew it was also a prison.

She was taken by the Spaniard to the Inca's court where the celebrations following the Chaco had begun. Gonzalo Pizarro paraded Tlalli before Manco Inca, forcing her to prostrate herself on the ground.

'Well, Manco Inca,' said the Spaniard. 'I found this girl alone on the road and have brought her before you. I will keep her. She will make a fine mistress for me.' He prodded her with his foot.

The Inca didn't like the interruption to the festivities. 'Who is she?' he asked.

'I believe she is the daughter of the Manari curaca at the village where the gold from the Temple is held,' said the Spaniard. 'I told her father I would have his daughter if he didn't return the gold and now I claim her as my prize.'

Manco Inca looked over to where Tlalli sprawled on the stone floor. She lay still, like a petrified stone at the Inca's feet, fearing death should she look on his face.

'Ah, Kusi Manari's daughter,' said the Inca. 'She should have come to me before now to be one of my holy Acllas.'

The Spaniard laughed, 'Holy indeed, but not for long. I will lock her in my house until she is ripe.' His voice boomed with lust and contempt.

Tlalli heard another voice, the soft voice of a young woman. 'If the girl was destined to be a holy Aclla you cannot have her, Spaniard.'

Gonzalo shouted, 'Do you allow a woman to dictate at your court, Inca?'

Manco Inca retorted, 'No ordinary woman, Pizarro, but Cora Ocllo, my Coya, my Queen. She has full authority when females are brought before the court.'

The woman spoke again. 'Take her to my chambers. She will go to the temple and be trained as a holy Aclla; that is her destiny.'

Tlalli felt herself being lifted from the floor and hustled out of the court. She had kept her eyes down throughout the entire ordeal and realised she owed her very life to the Coya.

Women bathed and dressed her in white robes, as worn by all the women of the court. She managed to conceal her jaguar talisman and hide it once more under the new robes, when her old clothes were taken away to be burned. Then they took her back to the Coya's chambers for an audience. Tlalli gasped at the magnificent splendour of the room. Sheets of gold lined the walls and woven tapestries hung from the furniture. When the Coya entered, Tlalli went down on the floor, scattered with animal skins and hides. She kept her eyes shut tight.

The Coya spoke to her. 'What is your name, girl?'

'Tlalli Manari,' she said in a shaky voice.

'You are very beautiful, Tlalli Manari,' said the Coya. Her voice sounded young and almost friendly.

Tlalli didn't know how to answer her, but said, 'I wish I was ugly and then the Spaniard would leave me alone.'

The Coya laughed at this and so did her attendants. 'Well said, young Tlalli. We will send you to the temple and you will be trained to be one of my hand-maidens. We will not let the lustful Gonzalo Pizarro have you, not if we can prevent it. Stand up, Tlalli, and let me look at you.'

Tlalli stood up from the floor, her eyes still downcast, fearful of the consequences should she look at the Coya.

'It is permitted to look at me now, as you will become one of my attendants,' said the Coya.

Tlalli lifted her eyes and could not believe what she saw. Cora Ocllo had long black hair and stood the same height as Tlalli. They could have been sisters, they were so alike.

The Coya smiled at her. 'Yes, we are alike and that could be very useful to me. But I will give you a new name to use in the court and the temple. I will name you Inguill: a name more befitting to your new life.' As the Coya turned away her dress shimmered; for it had been made with pure gold threads, studded with gem stones, pearls and pink mulla shells.

'Take Inguill to the temple and give instructions to the mamaconas that she is to be made ready to serve only me.' She turned back to Tlalli. 'You are under my protection and in return you will protect me with your life.'

Tlalli bowed low before the Coya. 'I will always serve you, Oh Coya, and give you my promise to put your life before my own.'

In her heart she remembered she had already given her oath of protection to Izella. Would the goddess continue to protect her so far from Mount Yaguar, and within the Inca's Royal palace and temple? Could she serve two mistresses?

Tlalli looked out of the barred slit opening in the Temple's high tower and down onto the main square in Cuzco. Doing so was strictly forbidden, and if caught she would be punished, as she had already been, many times by the mamaconas since she had been brought to live in the Sun Temple.

She had done everything in her power to transgress the rules and be returned to her father and her life in the Willkapampa. The mamaconas and even the other girls shunned her. She was not of Royal blood and only tolerated because her father was a curaca. The Coya's intervention had saved her from a terrible fate as Pizarro's mistress. But she hadn't seen the Coya again since that first day at the court when she had foolishly caused her own capture; that was weeks ago. The free spirit within her felt crushed, as she realised her father would now be powerless to help her.

20

Diego

April, 1931, Recife de Pernambuco, Brazil

Diego is very pleased with the advantages this trip has achieved. He's won a lot of money in the casinos of Europe. He is a far better card player than Bill and much luckier at the roulette wheel. But then, he's been practising the art of deception for a long time. He congratulates himself on being very clever, even employing the art of double-deception by being a good loser, thus gaining the confidence of those he wishes to deceive over matters far greater than the stakes in a card game. He will be doing them a favour; these people have more money than sense. Making money is in his blood. If they invest in him they stand to gain, like the people Bill introduced him to, who are now keen to invest in his South American mines.

His grandfather had made his fortune in South America seventy years ago. Trading in the deeds of gold and silver mines had proved an excellent currency and he had returned to Spain in 1860 a rich man. Armed with these deeds, Diego has now acquired professional surveys on the yield potential of some of the mines; paperwork which has cost him most of the money entrusted to him by Don Rodriguez. He rubs his hands together and grins to himself. He and Bill have convinced a lot of rich men that they would receive a good return on any investment in The Yaguar Mining Company. Of course, all this was just on paper; now he is expected to turn promises into hard cash.

There is a rap on the door of the cabin. A voice calls out from the passage, 'Alvarez, are you packed?'

'I'm ready, Bill,' he calls back, and he relocks his case. As he slides his jacket on, he checks that his double-barrelled Remington Derringer, neatly holstered under his arm, is invisible. South America can be a dangerous place and he is an excellent marksman. He opens the door.

'Come on, man,' says Leeds. 'We can't miss the farewell luncheon with the ladies.'

Diego puts his suitcase in the passage ready for the steward to unload and packs his leather zip case into a smaller bag which he carries. 'It's not lunchtime yet, surely,' he says.

'No, but I don't want to miss a moment from now until we land. Come on.' Leeds strides off towards the drawing room leaving Diego to follow.

Everyone is congregating in this room which has been their meeting and eating place for the last three days. Lady Grace and Christina Freeman are already at the table by the forward starboard window. They have turned their chairs to look down and follow the line of the coast. Leeds and Alvarez join them. The stewards arrive with an early lunch of sandwiches and cake.

'Hey,' says Bill to Kubis, 'It's noon. Does that mean our captain has lost his wager with Fleming?'

'That depends, sir, on our actual arrival time,' says Kubis.

Soon after the lunch is cleared away Bill calls out, 'Pernambuco dead ahead.' Within minutes the airship is flying right over the city. Diego first approached this coast by sea. This city is new to him. From the air he can see Pernambuco is built on a number of islands interconnected by bridges.

'Oh, this is more civilised,' says Christina. Diego smiles at her but she avoids his eyes.

'Yes, see the wide streets lined with trees and the grand buildings,' chimes in Grace. Diego looks down and sees people waving as they fly over the city.

The *Graf* reaches the landing site. There is no shed, only a short stub mast in the centre of a huge white circle marked on the ground. The passengers are still clustered at the windows anxious not to miss the view as the captain brings them down. Diego moves to be next to Christina determined she won't ignore him.

'Are you going to the Central Hotel?' he asks.

She turns to her companion, 'Are we, Grace?'

Grace replies rather formally. 'If Mr Watson has arrived, we will spend the night at the hotel. That's the arrangement.'

Diego acknowledges this information and the fact that Grace is in charge of their itinerary. 'If that is so,' he says, addressing both women, 'when you meet with Mr Watson, would you allow me a few words with him? I will have need of his services over the next few weeks and wouldn't want to use another carrier.'

Again, it is Grace who replies, 'Of course, Don Alvarez. I will tell him you wish to discuss business when we arrive.' Diego thanks Grace and he moves away from the window, wondering about this rather frosty exchange. Christina Freemen's previously friendly manner seems to have cooled. As the *Graf Zeppelin* touches down, almost without a tremor, he decides she must now be focusing her thoughts on being reunited with her fiancé. The thought makes him ponder how he could possibly change her mind.

He breathes a sigh of relief as the door to the passenger car of the *Graf* is opened and the stairway is pushed out to the ground. Passengers are shaking hands with one another in a last farewell. Diego has all the contact details he needs from those interested in his business proposition. He watches as Commander Eckener and Captain Von Schiller are greeted by the Brazilian officials.

The heat of a full tropical summer wafts into the car. Diego knows he must hold his nerve. He will stay in Rio for a few more days to make the business arrangements for the bond flotation with Eduardo Moreno's bank. Diego's immediate concern is to speak with Sam Watson, but he is very conscious of the two women who have journeyed from Europe to see him. Far from this being a problem he is already thinking about how to manipulate their inclusion in his original plan. After all, three rich investors must be better than one.

The passengers begin to file down the stairway to bid farewell to senior members of the *Graf Zeppelin's* crew. But well-meant sentiments are lost in the loud babble of chattering voices and shouting from the Brazilian ground crew. In the absence of a shed for the airship, she has to be tethered to the ground by her guide ropes and men will guard her night and day until she lifts off again.

All the security guards are armed with hand guns and rifles. Diego sees Eckener is appealing to the Ground Commander that no guns are fired anywhere near the airship. Diego finds this all very amusing and says to Bill, 'In a country where revolutions break out once a fortnight the airship's security looks a little shaky.'

'Hang the airship,' says Bill. 'What about our security?'

Diego laughs at this, patting his jacket. 'Don't worry, Bill. I will look after you.'

The heat on the landing field is overpowering. There is not a dot of shade but vehicles are lining up to take the passengers to their destinations. The baggage is handed out and the passengers begin to disperse. Diego keeps a watchful eye on the two women. He doesn't want to lose the opportunity to make his arrangements with Watson.

And then he sees him, getting out of one of the taxis. So abandoning Bill and his own luggage, Diego moves a little nearer to where Grace and Christina are standing guard over their baggage, looking hot and a little bewildered. He watches Sam embrace the girl. They kiss quite passionately and he feels a pang of jealousy. He waits until Watson is shaking hands with Lady Grace and he hurries to where they are standing.

'Hey, Watson!' he calls, 'May I help you take the bags to the car?'

'Hello, Alvarez,' says Watson. 'What are you doing here?'

'I have just had the pleasure of the company of these two charming ladies on the *Graf Zeppelin* flight from Germany.' Grace smiles to acknowledge this statement but Christina seems to have eyes only for Watson and she says nothing.

'Oh you have,' says Watson. He is obviously taken by surprise and Diego wonders what he is thinking. They pick up and carry two cases each and walk ahead of the women towards the waiting taxi.

'I'm afraid I can't offer you accommodation on this occasion, Alvarez,' says Watson, 'but I can take you to Rio if that's your destination.'

'It is, but I am with Bill Leeds,' Diego replies. 'I certainly wouldn't want to cramp your style with the ladies by staying at your home.'

Watson winces, and Diego smirks, remembering times he has stayed there when they were entertained by other ladies. 'Don't look so worried, Watson,' he says, 'your secret is safe with me.'

'I can take you and Leeds to Rio tomorrow.' Watson stops at the car and wipes the perspiration from his face. 'Tonight I am staying with the ladies at the Central Hotel in Recife.' He uses the local term for the city of Recife de Pernambuco. He places the cases in the trunk. 'I've enough room in the plane. Wait 'til you see my new baby!' The two women have caught up with them.

'What new baby is that, Sam?' says Christina.

The men laugh and Watson says, 'Her name is Vega and she flies like a bird.' Now they are all laughing and Diego politely opens the rear door for Lady Grace while Watson assists Christina into the opposite side. Diego races off to report to Bill Leeds who is sitting on his case mopping his face and neck.

'Christ, Alvarez, I'd forgotten how hot Brazil can be. What have you arranged for our transport?'

'We travel to Rio tomorrow with The Honourable Samuel Watson who has, I believe, just acquired a larger airplane.' He is pleased how events are working to his advantage. Now he waves forward the last remaining taxi.

As they climb in Leeds says, 'Let's hope the hotel is cooler than this bloody airfield.'

It is almost dusk when they arrive at the Central Hotel. Recife is on the coast facing the Atlantic Ocean. It is much cooler. Large ceiling fans running in all the rooms and open windows catch the Atlantic breeze. Most of the passengers from the *Graf* flight are booked into the hotel for this one night at least and the hotel serves a late dinner for them.

'This is just like still being on the airship,' says Grace when Diego and Bill find themselves once more at table with the three English aristocrats.

'Except that Sam is with us now,' says Christina. He is sitting next to her and she squeezes his hand. He leans towards her and kisses her cheek.

As the last course is cleared away Diego asks, 'Any one for poker?'

'Not me', says Grace. 'I am absolutely exhausted and only fit for sleep.'

'Me too,' says Christina. 'To think we were up at 6am to witness crossing the equator. Can you believe that, Sam? You should have seen the German Officers, they were so funny.'

The ladies stand up and the men follow suit. Watson places his arm around Christina's waist and faces the other two men. 'I suggest we all get some sleep. Tomorrow will be an equally exhausting day with a seven hour flight to Rio. I don't imagine you will find it as comfortable a ride as on the airship.'

Christina again makes a public display of her affection for Watson by kissing him on the lips and embracing him. Diego wishes it was him she looked at with such rapture. The women say goodnight and he takes advantage of their separation and touches Watson's sleeve saying, 'A moment please, before you retire.' He seems reluctant not to follow the ladies but returns to the lounge with the other two men.

Diego explains about the forthcoming bond issue for Yaguar Mining. 'We will be working in US dollars which will be so much safer than South American currencies. The issue will be for one million dollars and bonds go on sale on the 20th of April.'

Watson is listening intently. 'What sort of a return are you offering?'

'Mining is a long term investment,' says Diego, 'but I expect to be in profit within a year. So bonds will pay annually from then. We will offer a six percent return over ten years.'

'So it's not a get-rich-quick scheme,' says Watson, frowning.

Leeds chips in, 'There's no such thing at the moment. Alvarez' mines will offer a better return than anything currently available.'

'Well, gentlemen,' says Watson, 'I will think it over.' He stands up. 'I have just invested a lot of money in the purchase of my latest plane for my own business. But I will give your offer due consideration.'

'Well remember, the issue is a limited-time offer and there's bound to be a lot of interest. You wouldn't want to miss out on such a good investment,' says Leeds in a parting shot.

'Oh, I will let you know soon, it's just that now I have to consult with my business partner.' Diego and Leeds pause, waiting for an explanation.

He smiles, 'My future wife, The Honourable Christina Freeman.' He lowers his voice to a whisper. 'Her fortune is greater than mine for she has already inherited, not one, but two fortunes. We have agreed to work as partners in all things financial, although of course once we are married, I would have the last word. Goodnight, gentlemen,' and he leaves them digesting this rather modern concept.

Bill shakes his head in dismay. 'I hope he realises the implications of such a noble plan. If I had agreed that with Xenia I would be bankrupt now.'

'Well, well,' says Diego, 'and I thought I was talking to the organ grinder, but it turns out he is the monkey.'

Bill roars with laughter but Diego's face is inscrutable as he calculates how he might win the trust and possibly even the affections of The Honourable Christina Freeman for himself.

21

The Coya

Tlalli hated her life in the Temple. The Acllas were the daughters of Inca nobles, or like her, the daughters of tribal leaders from all over the empire. It was considered a privilege to come here and learn to serve the Inca and his family.

In her lonely cot at night, she stared at the cold stone walls of what had become her prison. She put her head under the thin blanket and ran her finger over the precious jaguar talisman. Only then could she remember happy days on the hillsides tending baby alpacas, or other days when she wandered through the forest collecting berries and leaves, smelling the damp sweetness and laughing at gaudy butterflies dancing in the dappled sunbeams. She could hear her mother's shrill laugh and her father's deep, soft voice, or hear Ispaca's clever animal calls, and see Paullu's laughing eyes as he trilled on his melodious panpipes.

When she thought of him, a sense of loneliness and longing lodged in her chest, until she could barely breathe. Cherished memories would tumble one on the other, stilling her aching heart and eventually lulling her to sleep. Morning brought her sharply back to reality as she was summoned by a mournful gong to follow the orders of this strictly disciplined life.

Outwardly, she appeared totally dedicated in her service to the Sun god, the Inca, and the Coya also. Inwardly, she tried to plan how she could keep her vow to Izella, and harass the Spanish intruders who had a great deal of influence in the Inca's court. Although she prayed to Izella daily, she began to think the jaguar goddess's powers could only be summoned in their own territory of the forest and the mountain. Here, in the Sun Temple at Cuzco, Tlalli felt completely alone.

The mamaconas trained the Acllas. Every day she was taught how to prepare special food dishes for the Inca, and how to serve these in accordance with the strict protocol attached to his sacred office. He did not lift a finger to do anything; even his food and drink was administered by the women who served him. His wives and other relatives were equally fêted and pampered, and the Acllas had to learn to do this. She also learned that some of the most beautiful girls would eventually be taken by the Inca as concubines or given to nobles as wives or mistresses. Since Manco Inca's close collaboration with the Spaniards they could also receive such favours from the Inca. She hoped the Coya's wishes would prevent this from being her fate.

Tlalli's special skill was working with fabrics. She received instruction on weaving and sewing exquisite materials which looked like silk or satin but had been spun from the fleeces of baby vicunas specially selected for their very fine coats. They also used cotton, which grew on the terraces. She worked with other Acllas who made all these rich garments for the Inca royal family to wear.

Today, she concentrated hard on her work at the loom, weaving a special cloth for the Coya. The yarn felt fine as gossamer and the yards of material slid into the basket like a golden cloud, so opaque as to be almost invisible. Along the edge, she wove an intricate pattern of tiny figures and shapes in a thread pure as gold. Tlalli loved the work, remembering her mother's teaching before she came to the temple. But she feared the strict mamaconas, who would bring a stick across the hands of any girl who made an error in her work.

The mamacona supervising the girls nodded her approval of Tlalli's completed work and she instructed her to take the finished material to the Coya's quarters. She waited outside until one the attendants beckoned her into the antechamber. It seemed like hours until they summoned her before the Coya. She knelt down stiff and taut with nerves, keeping her eyes on the material in the basket.

'Ah, it is Inguill, my little double.' The Coya laughed and all her lady attendants laughed with her. Tlalli's likeness to the Coya seemed to be the cause of their amusement. 'Stand up, Inguill, and show me your work.' Tlalli stood and trembling she carried the basket towards her.

'No, girl, come here,' said one of the ladies. So she went to the one who had spoken. The material was taken out of the basket by two of the women. It was so slippery and fine it fell in cascades of gold, shining all over the floor.

The Coya stepped forward and picking up one section she threw it over her shoulder, draping it round her. She twisted round until she was completely cocooned. Laughing she said, 'It is beautiful. I love it!' The Coya's attendants cooed and sighed over the sight of their mistress wrapped in the lovely fabric. She turned to Tlalli and said, 'Thank you, Inguill. I will have this made into a full-length gown and I shall wear it for the Inti Raymi festival.' She asked for the work to begin immediately, and the lady attendants who would do this began to fit and tuck the material.

'Inguill will stay here for the rest of the day,' said the Coya. 'I wish to know her better, and the work can continue while we talk. Come here, child. Sit by me while these ladies fuss with your exquisite handiwork.'

Tlalli sat on a low stool, sighing with relief that this great lady liked her work. The Coya stood for the gown to be fitted. 'Now, Inguill, tell me about your life before you came here, when you were a curaca's daughter.'

She felt tongue-tied by the Coya's attention but haltingly she began to relate her life with her family and all the things she had done when living in her mountain home. Like helping with the animals, gathering the fruits of the forest, and learning to weave with her mother.

'Oh,' said the Coya, 'so you weren't treated like a princess.'

'No, my lady, I suppose my brother and I were special children, because our father is the curaca, but we had to work like the other children in our tribe.' Tlalli didn't know what else she could have said. She thought the Coya might like to know about the jaguar cub.

'One day I saved a baby jaguar from a trap in the forest.'

'How did you do that?' asked the Coya.

She suddenly realised she couldn't say anything about saving the cub under the influence of the jaguar goddess. Her father's words about being misunderstood became all too clear. So she just told her that she released the cub from a hunter's trap and how the other children called her Jaguar girl. That led to her telling the Coya about the jaguars living in the mountain. 'I am sure the family must be descended from the sacred jaguar gods, Toquri and Izella.'

'Toquri and Izella? I know those names, but I have not heard them since I was a child,' said the Coya. 'Tell me what you know about them.'

So Tlalli related the folk tale she knew by heart, of the two brothers who set out to find their fortunes and found instead the truth about family love from the two jaguar gods. When the tale was finished, she felt very sad, for she was separated from the family she loved.

But the Coya was delighted with the story and clapped her hands. 'Yes, that is a wonderful story, Inguill.' She commanded an attendant to bring water, served in a silver bowl. Tlalli drank gratefully, for the story had taken a long time to tell. 'So you are a very special girl. You weave lovely cloth, you tell a fine story, and you can also talk with jaguars. What else is special about you?'

Again, she remembered her father's words, about keeping her special dreams and prophecies hidden. She wanted to confide in the Coya because she seemed like a friend, but decided to keep to her father's counsel. 'There is nothing else, my lady. I am not very special at all.'

They all smiled and laughed when she said that. 'Ah, but there is one more special thing about you,' said the Coya. 'You look like me.' All her attendants nodded but Tlalli cast her eyes down with embarrassment.

She shook her head. 'Oh no, my lady Coya, no one could be as beautiful as you. I am not beautiful at all.'

The Coya laughed again. 'But you caught the eye of our Spanish guest, Gonzalo Pizarro. He would have taken you for himself the day you arrived.'

She shuddered at the memory. 'I cannot thank you enough for saving me, my lady,' she said. 'I have pledged my life to serve you, but I think that man is very bad and I wish I could pay him back for his wickedness.'

A silence fell in the chamber and she realised she had spoken out of turn. The Coya looked quite sternly and lowered her voice. 'Hush, Inguill. We must not speak ill of our guests. You must keep such thoughts to yourself.' She lowered her voice to a whisper and spoke close to Tlalli ear, 'As I do.' For a second, they looked into each other's eyes. This lady, this great Coya, understood what Tlalli had dared to put into words.

Tlalli began to look forward to the festival of Inti Raymi. It would be held throughout the empire to celebrate the harvest. She remembered how the tribe celebrated back home, but sadly she realised on this occasion, her thirteenth birthday would go unmarked.

Here in Cuzco, the ceremony would be very special. Tlalli, and dozens of other Acllas, would be part of a procession. They had to practise their walk which was more like a dance. Acllas didn't usually mix with the men. Even to speak with a man not under the Inca's authority could be punished by death. But for the high purpose of the ceremony, the Acllas would join with the men and play their part in the sacred celebrations, which would continue over many days.

On the appointed day she felt very special dressed in a new white gown like all the other girls. The mamaconas called them to order as they lined up to leave the Temple. Tlalli carried bales of coca leaves, three in each arm. The narcotic leaves were normally reserved for use by the Inca, his nobles and chiefs of the tribes. She now knew they chewed the leaves because they had a hallucinatory effect. Today these bales would be part of the sacrifices. Like the precious llama meat, and the pots of chicha, the coca leaves would be burned in the sacrificial fires to the sun god, Inti.

As the lines of Acllas filed out of the temple in twos, the drummers began a slow beat and conch trumpets sounded out. Tlalli walked with the other girls, in time with the drums, pausing every few beats to lift up their hands and pay homage to the sun god. They reached a line of colourful canopies, covered with the brightly coloured feathers of jungle birds. Figures sat under the canopies shaded from the heat of the sun. They were dressed in the rich robes of Inca Kings and surrounded by their gold and silverware, cups for drinking and bowls for food, as well as wearing their royal jewellery.

The old Incas were attended by men dressed in silver tunics with gold amulets on their arms and legs, heavy gold earrings and gold medallion circlets on their heads. These attendants held fans made of swans' feathers, their sole task was to swat away the flies from the Inca kings. Tlalli lifted her eyes and realised with horror that the Incas' faces were decayed and their eye-sockets empty. Until that moment she hadn't understood that these were the mummified remains of previous Inca rulers. She quickly turned her head away from the gruesome sight.

The procession moved on with the slow-moving, dance-like steps of the Acllas, towards Manco Inca and his choir of men. They chanted to the sun god, a ritual begun in soft tones at daybreak, rising in volume until midday, and then growing quieter until the sun set.

Tlalli began to feel more in the spirit of the ceremony. Alongside the drummers a group of pipers began to play, and the joyous sound of the Andean pipes filled the air, reminding her of home. Cuzco was on a high plateau and all around, as far as her eyes could see, the beautiful landscape of mountains, valleys and forest stretched out to the furthest horizon. This was the first time she had been outside since her capture and she wanted to run and run far away from her life of imprisonment.

The procession stopped. She looked up and saw the Coya, surrounded by her attendants, high up on the hillside paying homage to Inti. The Coya lifted up her arms towards the golden sun and for a moment Tlalli saw her glow, surrounded by the rays of the sun and she looked like a golden goddess. The Coya's gown had been made from the cloth she had woven and she felt very proud. She knew then she could never run away, for she had pledged her life to the Coya.

The procession moved on and the haunting music of the Andean pipes filled her with longing and pricked at her eyes. One piper walked alongside her part of the procession. He played the quena, and there was something familiar about him. Yes, she was sure, it was Paullu! Her spirits soared. If Paullu had come here perhaps Ispaca, or her father, might also be in the dense crowd watching the ceremony and paying homage to Inti.

She became so excited she nearly lost timing with her partner in the walking dance. She began to take notice of the crowd as they moved out across the hillside. Hundreds of people had gathered and it would be impossible to recognise anyone, let alone be able to acknowledge them. But she had not heard a word from her family since the Spaniard brought her to Cuzco.

A warm glow lodged in her heart knowing that Paullu walked and played quite close to her. She didn't dare to acknowledge him but as she moved to his beautiful music she imagined she danced just for him. For one moment their eyes met in a brief smile of recognition. Then she lowered her head for fear of being seen. But in her heart she knew he had told her with his eyes, her family knew where to find her.

22

The Deception

During the week following Inti Raymi, the Coya summoned Tlalli to her
chambers.

'Come, Inguill, tell me more about your life and your family.'

Tlalli began with stories about her brother, Ispaca. 'He can mimic the
calls of birds and animals,' she said. 'He is a very good hunter, but he
often scared me and others into thinking a wild animal was close by. My
brother can be a very annoying joker.'

This made the Coya laugh although Tlalli felt sad remembering the life
she had be forced to leave. The Coya seemed fascinated by everything
Tlalli spoke of, as if she envied the life of freedom her new handmaiden
had previously enjoyed. Also the Coya appeared a little obsessed by
Tlalli's likeness to herself. Tlalli found she was summoned to the queen's
chambers almost every day. It became obvious Inguill, as she was called,
had become a favourite with the queen. Tlalli tried hard not to be the focus
of attention for she didn't want to arouse jealousies among the Coya's
followers.

On this day the Coya wore her finest gown and jewels. 'Inguill, I want
to take you into the court today. First you will be shown how to enter and
leave the Inca's presence.'

One of the ladies stepped forward and took Tlalli to one side. 'You
must wear a veil over your head, as we all do.' She laid a lace veil over
Tlalli's head and she could see only hazy outlines. 'We walk in a line
directly behind the Coya. I will put you in front of me so I can watch you,'
said the lady. 'Keep your head bowed low and when we reach the Inca we
have to go on our knees and remain there unless he tells us to move. Do
you understand?'

Tlalli felt overwhelmed at the thought of entering the Inca's court in
this strange fashion. She answered, 'Yes, I understand.' Her heart beat
faster as the Coya went from her bedchamber with all the ladies assembled
behind her. They began to process through the palace and passed under the
high, tapering trilithon archway into the court chamber.

Her legs felt weak and her hands trembled. Once they knelt before the
Inca, she could compose her thoughts better. She squinted through the
hazy veil to view the Inca sitting on a low stool at the top of a flight of
stone steps. His garments were made of gold cloth studded with jewels,
and on his head he wore the royal Inca fringe, called a borla, which was his
crown. He lifted his hand, and the attendants rose up and went to the back

of the court chamber, taking Tlalli with them. Only the Coya remained by the Inca and she moved to another low stool by his side.

Tlalli tried to look around. She could just make out many Spaniards in the court, including Gonzalo Pizarro and the man who had been with him when she was captured. She now knew this man to be his brother Juan, and her anger towards both these men sharpened.

The Inca began receiving petitions from his subjects, people who had waited days to bring their grievances to court. Among them she saw her father. She couldn't acknowledge him but she felt uplifted seeing him in the court and wondered if he had come to petition the Inca for her release. The first petitioner asked why a Spaniard had been granted land which previously formed communal land within his village used for growing crops for the community. His villagers had been forced to build a house for the Spaniard and now had to work for him. They were not paid and had no land to grow crops to feed their families.

The two Spanish brothers constantly interrupted the proceedings, disagreeing with the Inca's scales of justice, so most of the petitioners went away empty handed. Like the first man, others brought similar grievances, and the Inca seemed unable to right these terrible injustices. To her disappointment, her father did not even get a hearing, so she still didn't know why he had come.

It was Gonzalo who dismissed the unheard petitioners and then he began making his own demands. Two interpreters translated his words; one Indian and one Spanish.

'Well, Senor Inca, I think it is time you handed over more gold to me. This court still has lots of treasures and I want them.' Tlalli was horrified by his audacity speaking like this to the Sapa Inca. From the wave of murmuring and unrest in the court it was obvious the Incas there were equally appalled.

Manco Inca's reply came from the interpreter. 'You would turn me into a pauper. You have already taken all my gold.' Tlalli watched all the players in this scene, wondering what would happen next.

Gonzalo seemed unruffled by the protestations of the court and he laughed at them. He strutted right up to the Coya. 'What about your wife's jewels? I will have them.' Again, there were sounds of shock and disbelief from the court. But Cora Ocllo herself, removed all her bracelets, rings and necklaces, giving them to the Inca.

'Let him have them,' she said. 'Perhaps then he will leave us alone.' Tlalli wanted to run to her mistress's side, and do anything she could to prevent her making this sacrifice, but she dared not move.

Gonzalo's eyes widened with greed and he walked up and snatched the jewels from the Inca's hands. 'What a wise woman your queen is, Senor

Inca, but I doubt I will leave you alone for long.' He left the court with his brother Juan and they laughed together as they walked away.

Tlalli felt so angry that these people had humiliated the Inca and his Coya. Did the Inca really not know what they did in his country? She thought he probably did, for the Spaniards who terrorised his people now did the same to him and his family. She remembered the vow she had made with Ispaca and she hoped that others would find the courage to stand up against the Spanish thugs. But until the Inca himself did so, and turned against them, nothing would change.

As Tlalli lay in her cot that night she tossed and turned with terrible images in her head. A battle raged all around Cuzco. She saw Spaniards wearing metal armour and waving their huge swords. They sat on their horses and charged into lines of native Indians, slicing through them. Indians hurled volleys of stones from their slings and bolas, pulling the horses to the ground. Fire spread through the buildings in the city, and she could hear the pitiful cries of wounded and dying men. Three nights running Tlalli awoke trembling, fearful of her own part in this onslaught. She so wanted to confide in someone: her father, her brother, but there was no one she could tell.

On the fourth day, she came again to the Coya's bedchamber. When she arrived the queen was already listening to a messenger from the court. This man was a courtier and a cousin of the Coya. Tlalli heard him say, 'That Spaniard, Gonzalo Pizarro, said to our lord, "Come, Senor Manco Inca, you must have more gold hidden away; I want more gold!" We have grown used to him harassing the Inca every day. Well, today Pizarro became impatient quickly.'

The messenger continued relating Pizarro's words. "If you have no gold to give me I will take another of your treasures. I will have the lady Coya. Come, Senor Inca, give me the queen!" 'Of course,' said the cousin, 'the court was horrified at this demand and our guards grasped their weapons tighter.'

Tlalli, and everyone else in the Coya's chamber, gasped and looked to the Coya. She continued to sit very still, listening to her cousin, but she said nothing.

The cousin continued, saying the Inca had replied, "No! You shall not have my Coya. She is my full sister, my wife and queen. It is forbidden for any other man to touch her."

The messenger began strutting up and down, imitating Gonzalo's actions in front of the Inca's throne and speaking his words. "Bah! What heathens you are. The Spanish Church forbids marriage between brother and sister. You have been baptised into the Spanish Church of

Catholicism; your marriage is illegal! What say you to that Senor Manco Inca?"

Tlalli knew it was true that Manco and his relatives had all been baptised when the Spanish invaders had first arrived for the invaders had demanded this.

Cora Ocllo had turned very pale listening to her cousin. 'What does my Lord Inca say to this preposterous demand?'

The cousin told her Manco had said, "Cora Ocllo, my Coya, is the mother of my children and I love her dearly, you shall not have her." 'The Spaniard replied, "And I say I shall have her!" He shouted out, "Bring the Coya into court!"'

Cora Ocllo stood up, still serene and pale. 'What does my Lord command?'

The cousin seemed to remember his instructions, 'Ah, yes that is why I have come, for our Lord Inca has devised a plan. You are to dress one of your lady attendants in your clothes and she will be presented to the Spaniard. He is so drunk and stupid he will not notice the difference.'

Cora Ocllo sighed, shaking her head. Tlalli felt the Coya didn't seem convinced this ruse would deceive the Spaniard, but she also knew her mistress would not question the Inca's command. Cora Ocllo looked to her ladies. 'Who will do this for me?' She had only to command it and they would have to obey. All her attendants knelt before the Coya, saying they would take her place, but she turned to Tlalli. 'Your likeness to me is the greatest, Inguill. Will you do this for me?'

Tlalli's blood seemed turned to ice, knowing what this meant. Her fear of this man had followed her from childhood. Now her feelings towards him were also of anger and the time had come to prove her obligation to the Coya. She felt sure she could do this if she focused on her anger rather than her fear.

'I will do this for you, my lady Coya,' said Tlalli, barely controlling the tremble in her voice. The attendants quickly dressed her in a gown of shining gold and placed a heavy veil over her head. She was the same height and size as the Coya and the disguise transformed her into a very regal figure.

The Coya sent the messenger ahead to tell the Inca that she was ready to enter his presence. She spoke to Tlalli, 'Remember, you go to the Inca and obey only his words. I will not forget this sacrifice, Inguill. The Spaniard will soon tire of his obsession and you will be returned to us.'

The Coya sent four of her attendants to go with her into the court. This time Tlalli led the procession from the Coya's chambers. She swallowed the fear rising in her chest and kept reminding herself she was on a mission to save the Coya and to deceive the Spaniard. Failure was not an option, whatever the consequences to herself. As she went towards the Inca she stood straight and tried to walk like the Coya.

Gonzalo Pizarro did not hide his impatience. He stepped in front of the Inca, who sat on his low stool at the head of the steps, in the centre of the court. The Spaniard ran down the steps to Tlalli shouting gleefully. 'Ah, at last, the lady queen, come to me.' He did not wait or observe any dignity for her position as Coya, embracing her roughly and throwing off the veil. He kissed Tlalli full on the mouth and then stood back to look at her. She tried to stop herself, but a muffled scream flew from her mouth then she looked back at him with contempt. Gonzalo's brow knitted in a frown and his eyes turned cold and angry.

'This is not the Coya!' he shouted and he turned to the Inca in fury. 'I know this girl; she is a curaca's daughter!' He pushed Tlalli away throwing her off balance so she fell onto the steps. He kicked her and yelled at the Inca. 'Give me the Coya! I will have only the queen.'

The court chamber burst into uproar and Spanish and Inca guards began brandishing their weapons. The Inca stood up and called for silence.

The deception had failed and Tlalli had been totally humiliated. The lady attendants pulled her away out of the reach of the Spaniard who was venting his anger by kicking her as she lay on the ground. As she left the court, she caught a fleeting glimpse of her father and knew he had witnessed the spectacle. She fought back tears knowing she would be punished. She would bear that; what Tlalli could not bear was the realisation she had failed the Coya. She called on the spirit of Izella to guide and protect her, but since coming to the temple Izella seemed to have lost her power in the face of these terrible enemies.

Her punishment found her banished to the lowest part of the palace and not allowed to weave at her loom. Instead she was sent to the kitchens to work on the dirtiest tasks the mamaconas could find for her. These days proved worse than any she had endured so far. Everyone shunned her and the cooks only spoke to give her orders. 'Wash those potatoes.' 'Scrub the floors.' 'Sort and grind the maize seeds.' 'Wash all the pots and gourds!' And there were piles every day.

At dawn, she went with a group of other kitchen maids to collect water from the river that ran through the city. That at least allowed her a few minutes to escape from the oppressive prison the temple had become. This daily chore meant she could breathe in the outside world and see the citizens of the city collecting their water from the same place. Out in the open she found she could think better. She wondered what had happened to the Coya, for no one told her anything. She could only guess that she had been forced to go with the Spaniard and become a prisoner in his house, one of the other grand palaces in Cuzco.

As she walked back with the other girls carrying the heavy pitchers from the river to the side entrance of the temple, Tlalli hoped that Manco Inca would not tolerate such an outrage, and would turn against all the Spaniards in his court. Her anger resurfaced and she wished she was a man, a warrior like her brother and father. She would fight these usurpers with every last breath in her body; she would hold fast to the vow she had taken. She wanted to do this so much, but she didn't even know how to begin.

The next day she was summoned by one of the mamaconas. 'Your father is here to see you and has been given permission to speak with you,' said the mamacona. She sounded very disapproving but allowed her to go with the messenger.

When she saw her father she forgot about the palace rules and threw herself into his arms. 'Oh, Father, it is wonderful to see you again. Have you come to take me home?'

Father pushed her away from him, for they were in a passageway in view of people passing by. He found a quiet corner where they could speak more privately. 'Oh, that I could my daughter, but I'm afraid that is not possible.'

Tears welled in her eyes as she clasped hold of his hands. 'What has become of the Coya? I am banished to the kitchens because I failed in my duty to her.'

He whispered very quietly. 'The Spaniard has her, for now, but in a way it has brought things to a head. The Inca will no longer tolerate these people. I cannot tell you anymore but you must be brave, Tlalli, and patient for a little longer. I promise you things will change, and soon. I want you to be ready for what will surely come.'

'I understand, and I will be ready, Father, but there is something I must tell you.' She lowered her voice and spoke softly in his ear. 'I have had strange dreams of a huge battle.'

Her father looked up and down the passage to ensure they could not be overheard. 'Your dreams do not deceive you, daughter. I had a private audience with the Inca today and now I must go and do his bidding.' He pressed his hands on her shoulders and drew her to him kissing her forehead. 'I will get you away from here, Tlalli. Keep your ears and eyes open. You will know when the time comes.'

He hurried away, down the passage and out of the palace. She put her hand up to her neck and touched the jaguar talisman. 'Thank you, Izella,' she whispered and hurried back to her duties in the kitchen, now with hope in her heart.

23

Flight to Rio

April 1931, Recife to Rio de Janeiro, Brazil
We leave the hotel very early this morning. Sam has offered to take Diego and Bill to Rio but I wish they were not travelling with us. I am determined not to think about the Spaniard; he will eclipse my thoughts of Sam and that is not what I want.

'I know what this is,' Bill says as we arrive at the airstrip. 'It's a Lockheed Vega; I'd like to have one of these.'

Sam asks me what I think. 'I did wonder how we would all fit into the Jenny,' I reply and we admire the sleek stylish lines of the Vega, looking so modern with its high single wings. Sam opens the door into the fuselage. There is room inside for six passengers and the bags are all stowed in the rear.

Sam assists Grace and me to our seats and Bill and Diego sit opposite. Sam gets into the pilot seat and starts the engine. There is no winding of propellers and she is soon running ready to move off and we take a bumpy ride across the field to where we must begin the take-off.

Sam waits with the engine idling while we watch a biplane bounce across the rough grass and just make it into the sky before the end of the field. Now it is our turn and Sam tells us to hold on tight as he begins his take-off run across the field. As the speed increases, so do the bumps and jolts, and the noise from the engine is ear-splitting. We leave the ground and are up and away, gently rising into the blue Brazilian sky. The Vega has three big windows on each side and as we circle back over the area we have a wonderful view of the *Graf Zeppelin* mounted on the short stub mast.

'Looking at her, you could almost imagine the Martians have landed,' says Bill, shouting over the engine noise.

Grace looks wistful. 'If I had to travel all the way from Mars, I would insist on travelling by airship, not in one of these bone-shakers.'

'Oh, Grace, no,' I say, 'Sam's Vega is fantastic. The airship was lovely but this is the transport of the future.' Sam is wearing earmuffs and doesn't hear but he turns round and smiles and waves to his passengers now we are on our way to Rio de Janeiro.

We make one stop to refuel at Itabuna; other than that we are in the air for seven hours. Without being exactly rude, I try hard to ignore Diego, reminding myself that my interest in him is pure curiosity. As we near our destination I concentrate on the wonderful view and imagine I am a condor; that magnificent bird that rules the skies of South America. I pinch myself knowing I'm one step closer to Tlalli's homeland.

Rio is the capital of Brazil and Sam circles the harbour and the city to give us a tour. We can see the famous beaches of Copacabana and Ipanema, where the old Portuguese colonial buildings crowd together, with a few new high-rise properties, almost to the shore line. Between these and the harbour, a line of hummock hills juts out into the Atlantic, ending with the Sugar Loaf peak which rises up like a sentinel. This city of bays and peaks is surrounded by forested mountains, the highest being Corcovado. Sam says they are erecting a huge statue of Christ on the top of this mountain, which will overlook the city and dominate the skyline. So far, South America is everything I hoped: majestic and romantic.

Sam lands briefly at Rio's airstrip and we say goodbye to Diego and Bill, although I am sure we will see them again. Then we continue on to the hacienda as dusk is falling. By the time we reach Sam's home the sky is almost dark. I am surprised to see a line of burning flares, marking the landing strip on the airfield. Sam tells us they have been lit by the gauchos who live on his ranch. They look after the steers which Sam is hoping to breed, and he says I will need their help if I take on the horses for breeding also. The men would have been listening for the sound of the engine and lit the flares when they heard the aeroplane approaching. I don't know why, but I feel very strange, as if I am about to take a giant leap into this new life.

I am falling and as my body tenses I wake with a jolt. A dream floods back into my consciousness. It is a familiar dream that always leaves me feeling edgy. A child is in a dark cave; the child is me. Eyes are watching and I am very afraid. The eyes are big and golden. Animal eyes, and I'm sure I am going to die. That is always when I wake up. This dream is one of many which began when I first had my jaguar pendant. I try to collect my thoughts and stare without comprehending into this strange room. I push the dream images away and wake up properly; this is my first day in Sam's house.

It is already daylight. At the window I see for the first time what could be my new home. This beautiful house is called *Casa da Boa Vista*, which means house of beautiful views. It is built in the Spanish-Portuguese style, finished in white adobe, with staircases inside and out leading to terraces and balconies overlooking acres of adjoining land. Around the house are walled paddocks, then fields where I can see long-horned steers being marshalled to grazing by the gauchos on horseback. To the south is the city of Rio; to the north, the land gives way once more to tropical forest, and the views are stunning.

I was glad to say goodbye to Diego; his flirtatious advances are unsettling. When I left England five days ago I thought only of seeing Sam and deciding our future together. Now Diego's image is constantly in my thoughts and, try as I may, I cannot push him aside. What began as a puzzle over whether we had met before, is now a concern that we met at all; I am beginning to wish we never had.

There is a knock on my bedroom door. It's Sam's housekeeper. She sashays into the room with a tray of coffee. Rosita is a local woman probably in her twenties; honey-brown skin bulges from her white embroidered blouse, the low-cut neckline revealing her ample bosoms. Her hips sway under a full floral-print skirt and her long black hair falls around her face as she stoops to leave the tray on a low table.

I try not to stare. 'Thank you, Rosita.'

She mumbles something incoherent and her dark flashing eyes avoid mine. Is she shy or is she sullen? It is certainly in contrast to her manner last evening when she served us at supper. Then she was all smiles and chatter, but only to Sam and in Portuguese.

Half an hour later Grace comes to my room. 'Well,' she says, 'what do you think of your prospective new home?' She perches on my unmade bed looking cool and refined as ever in light cotton slacks and a fine embroidered blouse.

'I can't take it all in yet, Grace. There is still so much to see. I think perhaps I am overwhelmed by everything.' I dress quickly in an outfit that complements hers, although I'm sure I don't wear it so well. My answer to her was evasive. I have always wanted an adventurous life but now it is within my grasp I find myself holding back rather than embracing the opportunity. Perhaps this is not the adventure I wanted.

Sam appears looking fresh and excited. 'Come, we will take breakfast on the high terrace overlooking the paddocks and the airfield.' He leads the way up the white adobe staircase which is curved with an ornamental black iron balustrade. We look across to the field where five aeroplanes are lined up and Sam tells us his plans.

'It is difficult for me to be the pilot and run the business,' he says. 'I need to train more pilots. In fact, I am thinking about running a flying school and then expanding the taxi business using the men I train as pilots.' Rosita arrives with a tray of food and serves Sam first.

'And women?' says Grace.

'Oh, yes, of course,' says Sam, and he turns to me and takes my hand. 'Beginning with my lovely fiancée, Christina.' Rosita serves me burnt toast. I ignore this and continue the conversation.

'Yes, Sam,' I say, 'I really want to learn to fly like a bird!' Rosita hovers behind me facing Sam; her presence is irritating.

'And me,' says Grace. 'Airships are my first love but I'll never be able to own one. Maybe a plane, yes, now that is a possibility.'

I am really surprised at Grace's reaction. I had not thought she was the slightest bit interested in planes, but Sam has obviously opened her eyes to this new and convenient form of travel. Sam asks Rosita to bring more coffee and she leaves us.

I take the opportunity to talk to Sam about Perú and show him the information I received from the solicitor. 'Look Sam, these are the photographs of Uncle Peter's house from Mr Chambi in Cuzco.'

'Mr Chambi?' Sam seems vague about the details and only glances briefly at the pictures.

'I wrote and told you, Sam. Martin Chambi is the photographer who took Uncle Peter into the jungle and photographed the jaguar. They were friends and he has sent these pictures for me to see what the house is like.'

'Oh, yes, I remember now,' he says quite casually, as if it is not important.

I'm irritated by this so I say, 'When are we going, Sam?'

'Oh, are we going then? I didn't know it was decided.'

'Sam! I have waited all this time to see the house in Cuzco. Don't forget, it's my house now and I'm longing to see it.'

Sam smiles, 'Of course, my dear.' He leans across the table and takes my hand. 'And I thought you came all this way to see me.'

Grace gives me a funny look as if to say, I told you so.

'Oh, Sam,' I say, trying to make amends, 'you know I'm here to see you. But it would be silly to come all this way and not go to Cuzco.'

'I don't think you have any idea how far that is from Rio,' he says. 'It's almost as far as from London to New York!' I don't even know if they have landing strips there because it's up in the mountains. But, to please you, I will find out what facilities are available in that part of the world. Then I'll see what I can sort out.'

He quickly changes the subject. 'Tomorrow,' he tells us, 'we are going to Rio. It's Carnival time. I have booked us into a new hotel facing the ocean at Ipanema. They say you have not lived until you have experienced Carnival in Rio.'

'That's super, darling,' I try to sound enthusiastic realising I have said enough about Perú for the time being.

'We will probably stay all weekend. Once the carnival begins it carries on night and day,' he says with a laugh, 'So I thought we should have a convenient and luxurious bolt-hole at the hotel. I hope that is all right with you, Grace?'

'Oh, it couldn't be better, Sam,' she says. 'It will be something new for me to write about. The British and American magazines are hungry for features on anything Latin American.'

Rosita returns with the hot coffee and serves us. As we sit here talking I am struck by how much Sam seems to have changed. Before he came out here he seemed so young and... well, I suppose so very English. He had his dreams and ambitions but no real experience of life. Now, he is a man of property and is running his own business. He exudes confidence and seems to command respect from people like Leeds and Alvarez. In their eyes he is a successful businessman. He has acquired a deep tan and looks fit and muscular. The outdoor life certainly suits him, but I do still wonder about the parties that Diego spoke about. The boy I fell in love with has disappeared and I am not sure I know this new Sam; he is very different. If I am ever to feel at home here I will first have to learn to speak Portuguese.

I retreat to my room feeling deflated by Sam's attitude. I'm determined not to slip into the role of the compliant little woman in his life. I take my jaguar pendant from the jewel case and put it on in place of Sam's locket. Now I have arrived in South America, my thoughts of Tlalli are much stronger. I feel the shape of the jaguar with my fingertips and it seems almost to hum, as if it's trying to speak, to tell me something. My dreams have revealed Tlalli faced many trials and challenges. She was so young and so brave. I know whatever else happens on this journey I must follow the spirit that is calling to me. Then perhaps I will learn the secret of Tlalli's life.

24

Anas

1536, The Sun Temple kitchens, Cuzco, The Inca Empire.
Another full cycle of the moon passed. Tlalli rose from her bed before
dawn and went to the kitchen to start work. She was becoming more
despondent every day for she had not heard anything from her father. No
one spoke except to give her orders, so she had no idea what was
happening.

The kitchen was empty. Only a huge pile of dirty pots greeted her. She
set to work but in her head she tried to work out a plan. Her father's
cautious words led her believe the Inca had indeed turned against the
Spanish occupiers. What had father said? He had spoken with the Inca and
now must do his bidding. What could that mean? He had also told her to
be ready, and that she would know when the time came. Even her constant
prayers to Izella did not send guidance over when that might be, or what
she should do.

Oh, it was such a lot for her to think about. But her own senses told her
nothing would be easy for it never was. She had seen the battle in her
dreams and it would be cruel and terrible. Many would die on both sides.
Brave men, perhaps her father, or Ispaca or Paullu. That thought set her
trembling. What could she do? How could she help? At this moment she
was just a lowly kitchen maid, still a holy Aclla, but in disgrace.

As she scrubbed the cooking pots she thought about her beloved jaguars
living in the mountain caves, and the spirit of Izella who had helped her
rescue the cub from the trap. Before she came here her prayers to Izella
seemed to have been answered with the earthquake. That had kept the
Incas' treasure out of Gonzalo Pizarro's hands. But Izella's Spirit had not
prevented Tlalli being captured by the same man and now she was in this
terrible fix. Then she remembered wise words spoken by her father many
years ago, when she was just a little child. 'The ways of the gods are not
our ways, their wisdom is above our understanding. Always trust in your
gods and you will be delivered.' Why had she remembered those words
now?

'Oh, you poor little thing.' The voice, immediately behind her, startled
her for her mind had been a long way away. She turned round to find one
of the local women who helped in the kitchens. 'Look at your hands,
they're red raw,' the woman said.

Tlalli lifted the cleaned pot onto the wooden bench and inspected her
hands. They were indeed red and the skin cracked. The woman seemed

quite friendly, in fact she was the only person who'd said a kind word to her since she first came to work in the kitchens. She shrugged, as if the state of her hands was a small thing.

'Here,' said the woman and she pulled a little cloth bundle from her pocket. Unwrapping the folds she revealed a knob of balm and began to smooth it into Tlalli's hands.

She recognised the smell. 'Sarsaparilla,' she said, quite overwhelmed by this woman's kind actions. 'My mother used to make this balm and I always carried some. That is until I came to live here.'

'Hmm, you look like you could do with a bit of mothering,' said the woman. 'Leave those pots for today; I'll finish them. You sort the maize seeds for me. I need to grind them ready for the baker.'

'You are very kind,' said Tlalli rubbing her sore hands, grateful for the calming balm. She went to the table and began to sort the maize seeds, a job she had often done at home, discarding the husks and removing blacked seeds. 'What's your name, kind lady?'

The woman laughed, 'Lady, you say. That's not what I'm usually called. You can call me Anas.'

'Your kindness makes you a lady to me, Anas, and I thank you very much.' Tlalli felt cheered having someone to talk to and she kept a watchful eye to ensure nobody heard them or they would both be punished. She began the task of grinding the maize in a wooden bowl with a stone. 'Do you live here, Anas?' she asked.

'Dearie no, thanks be to Inti. I live in the city for I have six children to feed, but I come in every day.' As she spoke she washed and scrubbed the pots vigorously with her big strong arms. 'Usually I have to go to the market and collect some of the special ingredients the cooks need for the Inca's table. He has to have the freshest fruits and vegetables brought in from the forest daily. It's a good thing he's not here now, though we still have to feed these uppity Spaniards. I don't know what the head cook will say today, for the market was almost empty.'

'Why was that?' said Tlalli.

'Well, you wouldn't know unless you saw what's happening in Cuzco. The city is under siege and nothing is getting through to feed anybody. I think they're trying to starve us out!'

'Who is?' Tlalli asked.

'Why, 'tis the Inca's army and thousands of natives too. I heard they've come from right across the empire, and only the city walls to keep them out. We'll be murdered in our beds 'afore long.'

Tlalli wanted to yell with delight, but she could see Anas was very worried, so she continued to grind the maize seeds to a fine powder. 'I thought the Inca was still here,' she said. 'Where has he gone?'

'Coo, you are out of touch, poor girl.' Anas banged the cleaned pots down on the bench.

'No-one has spoken to me since I failed to convince the Spanish man I was the Coya,' said Tlalli. 'Do you know what happened after that?

'Dearie me, everyone heard all about that, you poor little wretch. That Gonzalo man took the Lady Coya back to his house. After that the Inca seemed to turn against these Spaniards. But he's been very cunning.'

'What's he done, Anas?'

She lowered her voice to a faint whisper. 'Well what happened was, another of that Pizarro family returned from Spain. I hear all this talk when I go to fill my water pots in the early morning at the river, or else I pick up the gossip in the market square.' She wiped her hands and began rubbing the pots with a dry cloth. 'This brother, I think he's called Hernando, he brought word from their King in Spain that the Inca and his people should not be badly treated and allowed to rule their own country. Provided of course, they keep giving all their gold and silver to the Spanish! I ask you, what sort of a deal is that?'

'So where is the Inca now?'

'Well, this Hernando demanded his brother Gonzalo return the Coya to her husband, and quite right too. But then, next we knew, the Inca and the Coya and lots of the palace courtiers and Acllas went off in a procession. It was said, they'd gone to perform religious ceremonies miles away. The Inca promised to bring this Hernando back a life-size statue of his father, the old Inca, made of pure gold.'

'And did he?' Tlalli was astounded by what Anas told her.

'No, course not,' she said, chuckling, 'It were just a ruse to get away and plan this rebellion. Trouble is the rest of us is stuck here, right in the middle of the battle ground, or so my old man reckons.'

Tlalli knew what she wanted to ask, but she could see Anas was split in her loyalty. Here in Cuzco the local Incas and Indians were under the rule of the Spaniards, caught in a trap, waiting for the battle to start. They would have to fight alongside the Spanish against their own people.

At that moment, one of the cooks entered the kitchen, demanding to know if the maize was ground ready for bread making. Anas gathered up the maize from the table. She didn't say another word and hurried after the cook. Tlalli put away all the pots, cleaned and dried by Anas. She touched her talisman. Thank you, Izella. Now I know you still answer my prayers.

25

The Rebellion

Tlalli felt very glad she now had a friend. They didn't speak often, as there was usually at least one of the cooks around. These men treated the women who worked in the kitchens very badly.

Today, Anas arrived early and Tlalli went with her into the cellar to collect cold chicha for the Spaniards' mid-day meal. 'It is good to see you, Anas,' said Tlalli, 'What is happening in Cuzco?'

The older woman tapped the barrels of chicha to select the best brew. 'It's what's happening outside that worries me,' she said. 'There must be thousands of natives camped outside the city boundaries. My old man said, of a night time there's so many campfires the hills around Cuzco look like the stars in the sky.' The two women worked together to fill the pitchers to serve the Spaniards at table.

'I wonder why they haven't attacked?' said Tlalli.

'Well something's got to happen soon. Food is running very low.'

'Why haven't the Spaniards attacked the Inca's army?'

'Spaniards? Lots of them have gone off to find more gold and treasure. There's only half as many here as there was a few weeks back.' She wiped her face with her apron. 'If the Inca wants to catch 'em short-handed he'd best hurry up and get it over.'

Tlalli too, was puzzled that the Inca army had not yet attacked the city if there were so many of them.

''ere, this'll make you smile. When I went to fill my pots at the river this morning, there were these two lads there. They offered to carry me and my neighbour's pots back to our homes.' Anas laughed. 'Well, I'd never had that offer before so I let him, so did my neighbour. All they asked for was a crust of bread. Good looking boys, both of them. I'd never seen them before.'

All at once, Tlalli perked up and thought this was perhaps something significant. 'What did they look like, Anas?'

'Hmm, well, the one who carried my pots was darker than the other and I think he was younger.' Anas looked at Tlalli. 'Come to think of it, he looked a bit like you, your colour and similar eyes. The other boy was older, taller.'

Tlalli began to hope, but she didn't say what she thought to Anas.

'Well, the funny thing is, when I came into work just now, they was in the market square. The taller one was playing a quena. Oh, I do love to hear that music. I think they were trying to earn more food. But like I said,

I never saw them before today, though where they came from is anybody's guess, 'cause getting in and out the city is restricted now.'

'I expect they are local lads trying to earn enough to eat,' said Tlalli. But in her head she was thinking: Could it be them? Have they come to find me?

'Well if they come back to the river tomorrow, I'll give them the Spaniard's left-overs!' she laughed a little too loudly and the cook came to the door demanding the pitchers be brought in immediately.

Later that day, Tlalli wondered how she could go to the river the following morning. If these boys were her brother and his friend Paullu, she needed to let them know she worked in the kitchen. Then she realised, of course, Father knows I work here, so perhaps this plan has already been devised. All she had to do was be there.

The next morning she arose long before the cocks crowed and made her way to the kitchens. No-one was about, not even the cooks. She collected two wooden pails and went to the rear entrance. Normally, they had always to be in pairs to leave the confines of the palace, even to go to the river, called the Huatanay. It flowed right through the centre of the city, the water feeding the fountains, and channelling to the various palaces and main residences. Then it ran down the hillside, watering the farming terraces, until drains took it back to the main river.

Tlalli did not have anyone to go with, but she hoped if Anas was there she would not be stopped or appear conspicuous. The dawn would soon break and others would come to the river. She hurried across the square and down towards the city wall where the riverbank was shallow, allowing people to lower their vessels directly into the flow. She kept in the shadows, with a watchful eye, looking for her friend. Then she saw her, coming from the opposite direction. She waited until Anas stopped by the riverbank before stepping out.

'Hello Anas,' she said.

The woman jumped. 'Oh, my goodness. You gave me a fright. What you doing out here this early all alone? Do the cooks know you're here?'

'No,' Tlalli replied. 'I left before they were about.'

'Whatever for, girl? You'll be in terrible trouble,' she grumbled. 'That's if they notice, 'cause the guards have moved from here up to the boundary. My old man was called back last night. They've doubled the guards on the walls.'

They began to fill their pails with water from the river. Tlalli looked around at the other locals who were arriving. Her Aclla headpiece fell away from her face and she saw two men approaching.

'Tlalli!' one of them called out, and her heart jumped. He was taller than when she last saw him but it was Ispaca. She knew this was the time she waited for all these months. He began running towards her.

A loud shout of command sounded out from the top of the city wall and Ispaca froze on the spot, still too far from Tlalli to reach her. She quaked, fearing Ispaca had been seen. But the alarm was not directed at him, but to the hordes of warriors outside the gates. A great hail of stones, fired from the rebels' slings, fell all around them. Simultaneously, the onslaught began on all sides of the city. There was momentary confusion around her, then Anas grabbed her arm, 'Quick, girl, we must take cover.'

Tlalli shook her off. 'You go back, Anas. I have to go a different way!' Anas' mouth dropped open speechless, but then Ispaca reached them and took Tlalli by her arm.

'Goodbye, Anas. Please don't say you saw me go.'

Paullu came up and grabbed her other arm and the boys began to run, almost dragging her away. She called back to Anas, 'I will never forget you, friend!' and they disappeared in the confusion around the riverbank.

They didn't have breath to speak and took the only route available, along the bank of the river, close to the water. All the soldiers seemed to be retaliating against the rebels outside the city, repelling their attempts to scale the walls and gates. The three fugitives crept towards where the river passed out of the city and the shouting and screaming increased. They waded out and hid in the tall reeds.

'Look!' said Ispaca, pointing up. The roofs of the dwellings inside the walls were on fire. One by one the thatched roofs caught light and the fires spread like lightning in a freshening wind. Tlalli didn't know whether to cry from joy or grief, as she remembered Anas, and all those who lived in the city.

She could see the faces of every soldier, rebel, and ordinary citizen look up towards the terrifying prospect that Cuzco could burn to the ground. Numb with shock, she felt the boys take tight hold of her arms again. Under cover of the battle she staggered, struggling on, being pulled through the river reeds, drawing further away from the city. Half wading, half swimming, they reached the far bank of the river and disappeared into the dark forest.

26

Paullu

Cuzco to Calca in the Yucay Valley, Perú. (Renamed by the Spanish)
They only just escaped into the cover of the forest in time, as the dawn
broke and daylight filtered through the canopy. Their clothes were sodden
through with river water, but they pressed on, following animal trails. She
had no breath for questions and allowed herself to be propelled forward at
a speed she could not have made on her own. The boys had marked their
trail in the manner of forest Indians, and knew where they were going.
After what seemed like forever, they slowed down and she flopped to the
ground gasping for breath.

'Come on,' said Ispaca, 'not much further, then we can rest.' She
staggered to her feet and while her brother ran on, leading the way, Paullu
picked her up and laid her over his shoulder. Then he ran after Ispaca.

She felt ashamed of her weakness, but she still wore the long robes of
an Aclla. Wet though, they had hampered her movement and sapped her
strength. Jogging up and down on Paullu's shoulder she marvelled how big
and strong he had become since she had last seen him. Ispaca too, had lost
his boyish looks and like Paullu, he had grown to be a man.

Ispaca had disappeared and as Paullu, with her still hoisted off the
ground, caught up with him again they stopped. Paullu let her down but
kept his arms around her, for she still gasped and struggled to take breath.
Here the forest gave way to granite rocks rearing up between the trees. The
rocks were full of crevices and Ispaca led them into a cave half hidden in
the undergrowth.

'We found this on our way to Cuzco and marked it out as a safe place
to rest.' It was dark in the cave but dry and surprisingly warm. The roof
was low and they wriggled further in away from the entrance.

'We can't risk a fire,' said Paullu, 'but I don't think we were followed.'

Ispaca laughed. 'The Spaniards and the traitorous Indians will be too
busy saving their burning homes to worry about us.'

Tlalli thought of Anas and her family of six children; they weren't
traitors. But she didn't say anything. She owed her freedom and her life to
her brother and to Paullu; two brave men. Her father would have wise
words of comfort when she reached home and she must focus on that.

'I truly thank you both for coming to my rescue,' she said, 'and I'm
sorry I put you at great risk. It was my own fault I was taken.'

'Too right!' said her brother and then he laughed again and she knew he
hadn't lost his sense of fun.

Paullu just smiled. 'I think that Spaniard would have found a way to take you, Tlalli, so it was not really your fault. It must have been very frightening for you.' He put his arm round her shoulder. 'I am so happy you are free.'

Tlalli shuddered. 'I am free now but I am still a holy Aclla; my life is forfeit to the Coya.'

'What! After they treated you so badly, sending you to work as a kitchen maid?' said Ispaca, sounding indignant on his sister's behalf.

'It was not so bad for me,' she said, 'not as bad as it was for the Coya, to be taken by that wicked man.'

'Well she is not with him now,' said Paullu. 'She is back with the Inca and they are at Calca leading the rebellion troops.'

She briefly wondered if she would have to go back to service in the Sun Temple when the rebellion restored the Inca to his throne. But now she wanted to be home again, with her mother and father. 'How long will it take us to return home?'

The boys looked puzzled. 'We're not going home, Tlalli, we are going to Calca,' said Ispaca.

She looked from one to the other, not understanding. Paullu stepped in quickly. 'Home is not as you remember, Tlalli. The Spanish troops have stolen land and homes across the country, massacring and murdering, burning whole villages to the ground.'

Tlalli grasped hold of her brother's arm. 'Please, no, don't say our village ... our families...' Her words trailed off as her voice began to catch and turn to sobs.

'No, no,' said Paullu gently. 'We left everything safe and most of our villagers journeyed with us to Calca, for all our men have joined as warriors led by your father.'

She looked deeply into Paullu's eyes for she was not consoled. 'My mother? The children?'

'They are safe in the camp at Calca,' he said but she sensed his sadness.

'Your family, Paullu, where are they?'

He sighed with a worried frown. 'My parents would not leave. Mother was too poorly to travel and father wanted to keep watch over our herds. We moved them both up to a hut where the herds graze, although we brought half the llamas with us to Calca. My parents are as safe there as anywhere and my sister stayed with them.'

Tlalli closed her eyes willing her tears away. She hadn't considered how things might have changed at home. To her, life in the Willkapampa had always seemed indestructible. She chided her selfishness thinking only of her own troubles. When she considered the destruction the Spaniards had brought on her homeland, the anger she had felt so many times since their arrival rekindled. She turned to Ispaca, 'And what of our vow, brother? Does the Spirit of the Jaguar not rampage still against these invaders?'

Ispaca looked despondent. 'We did try for a while sister, and we were successful in a small way. But there are too many of them, and too many traitors helping them, though thankfully not Manari men. When father returned from his last visit to the Inca we were told of the plan for the great rebellion, so now all our efforts are to work under father as his warriors and take part in the battles with all the other tribes to defeat our enemies. You saw the first strike on Cuzco today. Now, we must return with you to Calca. Then Paullu and I must go back and join father in the war.'

She had thought she was prepared, ready for life outside the Temple. She'd imagined returning home, going back to the mountain and empowering herself with the Spirit of the Jaguar goddess Izella, leading her people to vanquish the enemy. She realised now that was all a childish dream. The harsh reality was that the country's leader, Manco Inca, was now taking all the people into a terrible war and that many would die, had already died.

'What is it that I must do?' she asked them. 'How can I be a part of this rebellion?'

'You can help mother at the camp,' said Ispaca, then she saw the laughter in his eyes. 'Make a meal for fifty men from scraps of meat and yesterday's left-overs.' He laughed and rolled over on the hard granite floor of the cave. 'Oh, if only you could feed us as you did before all this began.'

She reached out and thumped him. 'You know what I mean, funny boy. I need to be part of the rebellion now. I am older and wiser than before. I need to put the vows we took into action.'

Paullu put his arm on her shoulder. 'Ispaca has told me of your dreams, Tlalli, and the vows you took. I know you believe in the spirit of the jaguar gods, and that is good. But we need more than dreams to get through this time, to win this battle.'

She wriggled back to the mouth of the cave and stood up, suddenly angry that her brother had told Paullu her secret, and in their apparent lack of faith. 'You just don't understand, neither of you!' and she ran out into the forest where dusk had begun to rob the daylight.

Paullu immediately came after her and he caught hold of her before she could run far. 'Stop, sweet Tlalli, don't run from me.' He held her hand firmly. 'I do understand, and so does your brother. We have been charged by your father with protecting you and returning you to Calca and your family. Your father places great importance on your gifts and your ability to lead us in your own way. Don't reject us. Ispaca just likes to rib you and make fun, don't mind him.' He took hold of her other hand and turned her to face him. 'You are very special, at least to me you are.'

Tlalli immediately thought of the Coya's words. Her gifts were also her burden. She turned her attention to Paullu. Standing with him, feeling him holding her close in a protective embrace, emotions began to stir within her. She felt blood pounding in her temples.

She looked into his eyes. 'Dear Paullu. I have been quite selfish over my imprisonment. I have allowed myself to forget how these times affect everyone else.'

'If I could, Tlalli, I would ask you to marry me. But now is not the time for such celebrations. For now I will content myself to say that I love you.'

Tlalli opened her mouth to reply then closed it again. She didn't know how to respond. Do I love him? Until now love had been something she felt only for her family. She knew about respect; she respected the Inca, the Coya, and the priests at the Temple. Friendship. She knew about friendship; the latest was with Anas. But love for a man, for Paullu?

'I can't answer you, Paullu,' she said, her voice breaking with emotion, 'except to say I am not free to return your love, for I am promised to serve the Inca and his Coya. Even though I am free because of you, I am not free to love you, dear Paullu.'

In spite of her words she felt him draw her towards him and she tilted her face to his. Their lips met in a brief, loving kiss. Everything seemed to fall away from her. The moment was sweet and beautiful, and she was filled with great calm.

Ispaca emerged from the cave, a shadow in the twilight. 'Come on, you two. We'd best press on before we are caught. Many more miles to go to reach Calca.' She heard him but looked only to Paullu. He turned, still holding her hand, and they followed after Ispaca. Night birds screeched and demonic insects buzzed, but Tlalli felt warm inside feeling the change in her heart. They followed Ispaca, now in single file, while around them, eerie creatures clustered and glowed green. She had only one thought: would she ever be able to change her future and be free to be with Paullu? Perhaps one day, but first she must keep vows already made and find The Spirit of the Jaguar once more.

27

Schemes and Dreams

April 1931, Rio de Janeiro, Brazil

'Tell me again, Eduardo, what is it that I must do?' Diego is in the Manager's office of The Bank of South America on Rio's Avenida Rio Branco. He is pacing up and down, tense as a tiger.

Eduardo raises his eyebrows. 'For a start, you must remain calm and keep your nerve, my friend.'

Diego swings round and sees the warning look in Eduardo's eyes. So he returns to sit facing the Manager's desk. 'Of course, Eduardo. It is just such a big responsibility to make money for investors.'

'Let me go through this with you once more.' Eduardo leans back in his executive chair. 'Invitations to apply for the Bond Issue have been mailed out to over one hundred individuals and companies who have already expressed an interest. Every major bank in North and South America, Canada, Europe and Australia has been notified. We have placed advertisements in every financial newspaper in all those countries as well.' Eduardo stops to take breath.

'You are doing a magnificent job, Eduardo, but tell me what response do you envisage? When are we likely to see any money? Until that happens this venture cannot even begin.'

Diego needs the capital to begin his mining operations. He intends to start with the largest mine in Perú, but it is a long way from Rio. That site, the Yaguar mine which he has never seen, appears to show the best return. The surveys on this and three other mines in Brazil, Mexico and Argentina have all been acquired, at no small expense. It was the only way he could have persuaded eminent people like Bill Leeds and Eduardo Moreno to back him. But Diego knows financial transactions at this level can be very difficult, almost like gambling with his very life.

'The official date for the floatation is tomorrow, 24th April,' continues Eduardo, 'so if everything goes to plan, we should see the result in two to three weeks' time.'

Eduardo's words are opening up visions of riches for Diego. 'And do you think we will raise the million dollars?' he asks, anxious to demonstrate his integrity, as if he does this type of thing every day.

'Absolutely,' Eduardo asserts. The hairs on Diego's neck begin to tingle. He can barely comprehend he is about to become a millionaire.

It is Saturday afternoon and now all the banks are closed. Fresh from his hotel Diego is making his way through the crowds along the promenade at Ipanema. It is Carnival time and all the hotels are full. Rio is a riot of noise and colour as thousands of people descend on the few square miles that make up the city centre and seafront. He is wearing a white silk samba shirt, like the musicians wear, with pleated ruffles on the arms edged with coloured silks.

He sways his narrow hips to the music playing up and down the Avenue. He feels his lithe muscles stretching against the black cotton trousers. Every group of dancers he meets sets him turning and tapping with the pulsating samba rhythm.

Jazz bands with trumpets, trombones and saxophones rend the air, alongside Spanish guitars, Latin drums and maracas. Together they fill the hot and sultry streets with the sound of samba rhythm. The city throbs as bodies sway and shake. Elaborate floats and costumes, a year in the making, parade through the city centre, competing to be the biggest, noisiest, most fabulous samba spectacle.

Diego is in his element; this is his world. He finds the rhythm of Latin dances hypnotic and just as passionate as the flamenco which fired his love of dance back home in Spain. He loves the intimacy of dancing so close to the beautiful South American women. But he also needs to think through his next move. If he is successful in getting control of all the funds he has to set up the mining operation. He has no experience in that field, but no doubt money will buy him all he needs; in fact money will buy him anything he wants.

Street vendors are displaying their wares. As Diego stops to look and buy, prostitutes strut along the pavement, vaunting deep plunging necklines, legs thrust through slits in narrow skirts, or completely on show under tiny tight shorts. He scrutinises the heavily made-up faces very carefully, for some are transvestites and it is sometimes difficult to tell the men from the girls.

'Hats, senor?' shouts a vendor selling brightly coloured hats and bandanas. Diego chooses a flat straw boater and sets it at a jaunty angle.

A girl nearby claps her hands, 'Oh, senor, you look so handsome! The hat, it suits you.'

Diego laughs and twirls, arms raised flamenco style.

The girl comes closer to him. 'You want some fun, senor?' She brushes his face with her hand. 'I can show you fun.' She laughs and thrusts her chest out towards him.

Diego smiles. In spite of his own sexual arousal, far from finding this exciting Diego shakes his head. His fantasies are of bedding princesses in bejewelled palaces and he turns to walk away.

'Hey,' she shouts after him, 'you crazy or something? For a moment he is tempted, but then he waves goodbye and continues, following the throbbing samba carnival. He works his way along to the far end of the seafront. There are as many couples dancing on the beach as in the streets; they are even in the water. Only further out, beyond the surf is the skyline free of writhing, bobbing bodies.

As the number of cafes and street musicians thins out, so do the number of people. It is very hot and Diego is tired and thirsty and he craves a long cool glass of beer. The last cafe still has tables to spare under pretty blue fringed parasols, and he slumps into a chair, quite exhausted. Here, there is a troupe of musicians playing samba rhythms, but in a softer, gentler style, with a Spanish guitarist, who also sings to the melodies.

He orders his beer and lights a black cigarillo while he waits to be served. The music is delightful, and he feels a glorious sense of self-satisfaction, as he listens to the strumming guitar. It reminds him of home and Spain. Not so very different from Rio; in fact Rio is a far more exciting place to be than Toledo ever was. His beer arrives and he downs the cool refreshing liquid quickly, quenching his thirst.

The encounter with the prostitute has left him feeling that, exciting as the carnival atmosphere is, it also has its unseemly grubby side. He should be aiming much higher. In the past when he had stayed at Watson's hacienda, the housekeeper Rosita and her younger sister Serena, had made perfect and discreet bedfellows for Watson's male guests. Clean beds and clean women are very pleasurable but such women are still beneath his social standing, not what he is really looking for.

As the sun loses its fierce heat the shadows lengthen. Diego is hot and sweaty and it is time to return to his hotel to prepare for the coming evening's entertainment. He is sure that tonight he will find a senorita to suit his mood.

As he makes his way back along the crowded Avenida, Diego passes other hotels which front Ipanema beach. On the first floor balcony of the Hotel Riviera he catches a fleeting glimpse of the lovely Christina Freeman. He is so surprised he stops abruptly. Yes, he sees her clearly now, leaning on the balcony, apparently watching a troop of dancers performing in front of the hotel. He calls up to her, but over the music and constant babble of noise she doesn't hear him. He waves his hat and calls again, but still fails to attract her attention, which is wholly on the dancers in their skimpy costumes. Then she turns and speaks to someone unseen by Diego. A moment later Sam Watson comes into view and Diego feels a pang of disappointment.

In those few seconds he had imagined himself wooing the beautiful blonde English girl from under the balcony and winning her heart, like

Romeo to Juliet. But she and Watson are now standing together, their arms wrapped around each other.

Diego is not to be deterred. He is used to having his own way. When fair means don't achieve, foul play can usually secure whatever he desires. He will soon have a million dollars at his disposal, so there is no reason to suppose he could not still have everything he wants; and he wants Christina Freeman more than anything in the world.

28

Perfect Timing

At 6 pm precisely, Diego strides into the Hotel Riviera looking very dapper in a dark suit and wearing shiny black patent leather shoes. His hair, beard and moustaches are slick with brilliantine. He has booked for dinner on the assumption that the English visitors will dine there before tasting the delights of the best night of Carnival; why else would they be in Rio? The maître d'hôtel greets him. 'Good evening, senor,' he says, with a slight bow of his head.

'Don Alvarez,' says Diego. 'I rang earlier to book for dinner. Tell me, do you have a Mister Sam Watson staying here? I believe he is with two English ladies.'

'Why yes, senor,' says the maître d'hôtel. 'How can I assist you?'

'They are friends of mine,' Diego replies. 'Would you be so kind as to ask Mister Watson if I could join them at their table?'

'I will enquire for you, senor. Please wait in the lounge bar,' and the man hurries into the hotel dining room.

Diego goes into the bar feeling pleased that his assumption was right. He is sure that Sam can hardly refuse his request. He orders a martini cocktail and lights a cigarillo.

The maître d'hôtel returns. 'Senor Watson says you are welcome to join them. Please follow me.'

In the dining room the party are seated at a table for four with one place vacant. Diego's timing is impeccable as they have not yet begun their meal. Sam stands to greet him, but Diego senses he is not best pleased by Diego's intrusion. He must be very diplomatic tonight for he knows things about Sam Watson that would shock the ladies and possibly create havoc in Sam's relationship with Christina. Diego is excited by the prospect of using this to his advantage, but first he must gain the trust of the lovely Christina and he will do this through the good offices of her confidante, the equally lovely, Lady Grace Drummond-Hay. She is a widow, and as far as he knows, she is not engaged to anyone.

As Diego takes his place at the vacant seat Christina is opposite him. He smiles politely at both ladies in turn, murmuring good-evening and his thanks for their hospitality. He senses a pause in their conversation and considers how he can charm his way into their circle. The waiter brings their wine order and Diego requests a second bottle and insists the whole order is transferred to his bill. Sam fills Christina's glass and Diego serves Lady Grace before filling his own. The music has enticed several couples onto the small dance floor which is set on a lower level and overlooked by the diners.

'So, my friends,' he says, breaking the silence, 'are you enjoying the Carnival?' He looks to Lady Grace, 'Madam?'

'Oh, the Carnival itself is spectacular,' she says, 'but we were just saying the crowds are overwhelming and the noise deafening! Rather like being in the middle of a circus.'

Diego nods his head in agreement. 'It is, as you say, a huge circus and indeed very noisy, milady. But it does have its origins in religion, of course.' He glances at each of the three faces. Even the cool Christina is showing some interest.

'Ha,' says Sam scornfully, 'you mean a celebration to the gods of fertility and virility?' Christina frowns at him and playfully taps the back of his hand to admonish him.

He defends his words. 'Well, you have to admit that nothing is left to the imagination. It's all on show in Rio; the good, the bad, and the downright ugly.' Sam takes a large gulp of his wine and Diego merely nods and smiles, agreeing without comment. He does not want to put a foot wrong tonight.

The soup course is served and consuming this breaks the conversation. As the plates are cleared away he says to Christina, 'Miss Freeman, you seem to enjoy and appreciate the lovely dance of the samba, yes?'

She seems taken by surprise. 'I do,' she answers, 'but how do you know that?'

'Oh I can tell these things, he says, 'I would say that dance is in your soul'. Her expression shows he has indeed awakened a desire in her, but then she casts her eyes down to her plate. Diego continues, 'Perhaps in a former life you danced for kings and lords.' At this she raises her head and her eyes look almost haunted, as if he has revealed an unspoken secret. He feels he has touched a nerve and hopes this has not caused her any pain. He quickly turns to Grace to change the subject. 'And what will you say about Rio in your newspapers, milady Grace?'

She smiles at him. 'Well it is, of course, ideal copy for sex hungry Americans but I would like to know more about the origins of the Carnival, Don Alvarez. The history must be fascinating.'

'After dinner, if you are interested, we can view the evening's entertainment and visit the beaches where the spiritual ceremonies are to be seen. But please, Lady Grace, call me Diego.'

'Oh, then you must call me Grace. Speaking for myself, I should be delighted to see these ceremonies.' She turns to the others, 'Sam, Christina, what do you say?'

Christina still seems withdrawn and Sam speaks for them. 'Well, Alvarez, provided there is nothing unseemly, we'll go with you.'

'Of course, that goes without saying.' Diego turns his attention back to Grace. 'Grace is a beautiful name and perfectly suits your ladyship.'

Grace smiles again. 'And you, sir, know how to flatter a lady.'

Their main course is served and conversation lapses while they enjoy their food. The dancers on the lower floor provide the entertainment. An Argentine tango is played and one couple give an outstanding performance which draws applause from the diners.

'We did not have to travel to Buenos Aires to see this dance after all,' Diego says to Christina.

She has turned her chair to watch the performance. 'I would love to be able to dance like that.'

'Oh, but you can'. He is pleased to have her attention at last. 'You only need a good teacher to show you the steps. The rhythm and movement are in your soul already.' The music changes to a samba beat. 'And samba? I know you would love to dance the samba,' he says with a flourish of his hand.

'Oh, yes, I would.' she replies.

He stands up. 'Wait here and watch.'

He leaves them and descends the half dozen stairs to the lower dance floor. Local dancers are employed by the hotel to entertain guests during dinner. Afterwards they are available to dance with the guests. Diego chooses a dancer wearing a short red dress with tiered ruffles. They join the other couples dancing on the floor. He has lost no opportunity since his arrival in Rio to polish his dancing prowess. He can hold his own with the local Cariocas in any Latin dance.

He twirls his partner, lifting her up in the air and twisting her round and round to the exotic beat. The music changes to a rumba and seamlessly the couple move together. Their hips sway and he pushes her away, then folds her back into his arms with a circular movement. They continue moving to the sultry staccato rhythm of romance.

The music ends and Diego leads his partner off the floor and returns to the dining room level. He is applauded by the diners and stops to bow and acknowledge this on the way back to the table. Christina and Grace are clapping their hands.

'Bravo,' says Grace.

'Wonderful!' says Christina, 'I didn't realise you are such an accomplished dancer.'

'Thank you, my dear Christina,' he says, delighted that she has apparently dropped her cold-shoulder attitude. 'But all it takes is practice.'

'And a natural rhythm,' says Grace, 'which you have in abundance.'

'And a natural way with the ladies,' scoffs Sam, 'which you also have in abundance.'

Diego laughs at this. 'Each to his own, my friend,' he says to Sam. 'You fly, I dance.'

'So there's no competition?' asks Sam.

'None whatever,' says Diego, and he turns once more to Grace. 'Would you like to dance, Grace?' The music is traditional tango again. She says she will try but only because she is fortified by the dinner wine. They go down onto the dance floor and Diego leads her gently in the basic steps of the tango.

'You could make a good living as a dance teacher, Diego,' says Grace as they come off the floor.

'It is a pleasant pastime,' he answers, 'but my job is to reopen the Alvarez family mines and make money for my investors.'

'And for you, of course,' says Grace.

'In the end, yes, I hope to make a good deal of money, my dear Grace.' As he says this he deliberately looks into her eyes, hoping to flatter and impress her.

'When and where will you start?' she asks.

'Perú. The most productive mine is there. All the readings are very good and that is where I must go, and soon.' They return to their table in the dining room. He pulls out Grace's chair and she sits down.

'Christina,' says Grace, 'Diego says he is going to Perú to open his gold mine. Isn't that a coincidence?'

Diego looks from Grace to Christina. 'What is the coincidence, ladies?' He notices Christina's complexion is flushed. Her wine glass is empty so he tops it up.

'Grace means I am hoping to go to Perú also.' Her words are slightly slurred and she is obviously a little tipsy. She leans towards Sam, snuggling close to him. 'That's if Sam will fly me there.' Sam looks taken aback as if wrong-footed.

'It's a very long trip to Perú,' he says, 'and time, my darling, is money.'

Diego senses a difference of opinion between them as Christina pouts with disappointment, but she's not about to let it rest.

'If you won't take me I shall find another charter pilot who will. I can afford to pay.' She empties her wine glass. Diego is surprised by this outburst but secretly he is pleased by her little show of temper. He had wanted to drive a wedge between the lovebirds but now it seems there is already a rift in this apparently perfect relationship.

Diego seizes the opportunity. 'May I perhaps make a proposal which would avoid the lady being disappointed and provide finance for such a journey.' He has directed his words to Sam but they are all waiting for him to explain. 'I need to travel to Perú myself to supervise the re-opening of my family's mine. I want to travel as soon as possible and I can, of course, afford to pay for your services, Sam. So please name your price.' It is

130

obvious that Sam is caught in a trap of his own making. Diego can't see how Sam can refuse to take him to Perú now that money is on the table. No doubt Christina would fly with them.

Even so, Sam hedges. 'Well, to Lima it would be at least two days' flying and then of course my return trip without a fare.' He um's and ah's, apparently thinking things through. 'I'll have to cost it out and let you know.' His annoyance and impatience are undisguised.

'Actually,' says Diego, 'although I need to go to Lima first, I really want to continue on to Cuzco.' Sam's frown deepens.

'Oh, Cuzco,' says Christina. 'That's where I want to go.'

'Do you?' says Diego. 'And what is your interest in that remote and ancient city?'

'I have inherited a property in Cuzco and I am very keen to see it before it is sold.' Diego is sure it is the wine that has loosened Christina's tongue. She continues, 'In fact now I have come to South America I am determined to go.' She looks at Sam as if he is an obstinate child and she is determined to have her own way.

Diego could not be more delighted. Although he will now have to pay quite dearly for the flight to Cuzco the fact that the beautiful Christina Freeman will be going also should give him plenty of opportunity to spring the perfect trap.

29

Black Magic

April 1931, Rio de Janeiro, Brazil

By the time we are ready to leave the hotel for our evening stroll it is nearly 11 pm. Given the grotesque nightmare I had on the airship, Diego's words about dancing for kings has unnerved me; it's as if he can read my mind.

I suppose I should be grateful to him for bringing forward my trip to Perú. Sam is very annoying; he will fly there for money but not just to please me. I think he really drank too much tonight, but perhaps he was a little put out by Diego's prowess on the dance floor.

The carnival is still thronging noisily along the Avenida and the seafront. We have to link arms not to be separated as a huge tide of people carry us along and I am giddy with excitement. Dancers wear the most outlandish costumes and all the shops are open. The keepers are shouting for trade from the doorways, trying to compete with the street vendors.

As we reach a jewellery shop I remind Sam of his promise to buy me a ring. I think he is anxious now to make amends so I must accept this as his way of apologising. Diego says this is the best jewellery shop in Rio, so we go inside to avoid the crush of people on the pavement. The shop is lit with oil lamps and candles creating a strange glowing ambience. Sam speaks to the owner in Portuguese. He is a small man with shoulder length dark hair. When he speaks his teeth flash with gold fillings, and I can't help but stare at him.

He brings out three trays of rings. I have never seen so many different coloured diamonds and settings, all solid gold or silver with bridge settings, or shaped like coronets. Some are in filigree swirls like the petals of flowers, or twisted like coiling snakes: so many different rings I find it impossible to choose.

'An engagement ring should be diamonds,' says Grace. She points to a row of rings fashioned like buckles, all different. Then I see a beautiful ring shaped like a flower. The central stone is a large pink diamond and each petal has three little white diamonds. The fit is almost perfect and the jeweller says it can be adjusted for me and be ready tomorrow. I cannot tell the price because I don't know the currency but it looks very expensive.

'Do you like it?' Sam asks me.

'Oh, yes. It is exquisite,' I say and my voice comes in a whisper because I am quite overwhelmed.

'Then you shall have it,' he says, 'but you must not be embarrassed if I haggle with this gentleman over the price, it is the custom here.' He smiles and kisses me on the forehead. I understand his meaning and go over to where Grace and Diego are examining a case of gold and silver ornaments.

'Look, Christina,' says Grace, 'these items date from before the Portuguese and Spanish invasions. Some were made hundreds of years ago by different races in South America.'

'This group here,' says Diego, 'was discovered in Perú and is of Huari origin.'

'Who were the Huari?' asks Grace. When she says this I remember Great Uncle Peter's letter when he explained the origin of my jaguar pendant.

Diego reads the card and translates the Portuguese wording. 'The Huari Empire arose around 600A.D. The Huari invented many practices later adopted by the Inca. They built stone buildings, paved roads, and perfected the mining and refining of gold and silver. These colourful, decorated pieces are examples of the work of Huari goldsmiths.'

We look at the beautiful artwork in the glass case. There are everyday objects like plates, bowls and cups ornately decorated with repeating patterns, and small replicas of birds and animals made in solid gold or silver finished with the same patterns. My eye is drawn towards a flat engraved item, very similar to my pendant. The head is in the centre and the four corners are the paws. The face is fierce, with fanged teeth and bulging eyes. I've seen this pendant in my dreams. My heart begins to pound and I feel very strange. I find myself saying, 'How much is the little gold pendant? I want to buy it.'

'Oh, I doubt it is for sale, Christina,' says Diego, 'but I will ask for you.' He waits while Sam concludes his transaction with the jeweller. I hear him say, 'Senor, the lady would like to know if the gold pendant in the Huari display is for sale.'

The jeweller quickly moves to the glass case, 'No, madam, none of these items are for sale. They are on loan from a museum in Lima.' I thank him and turn to Sam, desperate to hide my disappointment. Sam smiles at me but says nothing about my failed transaction.

'When will the ring be ready?' I say, trying to show how pleased I am. He says we will return tomorrow before we leave Rio.

As we go back out to the Avenida Diego says, 'If you still want to see the true religion of Rio we must go to the beach.'

'Lead on,' says Sam, 'but I trust we will not expose the ladies to anything unsavoury.'

Diego says, 'If you are not comfortable with what we see we can always walk away.'

'Well I want to see everything while we are here,' says Grace. 'This is an opportunity not to be missed.'

So we continue down towards the beach, arms linked as before. The area below the sea-wall is dark but is filled with a great throng of people congregating for the ceremonies. Circles of burning candles have been set into the sand, and men, women and children wearing long white robes, their heads also covered with white cloths, are walking slowly around the circles. As we come down the steps from the promenade I can see statues in the centre of the circles and that the people seem to be paying homage to these.

I know that Rio is a Catholic city and ask Diego, 'Is this a Christian ceremony?'

'Hardly,' he says. 'This is a spiritualist ritual for believers in Umbanda. They are paying homage to Yemanja, the ruling divinity of the sea.'

The believers swirl to the mesmerising beat of drums and call out, though I don't know what they say. Others make signs in the flat sands and also call to the night sky. Sam shakes his head and mutters under his breath. 'All mumbo-jumbo if you ask me.'

As the drumming intensifies individual dancers go into frenzies, twirling, stamping and chanting. 'They are attempting to call on the spirits to give them good luck and to drive away the devil,' says Diego.

We walk around the groups and move further across the beach. The drumming is fast and dancers with painted faces, some wearing grotesque masks, thrust themselves towards us as we pass. The air is filled with a sickly smell and it is quite intimidating. I am glad Sam is here to protect me.

Diego points towards some whirling chanting dancers. 'They are trying to communicate with Exu, who is the devil. What you can smell is cachaça, a local alcoholic drink they have brought to pacify the spirits. There are mediums here who will tell you your fortune by speaking with the spirits.' As we move further along the beach I wonder how he knows so much about this black magic.

An elderly lady is sitting on a stool surrounded by people anxious to consult with her. She wears a white dress and wisps of black hair escape from a round white cap pulled down over her ears. Golden bracelets jingle on her arms and remind me of gypsy fortune tellers at our own fairs back home. But most bizarrely, like a man, she is smoking a big fat cigar. Her eyes are closed and Diego says she is supposed to be talking with the spirits on behalf of a man who sits at her feet. The consultation seems to come to an end and the man thanks her. He seems satisfied with what she has told him. The party with him move away and we are able to come closer to her.

'So, who wants to know what the future holds for them?' says Diego

'Not me,' says Sam, 'It's all voodoo rubbish.'

Grace ignores Sam and links her arm with Diego's. She laughs. 'I will if you will.'

Diego pretends to look shocked. 'Oh, you little dare-devil, Lady Grace,' he mocks. 'Come, let us speak with this spirit medium.'

I feel Grace must still be intoxicated from the dinner wine to agree to submit to this but it is Diego who requests the first consultation, so we stand around and watch. He speaks to her in Portuguese and the woman casts her eyes over all of us, so I ask Sam to tell me what is being said.

'Diego has told her we are all from Europe and want to know what the future holds for us. He has said he's from Spain and has come to South America to make his fortune.' Sam sneers. 'Not sure that was a wise thing to say.'

The woman asks for money and Diego puts some coins in her hand. She draws on her cigar and closes her eyes. She blows the smoke over Diego and he wafts it away with his hand. The medium begins to mumble and chant as she did with the other man. This goes on for some time and I wonder if this is just a show for tourists. She speaks to Diego, but her voice seems altered, deep like a man's voice. I notice Diego seems quite anxious and yet very interested in what is being said.

'What does she say?' I ask Sam.

'Strange,' he replies, 'I think she is now speaking in Spanish.' The consultation continues for some minutes and I can see that Diego is rather unsettled. He keeps looking towards us, but Sam shrugs his shoulders to indicate he can't understand what she is saying. It ends, and Diego looks relieved to come away from the woman and I do wonder what she has told him.

'What did she tell you, Diego?' asks Grace.

'Oh, I am destined to be rich and famous!' He laughs and tells Grace it is her turn. She seems less keen now but Diego gives the woman some coins for Grace. She puts the cigar aside and stares into Grace's eyes. Then she goes off into her trance as she did before, muttering and chanting in a very theatrical way. Then she speaks directly to Grace, but in Portuguese.

'Tell me what she says, Diego,' Grace sounds impatient to know her fate.

'She says the spirits say you are too young to be widowed and that you should marry again soon.' Grace looks amazed at this and I am speechless. How could this woman have known Grace was a widow? She wears her wedding ring still but that would not have told the woman anything.

Grace recovers her surprise and asks, 'Do they say who I should marry?'

Diego is smiling and repeats the question to the woman in Portuguese. She gives an answer and Diego translates again. 'You know him already but he is not here with you.'

'Well,' says Grace, 'I wonder who he can be?'

'A lucky fellow, whoever he is,' says Diego, 'but apparently not me, I am jilted yet again.'

Grace laughs this off but I can tell she is preoccupied by the woman's words.

'Go on, Christina,' says Grace, 'it's your turn now.' I think she says this to take the focus from herself.

'I'm not sure I want to know about my future,' I say, but it is useless to protest as Diego is again crossing the woman's hand with coins and I am jostled in front of her. She looks into my eyes and I feel a sharp piercing like the prick of pins and the smoke from the cigar makes them water. The old woman utters strange words in a chanting fashion. After a while she starts to talk rapidly but I don't know what she says. Diego listens intently and interjects her flow with questions in Portuguese. It seems he has to be persistent to extract information from her.

'What does she say?' I ask, alarmed by her manner. Diego holds up his hand to me signalling that I should wait and soon it all comes to an end and the old woman falls silent and cannot be coaxed to say more.

We make our way from the beach back up to the Avenida where the noise and bustle of the carnival continues unabated, so it is not until we reach the entrance to our hotel that we are able to speak. The lounge is still open so we go inside.

'Please, Diego, I must know,' I say, 'was she genuine or was it all just a charade?'

'Oh, no, not a charade,' he protests, 'although I cannot give any guarantees of accuracy. But I am sure she was in communication with spirits.'

'Bunkum,' says Sam, and Diego shrugs.

'Did she say anything else during my reading?' asks Grace, ignoring Sam.

'No, Lady Grace, she did not,' Diego tells her. 'But I suppose a better interpretation would be that your destiny is with a kindred spirit and that you will know who he is.'

'Oh,' says Grace and then she sits back silent and appears in deep thought.

I still haven't had an answer to my question. 'What about me, Diego?

'Well, my dear, Christina, this was much harder to understand and I'm not sure that I do,' he says with an air of mystery. 'She said that the spirits, several spirits, had been waiting for you for a long time and that your destiny was here, in South America.' Diego pauses; I feel he is holding something back.

'And, what else?' I prompt him.

'One thing only,' he says. 'The Jaguar's spirit will guide you.' As he says this he looks very pleased with himself.

'The jaguar?' I repeat. 'Do you think she meant the jaguar pendant in the shop?'

He nods his head, 'I know it sounds very strange, but how did she know about it if not via a message from the spirit world?'

Sam laughs, 'She's probably in league with the jeweller, working on commission!'

'Oh, Sam, that's rubbish. You're very cynical,' I tell him, and then I think about my pendant and the one in the jeweller's shop and wonder if they are connected, like the two pendants in my dreams. I remember that Diego was the first to submit to the old woman's séance. 'You must tell us what she said to you now, Diego'.

'I told you before,' he says nonchalantly. 'My destiny is also in this continent and I will be rich and famous.' He laughs. 'I just hope she is right.'

Sam seems impatient and gets to his feet. 'I think it is time we all went to bed, so we'll bid you goodnight, Diego.'

Diego stands and bows to us and thanks us for our company.

'And you for yours,' Grace says on our behalf.

Once he has left us, Sam sits down again. 'A word with both of you before we go up,' he says, and I am alert to a possible problem. 'I am not so sure that our friend Diego was quite candid in his interpretations. I think there were things said he did not tell us.'

'Do you mean our readings were not as he told us?' asks Grace.

'I think your readings were as the woman told, but it was his reading which intrigued me.'

'You said she began speaking to him in Spanish, Sam,' I remember.

'Yes, but I did understand some of it.' Sam strokes his chin thoughtfully. 'Although I'm not sure I believe any of it.'

'What did she tell him?' I am impatient now.

'She said the spirits knew he had blood on his hands. He would have to seek their forgiveness if he was to save his soul for he had become an instrument of the devil.'

30

Ambition

May 1931, Rio de Janeiro, Brazil

Back in his hotel room Diego lights a cigarillo. He pours a whisky from the decanter provided for first class guests and sits down on the bed. He has been disturbed by the words uttered to him by the spirit medium. He has never been sure about these people. His friends in Rio all believe in the old religions and have explained the spirit culture to him. Even church-going, Catholic Brazilians pay due homage to the old spirit gods, and the words of mediums are revered and respected. The hundreds of people on the beach last evening bear witness to this undercurrent of belief and Diego is not about to test its validity.

He knows, of course, that she is right. He has murdered twice, but each time it was necessary to preserve his own life and liberty. In his book that is not a sin, so he hopes the spirits will understand and he will of course, ask for their forgiveness. To him, it is that simple. Provided he maintains Diego's identity he knows he will never be caught.

Now he has another ambition. He contemplates the beautiful English lady. Christina Freeman is engaged to that buffoon Watson. She is apparently a very rich woman and she is also exceptionally beautiful. There is something mystical about her and he has felt drawn to her since they first met on the airship. Now, he is obsessed with making her love him, for he wants to own her, body and soul. He thinks about making love to her and driving Sam Watson from her mind. His passions rise at the mere thought. Together they could have riches beyond their wildest dreams; her fortunes, his mines, and the investors' million dollars. How could she possibly resist him once he is able to get her alone?

It is three weeks since the flotation of the Yaguar Mining Company and Diego is impatient to know how much money has been raised. The next morning he hurries from his hotel to the Bank of South America for his appointment with Eduardo Moreno. His own funds are now dangerously low and everything depends on the success of this venture. It is the first step in his plan.

As he enters the Manager's office, Eduardo stands to greet him. 'Ah, Diego.' They shake hands. 'Please be seated, we have much to discuss.' Eduardo is positively beaming and Diego's anticipation means he can hardly breathe.

Eduardo begins, 'I am very pleased to report that the bond issue has been a total success, in fact, it has been over-subscribed by...' he hesitates, consulting the paper-work on his desk and adjusting his spectacles, 'by eight thousand dollars!' He looks up still smiling. 'Accordingly, we have issued bonds for a further ten thousand dollars. I'm confident these will all be sold very soon.'

Diego can feel his mouth opening and closing like a fish but eventually he finds the words he needs. 'One million, eight thousand dollars? Is that right?'

'Precisely,' says Eduardo, 'minus the bank's fees, of course, and I will need to administer the fund most carefully with you. It is my duty to protect our investors' interests.'

Diego has already worked out his strategy for dealing with the problem of securing as much of the funds as possible under his control. 'My intention is to go to the Yaguar site in Perú and re-open that mine as soon as possible,' he tells Eduardo. 'I have my quotations here for the new drilling equipment which my surveyor advised would be needed.' Diego opens the envelope he is holding and finds the quotation which he'd had drawn up. It all looks very plausible and he passes it to Eduardo.

'I shall hire workers on site, so I will require working capital to cover labour costs and this will be a considerable sum,' says Diego, 'but I'm sure the rewards will soon justify the expenditure.'

Eduardo studies the documents carefully and then he does some calculations on a pad. He is quick with the sums. 'Would two-hundred and fifty thousand dollars cover the set-up costs?'

Diego's mind leaps with delight but he is guarded in his reply, 'It would pay for the equipment, yes, but the running costs are as yet unknown, and the interval before we reap any income is also unknown. I would need access to more funds until that happens.' His voice is strident and confident but inside his shirt he feels perspiration trickle down his back.

Eduardo is looking thoughtful and nodding his head. 'I will open an account for you at our branch in Lima. You can tell the Manager there when you require more funds and he will contact me.' Eduardo looks pointedly at Diego. 'The bank will require written details of all your expenditure.'

'Of course, of course, Eduardo,' Diego says, 'you shall have everything in triplicate!'

'When do you leave for Perú?' Eduardo asks him.

'My good friend, Sam Watson, is owner of the British South American Air Taxi line, and he is awaiting my instructions. As soon as I have the money to pay him, we will go.'

'I will advance you ten thousand dollars immediately,' says Eduardo, 'but you must learn the art of shrewd business practice and obtain credit whenever possible. Preserving capital is of paramount importance.'

'I will always seek your advice, Eduardo, before making any financial transactions.' Diego stands to leave and the two men shake hands again.

'I am sure this venture will be most profitable for us all,' says Eduardo, 'the bank, the investors, you and me. Now, let's go down to my chief cashier and collect your cash advance.'

When Diego leaves the bank his briefcase is bulging with ten thousand dollars in mixed currency notes. He will go back to his hotel and lock the money safely away in his travel bag, but first he needs to visit a certain jewellery shop.

31

Warriors

1536 Yucay Valley, Perú
Tlalli looked down across the Yucay valley which had been her home ever since her escape from Cuzco with Ispaca and Paullu. It wasn't really a home, but the base camp for Manco Inca's fighting forces, the place to which the warriors returned for rest and sustenance after many days of fighting to reclaim the city of Cuzco. Night and day Tlalli prayed to the sun god Inti and the jaguar gods Toquri and Izella that her father, brother and now Paullu would return safely to her.

When Tlalli had escaped with the boys, it had taken them three days to reach the camp at Calca. They took a devious undercover route, for she feared being recaptured by the Spaniards, or that the boys would be imprisoned or killed. During the journey her attachment to Paullu deepened. He showed strength, resourcefulness and had declare his love for her. Tlalli wished sincerely she had not been promised to the service of the Inca's Coya. She wanted to be free to make her own destiny; to love Paullu and fight beside him and her brother. But Paullu seemed to understand her dilemma and the boys' lively humour kept them all cheerful during the journey.

When they reached Calca, she hugged her mother and little brother and sisters warmly. But sadly, her father had gone with the forward troops, already now entrenched in the battle to reclaim the Inca's capital city. Word eventually reached the camp that many of the Acllas had left the city by a secret road and joined Manco's temporary court. Tlalli kept away from the Inca's camp and stayed with her family. She wanted to wait until her father returned, hoping he would advise where her loyalties lay.

Before the boys left to join her father in the Manari fighting unit at Cuzco, Tlalli spoke to Ispaca about what part she could play in the rebellion. She couldn't go with them to join in the fighting and she couldn't go home to the mountain and the source of Izella's power.

'Just keep up the spirits of our followers, Tlalli,' said Ispaca, 'for we need their support.'

She wanted to protect the boys with the Spirit of the Jaguar. 'Come brother, Paullu also. Let us renew our vows, to keep our people free from Spanish rule.'

So Ispaca, Paullu and Tlalli went to the top of the hill at sunset. She held up her hands to the sky, just like the first time, and said, 'We must promise to fight against all who try to crush our way of life and our beliefs.

We must keep the secrets of our ancestors safe and hide our sacred treasures from thieves – even to the point of death. We must do this in the name of Inti the Sun God, and the jaguar gods Toquri and Izella, for we are under their protection.' She turned to her brother and Paullu, taking hold of their hands. 'Will you take this promise with us, Paullu?'

Both boys seemed unsure, and she sensed they did not believe as she did, but she knew they both loved her and wanted to please her.

Ispaca said, 'I will renew my vow with you, sister.'

'I also will take this vow,' said Paullu. 'It will connect us while we are apart, dear Tlalli.'

She felt content. 'Long live the Spirit of the Jaguar,' she whispered as they watched the sun go down behind the hilltop, 'for that is the name of our alliance. With this we will defeat our enemies.'

Ispaca and then Paullu, embraced her and together the boys went to fight under Kusi's command. Ispaca called back to her as they left. 'We will fight with weapons of war. You must continue the silent rebellion from here, Tilly. May the gods protect us all.' Ispaca and Paullu went back to Cuzco to fight alongside her father. She had seen them only once since then.

Tlalli remained at the base camp with her mother for many months. If the battle for Cuzco could finally be won by the Inca she still feared she would be returned to the Temple. As the weeks had stretched into months and the rebellion dragged on, she began to wonder if this current awful waiting would ever come to an end.

She tried very hard to bring others into the alliance she called, The Spirit of the Jaguar, but the camp was full of women and children and old people. They only wanted an end to the war and their miserable existence at the campsite. Few would listen to her rallying cries or show any interest in the power of ancient gods. She began to lose her faith, for her prayers to Izella brought no sign that the jaguar goddess even heard her.

Three months ago Ispaca and Paullu had returned to collect fresh supplies. Tlalli began once more to have hope as she listened to their tales of victory. Everyone gathered round the campfire, as an excited Ispaca spoke to his relatives. 'We are winning! During these first few months the battle has all been in favour of our rebel army. We've destroyed the roofs of many buildings, leaving them useless to the Spanish forces.' The two young warriors delighted in telling their admiring relatives how well the battle was going.

Paullu said, 'Best of all we have taken possession of Sacsahuaman, the fortress citadel built on the hill-top, immediately behind the city.'

Tlalli turned her head from one to the other, hungry for news of the battle and so proud of her two warriors.

Ispaca continued. 'The Spanish and the native traitors are besieged within the city. We have them completely surrounded and attack them with our lethal projectiles and our bows and arrows.'

Paullu told them. 'We have re-routed the city's water courses and flooded the fields and terraces, so when the cavalry charge out to slay us, the horses are bogged down. We dig pits and build barricades to stop any cavalry charges from succeeding.'

Ispaca said, 'Father says those not killed by us will starve, for we have cut them off from the outside world.'

Tlalli briefly thought again of Anas. She remembered her as a resourceful woman who would find a way to survive, so she pushed the image of her and her children away.

All too soon, Ispaca and Paullu had to return to the fighting, taking fresh supplies of food and weapons. She sighed; it had been weeks since they left and little news had reached the camp since then. She continued to say her prayers, hoping for news of a victory. But Izella remained silent.

32

Turning Point

Tlalli came up to the hilltop every day looking for signs that her loved ones might be returning: her father, whom she adored; her brother, who was her dearest friend; and now Paullu. Since the day of their first kiss in the forest, she had thought about him constantly also as a loved one. Although she had not spoken words of love to him, he had to her. It was with great sadness she realised she could not, and perhaps never would. Remote from her home and the mountain which fed her belief in the power of the jaguars, she didn't know what the future held for her. Could the ancient gods still help them overcome the Spanish army? Could their lives ever be as they once were?

A movement on the road below caught her attention. Tlalli shaded her eyes until the figure came into focus. A lone runner moved up the valley towards the camp. She gathered up her skirts and ran to intercept his route into the camp. As their paths crossed she had to turn and run beside him for he didn't slow his pace. He looked young but she didn't know him or his tribe.

'What is happening in Cuzco?' she said. Up close, the boy's face looked haggard, grimed with mud, his hair matted with dirt. He had welts, sores and bruises on his skin, eyes sunken and dull. It was then she saw the boy had only one hand. His right arm had been severed at the wrist and bound with cloth stained with dried blood.

He slowed to a walking pace. 'The battle has turned against us and we have lost many warriors,' he said.

Tlalli's blood turned to ice hearing these words. She stumbled, struggling to keep pace with him. 'Do you know the whereabouts of my tribe? They are Manari.'

He shook his head. 'Many of our army are dead or captured and it is said the prisoners are slaughtered by the Spaniards, or like me, they are maimed.' He held out his injured arm towards Tlalli.

'Did you lose your hand in the battle?' she asked, fearing his reply.

'I was taken prisoner with about a hundred others. The Spaniards cut a hand off every man and sent us back as a warning.' The boy spat on the ground and uttered a curse on the enemy, and then he resumed running towards the camp.'

Tlalli watched him go. She tried to supress the unwelcome realisation creeping up on her that the Inca's mighty army could lose the fight for Cuzco and worse still, the warriors might never return. She went back to her camp, reluctant to tell her mother and relatives, what she had learned from the unfortunate boy.

She spent the following days near the entrance to the camp. Every day she watched little bands of listless men return from the fighting, sick and injured men, struggling to walk and helping one another on the last part of their journey. The once proud and eager warriors limped and shuffled into the valley, grateful for the gourds of water provided by Tlalli and dozens of other women, all hoping to find their own people among the few who made it back before they died on the trail. Some men, the not so badly injured, or farmers who had never been cut out to fight, had been sent back to plant crops for the coming season. The fight could not continue without food to feed the army or its families.

Day after day Tlalli continued to tend to the sad groups arriving at the camp and she stopped looking for her own loved ones, too frightened to think they might never return. She began ladling out water to the latest group when the boy whose cup she filled lifted his head and spoke to her.

'Hello, Tlalli,' he said, and she looked into Paullu's eyes. She stood motionless, too stunned to speak. He looked so different; covered in dirt and mud, thin, aged and weary almost beyond recognition.

At last she found her voice and grasped at his arms. 'Oh, Paullu, how wonderful you are here at last, but where are Ispaca and my father?'

Paullu stood up and took her hand, leading her away from the others. 'Dear Tlalli, your father fights on, for he is the commander and must stay with the remaining warriors for now.' He hung his head and then clasped her hand tighter. 'I am sorry to tell you that Ispaca is dead.'

Tlalli cried out, 'No, oh, no! Not my dear brother, not dead?' Tears flowed freely down her cheeks and she shook uncontrollably.

Paullu put his arms round her shoulders and held her close to him, trying to comfort her. 'He died a hero, Tlalli. He saved your father's life in the middle of a battle; he was a great warrior.'

Tlalli could not control her tears. 'Tell me what happened please, Paullu.' And they went to a hillock and sat, their arms entwined.

Paullu began, 'Six Spaniards came out in a cavalry charge onto the terraces below the city wall. They caught us unawares and Kusi fell. Ispaca went to help him to his feet when a Spaniard wheeled round on his horse and charged towards both of them.' Paullu stopped to control his own emotions for Tlalli could feel his hands shaking.

'I saw your brother deliberately stand in front of Kusi and take the blow from the Spaniard's sword. Ispaca fell dying, and I believe Kusi would have died also except that your Uncle Tutsi went forward with his bolas sling and hurled his stones. The cords immediately entangled the horse's legs and brought the animal down unseating the rider. Kusi scrambled clear and caught up the Spaniard's sword, lost when he fell from the horse.

Your father drove the sword into the Spaniard's neck and killed him! And so he avenged his son.'

Paullu stopped speaking to comfort Tlalli and she looked up into his face. 'I always knew Ispaca to be brave and I will remember him for this unselfish act. But, Paullu I am so relieved that you are here, and I pray my father will soon return safely.'

'I pulled Ispaca clear from the fight and held him in my arms.' Paullu's voice trembled and he choked on his words. 'He told me to take his jaguar talisman and give it to you.' He pulled the jaguar, still on its hide thong, from his pocket and gave it to Tlalli.' Then Paullu said, 'Ispaca's dying words were for you, dear Tlalli. He said, "Tell Tlalli to keep our vow and continue the fight in the name of The Spirit of the Jaguar. I should have believed more but Tlalli will know what she must do. Please help her, my friend." Paullu held her close and looking deeply into her eyes he said, 'All this was important to Ispaca and now it is important to me.'

She took the talisman and shook her head. 'It was supposed to protect Ispaca,' she said, tears spilling down her cheeks.

'Don't lose faith, dear Tlalli. Without you, I wouldn't want to go on,' said Paullu and he held both her hands to stop her trembling.

'Until my father returns to us, will you wear Ispaca's jaguar, Paullu?'

'I would be honoured to do so,' said Paullu. 'When your father comes back I will return it to him.' She took the talisman and placed the hide thong over Paullu's head. They looked into each other's eyes and an understanding passed between them.

Tlalli and Paullu walked on into the camp and she grieved openly over the death of her brother.

Paullu said, 'You know, Tlalli, I never wanted to be a fighter, I am a musician and a herdsman. I have to return to our homeland with the farmers to grow this year's crop of maize and potatoes. What will you do?'

Tlalli felt ill thinking about Ispaca's death, and of her father still fighting on, but thoughts of her home soothed the jagged edges of her ravaged mind. 'I would like to go with you,' she said. 'I can work the land as well as any man.' She caught hold of Paullu's arm. 'One day, I may have to go back to serve the Inca or the Coya.' She looked around the camp as if in fear. 'But until that day I am free to make my own life.'

Paullu smiled, illuminating his dirt streaked face and he took her hand. 'I will look after you, Tlalli. If I could, I would marry you. That's if you want me.'

'Oh, Paullu, that would make me very happy, but I am a holy Aclla bound to the Temple of the Sun and that cannot be undone, even if I never return to that life.' She began to cry again; her future seemed hopeless.

'I love you, Tlalli,' said Paullu, 'and love can move mountains. We will find a way.'

Hearing him declare his love for her, Tlalli felt a glimmer of joy in her heart. She could speak no words of love but pressed his hand tightly. 'I will come with you, back to the Willkapampa. Perhaps, as you say, we will find a way to stay together.' She thought perhaps, once back home, she could reignite the Spirit of the Jaguar and continue the struggle against the enemy now with Paullu at her side.

33

Revelations

May 1931 Sam's hacienda, Rio, Brazil

Sam has been rather disgruntled since it was decided we would all go to Perú. He's gone to Rio to collect Diego, for this trip is really all about his gold mine, otherwise I doubt I would have being going at all. I think Sam just wants to fly off with Diego and leave me here.

I have tried to explain to him that inheriting Uncle Peter's estate is not just about accumulating his wealth; that I have a deep emotional attachment to his memory and need to visit his home to pay my respects. I can't tell Sam about my dreams. I'm sure he would laugh at me, but that is really my driving force.

And then of course, there is Diego. I keep telling myself that what I feel about him is mere infatuation and I must not be blind to his duplicity. Perhaps Perú will bring some of the answers I seek about this man and I can finally free myself of this dangerous situation.

This last week has been a flurry of excitement. Grace, who is usually so calm and collected, has been in a whirl of anxiety that we should have the right clothes and sufficient of them for what might turn out to be rough terrain. She has also spent a fortune on long-distance telephone calls to her co-correspondent at Hearst Newspapers in New York. His name is Karl von Wiegand and she has been seeking his advice on the features she hopes to write about Perú and its treasures.

Since we left London, several weeks ago, Grace and I have become much closer and I do believe we have developed a friendship based on trust and mutual understanding. I have confided some of my wavering feelings about living permanently in South America and the enormous commitment I have made in agreeing to marry Sam. I don't know what she would say if she knew Diego was at the root of my muddled emotions, even though I've discovered there is much to disapprove of in her life.

Grace has confided in me that she and Karl were once closer than just colleagues. She told me that shortly after her husband Robert died, she went to New York to work for Hearst Newspapers. That's when she met Karl. For a while they were almost lovers and Grace tells me she completely lost her head over the affair, and it was an affair, for Karl is a married man. I think she is prompted to talk about this because of the reading from the spiritualist medium.

We are upstairs trying to finish our packing. Grace sits on her bed and looks so unhappy. She continues her story. 'Towards the end of '28 Karl said we had to stop seeing each other. He said his wife was mentally unstable and he could not leave her for fear of what she might do to herself.' Her voice shakes and she turns her head away on the pretext of blowing her nose.

I ask, 'What did he mean by mentally unstable?'

'Who knows?' She humphs. 'He says her nerves are very bad, but whatever it is, she has a tight hold over him and she won't let go,'

Now Grace looks more angry than upset. I can only sympathise. 'Oh, poor Grace, how awful for you.'

She continues her sad story. 'A few months later William Hearst appointed both of us to go on the *Graf Zeppelin* Round-the-World-Flight and we found ourselves thrust together again.'

I have to admit to being enthralled by this tale of illicit love and amazed at Grace's involvement. Until now I had no idea. 'What happened during the flight, Grace? Do tell me.'

She shrugs. 'There's not much to tell. To begin with he was rather distant and obviously wanted to keep our relationship on an entirely professional level. But when we landed in Japan and spent some time there off the airship, he became friendly again. I really thought I had won him back.' There is a wistful look in her eyes.

'Wasn't the airship grounded at one point? Didn't you lose contact? The papers said the *Graf* was lost.'

'Yes, all that and more,' she tells me. 'After we left Japan, we were blown off course by a storm. The *Graf* lost altitude and we came down in the sea near some deserted islands. Luckily, by then it was calm or I think we might have been swamped and drowned. But I never thought it was the end and I spent my time bolstering spirits and telling the men to have faith in Commander Eckener.' Grace looks wistful over her memories and of course I know how much she respects the Commander.

'I wonder you didn't lose faith yourself, Grace. You really are very brave.' My admiration is undiminished by her illicit affair.

'Well, of course, the Commander repaid my faith by getting the airship up in the sky once more. After two days we re-established communications with the world and continued on to Los Angeles.'

'And Karl, did he remain friendly?' I am almost afraid to hear her answer. When she does her voice is cold and brittle.

'Before we reached the West coast Karl received a telegraphed message from his wife. She said she would travel to Los Angeles and meet up with him when the airship landed.' Grace looks at me and I can read the unhappiness in her face. 'And that's what happened. Now I only see him if our paths cross professionally.'

'So what do you make of the clairvoyant's prophecy about your love-life?' I so want to give her hope. 'Surely that must be a sign that you do have a future with this man!'

'You don't really believe in all that, do you, Christina?' She still seems unconvinced.

'Why not? Don't you think it significant that she spoke of your association with a man not present? How could she have known?' Grace doesn't answer me but I can tell she is thinking over the woman's words.

Sam and Diego should be arriving soon and I go to the kitchen to see if Rosita has prepared the cold lunch I ordered. I still find she is sullen with me but Grace insists that I give her the instructions regarding the housekeeping and that Sam tells Rosita to consult with me over menus and timing. My Portuguese is still poor but I am learning. She looks at me with those big black eyes pretending she doesn't understand me. Now she tosses her head and flounces across the room to fetch the plates I have asked her to use.

I can hear the sound of the Vega approaching and I go outside. Sam circles the plane round the house. I wave and hurry over to the airstrip as he touches down. The two men leave the plane and walk towards me. My heart is beating fast but I don't know which man is causing this feeling; like Grace, I too have a guilty secret.

As they approach there is really no contest. Sam strides towards me. His athletic physique is so manly and he is a head taller than Diego who is darker skinned and with jet black hair. His beard and moustaches give him an air of mystery, like a theatre magician, and yet I am still hypnotically drawn to this strange man. It is as if fate has brought us together for a specific purpose over which I have no control.

Sam takes my hand kissing the lovely engagement ring and we walk back to the house.

Diego asks: 'Are you ready for our epic journey, Christina?'

'Well, I hope so,' I reply. 'Grace and I have bought ladies' versions of the latest safari style suits, with slacks and proper walking boots. I'm afraid we will not look very elegant.'

They both find this funny and Diego says, 'Well, there will still be opportunities to look elegant in Lima. I'm told it is a very modern city, no different from Rio or Buenos Aires, so I hope you have also packed your dancing shoes.' Sam groans at this and I know he is still put out over the dancing.

We take lunch in the cool dining room and the talk is all about the successful flotation of Diego's mining company. We've all invested a moderate amount of money in the fund, with Sam insisting it was not more than we could afford to lose if Diego's mining activities are not profitable.

150

I notice Rosita seems familiar with Diego and responds to him as she does to Sam. They speak about someone called Serena, whom I do not know. Sam and Diego obviously do, and I feel unsettled. 'Who is Serena?' I enquire.

Sam answers me. 'She is Rosita's sister. She works here sometimes if Rosita needs help.' He is guarded and does not explain further.

'Oh, that's useful,' I say, 'and keeps it in the family.' I notice Sam and Diego make eye-contact. For a brief moment a danger sign passes between them as if to say no more, and then it is gone. I do wonder under what circumstances Rosita might have needed help.

We have finished eating and Sam stands up. 'Would you all please excuse me,' he says. 'I need to go to the hangar and check the Vega is ready for an early start tomorrow.' Grace also excuses herself to finish her packing. I am left alone with Diego who has moved to the big sofa by the window. I intended to follow Grace but he speaks to me. 'Are you really looking forward to our trip, Christina?'

I feel obliged to go and sit beside him. 'Well, yes. I've heard such a lot about Perú and the Inca finds of recent years. It all sounds so amazing.'

'Tell me,' he says, 'have you thought much about the words of the spiritualist medium on the beach in Rio?'

He looks at me with his dark flashing eyes. He is close and I feel a frisson of excitement, a forbidden thrill which also frightens me. 'Do you mean her saying my destiny is here, in South America?'

'Not just that,' his voice is low, almost a whisper and he edges closer to me. I again think about that other Spaniard on the ferry long ago; they are fused together in my mind. He continues, 'I mean the message to follow the spirit of the jaguar, that it would guide you in a quest?'

'Quest?' I repeat, not really following his meaning. I would not have guessed what would happen next. He puts his hand into his pocket and then places something in my hand. I can feel the shape and when he withdraws his hand there is the little golden jaguar pendant from the jewellery shop. I gasp with surprise and stare at the piece. I do not even realise he has taken my hand in his.

'My dear, dear Christina,' he whispers. 'Oh, that I could win your heart with my little gift,' and for a brief moment his lips brush my hand and his touch is electric.

I nearly succumb, so powerful is the emotion of this moment, but I regain my sanity just in time and stand up, still holding the pendant. I tremble, close to tears and turn away from him.

'I cannot accept this, Diego,' I say, holding my voice as steady as I can and I offer it back to him. 'I thought the jeweller said the item was not for sale.'

He smiles so casually, 'Every man has his price, my dear. Please don't refuse my gift, Christina,' he says softly. 'I know you belong to another, for now, but please keep the jaguar. Think of it as a gift from the spirits. I am sure it was meant for you and no other.'

Why do his words echo my own thoughts? I look down at the tiny gold piece in my hand. It is as if the benign image of my jaguar pendant has found its mate, for they are so alike, male and female. Diego stands up next to me and closes my hand around the pendant. 'Forgive my clumsy effort to win your heart. I am sorry if I have offended you. But keep the gift, please. I'm sure it will guide you to help us find the gold.'

My thoughts are all in confusion. 'Gold?' I repeat, as if he is talking in riddles.

'The gold in the mine, and precious stones too.'

'I don't think we are going to the mine with you, Diego.'

'Oh, but you must, Christina!' he is insistent. 'I cannot find them without you.'

I am embarrassed now and really out of my depth. 'Let's wait until we arrive,' I say, anything to end this discourse. I move away from him.

'But you must keep the jaguar, I insist. You must carry it with you always. It will protect you.' His face is quite serious; I cannot detect any jest or humour there.

I know I cannot give it back. 'Very well, Diego. I thank you for your generosity but I have nothing to give in return, certainly not my heart.'

He moves towards me again and puts his hand on the pendant. 'It is a token of my feelings for you. I know you are betrothed to Sam but I must declare my undying love for you. I know I should hold my tongue, but that would not stop me loving you.'

'Please, Diego, you must not say such things!' My face is burning.

'Too late, it is said, and I will not apologise. I live in the hope that you may have a change of heart.'

With that he bows and opens the door to allow me to leave first. I hurry from the room still flustered and confused. I am startled to find Rosita outside in the hallway. She gives me such a look, almost of triumph, as she enters the room to clear away the lunch. Rosita does not understand English but I am afraid some things are obvious, in any language.

34

City of Kings

Lima, Perú

This is the second day of our flight to Lima, the capital of Perú and the journey seems endless. On the *Graf Zeppelin* I was hardly aware we were flying and we walked around as if we were in a hotel. In the aeroplane we have to remain in our seats and are, at times, buffeted by turbulence. Loud engine noise precludes any meaningful conversation and we are reduced to shouting or sign language. Most of the food we brought with us has been consumed and I keep dozing off in my seat.

Sam has been wonderful. Yesterday he flew the plane non-stop until we reached Porto Velho which is close to the Brazilian border with Bolivia. This was our re-fuel and overnight stop. The accommodation was very plain but I slept from sheer exhaustion.

Diego has been very quiet throughout the journey and I wonder what he is thinking. He sits on the opposite side of the plane and when he catches my eye, he smiles. He is so obvious, I'm afraid Grace or Sam must realise he is in love with me. I suppose I am flattered, but I absolutely must not encourage him. I worry now that I accepted the jaguar pendant, although I cannot say I am sorry to have it. I am wearing both my jaguars and I reach inside my blouse and touch them. I'm more than ever convinced these were Tlalli's jaguar talismans. I wonder again, what is the spirit of the jaguar? What will happen to me and when?

For most of the last two days we have seen nothing but forest and I feel very close to Tlalli as if I am alive then and not in a dream. This whole continent is one huge rainforest. Some areas have been cleared and there are villages and settlements, savannahs and even some desert. Occasionally we see winding rivers, rapids and falls, but the forest always returns and overwhelms the landscape.

This afternoon as we cross the border into Perú the scenery is changing. Mountains have begun to appear as if growing out of the forest. They rear up towards us from the green canopy. Sam says these are the Andes. This is the landscape I see in my dreams. Although it is not apparent from the air, the forest continues in the deep gorges between the mountains and I know this was Tlalli's home.

The Vega is flying at a higher altitude now; I can feel the difference in the temperature and I wrap my blanket round me as I look at the snow-capped mountain tops as we fly through the range. They look like pointed crystal towers in a sea of green; such a strange landscape. The cold makes me feel so sleepy, so strange, as if I am falling ...falling...

Sam lands the Vega on the airfield at Lima, which is called the City of Kings. The afternoon sun is baking hot and we emerge from the plane stiff, sweaty and rather grubby. All I want is to soak in a warm bath and wash away the fatigue of the long journey. Everyone is similarly affected and Sam in particular seems irritable and short-tempered. A taxi takes us into the centre of the city to, we are told by the driver, the best hotel in Lima. After booking in we are taken to our rooms via the staircase as there doesn't appear to be a lift.

'If this is Lima's best hotel I wonder what the worst is like,' says Sam looking as if there is a bad smell under his nose.

Diego agrees with him. 'I expect the driver gets a commission for all the guests he brings here. Do you want to find another hotel?' We have entered the first of the four rooms we have been allocated and I look around. The furniture is plain with only rugs on the wooden flooring.

Grace walks over to the bed and pulls the covers back. She sits on the edge and tests the mattress. 'This bed is clean and comfortable enough,' she says, 'besides, it is too late in the day to go traipsing around to find somewhere else.'

Diego shrugs and says, 'Her ladyship has spoken, and I do agree with her.' So we open up the other rooms and I select mine which is next to Grace's room.

None of them have a bathroom and there are only two on the landing. I am grateful when the men insist Grace and I bathe first. Unfortunately, the plumbing system seems not able to cope with running two baths at the same time. Eventually I settle for half a bath of tepid water and forgo washing my hair until tomorrow. As I wash, my mood is lifted, and I remember that on the last part of the journey I fell asleep and had a dream. I recall the images very clearly and I hurry with my bath so I can write them down in my journal before they fade.

Journal entry 18th May 1931

We crossed the border from Brazil into Perú. As I viewed this stunning landscape of forests and mountains with glimpses of wild rivers and cascading falls, wonderful as it was, I was so tired I drifted asleep and into a dream.

In the dream I was the native girl Tlalli again, only now she is older. She is with a man. I truly feel this girl's emotions and I think her thoughts; looking back now outside the dream, it all seems very strange. She is in love with the man and he with her. They seem to be escaping from a bad situation. They are with other people all looking for a new home where they will be safe. I think they were fleeing from the Spanish invaders.

There is one image which is very clear, and I know this place. A deserted city is on the top of a green mountain. It is the one Uncle Peter wrote about to me all those years ago and this confirms my belief that my dreams are of a life in Perú. I am seeing it through the eyes of Tlalli.

Neither Sam nor Grace nor anyone else will stop me from finding out everything I can about this mystery but I'm not sure who to confide in. Perhaps Mr Chambi, the photographer can help me. But first we have to get to Cuzco.

Reluctantly, I leave my journal and go to find Grace. We go down to the dining room where Sam and Diego are in the bar. Diego smokes his cigarillos; the smell from them reminds me of Daddy's cigars and pipe. We move to a table and are served from a Spanish menu which Diego guides me through.

As we eat I am very excited to realise my long awaited visit to Perú has begun. However, it is a concern that Sam still seems unenthusiastic. 'Are you looking forward to the next few days, Sam?' I ask. His reply astounds me.

'I may not stay with you after all.' As he says this, it is clear he is very agitated.

'Whatever do you mean, not stay with us?' I am very put out by his sudden change of mind.

He turns to me. 'Look, Christina, I need to be back in Rio to look after my business interests. The opposition is fierce in charter flights and I can't be stuck out in the back of beyond for several weeks.'

I really don't know what to say and am near to tears. I remember the boy Sam, who was so interested in the history of Egypt, Vienna and Paris when we first met. I was right in thinking he has changed. By now my initial upset is turning to annoyance, particularly that he should say all this now, having just endured a long flight.

'Well, I'm not returning,' I say, with more courage than I usually show. 'I must see my house in Cuzco, and if I want to I will tour around the area. There is so much I want to see there.' I know my annoyance is obvious but I scarcely care.

Sam looks black, and I do believe he expected me to say I'd go back with him, but I have confounded him and stood up for myself. I have the advantage of knowing I am not financially dependent on him and perhaps never will be as my investments are in trust. Even so, I am shaken by my words and it must be obvious to all of them.

'Diego, please be so good as to ask for another bottle of wine,' I say, and he, also being diplomatic, leaves us to fetch it rather than call the waiter. I turn to Grace, 'Can I have a cigarette please?' I see my hand is shaking as she offers me her pack of Black Cats and a light. I sense she is rather amused by my taking such a stand.

'I suggest,' she says, 'that we leave our decisions until tomorrow. We are all very tired and a bit fraught, so it's not a good time to change our arrangements.'

Diego has returned with the wine and pours it for us, 'You are so wise, dear Grace,' Diego says. 'Tomorrow is always a better day.' As he sits down he lights up another cigarillo. 'The fact is, tomorrow I have to visit the manager of my bank here in Lima, to arrange to receive the money I need to start my mining project. So although I will travel with you to Cuzco, after that, you two ladies will be on your own.'

'I'm sure Mr Chambi will look after us,' I say. 'If we have a guide to accompany us, we will be quite safe.'

'We'll look into it tomorrow, Christina,' says Grace. 'Tonight, all we need is a good night's rest.'

She is obviously trying to smooth things over between Sam and me but we are still looking at each other like two cats sparring for a fight. I am very upset by his manner and begin to feel there is something more than just his business interests behind all this. I extinguish the cigarette and drink all my wine rather quickly.

'Shall we go to bed now?' Grace asks me. I stand up and realise the wine has gone to my head. I take her arm and say, 'Goodnight, Sam.' I wait for him to kiss me because he always does. He places a kiss on my lips but there is no warmth in it. I say goodnight to Diego and avoid his eyes; I have enough emotions to contend with and know his look will confuse me more. I walk away with Grace and feel a wave of utter misery in my heart, but it is overshadowed by the thumping ache beginning in my head.

I wake, and the room is dark. I had been dreaming but before I can recall its threads I am startled by a noise; a soft tapping on my door. I slip from the bed and go to the door. Then I hesitate, for by now I am wide awake, the dream forgotten.

Suppose it is Diego? The tapping is repeated and I hold my breath. If it is him, it is best I say nothing and feign sleep. I hear a voice, almost a whisper, 'Christina! Are you awake, Christina?' It is Sam and I am tempted to maintain the charade of sleep, but I weaken and unlock the door, opening it just a little.

There is a dim light in the hallway, and he stands there wearing a silk dressing-gown over his pyjamas and looking dejected. 'Please can I come in?' he says.

I frown. 'It's the middle of the night, Sam. You woke me up.'

'I'm sorry,' he replies. 'Please let me in, Christina.'

I step back and he almost barges into the room, quickly closing the door. Before I have time to walk away, he catches hold of me and wraps me in his arms. I open my mouth to speak and he silences me with a kiss. He holds me close to his body and I feel intense emotions in his lips. Sleep has already softened my anger and in the warmth of his intimate embrace resistance seems futile.

He moves his hands across my back and down to my hips. Through my thin nightdress I feel his finger-tips knead my rounded buttocks pressing me closer to his groin.

He murmurs, close to my ear. 'Let me love you, Christina, oh, my darling.'

I want to, oh God, I want to, then I remember Rosita and I push him back saying, 'You undervalue my love for you, Sam. This is not the time or the place to start married life,'

He protests, 'But we love each other, don't we?'

'Yes, Sam, but I want us to do things properly. I don't want to be taken in a seedy hotel room like a common prostitute.' I walk away, feeling embarrassed and edgy. I go and sit on the side of the bed.

He quickly joins me and puts his arm around my shoulder. 'I want to show you how much I love you. That can't be wrong surely, not in this day and age? Besides, we are engaged.' He says this as if that gives him certain rights and I begin to feel annoyed.

'Why should this day and age be different to any other?' I say. 'Are you calling me old-fashioned?'

He begins walking round the room, clearly agitated. 'I wanted to spend every minute I could with you during your visit, Christina. And now we will be parted for several weeks while you go on this...this...adventure. I suppose I resent that; it's something I didn't expect.' He speaks as he walks to and fro, hardly looking at me.

I wish to bring this confrontation to a halt. My head is still aching so I try to placate him. 'It will only be for a few days, Sam, not weeks. Why don't you come with me?'

'No,' he says, quite emphatic. 'I have to return to Rio, I have other commitments for flights and to see prospective pilots about employment.' Now he is the one getting annoyed. 'This is not a pastime, my dear; it is my business, my livelihood.'

I detect a condescending note which annoys me again. I know he is not short of money as his father finances his business. I too can be patronising. 'Of course you want to return to your home, Sam, I understand. You will be very well looked after by Rosita, and her sister Serena.' I say this because I have an unacknowledged fear that these women's duties may extend from the kitchen to the bedroom. The very thought enrages me with disgust, and if I am honest, jealousy.

'What's that supposed to mean? Sam speaks accusingly, so perhaps we should have this out now.

I shrug. 'Rosita is very friendly with you and she obviously resents my presence,' I say. 'I think she is in love with you.'

He laughs, but I know I have caught him off balance. 'How can you deduce that from the way she looks at me?' he protests. 'I could say the same to you about Diego. He looks at you like a grinning, hungry wolf!' He raises his voice and I fear he will wake everyone in the hotel. He continues his onslaught. 'Perhaps I should deduce that he is in love with you; or perhaps he is just full of lust!'

He has turned the tables on me and I am now disadvantaged in the argument, but I must keep my composure, or what is left of it. I shrug again, 'Maybe he is,' I say. 'I am used to men falling in love with me, but you are the only man I am in love with, and now we are having our first argument.' I find a handkerchief and although I am not crying I blow my nose and wipe my eyes. It has the desired effect. He looks a little abashed and I hope I have deflected him from more talk of Diego.

But unfortunately he continues in the same vein. 'I hate the way he looks at you and smarms his way around both you and Grace.'

'There you are!' I say. 'He's the same with Grace. It's just his passionate Latin way.' I hope I have said enough to stop this train of thought in him, but I do worry that Rosita might have told him about my close encounter with Diego at the hacienda.

He won't let it go. 'If I leave you here with him, I am afraid he may try to seduce you away from me.' He holds out his hands as if appealing to me.

'Oh Sam! Please give me credit for some sense. You must not let jealousy cloud your judgement.' As I say this, I know I am guilty of the same offence, but I must follow through. 'I will be with Grace, and with Mr Chambi also. Besides, Diego is only going with us to Cuzco then he will go off to his mine and Grace and I will visit Uncle Peter's home and perhaps tour the area.' I sigh. 'Then in a few days you will return to collect us.' I wonder if now I have said enough, or perhaps too much, but I am tired of the argument and want to sleep.

'No more talking now, please,' I say. 'We'll make the final arrangements in the morning.'

He looks reluctant but comes to me and kisses me again, this time gently. 'I'm sorry for my outburst, darling,' he says, 'but I do love you and am so afraid I will lose you to another man.'

'I love you too, dear Sam,' and I kiss him back.

He goes to the door and once outside he turns to me. 'Sweet dreams, my love,' he says and blows me a kiss then closes the door very softly. I do not even hear him walk away and breathe a sigh of relief that we seemed to end on a conciliatory note.

Sweet dreams indeed. I lie back in the bed and try desperately to remember what I was dreaming when Sam's knocking woke me. I close my eyes trying to forget everything that has just happened. If I can remember something of my dream, perhaps just one image, it may be enough to take me there once again.

35

The Farmers

1537, Yucay Valley to Vilcabamba, Perú.

The following day Tlalli and Paullu set off with the other farming families, all travelling back to their homes scattered across the land. Without food to feed the army and the nation they could not hope to win the war.

Before leaving the camp Tlalli told her mother, 'I will go home with Paullu to help with the crops.' Neneti kissed Tlalli goodbye.

Tlalli was still grieving for Ispaca and she felt sorry to leave her mother but she was not sorry to be leaving the wretched camp. As they walked Paullu told her, 'Now the battle for Cuzco has dragged on for so many months, herdsmen like me and the farmers have been charged with refilling the empires' store houses.'

Tlalli looked up into his eyes. 'I hope when we return to Yaguar Mountain I can rekindle the Spirit of the Jaguar, Paullu. Then I can fight alongside you.' Paullu pulled her towards him and kissed her but he didn't answer her bold statement.

The journey would take many days. As they left the Yucay Valley the path was straight and the hills barren, with few bushes or trees. Paullu led the group, keeping below the skyline, and he played his quena to cheer them on their way. Tlalli helped the women who had children and babies with them, carrying little ones on her shoulders. Paullu told them, 'When we left Cuzco, I heard that the Spaniards there were expecting reinforcements of fresh cavalry from Lima and this would be their road.' So the men took turns to scout ahead.

On the third day the landscape began to change. From the rolling hills and valleys of the Yucay region they encountered the high mountains and deep gorges of the Willkapampa. Paullu had been scouting ahead with two other men and Tlalli walked with the women. They carried their belongings in baskets on their backs and in woven cloths held by the corners. A shout went up and she saw Paullu running back towards them.

'Quick! Hide in the bushes!' he urged. 'Horsemen are coming this way.' Their group numbered around twenty: men, women, children and babes on their mother's backs. They scattered, driven by fear, into the thick vegetation at the side of the road where the ground fell away towards the forest.

Tlalli and Paullu scrambled into a thicket of thorns catching their clothing and tearing their skin. They heard the drumming of hooves even before the horses came into view; huge animals snorting and stamping, trotting in unison and carrying their awesome riders. They moved above the level of the people hiding in the bushes. Tlalli looked up and saw the huge horses carrying soldiers in full battledress, wearing helmets, armoured breastplates, even armour on their legs. She counted at least thirty riders, all wearing swords and scabbards and carrying long lances flying the Spanish colours that fluttered in the wind. With the arrival of these reinforcements she feared the siege of Cuzco by the Inca's army could be broken and the battle lost.

The riders had barely passed by when she felt Paullu move closer to her. She looked at him with surprise and then with shock. He held his knife and he lunged forward as if to strike her. With a sharp swift blow the knife plunged into the ground inches from her leg, straight through the back of a viper just below the head. The tail whipped round and she felt the lash of the snake's body as it twisted and turned in its death-throes. Paullu's other hand clamped over her mouth to stifle her involuntary scream, which would surely have been heard by the riders on the road. The snake continued to convulse and its tongue was barely a hand's width from where her leg had been a moment before Paullu's timely action.

Tlalli shook with relief for the soldiers had passed by. Thanks to Paullu's sharp eyes and quick thinking, the snake lay dead. She felt under her tunic and clutched her jaguar talisman. Paullu had saved her life. Perhaps now he wore the jaguar talisman, he also had been given the power to protect her.

Once they were sure the horsemen had gone, they scrambled back up on to the road and helped the mothers and children out of their hiding places and continued their journey. As the sun went down they left the old Inca road and moved into the forest to make camp for the night. Tlalli made a fire and the travellers found wood to keep it alive. They foraged close by for food and roasted wild potato roots and cooked the snake that Paullu had killed. The gaudy forest butterflies had folded their wings but now moths appeared, like ghostly mimics dancing round the flickering firelight. As the travellers shared their meagre supply of food they talked.

'What will happen when those Spanish soldiers reach Cuzco, Paullu?' asked Tlalli.

'Manco Inca has already moved to the fortress city Ollantaytambo. I think perhaps the siege may be abandoned and the forces moved there so they can protect Manco from capture.'

A farmer called Saqui spoke. 'You are right, Paullu. They need to protect the Inca.'

'What can the Inca do now?' asked another of the farmers.

'Manco will want to re-group the armies and keep them ready to fight again,' said Paullu, 'but I am afraid the fight for Cuzco may already be lost.'

Saqui spoke again. 'If we are to raise crops to feed the army, should we not work together? Our homelands are deserted. Alone, we won't be able to defend ourselves.'

'You're right,' said Paullu. 'It's best we keep together, but we need to find a place that is safe.'

Tlalli began to worry. She wanted to go back to her home village and the mountain.

An older man spoke up. He had lost an eye in the fighting and looked quite fierce. 'My name is Zolin. Did you ever hear tell of the old sacred city? It was built by the ancestors many years ago. It is hidden on the top of a mountain and is very difficult to find.'

'I've been there once,' said another man. 'I am called Atl. When I was a boy, my father took me and my brother there. Even then, the climb proved hard going, for the old road had been lost under fallen rock. The city is deserted and has been for many years.'

The one-eyed farmer called Zolin said, 'If we can find it we would be safe there and could perhaps raise crops also.'

'Why are there no people there now?' asked Tlalli. This tale of the old deserted city intrigued her.

The farmer who said his name was Atl answered, 'It was abandoned many years ago and no one knows why the old Inca left and took the people with him.'

'What do you say, brothers?' said Paullu. 'Should we look for this place and see if it is a safe refuge for us to grow crops? Or should we all go our separate ways back to our homes?'

'I say we should stay together,' voiced Zolin.

'Yes, and look for the sacred city!' said Saqui.

'Yes, yes, and we might send word to gather others to join us,' said Atl.

Tlalli realised she had to go along with the majority. After all she would need lots of men to carry out her plans.

'If the Spaniards have not found this place, we could grow food there for the army.' Then she thought about Ispaca and the vow they had taken, and she said, 'Perhaps we could start a resistance movement from the safety of the mountains.'

The farmers rallied to Tlalli's words, adding to her growing confidence that her mission might now begin. Speaking out had been a gamble but it appeared to meet with acceptance. As they journeyed on, everyone was talking excitedly about how they could be resistance fighters, not just farmers, from the safety of the old city in the mountains.

36

Devious Minds

May 1931, Lima, Perú

Diego is awake very early, in truth he has barely slept at all. He is acutely aware that the plans he makes today could spell success or disaster for his future prosperity, indeed, for his very life. Today he will visit the bank manager in Lima. Whilst Eduardo Moreno has so far proved infuriatingly professional and apparently incorruptible, no doubt officials in these far-flung outposts might be more open to a little financial incentive. In Diego's experience, money changes everything.

He hopes he can avoid opening and operating the mine at Yaguar. No one has set foot on the site since his grandfather's time. In fact he doesn't know for sure if the mine was working even then, over fifty years ago. All he has is the map showing the location, and the deeds. Yaguar Mountain is in a very remote part of the Andes, north-west of Cuzco on the edge of the Vilcabamba, where the Andes begin their descent down into the jungles of the Antisuyo; by all accounts an isolated and inhospitable terrain.

None of the other hotel guests are about so Diego goes to the bathroom to begin his preparations for the day. He immerses himself in the water and his thoughts return to Christina. He pictures himself caressing her lovely young body and running his hands through her beautiful blonde hair. As he shaves and preens his hair and moustaches he admires himself in the mirror. How could she fail to be attracted by his charm and good looks? He only hopes Watson goes through with his plan to return to Brazil.

The only other problem is the presence of Lady Grace. She is very astute and worldly-wise; not a person easily deceived. By the time he is dressed ready for his day and descending the stairs in search of an early breakfast, he has decided to trust to luck that soon only the two ladies will still be in Perú.

He makes his way to the Lima branch of The Bank of South America. It is housed in an imposing colonial building in the city centre. He asks to see the manager and after only a few minutes the man comes to greet him. He is short, and a mestizo; as are the majority of businessmen in this capital city. It is easy to tell the mixed-blood nationals from those of pure Spanish descent, both from their colour and features, but also from the lackadaisical nature of their mixed culture.

'Ah, Don Alvarez, what a pleasure to meet you,' he says shaking Diego by the hand. He is smartly dressed wearing a heavy cologne, but Diego detects a whiff of body odour from his clothes. 'I am Fillip Cabello, manager of this branch. I have heard so much about you from my colleague, Senor Moreno in Rio.' Although the man's first language is Spanish, Diego is aware of his bloodline and will use it to his advantage. As a pure Spaniard himself, he feels he has an edge of supremacy over this odious little man.

Cabello orders coffee and ushers Diego into his palatial office. The coffee is served from elegant silverware into bone china cups by a young girl who also offers Diego a plate of pastries. Cabello dismisses her and the two men drink their coffee eyeing each other over the manager's large desk.

Diego watches him carefully. 'No doubt Senor Moreno has explained why I am here.'

'Oh, yes he has,' says Cabello, nodding his head. 'You have come to Perú to reopen a mine in the Vilcabamba which belonged to your grandfather. He tells me this mine has been recently surveyed and has new potential?' He phrases this as a question then immediately follows with another. 'Tell me, Don Alvarez, have you ever been to this area yourself?

'No, this is my first visit to Perú.' Diego decides to tread carefully before laying out his plan. 'I have been entirely in the hands of the surveyor but he assures me that specialist drilling equipment will find new seams in this mine.'

Cabello looks thoughtful. 'Many prospectors have come to Perú over centuries looking for gold and silver. Some areas have been mined so extensively they are turned into wastelands.'

'And this site, at Mount Yaguar, would you include that?' Diego is now on his guard.

Cabello shakes his head. 'I don't know of any mining in that area, certainly not in living memory. The problem is that it is very remote; there are not even any modern roads leading there. Your surveyor would have had to travel by mule with an Indian guide even to find it.'

Diego is a little shaken by this for he knows that the surveyor never even came to Perú, but he makes a calm response. 'The Bank of South America stands to make a great deal of money from my venture. Are you saying that there is no more gold to be found in Perú?'

'Oh, no, I am sure there are a lot more mining opportunities in the outlying areas but this terrain is so remote, and without roads or access for motor vehicles the costs may outweigh the returns.'

Diego begins to realise he must not underestimate this man. He will have to think on his feet if he is to obtain more of the investors' money. 'I have already paid dearly for my survey of this mine and several others I own throughout South America. On the strength of their projection, your employer, The Bank of South America, has now obtained over a million dollars for me to turn my surveys into a profitable venture.' Diego walks round the desk, standing over Fillip Cabello. 'I could, of course, abandon this Perúvian project and concentrate on other mines in Mexico and Brazil.'

Cabello is perhaps now thinking of his own position and says, 'If the bank would release additional funds for you to set up better transportation links your project could be made profitable.'

Diego feels Cabello is beginning to get his drift. 'I am sure your word will carry a deal of weight with the bank. I will ensure your cooperation is well rewarded.' Diego returns to his seat. The smile playing round Cabello's mouth tells him the man understands him perfectly.

Diego returns the smile and continues the discussion as if nothing has passed between them. 'I need to be out there soon, with the new drilling equipment and a good workforce. Can you recommend a site engineer I might employ?'

'You will find the best people in Cuzco. I will give you contacts. That will also be the best place to arrange your transport.' Cabello appears optimistic. A bargain has been struck without a word suggesting bribery being spoken. 'I will speak with Senor Moreno on the telephone and request more funds for your... expedition, Don Alvarez.'

Diego nods, acknowledging the subterfuge; he now has Fillip Cabello on his side. He presses on to the next issue. 'The charter pilot who flew me from Rio has agreed to continue to Cuzco. He is concerned about the landing facilities.'

'The facilities are not very good for the area is surrounded by mountains and Cuzco itself lies at 10,000 feet. But there is a small airfield suitable for charter planes to land and take off. For a price, I could arrange it for you.'

'Excellent, Senor Cabello. Perhaps you can add the cost to the request for additional funds.'

'Of course, Don Alvarez, and I will have the next instalment of cash available for you to draw from the branch in Cuzco, and then your venture can begin.' Cabello shakes Diego's hand and guides him out of the office to the door of the bank. 'Ring me later, and we can tie up all the details for your charter pilot to land at Cuzco.'

Diego leaves the bank calculating his success and mentally rubbing his hands together. All this talk of mining equipment and transportation has, on paper, more than doubled the funds he needs just as he had hoped.

It is afternoon before he catches up with his travelling companions. 'I trust you have had a fruitful day in Lima,' says Diego.

'Yes and no,' says Sam. 'It would seem that Christina is still hell-bent on this mad adventure.'

Diego looks at Christina. 'Are you still going?'

'Of course we're going,' she says. 'Sam can fly us there tomorrow.' Her tone is very abrupt. Diego looks from one to the other.

Sam doesn't look best pleased and says, 'Apparently the airfield at Cuzco is privately owned and the fees to use the facility are high.'

'My dear Sam,' says Diego, 'my own enquiries at the bank resulted in the same conclusion, but the manager there has offered to broker an arrangement with the owner. I would be pleased to cover your fee if you will allow me to travel with you.' He hopes his suggestion will force a decision between them.

'Very well, I will fly you all to Cuzco tomorrow.' Sam says this as if making a big concession. 'But that is as far as I go.'

'Thank you, Sam,' says Lady Grace. Diego recognises her conciliatory tone. 'Once we reach Cuzco I'm sure our arrangements will become clearer, so there will be nothing to worry about.' Grace takes Christina's arm.

'Thank you, Grace,' says Christina. 'I'm sure it will work out perfectly and I will at last see Uncle Peter's house, which of course is now my house.' Diego sees her look pointedly at Sam, her eyes are sharp with supressed anger.' She turns her back on both men and walks away with Grace.

37

City of Gold

Cuzco, Perú

At last we are on our way to Cuzco and my excitement is growing. We leave the coast and fly inland and very soon are once more over the mountains. They fill the horizon from every window and I am again enthralled by how magnificent this part of the world really is.

In spite of my annoyance at Sam's attitude I have to admire his ability as a pilot. That he is able to navigate in such difficult terrain is truly wonderful. I just wish he would change his mind and stay with us. I cringe, thinking about last night when he came to my room. Was I right to refuse his advances? If I love him, as I say I do, perhaps I should let him make love to me. Maybe I am still not entirely sure he is the one for me.

After I went back to sleep I fell into another dream. The girl Tlalli was with the man she loves, and they were trying to find safety from the Spanish invaders. I still find all these dreams confusing, some disturbing. Yet I'm sure that someone, some spirit, is trying to communicate with me, so I write all these thoughts in my journal and hope that eventually I will unravel the truth.

We reach our destination quite soon and Sam makes a circular tour round Cuzco. I marvel at this city in the mountains, known as the City of Gold. Grace's handbook says the original pre-Spanish city was built in the shape of a crouching jaguar, a spectacle only visible from the air. How strange. In a time when men could not fly it must have been constructed so just for the eyes of their gods.

Sam calls Diego up to the front. He is in radio contact with the airfield but they are speaking in Spanish. Diego acts as interpreter and Sam is guided to the field. He again demonstrates his skill landing the Vega in such a tight space and I am very proud of him.

We are surprised to see a car waiting. Diego speaks with the driver who tells him the manager of the Cuzco branch of The Bank of South America sent him to collect Don Alvarez. Diego arranges to take us all into the city centre.

'Will you come with us, Sam?' I ask, 'At least for something to eat and to rest awhile.'

'No, Christina,' he replies. 'I think it would be best I return to Lima now.' He seems impatient to be off again. 'I need to refuel and check the Vega and get a good night's sleep before my long trip home tomorrow.'

I feel he is still being obstinate but then so am I. I have to trust this disagreement will not permanently dent our relationship and that Sam will be waiting for me after my stay in Perú. I am certainly not going to beg and plead with him anymore. I step towards him and say, 'Goodbye then, Sam.' He takes me in his arms and kisses me so passionately I am tempted to climb back into the Vega.

'Goodbye, my darling,' he says and I know this is hurting him as much as it is me. I turn away, determined not to cry and walk over to where Grace is waiting with Diego. Sam gets into the Vega and we all wave to him. I stand watching him take off and wait until the plane is just a speck in the sky.

'So, where do we go from here?' says Grace. I turn to her with the biggest smile I can muster.

'We go to Mr Chambi's studio and hope he can recommend somewhere we can stay.' I had written to him when we were in Rio but there had not been time to let him know exactly when we were coming.

'Well I'm expected at the Bank,' says Diego. 'I think they've arranged my accommodation also.' We all travel in the back of the car and as we enter the city I can see most of the buildings are Spanish colonial, of the type we found in Lima. There are also stone walls which look older, made of huge slabs of solid black granite. Strangely, I know these were here before the Spanish arrived and are all that is left of the original city, and I am overwhelmed with sadness.

Diego instructs the driver in Spanish and he seems to know where we want to go. He stops in one of the main streets and I can see this is a photographer's studio, with photographs displayed in the window and on the walls around the door.

'Please let me enquire if your Senor Chambi is here, otherwise I will find you a hotel,' says Diego.

'You are very kind,' answers Grace and we watch him disappear through the open door. My heart is in my mouth and it such a relief when we see Diego come out with another man. Diego says this is Senor Chambi and Grace and I leave the car.

He is just as I imagined him to be. Uncle Peter's story about this man has been in my mind all these years. How they went to the river together to photograph the jaguar, and how Martin Chambi was also a renowned portrait photographer and the darling of Spanish aristocracy in Cuzco. That is why I feel we will be safe with this man.

I remember my dream of Tlalli's father when he gave the jaguar pendants to his children. Martin Chambi's face is just like the father's: dark with humorous eyes, his skin lined and weather-beaten. When he smiles his face crinkles like a walnut. He is dressed in an immaculate dark suit, shirt and tie, a modern businessman through and through. I step forward and he shakes my hand.

'My dear Senorita Freeman,' he says in quite good English. 'We meet at last. Your uncle often spoke of you and your father. I feel I know you already.'

I introduce Grace and tell him why Diego is with us. 'Yes, I suppose I should be getting to the bank and leave you with Senor Chambi,' says Diego. He agrees to find out where we are staying and to keep in touch. He returns to the car and is gone. I feel a pang of loss as the car drives away but turn my attention back to Martin Chambi.

We go inside the shop. It is also his portrait studio, and his living accommodation. His work is everywhere: on the walls, up the stairway and on easels around his reception area. There are photographs of beautiful ladies in Spanish style dresses, some in wedding dresses; family groups, all very formal and beautifully posed. But in between these are landscapes of the Perú I know from my dreams: mountains and valleys, gorges and rivers. Also, Perúvian people: working at their daily tasks or posed for family portraits wearing their traditional dress. Far from looking strange to me I feel I know them all and am comfortable in their company.

We sit on an old horsehair sofa and a Perúvian lady serves us with a refreshing drink. She is Martin's wife and the drink is a local brew called chicha. It is alcoholic so I only sip a little.

'Thank you for your letter, Senorita,' says Martin. 'I hoped you would come soon and now you are here. I have arranged for you to stay in the home of Senor and Senora Montez.' He stops and calls his wife, sending her to this house to tell the owners we have arrived. Martin continues, 'I photographed their daughter for her wedding three years ago and she now lives in Lima. Their home is enormous and quite close to your uncle's house.'

'I do hope we will not be inconveniencing the lady and gentleman,' says Grace.

'Oh no, I spoke with them only yesterday and they are looking forward to having you. They have plenty of servants so will be only too pleased to know you have arrived.'

Thank you so much, Senor Chambi,' I say. 'When can we view Uncle Peter's house? Although you realise, I am the owner now.'

'Of course, you are, Senorita Freeman. I can take you tomorrow if you wish,' he says.

'That would be wonderful, thank you,' I reply. 'I wanted to ask you if it would be possible to also see some of the area around Cuzco while we are staying here.'

'I would be delighted to arrange that for you,' he says and his eyes light up with enthusiasm. 'Do you know anything about our history?' he asks.

'Some,' I say. 'Uncle Peter told me a little when he visited us when I was twelve and he wrote me several letters over the years with more information, concerning his exploration trips.'

'Wonderful man, your uncle,' he says sadly. 'I do miss him, and our trips into the interior.'

'Where did you go?' I ask catching his enthusiasm.

'Lots of places, wherever there was a dig or news of a new find, but nearest to here is Machu Picchu. Have you heard of it?'

Grace answers him. 'Oh, yes, we have. Discovered by an American in 1911, I think.'

He laughs. 'Oh yes, the Americans like to say he discovered it, but it was never really lost. The local people have known about it for hundreds of years. But knowing how destructive foreigners could be they learned to keep a lot of things to themselves.'

'We really would like to visit Machu Picchu if possible,' I say more in hope than expectation.

'Can you ride horses?' he asks.

'Why yes,' I say and glance at Grace. She pulls a face but I know she did ride when she was younger.

'There is a new rail link from Cuzco as far as Ollantaytambo,' he says, 'but none from there to Machu Picchu. The roads are not good for wheeled transport so horseback is the best way to travel. I can arrange good mounts for you.'

'How long would it take?' I imagine having to camp out and know Grace would not be in favour of that.

'We can travel on the train to Ollantaytambo and pick up the horses there. If we stay at a guest house overnight at Aguas Calientes we can go to Machu the next day, stay over a second night and return on the third day. How does that sound?' He makes it all sound so simple.

'Well, we shall be here for at least a couple of weeks, so that sounds perfect, Senor Chambi,' I say. 'Please let us know tomorrow when it would be convenient for you to take us.'

'Delighted,' he says. 'Now I will escort you to Montez' house, I'm sure they are longing to meet you.'

When we go outside Senor Chambi summons a boy with a handcart and all our luggage is loaded on to this. We walk through the streets of Cuzco, following the boy with our luggage. We turn into a street with large Spanish style properties and all the houses are detached with lush gardens surrounding them. The boy stops at the house where we are apparently to stay. It looks very grand with stone steps up to the front door. Tall pillars stand either side of the door with an arch above. We mount the steps and ring the bell. A Perúvian girl in a maid's uniform answers the door and we are ushered inside. Senor Chambi supervises the unloading of our luggage and pays the boy for his trouble.

Inside the house the grandeur continues. In the centre of the entrance hall is an enormous staircase which widens out at the foot with curved brass handrails, and on either side, are two life-size statues of Grecian maidens on raised plinths. The head of the staircase leads off to left and right in a balcony which continues round the upper floor. From the ground we look up and see a beautiful glass roof with coloured panels, filling the hallway with colour and light.

The maid leads us into a palatial drawing room with ornate wooden furniture and rich fabrics. The owners, a rather elderly Spanish gentleman and his lady wife, have stood to greet us. Senor Chambi makes the introductions and we are soon seated and being pampered with coffee and pastries. They converse in Spanish and Martin tells us that Senor and Senora Montez do not speak English but that he has told them what our movements will be tomorrow. He will call for us at 11 o'clock to view the house of Senor Bosworth, as they knew him. After tea the maid, whose name is Maria, returns and takes us up to two lovely rooms on the first floor. Maria seems to understand us well and runs baths for us and unpacks our garments, hanging them in the wardrobes, as if we will be here for a month.

38

Tlalli's Testament

June, 1931 Cuzco, Perú.

I wake very early the next day and the sun is shining brilliantly into my room. When Tlalli came to Cuzco she was a virtual prisoner, living in the Sun Temple and being trained to be one of the Inca queen's attendants. This is what I have written in my journal some time ago when this dream came to me. I think this must have been after she found the Inca's treasure in the mountain cave, although the dreams came to me in a different order. That has been my difficulty in working out Tlalli's story – the dreams are always random.

I dress and go down to the kitchen to find the maid Maria. She is surprised I am up and offers me coffee. Tea doesn't seem to be on the menu but coffee is grown locally and tastes good, so I content myself with that and drink it in the big kitchen. She picks up a basket and I understand that she is going shopping so I ask to go with her.

The market is full of colour. The stall-holders display their wares in woven baskets set out on the cobbled square. The women mostly wear black bowler hats and wrap themselves in bright coloured blankets; indigo blue and cochineal red splash across the scene like regimental flags. There are purple passion-fruits and a small orange-and-green fruit I don't recognise is cut for us to sample; it tastes like melon. There are green and yellow bananas and wild scarlet strawberries and well as yellow corn, maize and dozens of different potatoes.

My attention is drawn away from the fruit sellers to a lone man playing a flute. His music is haunting and seems to echo with long plaintive notes quite different from an English flute. A crowd jostle round him and he collects coins thrown at his feet. The music finishes and he bows and smiles to the listeners who soon move on. I step forward and throw a few coins. He bows and collects his bounty mumbling his thanks in Spanish. As he stands up I see his face and am arrested by his deep black eyes full of intensity. A smile curls at the corner of his mouth but there is nothing sinister in his expression and I return his smile.

Maria tells me she has finished her shopping and we return to the house. I go upstairs and tell Grace about my trip to the market. We are summoned for breakfast by a gong banging in the hall and go down to join our hosts. It's amusing to find that although we don't understand each other's language we can make ourselves understood through signs and laughter. Senor Montez and his wife were apparently very fond of Uncle Peter.

At 11 o'clock Senor Chambi arrives to take Grace and me to Uncle Peter's house. He tells us that the housekeeper is still looking after the property which is what I had arranged through the solicitor. This was thought necessary in view of the large quantity of antiquities still in the house. It is daunting to think all these will have to be sold but I am so anxious to see everything while it is still there.

The house is in the same street as Montez House, a few yards further up on the opposite side. The front garden is so overgrown it is not until we reach the front door that the walls of the house become visible. Like Montez House, the adobe is a creamy white although this house seems in need of a coat of paint if not more intensive work. The steps up to the front door are worn and broken in places and the door itself was once bright blue but now the paint is peeling away. I am surprised, as I know Uncle Peter was not short of money.

Senor Chambi seems to read my mind. 'The house is not in the best of health,' he says, 'but in the last few years neither was your uncle.'

'We had no idea,' I say. 'Uncle Peter's letters were few and far between but I never realised he was so ill.'

'I can imagine,' says Senor Chambi, 'and his friends were forbidden to write to his family regarding his deterioration. He refused to spend any more money on the house and spent his final months translating old documents he had found in the house some time ago.'

He rings the bell and we wait for the housekeeper. When she opens the door I am surprised again, this time by the apparent antiquity of the wizened old lady standing in the hall. She is dressed in black and Senor Chambi introduces her as Senora Barros; she was Uncle Peter's housekeeper for forty years, his entire residency in this house. We go inside.

They converse in Spanish, Senora Barros goes to the kitchen and Senor Chambi begins by insisting Grace and I call him Martin. Then he takes us on a tour of the house. It smells musty, like an ancient church, and he tells us that for the last two years Peter did not use the second floor rooms as the stairs become too much for both him and Senora Barros. There is a sweeping staircase much the same as in Montez house, but the whole place seems so dilapidated, and I have to admit, depressing.

We move into what appears to be a drawing room. I had set such store on coming to this house and probably expected too much. There are however, lots of artefacts, mostly on shelves and tables gathering dust: pottery of exquisite colours and designs; drinking vessels in the shape of heads, which remind me of Toby jugs, some in the shape of animals. They are not all perfect; some have chips or cracks. There is silverware, fashioned into bowls, plates and jewellery, all intricately engraved with pictures or patterns.

'Are these from the time of the Incas?' asks Grace.

'Most are much older than Inca,' says Martin, and he picks up a ceramic beaker with bright geometric patterns and animal shapes in repeating patterns also. 'These date back to the Nazca, about 500AD, nearly a thousand years before the Inca. Pieces like this one were buried under the sand in the desert regions along the coast. Whole settlements and ancient tombs have been found only recently. Sir Peter went with the early explorers and brought some of these pieces back.'

Grace examines the ceramics with great interest. 'Fascinating that they have survived so long,' she says.

'Fortunately they were buried already at the time of the conquest,' Martin explains. 'The conquistadors took everything of value they could lay their hands on, mostly of course, gold and silver. They melted down beautiful pieces of ancient art and turned them into bullion bars; that was the only worth they put on them, they had no appreciation of the priceless art and history they destroyed.'

I am reliving everything he tells us through the eyes of Tlalli. Her people risked their lives for the beautiful Inca treasures that were hidden in the sacred mountain to protect them from the greed of the Spanish conquistadors. Because I know it would sound so implausible, I say nothing. Senora Barros brings us coffee and biscuits so we pause to enjoy these.

Grace says, 'You will need the solicitor here to draw up a detailed inventory of all these items, Christina.'

Martin adds, 'May I suggest it is all valued by an expert before it is auctioned. Your uncle would have wanted you to obtain the best possible prices.'

'Yes, of course,' I say, 'but I am in no hurry.' We move on to see what else Uncle Peter has left for me to find, for I feel sure he knew I would come here in person.

Martin takes us into what must have been Uncle Peter's study. There is a big mahogany desk by the window and an upholstered chair faces the light from the rear garden. Through the window I see a huge fig tree and bougainvillea climbing over sun-warmed walls. Magenta blooms illuminate the mass of green with splashes of colour.

I sit at the desk as Uncle Peter would have done and survey his line of pens and a pewter ink well. There is a pile of writing paper on the blotter. To one side is an old Spanish/English dictionary and on the other is a scroll, rolled but with a broken seal. It is yellow with age and I wonder about the contents.

Martin breaks into my thoughts. 'This was the work which engaged your uncle's attention during his last few years.'

'What was he doing, Martin?'

'First, I will tell you how this all came about,' he says and he sits on a small chair next to the desk. 'A few years ago Sir Peter decided to have some work done at the back of the house. The wall in the kitchen was very damp and the plaster was crumbling. The men started work, intending to re-plaster the inside, but when they removed the old plaster they revealed a pre-Columbian wall underneath.'

'You mean an Inca wall?' I say.

He nods. 'Many Spanish properties were built on top of Inca stonework. The fact was, these remains were so strong and well-built it was impossible to demolish them. So the Spanish builders added their walls to the original and then plastered over, completely covering the original structures.'

I can see the wall in my mind, so am not surprised when he says, 'There was an ingle nook in this wall and it contained a wooden box; not a small box it was big enough to hold many scrolls, like the one you see on the desk.'

My hand falls on the rough parchment scroll. 'But the Incas didn't have paper, parchment or any written language,' I say.

'Quite right,' says Martin. 'I was present when your Uncle opened the box. The manuscripts it contained were written by a Spanish chronicler, and are all dated around 1600. This man spent many years talking to native Perúvians and writing down their stories.'

Now I remember the reference to this find in Uncle Peter's last letter. Grace asks, 'How did the manuscripts come to be hidden in the wall of this house?'

Martin tells us. 'When Sir Peter made enquiries it seemed the original house was once lived in by a Spanish chronicler called Martin de Murua, a Jesuit Priest. He came to Perú and wrote a history of the events surrounding the conquest. These scrolls appear to document the lives of local people and pre-date his main work. At that time the Spanish authorities would not have been interested in the stories of the native population. In fact he may have felt it unwise to reveal them. Whatever Martin de Murua's reasons were, Sir Peter concluded it was he who hid them behind the plaster board.'

'What an amazing find.' I am anxious to know everything these manuscripts say.

'Your uncle decided to translate them from the old Spanish used by Martin de Murua into modern English. But unfortunately, he died before completing the work.'

'Can I see them?' I'm afraid to touch the yellowing parchments in case they fall apart in my hands.

Martin Chambi comes to the desk and opens the draw on the left side. 'These are the translations he had completed.' He lifts out a sheaf of papers filled with the handwriting I am familiar with from Uncle Peter's letters. At the front is a list with the names of the contributors and a brief history for each. Martin opens the drawer on the right side of the desk. 'These are the manuscripts not yet begun. I think he was about halfway through them.'

'And this one, on the desk?' I ask him.

'That is the one he was working on when he died.' Martin looks out on to the garden, apparently remembering that time. 'He said to me this one was very special and that he wanted to finish it to send to you.'

'Do you know why, Martin?' Although I ask, I already know the answer.

'He told me it was to do with the present he had left for you with your father, many years ago, a golden jaguar pendant.'

My hand flies to my throat and I pull out my pendant, careful not to reveal the second one. 'This one,' I say, remembering the contents of Uncle Peter's last letter. I feel almost breathless with anticipation.

Martin inspects my pendant. 'I do remember it. When Sir Peter acquired it at auction it was listed as of Huari origin, or Warri as the native Perúvians call it.'

Grace intervenes. 'Like the one we saw in Rio,' she says. 'That was Huari also, but it wasn't for sale, was it, Christina?'

'No.' I say. I feel very guilty not telling Grace I have it, but how could I possibly explain Diego's gift?

Martin steps forward and turns to the list fronting Uncle Peter's manuscript. His finger points to the last entry: 'My Grandmother's story of the Sacred Jaguars as told by Paullu Manari Yapanki in the year 1601.' For a moment, my heart seems to skip a beat then beats twice as fast and I tremble. I know I am very close to finding the secret of Tlalli's life.

39

The Sacred City

1537. The Road to the Sacred City, Vilcabamba, Perú.
When Tlalli awoke the following morning, she felt sure Izella had visited her in a dream, filling her with hope and reassurance that this decision had been right. They broke camp at first light and began on the trail to find the lost city.

Atl, who'd said he'd been there as a boy, had a rough idea of the direction they should take. 'We need to follow the river beyond Ollantaytambo, then strike out to the west, but it will not be easy to find.' Landslips and floods made progress arduous, but Tlalli's spirits grew high. She had a purpose and the group became closer in the warmth of their comradeship.

Most of the road had disappeared. Erosion from heavy rains, rock falls and the constant encroaching vegetation of the forest had obliterated the trail. Paullu forged ahead with the other men for many hours. When they reached the trail to Ollantaytambo, they took the opposite direction, down valleys, over passes and on towards their hoped-for destination. They began to climb. The men hacked away with sticks and cut through thickets to find any sign of what was once a broad Inca road leading up into the cloud forest.

They had been climbing for hours. Tlalli helped the women with babies and children as they struggled on up behind the men, through the narrow pathway they had made. They fought their way round decaying tree trunks masked by thick undergrowth and they hacked down stunted trees that blocked their passage. Eventually they reached a higher altitude, but they were exhausted by their efforts and from the heat of the sun, for no tall trees grew on this high plateau. Everyone was tired, hungry and very thirsty.

Tlalli grew anxious, worrying that perhaps this had not been such a good plan. She looked around and realised this place reminded her of the forest near her home. At this altitude, the cloud forest bears, who fed on the pureos cactus filled with sugar, made their home. She shaded her eyes and saw the same plant growing here. She showed the women how to cut the cactus, avoiding the sharp thorns, and they sucked the sugary liquid just as the bears did. With great relief, the little band of travellers rested and enjoyed the bounty provided by nature. Tlalli sat close to Paullu, and they watched with delight as the air filled with dozens of hummingbirds and butterflies, seeking nectar among the flowering shrubs and plants.

They set off again, climbing up the mountain. After many more hours trekking, and as the sun began its descent to the west, they scaled the final ridge. The ground flattened out and then sloped gently down the other side of the ridge. Tlalli thought she had been transported into another world as they looked down on a massive shelf, seemingly carved out on the very top of this mountain. She stood perfectly still, unable to find any words to describe what she could see, for this place had been completely invisible until they scaled that final ridge.

The sun had lowered in the sky but still shone on them. A gap between the peak of this mountain, and another from a higher mountain behind, allowed the rays of the setting sun to splay out and cast a golden glow across the shelf. Within this almost circular place lay the remains of a city. The ancient structures seemed to light up and shine like a celestial crown on the mountain top. Tlalli fell to her knees. Words failed her, and everyone in the group bowed down.

'Thanks be to Inti who has brought us to this palace in the sky,' said Paullu and they lifted their arms and paid homage to the setting sun. Tlalli felt the glory, but she shivered, for in that moment the deserted city seemed full of many ghosts.

She could see the houses and buildings had been made of stone in the traditional style. The timber roofs remained but the thatch had long since rotted away. Vegetation grew over many of the structures. Even so, the outline of roads and steps separating the buildings were visible, marking out the original shape of the city. In places the grasses looked short as if still tended. Then she spied a movement and she shaded her eyes. 'Look,' she cried, 'llamas and alpacas!'

'And I see vicuñas!' said another woman.

'We must keep silent and move quietly,' said Paullu in hushed tones. He directed Saqui and Atl to follow him. 'Praise to Inti, for he has given us a new home and provided for us.'

Paullu and the two men with him set about corralling the animals in one of the empty houses. Paullu was a skilled herdsman, and using his bolas to ensnare their legs, he captured six good alpacas and two with young. Tlalli ran to him to see the animals. 'Now we shall have milk,' he said.

'And fleece to spin and weave,' she said and they hugged with the joy of this miracle.

The men inspected what had been terraces where crops had once been raised. Here, tangles of brambles and weeds grew, but in between they found potatoes of many different types, still growing in the rich soil. It seemed this mountain retreat had been chosen as it was well below the snow-line of the higher mountains, but it rose up from the valleys, which sometimes became unbearably hot. The men dug some tubers and brought them to where the group had set up their camp, a house shell on the edge of the city.

Tlalli and the other women explored some of the deserted homes. They found pitchers and bowls and even cooking pots and utensils left behind by the inhabitants. Others looked for water and found the ditches and rivulets which had once provided irrigation to the terraces and supplied the city.

'There must once have been a spring up here which provided the water,' said Paullu, 'but it is dry. Rain alone would not be sufficient for a city of many people, especially in the dry season.'

'Will it be enough for us?' asked Tlalli.

'I think so,' he replied, 'but we must find a new source to provide more water if we are to grow many crops.'

Although some of the men were older than Paullu, the new inhabitants of the sacred city seemed to turn to Paullu and Tlalli to lead them and organise the work necessary to make some of the houses fit to live in once more. In the weeks that followed their arrival, they cleared the terraces of weeds and even planted maize and corn. Tlalli had found a cache of seeds in a cave. The cave held a tomb and contained sealed jars of seeds next to the relics; these were intended to sustain the dead in their afterlife. She led them in prayers of thanks to these ancestors and they took the seeds which had survived their long incarceration and were still fertile.

The animals proved useful to clear more terraces for they ate the vegetation. Other men cleared all the water runs and they searched the mountain and found a new spring of clear running water.

One of the empty buildings had once been a Sun Temple. After many days Tlalli plucked up her courage and entered. Her experience of life in the temple at Cuzco was still fresh in her mind. She looked around the empty building thinking that at one time the walls would have been lined with sheets of gold and the altar adorned with gold and silver statues. The priests would have made sacrifices to the sun god, Inti. Perhaps even the Jaguar gods had once been worshipped in this place. Tlalli liked that thought, yet she was reminded how the jaguar's power had seemed to wane since she had moved away from her own mountain home.

Nevertheless, she knelt before the empty altar and touching her talisman said a silent prayer to Inti, asking for the Jaguar's strength to empower her, and keep her true to her vows. She closed her eyes and felt the silence around her. She experienced an overwhelming spiritual presence telling her to begin the fight back. She heard a sound and looking up she saw that Paullu had entered the temple.

'Ah, Tlalli. I thought I might find you here.' He knelt beside her. 'What are you asking, my love?'

She placed her hand on his. 'We must begin our work against the Spanish from this sacred city, Paullu. Can we trust this band of people we have brought with us?'

Paullu laughed. 'If not these friends, who else could we trust? Even though they are just farmers, I know they want to continue fighting. Like us, they have lost so much already. What do your gods say? What do you want to do?'

Tlalli shuddered. 'This place is full of ghosts but the gods seem to say more towns and villages will be full of ghosts if we do not act now.'

They stood up and he took hold of her shoulders. 'Then we shall. I have already spoken with Saqui and he is with us. But this is your mission, Tlalli. You must show the way, not me. I will be beside you, but you must lead.'

Paullu had shown her in everything he did that he loved her and she knew he was right. This was her calling and she must follow her instincts and lead, even men as old as her father. This would be her greatest test. If she could do this, she would know the Jaguar gods were still with her.

Later that evening, when everyone came together, Tlalli asked the men to go with them to the open air altar above the city. Just as on the first day they arrived, the evening sun shone between the two mountain peaks lighting them from behind, and spreading its rays across the city like a translucent mantle of gold. They climbed a series of huge steps to a large flat area like an open temple. Here, a representation of the mountain peak directly behind them had been carved in solid granite. Paullu traced his hand over the peaks and shoulders of stone. 'The stonemason's tribute to our natural world,' he said. 'This has always been the mark of our people when they build.'

'We are surrounded by so much beauty,' said Tlalli, 'it is good to reflect on Viracocha's creation. This is a sacred place.'

They all sat close together beneath the stone effigy of the mountain peaks and the condors flew around their heads, hovering in the thermals created by the rocks and then swooping away across the valleys.

The men looked to Paullu to hear what he had to say. He began, 'We have asked you here to listen to Tlalli. She has a mission and wants to know if you are willing to join us.'

Saqui and the other men, about fifteen in all, turned with surprise to Tlalli, and then she spoke. 'I know you are thinking I am just a girl, and a young girl at that. I have to tell you that I have been given a mission but I need your help.'

There was a wave of whispers through the group. They ranged in age from young boys up to men older than her father. Some chewed coca leaves, some looked at their feet clearly embarrassed, while others seemed amused. Tlalli pulled out her talisman and focused on the face of Izella, so serene and composed – and that gave her the courage she needed.

'Since I was a small child, I have been visited by dreams. I knew of the Spaniards before they reached our country. My dreams told me how ruthless and savage they would be.' All eyes were on her now. 'My father, Kusi, who is the commander of the Manari fighting unit in the battle you have all endured, he gave me and my brother these two talismans.' Paullu had withdrawn his also from his jerkin. 'They represent the ancient Jaguar gods, Toquri and Izella. Do you know the legend?

The group gave their replies. 'Aye. Yes. I do.'

Tlalli continued, 'Izella has given me many signs to tell me what I must do.' The men had fallen very quiet. 'I must do everything in my power to protect our people, our way of life, our culture and the right to worship our own gods and govern ourselves.' She looked around the silent group. 'Our sacred treasures are being stolen by these invaders, and worse still, our people are being stolen to be slaves and servants to the usurpers. We are impoverished, robbed of our traditional lands and our ability to sustain our families with crops and animals.'

All the while Tlalli spoke, she felt she grew in the eyes of those around her. She could see in their upturned faces their conviction she was indeed a mouthpiece for the gods, and they believed every word she said.

'First, we must find a safe route from here onto the surrounding roads. We must not be followed back to this place; that is very important. Then we will send out raiding parties to ambush any small groups of Spaniards using the roads, especially those who have taken possession of land on which to build homes outside of the cities or towns. We will pick them off, one by one!'

Paullu stood up facing the group. 'Any of you who do not want to be involved in this work must say so now. We will not hold it against you provided you do not betray us.'

Saqui stood up. 'I am with you, Tlalli and Paullu. What is the name of this great mission?'

Tlalli smiled at him. 'Thank you, Saqui, for being the first to join us. We are called 'The Spirit of the Jaguar', and we are the first secret rebel movement against the Spanish invaders. Our other mission is to enlist the help of brothers and sisters throughout the length and breadth of the land. But never forget, secrecy is imperative. Be sure you know who you can trust.'

They rose to their feet like a wave, shouting approval of Tlalli's plans.

'Count me in!' shouted Zolin.

'I'm with you!' said a younger boy called Ollin.

'Thanks be to Inti, you're a little marvel!' yelled Atl.

They crowded round and were making so much noise that their womenfolk came up to where they had gathered to know what all the shouting was about.

'Tell your women what we have agreed,' Tlalli said. 'We have to be all in this together or our plans will not succeed.'

After a while they quietened down and gradually dispersed. Paullu put his arm around Tlalli's shoulder and drew her close to him. She felt at peace, as if a huge weight had been lifted from her. She could put aside all her doubts over how to begin on the role she had been given by the Jaguar gods. They looked into each other's eyes and they kissed. Tlalli felt sure that Paullu would share the burden with her and be her mate for life.

40

Perúvian Railway

June 1931, Cuzco, Perú.
When we return to Montez House I am clutching a bag with Uncle Peter's transcript of Tlalli's story. I am anxious to begin reading but as we approach the front door I am surprised to find Diego is waiting on the doorstep, his hand on the knocker. As always, he is immaculately turned out wearing a grey suit and black fedora which he removes as we reach the top of the steps. Maria opens the door looking bemused.

'Oh, it's all right, Maria, we know this gentleman,' I say, and we all enter the house.

'We have just been to see my uncle's house,' I tell Diego. 'Martin is going to take us to the museum here in Cuzco later, to see if they want to purchase any of the artefacts.'

'That is very good news,' he says. 'I came to tell you I have acquired the services of an Indian guide. He seems to know the location of the Yaguar Mountain and will take me there. But first, we are going to visit Machu Picchu. I wondered, would you care to come with us?'

Grace says, 'Thank you Diego, but I think we are going with Senor Chambi, by rail to Ollie... what was the place, Christina?'

'Ollantaytambo,' I say.

'Yes, that was it,' Grace continues. 'Then we will go on horses to see the ruins.'

Diego nods his head. 'That is my plan also. When are you going?'

'Tomorrow,' she says. 'The train leaves here at eight in the morning, so it will be an early start.'

Diego looks delighted. 'I will see you at the station, ladies.' He looks at his pocket watch. 'I will be there with my guide. His name is Egecati.' He puts his hat on and steps out of the house, trotting down the steps with an agile spring. I am left pondering on the name Egecati.

The taxi weaves through the narrow Cuzco streets in the early morning light. Grace and I are carrying only one bag each with spare clothing and toiletries. We are wearing our safari suits with slacks and ankle boots. I am so glad we bought these as they will be ideal for riding the horses later.

At the station the steam engine chugs and hisses and the local people make a deal of noise as they clamber aboard the rear carriages. The windows have no glass and the cacophony continues unabated with chickens squawking, dogs barking and children wailing, while the adults shout to restore order and find everyone a place for the journey.

The first two carriages do have glass windows and proper seats and we are guided into one of these. I catch sight of Diego on the platform and he approaches us. Behind him walks a Perúvian man. He wears a battered trilby hat and a bright woven poncho over faded trousers. There is a string bag on his back from which flutes are just visible and he carries a stout stick. I recognise him immediately; he is the musician from yesterday's market.

Diego speaks to the guard and his guide is allowed to enter our carriage. Once there he sits cross-legged on the floor and cannot be moved. Martin Chambi knows this man also and they speak in Spanish.

Martin says, 'Egecati also speaks quite good English.'

'Where did you learn English?' Grace asks the man sitting on the floor and we are surprised when he answers her quietly but without hesitation.

'Many foreigners come to Perú speaking English. I learn from them as I guide them around the mountains.'

I have to admit to being impressed by this man. 'And you are also a musician,' I say. 'I enjoyed your playing in the market.'

'Thank you, Madam,' he says with a little bow of his head. 'That was my quena flute but I also play the quenacho and the antaras; my panpipes.'

To me, his English is faultless if heavily accented. 'So we will be entertained as well as guided by you, Egecati.'

'I hope you will enjoy your trip, Madam.'

At last the guard blows his whistle and the engine pulls us away from the station. Martin says the journey will last about two hours. The countryside through which we pass is one of infinite variety: deep valleys which are green and lush and rocky plateaus barren and grey. In between on the hilly slopes manmade terraces have been cut, some of which show signs of agricultural crops or grass for pasture, while others have reverted to a wilderness of scrub and wildflowers.

The train runs alongside a big river which Martin says is the Urubamba and we will follow its course all the way to Ollantaytambo. I stare at the river and feel I know every twist and turn, every rapid and fall. I have dreamed of this country many times, not really understanding the true meaning of the dreams. But last night I read Tlalli's history in Uncle Peter's translation. This place was her world and now perhaps it will be mine.

This account had been made by her grandson to the Spanish chronicler. It has both thrilled and disturbed me although not everything was revealed. The exact location of the mountain for instance, that seems to have been cloaked in mystery as the name was only used locally. But it was called

Yaguar Mountain and I wonder if this is the same location as Diego's mine.

The place she called the Sacred City must have been Machu Picchu. I really hope our visit will confirm this to me. At a time when the Perúvians had no written language and when folk legends were passed down the generations by word of mouth, it is indeed a miracle that Tlalli's story came to be written. So some Spanish people did do good things as well as all the wickedness that prevailed during her lifetime. But of course Uncle Peter had not completed the translation and so Tlalli's story has no end.

The scenery visible from the train changes again and higher mountains appear on the skyline, towering over the river and our adjacent railway line.

'According to my guidebook Machu Picchu was discovered in 1911 by the American explorer Hiram Bingham,' says Grace. She is always a mine of information on our travels. She addresses Egecati and perhaps wants to test his knowledge.

He grins and nods his head in agreement. 'Yes, Madam, you are right but our people always knew it was there.'

We had this conversation with Martin yesterday but Grace takes the argument forward. 'Why did they not live there then?'

'The city was deserted long before the Spanish first arrived,' he says. 'It is said the great Inca Patchahuti built it as a summer palace. When he died everyone left. The city no longer had a purpose.'

Grace looks perplexed. 'Oh, well that's not what Mr Bingham says and he is a world authority on these ruins.'

Egecati answers this by raising another point of interest. 'Andean history is woven with many legends and the truth is sometimes hard to find.'

This sparks off a train of thought in me and I reach into my blouse to touch my jaguar pendants and say, 'Do you know any legends about sacred jaguars, Egecati?'

He lifts his dark eyes to mine and I feel their intensity. 'Oh, yes,' he says. 'I know the Legend of the Jaguar, but it is a very old tale and very long.'

'Please tell it to me, Egecati. I would love to hear such a story.' I sound a little pleading but suddenly it is very important to know this legend, and so he begins.

41

Aguas Calientes

Ollantaytambo, Perú.
'Wake up, Christina! We're nearly there.' Startled, my eyes open wide to see Grace looking at me intently. 'Fancy you sleeping through Egecati's fascinating tale.'

It was true, I had fallen asleep. I also realised I had heard the story many times before. The memories of another me are reawakened now I have returned to the country of Tlalli's birth – my birth. All my scattered dreams, all the strange intuitive feelings of déjà vu, begin to make sense. The puzzle pieces of my fragmented past, dare I think - past-life, are falling into place. Egecati's Legend of the Jaguar was at the heart of my story, Tlalli's story; an intrinsic part of me.

The train is drawing closer to what is called the sacred valley. There are mountains all around. Some reach so high their snow-capped peaks disappear into the clouds. Diego has been sitting opposite me throughout the journey. It was in an effort to avoid his eyes that I closed my own and seemed to sleep.

'Egecati, my friend,' he says to our guide, 'do you think your jaguar legend refers to the site of my goldmine at Mount Yaguar?' This question is also uppermost in my mind.

The old Indian turns to face him and seems to weigh Diego's question thoughtfully before answering him. 'There are thousands of mountains in the Andes. Many do not even have names except to the local people.' He looks at me then back to Diego. 'If it is, your hopes of extracting gold there will be more difficult.'

Diego looks alarmed. 'Why is that?'

'You will need the help of local people. They will not work on any sacred site.'

'I thought all the indigenous people converted to Catholicism when the Spanish rule began,' says Diego.

It is Martin who replies. 'Andean Indians are of course all Catholics. But the old religions never died, they just went underground.'

'Now that really is interesting,' says Grace. She is trying to find something different to write about in her newspapers. 'Can we see the old Inca religions at Machu?'

Martin shakes his head and lowers his voice. 'Oh, no, the ceremonies are illegal. But I'm sure Egecati could take you to see them if you promise not to reveal the sites, although you will have to pay for the privilege.'

Diego laughs at this. 'I don't think your Indian friends are as simple as they appear. They know tourists come with fat wallets and they of course are poor.'

My mind is still taking in Martin's suggestion. I turn to Egecati. 'Could we see one of the ceremonies?' I ask him.

'If you want to see a ceremony we could travel to the sacred site after your tour of Machu Picchu,' he says.

Curious, I ask, 'What would we see, Egecati, what ceremonies?'

Egecati looks around the carriage to ensure he is not overheard by any local Spaniards or mestizos and lowers his voice. 'We may see the Inca ceremony of Inti Raymi, for this is the time of year it is held.'

I shudder as he says this and yet I am enthralled. I recall one of my constant dreams as I danced past the relics of ancient kings and stretched my arms to the rising sun in an act of worship. Was that just a dream? If I see this ceremony now, as a spectator, will I know if it really happened to me? I feel I absolutely must go to this place with Egecati.

'Oh, I don't know if we can do that,' says Grace. 'It will extend our visit considerably.'

I am panic-stricken. 'Oh, Grace yes, we must go.' I try not to convey my mounting anxiety at the thought of losing this opportunity. 'Besides, think what a fantastic feature it will make in *The New York Times*.'

Grace seems to consider this. 'Hmm, well, if the travel arrangements are satisfactory perhaps we'll go.'

Diego intervenes. 'Is this place near my mine-site, Egecati? You know I have to travel there also.'

Egecati nods slowly. 'It can all be done in the time we have, sir.' I sense he is cautious not to break faith with these sun worshippers by telling us too much, particularly as Diego is Spanish.

The train begins to slow down as the line funnels into a narrow valley alongside the vibrant Urubamba River. The backdrop is one of forested hills and mountains on all sides. The train begins to lose the rattling pace which began when we left Cuzco and the steam engine slows to walking pace as we enter the station for Ollantaytambo. The carriage doors fly open and the Indian passengers begin jumping out even before the train stops which it does with a jolt. Everyone now streams onto the wooden platform in a babble of voices and clatter.

Martin and Diego jump out and assist Grace then me from the carriage. Egecati hands our baggage down and we give him money to hire the ponies for the rest of our journey. There are grazing patches near the station with good strong ponies and donkeys for hire and Egecati will select suitable animals for us.

I look around and realise how poor this country and its people are. When Tlalli and Paullu came here Ollantaytambo was a fortress town but now the old Inca ruins have fallen into disrepair. Martin tells us that like most of the ancient buildings in Perú, over the past four hundred years they have been abandoned, destroyed or built over.

He says, 'Perú may now be an independent country again but the struggle to reclaim our Inca heritage has a long and difficult history. Maybe in time, that will happen.'

I think of Tlalli, and what she began. I wonder if, in her place, I could have been as brave. Beside the station there are market stalls just as there were in Cuzco. Vendors are shouting out their prices selling local produce and hand-made goods. There is home-made cassava which is an alcoholic beer, sold by the glass and consumed in copious quantities by all the men and some of the women. Breads, fruits and even cooked potatoes and other hot foods are all on sale.

I choose a bright red scarf woven with a black design. Between my fingers the material feels soft as silk. The woman is spinning with one hand as she sells her goods. Martin tells me she says it is made from baby alpaca. I know this feel as if I had woven it myself; it is warm like a mother's embrace.

Egecati comes along the track leading the ponies. Diego calls out, 'So, Egecati, my friend, have you found reliable equines for the ladies to ride?'

Egecati nods. 'I have selected the best available for you all. I hope you will think so when you ride them.'

Diego looks pleased. 'I practically lived on horseback until my father bought me my first car in 1926.'

'I thought you were adopted as a child by your uncle,' I say, recalling him telling us this back at the hacienda.

He frowns. 'Of course, this was my adopted father, Don Rodrigo Chavez. But he was, of course, like a father to me.'

I am curious to learn more of Diego's background which has so far been a blank canvas. 'Didn't you also say you had a brother?' Diego retains a calm façade but I sense he is not comfortable with these questions from me.

'Yes, we were cousins and I became his adopted brother. He was Roberto Chavez, Don Rodrigo's son.'

'Oh.' I must look surprised but I decide to remain silent. I need to think. The name is familiar and I am trying to place it. My instinct tells me Diego did not intend to tell me this but he probably thinks the name will be of no consequence to me. It is, but I don't know why.

Grace says, 'It's a long time since I did any riding so I hope I won't disgrace myself.'

Diego takes hold of Grace's hand and squeezes it. 'I am sure you will not, dear Grace.'

I see he is working his charm on her. I am beginning to know this man very well. Yet I do wonder how genuine his sentiments are. When he does it to me I can't help being taken in and flattered by him. I find his silver tongue very seductive and yet I am sure he is working his own agenda with every word he speaks.

Egecati has been very efficient and the four ponies are saddled ready for us to mount. He has a young boy with him to help and mind the animals. Each pony carries a sheaf of alfalfa for the grazing is poor on the mountain.

Diego helps me mount a little piebald called Juana. She is very sturdy with thick legs and a broad back. Grace looks uneasy on a brown pony. Hers has a long thick mane like a Shetland, which covers the eyes, and I wonder if this pony will be able to see where she is going. Egecati tells the boy to lead Grace's pony and assures her she can dismount and walk when the pathway is not too steep.

Martin's mount is a stocky grey animal which has a broad back and looks very calm but Diego rides the biggest pony, a black, which is almost a horse, a stallion with a frisky disposition. He will have ample opportunity to impress us with his horsemanship to keep this equine in order.

We set out at a steady pace along the road and I soon realise why wheeled transport was not recommended. The track climbs steadily into the mountain range. In places the road almost disappears where subsidence has washed it away. Egecati and the boy are walking, and lead Grace and me across the difficult passages, guiding the animals with skill and patience. Sometimes the road goes downhill and the river is never far away.

Grace dismounts and walks some of the way. I don't think she is as comfortable in the saddle as I am. At home I spent hours riding on the downs around Madeley Hall and I feel very comfortable on this little piebald mare.

After about two hours we arrive at our destination and night stop. This place is called Aguas Calientes. It is just a tiny hamlet and Egecati leads us towards a row of houses. The little dwellings look as if they have grown out of the hillside, no two alike. They are made from stone and form the street. There are a dozen perhaps, all that there is of this quaint little place and I wonder where we will stay. We ride on, with the roar of the river on one side and round a bend in the road, which is just a rough paved track. A much larger house stands alone, facing the river. This too seems built into the mountainside. This is the guest house where we will stay for a couple of nights. The Andean people are efficient builders. Egecati tells us they use local quarried stone and reuse material from abandoned buildings or old walls. New properties, like this one, blend into the existing landscape and don't look new at all.

'The Incas were master architects and builders,' says Martin. 'Today our craftsmen still use some of their methods as did their fathers and grandfathers before them.'

At the door we are greeted by the owner. He is dark skinned with jet black hair and is rather rotund. He puffs and blows as he carries our bags up the stairs to the first floor. But he is good humoured enough. Egecati and the boy take the ponies round the back to stable them for the night.

I don't think things have changed much here since the days of the conquistadors. The Spanish still consider they are the ruling class, the mestizos run the businesses and the Indians do all the dirty work for little return, even though this was originally their country.

My upbringing as an English aristocrat does not equip me for such radical thinking. I have always had servants and I know these class divisions exist in all societies. But here, in Perú, the divisions are very marked and I discover I have a strange affinity to these lowly Andean Indians for they are the disinherited heirs of the Inca race. They have an amazing dignity and I wonder again about Tlalli and her family; I feel very close to her.

We take refreshments at the guest house. Diego is still with us but I think Grace wishes he was not. 'I thought you were anxious to get to your gold mine, Diego,' she says to him.

'Indeed I am, Grace,' he replies. 'But I need Egecati as a guide so I must wait for him.' From this is seems obvious that we shall have Diego's company for many days if we go to see the Inti Raymi ceremony.

Grace has brought her camera and as it is still light we go for a walk beside the river, making our way back towards Aguas Calientes. We take photographs of each other with the stunning scenery as a backdrop. This little folding Kodak camera is so clever. It takes twelve pictures on a little spool of film. Martin has promised Grace he will develop her films when we return to Cuzco.

When we walk back to the guest house, I seek out the owner who is now puffing and blowing in the kitchen, shouting at his poor cowed little wife who is organising our dinner. 'Please would you set a place for our guide, Egecati,' I ask him. His mouth drops and his eyes widen, as if I had requested a cockroach at the table, but I insist. I have grown very fond of Egecati. I consider the old Indian more as a friend than a servant. He is just like the shaman whose name he carries, from the jaguar legend.

Dinner is ready at six o'clock and Egecati joins us. Even Diego is tolerant of my attachment to his Indian guide although I think he would indulge me in anything I wanted. He looks at me with his devilish smile but I look away.

Grace says, 'What are we eating?' She is poking at the food on her plate with her fork, displaying a look of distaste.

Martin tells her, 'The meat is guinea pig.'

Grace sighs. 'In France they eat horse. In Japan they eat dog. So I suppose guinea pig is better than those and at least it makes a change from endless chicken,'

Subconsciously, I avoid the meat, but my mind has returned to the puzzle over Diego and his cousin, Roberto Chavez.

42

Rebels

1537-38, The Sacred City, Vilcabamba, Perú.

The next morning, as the sun rose, Tlalli, Paullu and Saqui set out on a reconnaissance mission. Tlalli looked around. 'This is still a beautiful city and so far the Spanish have not found it.'

Saqui spoke up. 'Today we will find safe routes in and out of the city.' They had originally reached this place from the east, but now they worked their way south with Saqui taking the lead. He told them, 'We will stay in the mountains where the Inca road-builders have created pathways through these ranges.' Saqui spat on the ground as he and Paullu hacked at the vegetation blocking the old path. 'Once these trails were kept repaired and in good order.'

Paullu nodded. 'That was until the wretched Spanish invaders showed up.' They stopped and mopped their brows with their sleeves. Tlalli gave them water from the leather bottle she carried saying, 'They have overturned the ways which allowed our people to live well.'

'They are fools,' said Paullu, 'but they are strong and we must learn to outwit them.'

'I doubt they would risk their horses up here,' said Saqui. 'They will take the easy road by the river or through the lower passes.'

'So we must set our traps or ambushes from these higher places,' said Tlalli. They had reached the remains of an old Inca stopping point. It could hardly be called a settlement, but the stone walls showed there had been roofed structures which could have housed a tambo for supplies and shelter for travellers. 'A camp, maybe?' said Paullu.

'Or a lookout post to guard against unwanted intruders reaching the sacred city,' said Saqui.

Tlalli felt excited. 'That's exactly what we are looking for.' The old camp site had been built into a steep hillside, overlooked by a high ridge. They started to climb up and from the top they had a perfect view of the surrounding countryside from horizon to horizon in every direction.

Paullu said, 'I can see the river from here and the road from Cuzco winding beside it.'

'We will stock this place with food and weapons, then we can keep the city safe,' said Tlalli.

Saqui climbed back down to the campsite and was digging around the bushes. 'Come and look at this,' he called out. Paullu and Tlalli climbed down and went over to him. 'See,' he said. He had slashed back vines and creepers from a rocky outcrop and revealed a fresh water spring, bubbling up from the ground. 'This is why the camp was sited in this place.'

'Another sacred sign,' said Tlalli.

On their way back to the city they made a double detour, leaving almost invisible marks on tree bark and camouflaging any signs that humans had passed that way. Once back in the sacred city they called everyone together and Tlalli spoke to them.

'We have found a stronghold we can use as a base. It is vital you all know how to reach this place and how to cover your tracks. I'm going to call this place, Winay Wayna, forever young, for that is what we are and what we wish for our people,'

Throughout the rest of the day Paullu and Saqui took people back and forth to the site now called Winay Wayna, showing them how to disguise their tracks and cover any sign of their passage through the cloud forest. They took tools and weapons to hide and took turns being lookouts from the high ridge. Tlalli organised the women to prepare foods that could be stored at the campsite also.

The following day, Paullu and Tlalli took Ollin and two of the other younger men with them. From Winay Wayna they travelled towards the road from Cuzco, again fighting their way through the virgin cloud forest. Here a section of the river ran between the mountains, and the Inca road had been carved higher up the mountainside, overlooking the river. It ran through a pass between two high peaks; a perfect place for an ambush. The rebels staked out hiding places on the two peaks and began collecting rocks and boulders to throw down on anyone passing below. Now they would be ready for an attack on any Spaniards moving on the road.

They worked in small groups. Three days running they kept watch from Winay Wayna and then moved up to the twin peaks and waited. On the fourth day they spied a group of men moving up from Cuzco, two men on horseback and two others driving llamas, fully laden. Spaniards didn't often move about the country without an escort, and this presented the perfect opportunity to test their plans.

Paullu and Tlalli hid on one of the peaks. They watched the men approach the pass. The travellers stopped and sent the men with the llamas on ahead. 'Wait for my signal,' Paullu told the two men with them. Saqui with two more men lay hidden on the other peak.

The Spaniards did not enter the pass until the men with the llamas, who were Indians, reached the far side. As the horsemen entered the narrow road Paullu, who was almost as good a mimic as Ispaca had been, sounded the cry of the condor twice. The Spaniards moved directly below them as they began their assault with boulders and rocks. Tlalli's head spun, first with fear, and then with elation. At last she was waging war on the hated Spanish invaders. She tried to imagine these men were Gonzalo and Juan

Pizarro. How she hated them and all Spaniards for their cruelty to her people. Quite spontaneously, she found herself shouting out, 'Death to the enemy!'

She saw the Spaniard's horses rear in fear and unseat their riders but the men were caught by their stirrups. She was mesmerised watching the horses bolt out of control and gallop right over the edge of the ravine, dragging their riders with them. They plunged into the fast flowing waters of the Urubamba. Horses and riders would have died almost instantly. As the llama drivers scurried down the steep bank towards the river to find their masters, Paullu, Tlalli and their accomplices, fearful of being seen, disappeared into the cloud forest and eventually back to Winay Wayna. As darkness fell they returned to the sacred city. They celebrated with the group. Tlalli spoke to them, still flushed with triumph.

'Our first mission and a complete success!' They drank chicha made by the women from berries and maize.

Paullu spoke to caution the group's excitement. 'I hope you all realise there can be no going back now. We have killed two Spaniards and soon it will be known rebels are active in these mountains. Remember, all strangers are our enemies, Spanish or Indian; take no chances.'

He spoke to Tlalli later that night. 'I heard you call out. It sounded like a battle cry.'

'It was, Paullu. Once I hurled the first rock I felt brave, like a jaguar is brave.' She looked into his eyes. 'I know the Spirit of the Jaguar Gods are with us. I feel it in my heart.'

Paullu pulled her to him and kissed her. 'Yes, I feel it, Tlalli. But we must not be over-confident. Soon, the Spanish will begin looking for us, and we must be ready for that.'

Many moons passed and Tlalli and Paullu remained at the sacred city living as man and wife. From there they went out on longer journeys with their rebel groups. They grew crops on the terraces as they cleared more of these for planting. This provided enough food for the group but Tlalli began to see they could never grow enough to feed an army.

The time for Inti Raymi was fast approaching. She realised this would also mark her sixteenth year. She had grown from a child to a woman and now felt the responsibility for the group rested firmly on hers and Paullu's shoulders. But thoughts of home and family still beckoned.

One evening, when they were all gathered together after sharing their food, the group recalled the success of their work. 'We have made many attacks on Spanish travellers,' said Saqui, 'and killed eight men this last moon alone.'

Ollin recalled, 'Most successful was our night raid at the village where the Spanish had demanded a church built to their god.'

'Yes!' said Atl. 'I took great pleasure in torching their accursed church and watching it burn to the ground.' It had been built by the local Indians under duress.

Tlalli clapped her hands, remembering their jubilation that night. 'Thankfully, we rescued those who would follow us, and brought them back here.'

Paullu remained sombre as he recalled. 'That night we slayed the Spanish priest left in charge of the village. I don't think the Spaniards will tolerate our activities much longer. I fear we are in grave danger of being discovered here soon.'

Over the next few days Tlalli sent trusted spies out to discover what was being said locally. When they returned, Zolin, who had led the spies, told them.

'News of our rebel group has spread around the region. I heard it said, "They are led by a female who changes her form from human to feline and calls her rebels jaguars."'

Tlalli laughed at this, knowing she had never done this during a raid, but she was not sorry that her rebels had become so feared by the Spanish, with a reputation which reflected the bravery of their followers. All this time her confidence and determination as their leader grew. She showed no sign of wanting to give up her struggle against the invaders.

But Paullu was worried for Tlalli. 'We should move on soon,' he said. 'Saqui tells me he and the others want to try and return to their home villages and find their own families again. But you and I have other work to do. We must find the Inca and follow his lead in our fight against the enemy.'

'Yes,' said Tlalli. 'The longer we stay here the more the people in this city are in danger.'

Paullu agreed, 'We have been safe here, but we know little of what is happening elsewhere.'

Tlalli reached out her hand to him. 'I long to see my mother again and to know if my father survived the fighting. You are right as always, Paullu.'

Tlalli's love for Paullu grew. She felt overwhelmed by her deep feelings for him for she loved him so much. Since they came to the city they had lived together. It would have been condemned back home because they were not formally married, but isolated from the outside world, they had become refugees from a terrible war. Now they planned to return to that other world and she didn't know what would happen when they got there.

That night Tlalli had another dream. She puzzled over the strange pictures in her head.

A group of people were standing where she had stood when she first came to the sacred city. She could see men and women, who wore strange clothes, and had come on horses. They didn't seem to have weapons and some looked like Indians and some were fair. There was one woman whose hair was golden, like the jaguar's coat. She was white and very beautiful and Tlalli felt spiritually close to her. The group were talking together and she could understand them. The fair lady said, 'You say the Spanish never found this place, Martin?'

An Indian man answered her, 'No, Christina, it remained undiscovered until 1911.'

'Of course it did,' replied the beautiful, fair lady called Christina. 'But I knew that, I always knew that.'

Tlalli awoke with the strangest feeling, as if she had been dreaming about herself. She knew this dream had spoken of the future, telling her that the sacred city would always remain a safe haven, but only if she continued to face the Spanish aggressors and fulfil her vow. The Spirit of the Jaguar guided her once more, sending her messages in her dreams. The fight would go on and she must not be afraid.

They told the other rebels of their decision to return to the outside world. 'What will you do?' Paullu asked them. Most of the group said they would also leave in the coming weeks. Rebel activities would be put aside for now while they all journeyed back to their homelands across the Empire. They each promised to continue rebel activity within their own areas. The sacred city would once more become deserted, left to the gods and the sleeping ghosts.

Tlalli and Paullu were the first to leave. They took one llama laden with food and some cloth garments the women had made by spinning and weaving during their time at the hilltop citadel. They bade goodbye to their friends and began the descent down the mountainside.

Paullu said, 'We will go to Ollantaytambo; perhaps there we can find out what has been happening in the struggle against the invaders,' He led the way and Tlalli followed, leading the llama on a length of rope. She remained hopeful that soon they could return home. They kept out of sight, taking a path parallel to the road but under cover of bushes and trees. When they reached Ollantaytambo they hoped to learn if the Inca's armies had survived or did the Spanish invaders now rule the land?

43

Machu Picchu

June 1931, Machu Picchu, The Sacred Valley, Perú.
I am awake early on this beautiful June day. Grace and I are sharing a room and from the window I look out on the magnificent Urubamba River. The sun shines on the tops of the mountains though the valley is still in deep shadow. Today looks perfect for our trek to the top of Machu Picchu.

I have dreamed of this city and that is a strange feeling. In my dream it was already abandoned and I was with others, taking refuge from an enemy. Now I have read Tlalli's story I know this enemy to have been the Spanish conquistadors and that I was with Paullu. I hope that when I see these ruins the memories will come back and I can fit them into the other threads from my dreams.

Because we are constantly on the move it is impossible to keep my journal. But it is no longer important. My aim now is to link my dreams with Tlalli's testament. I find this whole quest exciting, exhilarating even, but I dare not share my thoughts with anyone, not yet. The guest house owner loads a packed lunch into our saddlebags and we eventually set off. Martin leads the way and Egecati follows him on foot, then the boy leading Grace's brown pony. I follow on the piebald and Diego brings up the rear on his black stallion.

In the days of the Incas there were no horses on this continent. Egecati tells us they used llamas as pack animals or carried everything on their backs. The rulers were transported on litters carried by servants, even into battle, when they would direct the troops from their high vantage point. These ancient tribes didn't even use the wheel. I can imagine that living in this mountainous region wheeled vehicles would have been of little use.

This harsh and beautiful country is all around me and I drift back into my dreams. The girl Tlalli, who I truly believe was me, has taken me back into her time. Through her eyes I see all these things in a world so very different from my own. A voice startles me.

'I think my stallion has taken a fancy to your little mare.' It is Diego. I was so preoccupied with my own thoughts I had not seen him come alongside me. 'He obviously likes beautiful female company.' Diego beams his warm seductive smile at me. 'As, of course, do I.'

'You are a born flatterer, Diego, and I will not encourage you,' I say flicking my pony's neck with the reins.

He laughs, throwing his head back in the way which always reminds me of the young man I met on the ferry boat all those years ago. And then it comes to me, like a revelation: Roberto Chavez. I remember writing his name in my journal after we came home. I wish I could verify this fascinating fact. All my journals but they are boxed up at Madeley Hall, thousands of miles away. So was it just a strong family resemblance made me think Diego was him?

I need to question him carefully. 'Tell me, Diego, your adopted brother – your cousin, is he still in Spain?' I glance in his direction. A look of alarm spreads over his features and then almost immediately his face is composed once more.

'No. Unfortunately my cousin is dead. Why do you ask, Christina?'

'Oh, I am so sorry.' I feel almost bereaved myself. 'Forgive my intrusion into your family's grief. When you mentioned his name I knew I had heard it before. I am sure that was the name of the young man I met on the ferry. When was it, six, no, seven years ago?'

Diego is no longer looking at me. His eyes are fixed on the trail ahead and I can't work out what he is thinking. I am determined to have an answer now that I have remembered this link. 'You may recall I spoke of the meeting when we were on the *Graf*.'

He doesn't react immediately but then he nods slowly as if he is also remembering. 'Yes, of course, and you were just a little girl.' He beams his smile, once more charming and suave. 'What a coincidence. Roberto did travel on the ferry across the English Channel when he went to the university at Oxford. But how strange that you met and that you have linked him to me.'

'I thought you were him,' I say.

He looks at me as though I am still that little girl. 'Well, in looks we were very alike.'

I still feel it was more than that. 'And in other ways, was he like you in temperament?' He laughs that way again.

'Roberto was a rogue. I suppose one could say he was the black sheep in our family.'

'How did he die?' I am surprised how upset I feel at this loss. I had carried his image in my head for a long time after our brief encounter. He had featured in my adolescent fantasies of love. Then I had forgotten all about him, until I met Diego. He has awakened memories of the handsome Spanish student, dressed like a dandy, and now I am sad to know he is dead. The opportunity to learn the answer to my question is for now denied, as the pathway has become too narrow to ride side by side, and Diego drops behind again.

I must concentrate on the trail as we begin scaling the steep mountainside. It zigzags, making the ascent easier but the journey longer. We have to stop several times while Grace's pony is coaxed up the steep rocky gradients. Halfway up we dismount and drink copious amounts of water. Diego goes to talk to Egecati and I stay with Grace. The climb is taking its toll on both of us but she is not coping well.

'I thought I was fit,' she says looking quite exhausted, 'but my muscles ache already.' I am not so affected but the going is arduous. I see that Egecati carries a pouch of leaves. He puts some in his mouth and chews them constantly. He gives some to Diego and tells him to fold them into his cheek and chew them into a cud. Egecati says to chew them slowly and the juices will eventually mix with his saliva. This is coca and its mild narcotic effect is reputed to calm the nerves and improve stamina. It was used by the Incas and today most Indian men seem to use it all the time. Again, I feel this is something I always knew.

Grace and I decline the offer to try it and smoke cigarettes instead. Diego says the coca tastes disgusting and he lights up a cigarillo. I am once more reminded of Roberto and determine to find out how he died.

We resume the journey and one more hour of this winding trail brings us to the top. How clever the men who built this city were, for it remained completely hidden until we scaled the final ridge. Now, it is as if we have been transported to another world. The ruins are contained on a grassy flat plateau which spans the top of this mountain. Its peak is a rocky outcrop at the north end, but the peak of Huayna Picchu rises immediately behind Machu, as if it is the guardian of this magnificent place. We dismount from our ponies and stand still and silent, overawed by the scale and detail of the ruined city.

Neat rows of what were once houses and other structures, evidence of paved roadways and flights of steps, are all emerging from their hiding places. Restoration work is still going on, clearing hundreds of years of growth by natural vegetation, trees and erosion, which has covered the city and kept it hidden, but also kept it safe from plunder by the invading Spanish. Apart from local Indians, no one knew it was here until Hiram Bingham arrived in 1911.

Martin sets up his large plate camera on a tripod and we pose for photographs. Then we loll on the grass, eating our packed lunch, absorbing the scene before us. The site faces south and captures the sun and the warmth of the day.

Grace reads from her travel guide book and gives us some facts from its pages. 'The Spanish conquistadors never found this place,' she tells us, 'which is why the ruins are so complete.' She looks pointedly at Diego. 'The Spanish destroyed so many Inca towns and cities it is a miracle there is anything left to see.'

Diego is stretched out on the grass, his hat tipped back and he is chewing on a grass stalk. 'I can't defend the actions of my countrymen from four hundred years ago,' he says dismissively. 'Besides, most of the conquistadors were uneducated brutes and only interested in finding treasure. They considered the natives were illiterate heathens who must be converted to Christianity.'

Martin nods his head in agreement. 'Anything connected to their religious beliefs was destroyed and of course, their treasures were stolen. The Incas had so much gold they lined the walls of their temples and even paved some of the streets with gold. There was said to have been a garden at the Sun Temple in Cuzco made entirely of flowers, trees and statues all in solid gold. The workmanship of the goldsmiths was remarkable; their skills had been passed down from previous civilisations over thousands of years.' I detect in Martin's voice pride at what was, but also grief over what was lost.

Grace is still consulting her book. 'It says here that the Spanish melted all the beautiful items into gold ingots stamped with the King of Spain's seal. Some were shipped back to Spain, the rest divided between the conquistadors according to their rank. They also received land and the native Indians became their slaves; the Spaniards who settled in this country became very rich men.'

'Surely not all the gold and silver treasures disappeared?' Diego is addressing Martin. 'Perhaps there is still treasure to be found.'

Martin smiles at this; his brown face crinkles and his dark eyes shine in the sunlight. 'I think you refer to Manco Inca's lost treasure. Many have come to these mountains seeking this fabled stash of gold but as told in Egecati's legend of the jaguar, they are more certain of losing their lives than finding lost treasure.'

I know I have been here before. All the emotions I have today about this place I have experienced before. That is as far as my thoughts will take me and I join the others as we walk towards the ruins. The boy will mind the ponies until we are ready to leave.

As we walk among the ruins and follow the paved pathways I think about Diego's question and Martin's reply. Diego came to Perú to find gold and silver in an old mine which apparently belonged to his grandfather over fifty years ago. But who owned the mine before that? I have read Tlalli's testament, as told by her grandson. It tells how she found the Inca's treasure in the old Warri mine and she was the only person who knew where it was. I wonder, did she ever recover it? The story, as translated by Uncle Peter, doesn't say what happened to it. Tlalli tells it was guarded by the jaguar. I had concluded this from my dreams but the written story is my confirmation that it really happened; either way, I don't know the end of her story, and I wonder if I ever will.

We walk through the ruins to the far side of the city, to the north-west lip of the bowl. On the left is a raised monument. It echoes the shape of surrounding mountain peaks; lovingly carved by the Inca stonemasons. I know I was here with Paullu. We were in love; we were very happy and we had music. As if Egecati reads my mind he begins to play his panpipes. The notes are joyful yet haunting and in my mind it is Paullu playing to me, oh so long ago.

The sun has begun its descent into the west. We must start our journey back down the mountain to reach the guest house before dark. I walk with Egecati, anxious to learn more about going to see the Inti Raymi ceremony. The guide says, 'We will trek by horse about half a day to reach the sacred site.'

I ask about the price. 'You said it would cost us a lot of money, Egecati. How much money?'

He explains: 'They pay many people to act as spies and guard the sites from the police. They could be imprisoned and the sites destroyed without this protection. I think some local officials are bribed to turn a blind eye and all that takes money. I think we may need about twenty Libra.'

A Libra is roughly the value of a sovereign and to me this is not a large sum. I decide I will pay without asking the others. I feel it will be worth the cost just to see this ancient ceremony.

Diego comes alongside us. 'We could all go together to view this ceremony and then Egecati and I will continue on to the mine site.'

It seems a reasonable plan and Diego and Egecati discuss the details. Martin will come with us and then accompany Grace and me back to Cuzco. We find the boy and our ponies grazing peacefully at the top of the rise and we mount up for the journey back.

Going down the mountain path is not as easy as I expected. The ponies shy on the steep gradients as their hooves slide on the loose stones. We have to dismount and coax them down to the next level. Grace's pony is particularly nervous and the boy helps her by holding the reins. She has just remounted when suddenly, without warning, the little brown takes off leaving the path and trying to bolt across a ridge. I hear Grace shout out in fear and the boy runs after her. But the pony is too quick and almost gallops out of control. It stops suddenly at the far end of the ridge, facing a vertical drop. Grace screams as she is unseated, luckily falling to the ground and not over the precipice. We all dismount in great alarm and I hold on to Diego's reins and mine while he and Egecati run to help Grace.

I want to go to her but it is all I can do to hold the two ponies on the path as they sense the alarm around them. I am so afraid that Grace may be badly injured. Diego seems very attentive and is examining her limbs and head. Now he picks her up in his arms and carries her back towards me. I feel so anxious but witnessing Diego's quick reactions and gentle administrations at this moment I feel I could forgive him anything.

Grace is fully conscious, in fact she is laughing, which is such a relief. 'Oh, Grace, are you hurt?'

'No, no,' she says as Diego lowers her feet to the ground. She winces as she tries to stand. 'My ankle hurts though. Just a sprain, I hope.' She is trying to make light of it but it is obvious to me she is in a deal of pain. I examine the joint and see it is beginning to swell and bruise. Egecati has soaked a dinner napkin in cold water and I wrap it round her ankle. 'You must ride my pony. She is not so skittish,' I say. Diego insists he will lead Grace on the piebald and I will ride his pony. The boy is charged with bringing the naughty brown pony back down and so we continue the return journey somewhat subdued.

We eventually return to the guest house and Grace is helped to bed with aspirins and hot tea made from herbs which the owner's wife says will help her sleep. I dare not even contemplate tomorrow and the thought of having to cancel our trip to the Inti Raymi ceremony.

44

Ollantaytambo

1539, Ollantaytambo, Perú,
Paullu took a parallel track at a distance of about fifty paces from the stone-laid Inca trail. At times they hid in bushes, as columns of Spanish soldiers and native auxiliaries moved on the road. These men were enemy troops, all travelling in one direction: from the Vilcabamba towards Ollantaytambo. The wounded were carried on makeshift litters, others looked battle-weary.

Tlalli and Paullu found a narrow trail further away from the road, high up the side of the valley that led towards the city. The trail took them to a terrace with good grazing for their llama, a place where they could not be seen. Tlalli shared out the last of the bread they had brought with them.

'Listen!' said Paullu.

She kept perfectly still, her heart racing. A faint tinkling sound reached her ears. 'Bells?' she whispered.

'Alpacas,' answered Paullu, 'and maybe a herdsman with them.' They stood close to their llama, which was tethered to the ground on a short picket. Paullu clasped the knife hilt at his belt. The animals came into view from the hillside away from the road; their bells pealed in a familiar chorus. The animals seemed to know where the grazing was good. Their llama bleated as if greeting his fellows.

'Are they alone?' said Tlalli.

Paullu shook his head. 'They are too valuable to be left unguarded on the hillside.' As he said this a young boy came into view. He looked about ten years old and didn't see them until he came about twenty paces distant. His herd had fanned out on the terrace and two had come over to smell the strange llama on their grazing patch. The boy stared at them as if uncertain what to do and he raised the stick he carried.

'We are friends,' called Paullu. 'Don't be afraid, we will not harm you or your animals.'

The boy lowered the stick. He looked relieved and came closer. 'What are you doing here?' he asked. 'You are not from these parts. Where have you come from?'

'Oh, we have been on the road for many months and we don't know what has been happening in the cities,' said Paullu. 'Can you tell us?'

The boy seemed surprised. 'Do you really not know what has happen here at Ollantaytambo?'

Paullu answered him. 'The last we knew Cuzco was still under siege by Manco's forces. He had come to this city to hold out against the Spanish invaders.'

'You are certainly out of touch,' said the boy. 'How do I know you're not spies? They are everywhere now the Spanish hold Ollantaytambo. It is said there are rebels in the mountains.'

'We are certainly not spies,' said Paullu. Tlalli didn't say anything, knowing Paullu would speak with caution. 'But if the Spanish have taken this city where is the Inca? Is he dead?'

The boy laughed. 'Not Manco, he is much too wily to be caught by them. He retreated into the Antisuyo with his family. The Spanish wouldn't follow him into the jungle, not with all the tales of deadly poisoned arrows and cannibals.'

They laughed also and Paullu said, 'Their horses would not survive in the jungle. So is he still there?'

'Word eventually reached us that he had crossed the Chuquichaca Bridge into the valley and moved up to Vitcos.'

'Still jungle territory,' said Paullu, 'but within the mountain range.'

'We know it well,' said Tlalli. 'It is our homeland, though we left there a long time ago.'

'Well the Spanish soldiers followed him and there was a battle at Vitcos, burning the city to the ground. But the Inca slipped away again and disappeared with his family,' the boy told them.

'You seem to know a lot, boy,' said Paullu. 'What's your name?'

'I am Tenyoa,' he replied. 'Most of the people at Ollantaytambo have been forced to go and fight for the Spanish. I am fortunate being a herdsman, so I am allowed to remain here to look after the alpacas, but my friends and family who had to go and fight have told me what happened.'

'So have they tracked Manco down yet?' Paullu asked.

The boy nodded. 'He went to the Willkapampa city in the jungle. They built lots of barricades and everyone thought he had turned it into an impenetrable fortress. That young Spaniard, Gonzalo Pizarro, led a huge army from here and they went determined to capture him.'

Tlalli had clasped tight hold of Paullu's hand at the mention of Gonzalo Pizarro, and he put his arm round her shoulder. He asked the boy if he knew what had happened.

Tenyoa gestured towards the road. 'You must have seen the men returning from the battle. They have been trickling in for days.' He certainly seemed at ease now and had become quite friendly. 'My older brother came home yesterday,' Tenyoa said. 'He told us that after a terrible journey through sickly heat, where they were eaten alive by insects and ambushed by the natives who live there, they came near to the fortress town. After a fierce battle only one heavily fortified bridge across a precipice remained to enter the city. Eventually the Spaniards figured out a way over and stormed the fortress.'

'So they captured the Inca?' said Tlalli, holding her breath.

'Apparently no,' said the boy but he was not laughing this time, 'Manco is thought to have slipped back into the Antisuyo jungle again. But they found his Coya still in the city mourning the death of two other brothers. She has been brought back here as a prisoner.'

'Oh, no, poor Cora Ocllo, my dear lady Coya.' Tlalli could not hide her distress. 'What will become of her?' She boiled with anger and pleaded with Paullu. 'We must do something to help her.'

Paullu turned back to the boy. 'Do you think we could get into the city with you when you return with the animals?'

The boy shrugged. 'I suppose we could try if that's what you want. If we wait until it is nearly dark I expect I can get you past the guards. But after that you will be on your own.'

45

Cora Ocllo

At a tambo where they could barter for chicha and hot gruel straight from
the pot, Tlalli and Paullu found lodgings in the city. They had been given
space in a shack behind the house where animals were kept at night.

'We should move on, Tlalli,' said Paullu. 'I could be made to fight for
these Spaniards against our own people.'

'I know it is a risk,' she replied, 'but I need to know what will happen
to the Coya. I cannot stop thinking about her.' Tlalli wrung her hands,
remembering her oath to put the Coya's life before her own.

'According to the boy, Tenyoa,' said Paullu, 'the Pizarro brothers are
waiting for their elder brother Francisco to arrive; he is the leader of them
all.'

'He will vent his anger over the way the rebellion is continuing and
Manco Inca's escape.' This worried Tlalli more. She could not understand
why Manco Inca had left Cora Ocllo to this dreadful fate.

They didn't have to wait long to find out. Later that day, a great deal of
noise and shouting erupted in the streets. Tlalli and Paullu crept out and
mixed with the crowd of onlookers. Dozens of Spanish soldiers in full
battle armour rode into the city; the metal horseshoes clattered on the stone
cobbles.

'Look!' called a young boy in the crowd, 'Pizarro thinks he is the Inca!'
Sure enough they saw Francisco Pizarro brought into the city from Lima.
He sat on a golden litter held by twelve natives who carried him along very
smoothly, for they were trained to walk with a special gait to give the
ruling Inca a perfect ride. Now the triumphant Spaniard had claimed this
privilege for himself.

The local Indians lined the road. Tlalli felt her frustration rising as the
people were completely overawed by this spectacle. They seemed to
believe the stories that these white men were indeed gods, Viracochas,
come to replace the Incas. The people threw themselves down on the
ground as they had always done for Manco and his ancestors. She could
see this Francisco was not young like his brother Gonzalo but an ugly old
man, his face lined and weathered like the crocodiles in the rivers of the
Antisuyo.

Paullu moved closer to Tlalli to protect her, for within the ranks of the
native auxiliaries who now fought with the Spanish troops, they saw
Canari warriors with blowpipes and bows and arrows. Most of these tribes
had declared as sworn enemies of the Incas, and now aligned themselves

with the Spanish Invaders. Tlalli felt their presence here signalled a bad sign.

The parade marched on, then up a steep slope into the palace fortress, where the Spaniards had taken command. Tlalli and Paullu went back to the tambo. There, all the people talked about was what this elderly leader would do next, and what would become of the Coya. That night Tlalli slept only fitfully in the animals' quarters. Tomorrow they would have to move on or risk being made to work for the Spaniards.

The following day began with more shouting and confusion outside the Tambo. The boy Tenyoa, who had helped them on the first day, appeared breathlessly in the doorway of the shed.

He yelled, 'Quick! You must come to the main square if you want to help the Coya!' and then he was gone. They wasted no time and went out into the street. They fought through the crowds to reach the square for it seemed everyone in the city was moving in the same direction. They were pushed back and Paullu hoisted Tlalli onto a wall and climbed up beside her.

Over the heads of the crowd they looked to the centre of the square and saw a raised platform, paved with stone. In the centre a tall wooden stake had been erected. A gasp of astonishment went up from the crowd as they saw their Coya, Cora Ocllo, being dragged to the stake by Canari tribesmen. These wild rough men handled her brutally, tying her to the stake. They had long whips and began to beat the Coya.

'A shame on you wicked men!' called out a woman in the crowd. 'Will no man here defend our Coya?' Before anyone could even move guards swept down on the crowd pulling the poor woman away.

Tlalli turned her head and buried her face in Paullu's chest. 'Oh, no, Paullu this is terrible. What can we do to stop them?'

For once, Paullu was unable to give her any words of comfort. 'You saw what happened to the woman. It is useless to try to prevent this terrible torture.' They could see across the square to where the leading Spaniards were viewing the spectacle of Cora Ocllo's terrible torture by the wild Canari.

Tlalli looked at her former mistress and she felt anger, pity and fear. Most of all she felt powerless and hated herself for being a coward. Cora Ocllo seemed not bowed by the blows rained upon her. She held her head up and did not flinch as the whips cut into her skin. The men with whips were replaced with others, further back. They raised bows to their shoulders and began to pelt her with arrows. The arrows entered her small, fragile body and impaled her limbs.

The crowd were almost silent, appalled and hypnotised by this dreadful public execution of their own Coya. It was then that she spoke her only words, raising her head and voice towards the watching Spaniards. She spoke her native tongue; the crowd understood and the Spanish men soon would.

'You take your anger out on a woman? Hurry up and finish me off so that you can satisfy all your desires.' Within a few minutes she slumped within her bonds and was declared dead to the crowd of onlookers.

The crowd dispersed almost in silence. Tlalli beat her fists on her chest and hot tears of anger streaked her cheeks. She was utterly destroyed by what she had witnessed, as if the Coya's death symbolised the end of the world she had always known.

They fought their way back through the crowds. Tlalli could see dismay on the faces of people around her. What frightened her even more showed in their resignation, the almost passive acceptance by the people of their fate, as if they had lost the will to stand up to the Spanish invaders. Perhaps the blood-line she carried from the fiercely independent Manari jungle tribe made her different, but she was not ready to submit to the will of these foreigners. She would continue to oppose them whatever the cost. The Spirit of the Jaguar awakened within her once again. She would continue the fight against the invaders, begun when the Jaguar first came to her. The fight had begun back in the mountains with the rebels she had led. Now she was older and wiser and ready to face her destiny.

Tlalli and Paullu scrambled back to their lodgings where they quickly threw their meagre belongings into bundles, roping them to their llama. The sentries had been diverted from patrolling the roads to help control the crowds, so they hurried out of the city, back to the path used by the shepherd boy who had helped them. They kept to the trees and shadows, hoping not to be seen by the soldiers.

When they had climbed a long way up the hillside they stopped in the lee of a high ridge to catch their breath. Tlalli's anger over the cruel execution of the Coya had not lessened. She looked down on Ollantaytambo. Up here the air was clear and full of the sweet scents of wild flowers, the hum of insects and the whirling beat of hummingbird wings, but these could not soften the hatred boiling inside her. Her need to avenge this wicked act was growing.

They looked back down to the valley. They could see Spanish soldiers moving towards the great Urubamba River. Some native Canari tribesmen went with the soldiers, carrying a litter on which lay a bamboo casket. She couldn't be sure from this distance, but the uncovered casket appeared to contain a body, so it must be the bruised and bloodied remains of Cora Ocllo. When the men reached the river they found a shallow reach and pushed the casket out with long poles into the fast-flowing current, travelling westwards, towards the Vilcabamba.

Tlalli was puzzled. 'Why are they doing this? The Spanish murderers usually burn royal Inca victims to prevent worship of the relics.'

Paullu shook his head. 'All I can think is that they want to flush Manco out. He has disappeared but is probably following the path of the river. News travels fast and they know he would want to retrieve her body.'

'Then we must stop them.' Tlalli' eyes sparked and glinted with her supressed anger and determination.

'I don't see what we can do against so many.' He did not seem to share her enthusiasm for such a hazardous task. As they viewed the scene below the soldiers turned and marched back to the city. Only the hated Canari, about eight men moving along the bank, followed the casket as it bumped its way over sunken rocks through the shallow margins of the river. Tlalli looked up into Paullu's face hoping he would see what they must do. 'Very well,' he said, giving way to her unspoken pleas. 'Maybe we can do something.' As they set off again, Tlalli's face showed her renewed determination. If they could stop the Spanish from capturing Manco Inca, it would help her deal with the dreadful execution of Cora Ocllo.

46

The Midas Touch

June 1931, Aguas Calientes, Perú.
Tonight Diego's mood is euphoric. All his planning and scheming over the past two years is coming to fruition. Before leaving Cuzco he visited the local branch of the bank. Cabello had made good on his word and Diego now has over half a million US dollars, some in Perúvian currency, stashed in his travel bag. He has to keep pinching himself to be sure he is not dreaming.

Now comes the next stage of his scheme: how to obtain even more of the investors' money in cash and spend as little as possible laying a false trail of his mining exploits. He knows he should be concentrating on this and nothing else, but the opportunity to include the gorgeous Christina Freeman in his plan is too tempting, one he must follow, and he will do so tonight.

They take supper at the guest house in the tiny village of Aguas Calientes without Lady Grace. She is still resting after her little accident today, so Christina is without her chaperone when they sit down to dine. Diego has instructed his guide, Egecati to stay with the ponies all night and ensure they are fit for the journey tomorrow. So there is only Senor Chambi here and Diego is confident he can shake this wily Indian off his tail.

Diego fills their wine glasses as the meal is served. 'Ah, my dear Christina, I hope our plans to travel to the Inca ceremony tomorrow are not in doubt?' He can't take his eyes off her. She looks ravishing in a pale blue silk dress with a long string of pearls tied in a loop at her neck and cream leather court shoes on her dainty feet. He thinks about the silk stockings she is also wearing and imagines her taking them off.

'I do hope so, Diego.' She answers his question and doesn't seem to realise how alluring she is to him. 'Grace says she will have to rest for a couple of days before she can go anywhere, even back to Cuzco. So I may as well keep to our original plan and she will wait here.'

Diego is delighted and asks, 'So do tell me why you are so anxious to see this ancient ceremony?

She pauses, as if deciding how to answer his questions and she sips a little wine. Before she can say anything she looks across the table at Martin Chambi. He appears not to be listening to either of his dining companions. His eyes are glassy and his food is untouched. Christina's face is immediately full of concern. 'Are you feeling all right, Martin?'

'My apologies, Senorita, I don't feel at all well.' He rises from his seat and seems to sway as if he is drunk. Diego jumps up and steadies him.

'I will take Senor Chambi to his room, Christina,' he says. 'Please excuse us, I will be back shortly.' Diego's heart is beating fast. He is sure no one saw him add the powder to Chambi's drink. Drugs are so easy to obtain in this country and once he gets Chambi to his bed he will sleep off the effects with wonderful dreams of his own. Diego returns to the dining room as quickly as he can. Now he has managed to get himself alone with Christina he must not waste one minute of this heaven-sent opportunity.

She is still concerned about Martin Chambi. 'Is he ill, Diego? Does he need a doctor?'

He must reassure her quickly. 'Oh, no I don't think so. He is not sick or in pain. I think he was just overtired. He went to sleep as soon as he hit the bed.'

She shakes her head looking mystified. 'How very strange, he seemed perfectly all right a few minutes ago. I hope he will have recovered by tomorrow or I'm afraid we will have to cancel our arrangements.'

Diego is quick to reassure her. 'That won't be necessary. Egecati is our official guide and you will of course have me to protect you.' He smiles but checks himself from being too familiar.

She returns the smile. 'But who will protect me from you?'

He tries to be serious. 'I do assure you that my intentions are completely honourable. I respect you too much to trifle with your affections, Christina.' This trite little speech seems to reassure her and they continue with their supper.

'There is something else I need to ask you, Diego.'

'And what is that, dear lady?' His tone is smooth as silk and he looks straight into her eyes.

She takes a deep breath and says, 'What happens when Sam gives his parties at the hacienda?'

He gives a little chuckle and wags his finger under her nose. 'Ah ha! Do I detect a note of disapproval?'

'That depends if there is anything of which to disapprove.' She sounds indignant. 'You told me the parties were for Sam's men friends. So I have concluded that Rosita and Serena are the only women present.'

'But they are servants,' he says, endeavouring to take the matter seriously.

Christina shows she certainly doesn't find it funny. 'They are also attractive women. I know what happens when a group of men are drinking together and women are present – any women.'

Diego is delighted she is finding fault with her handsome fiancé. 'Umm, Sam does give very good parties and of course everyone stays overnight,' he says, 'but that doesn't mean ...'

'There are you! I knew I was right.' She looks appalled.

'Oh, Christina, surely you are not accusing Sam of dallying with his servants?'

'Well, Rosita obviously doesn't like me and now Sam has abandoned me and hurried back to her in Brazil, so what am I supposed to think?'

'Oh dear, it certainly looks bad for the Honourable Sam.'

'So you agree with me that it looks bad?'

'My darling Christina, I always want to agree with you and never to cross you. But I cannot bear to think that Sam would be unfaithful to you. You do not deserve to be treated so cruelly.' He maintains an air of diligent concern for her feelings. She is now almost ready to be wooed away from the 'dishonourable' Sam; Christina's feelings of jealousy will drive her straight into his arms.

'I must help you to forget this unsavoury business for now and enjoy the delights of Perú.' He puts out his hand and touches her arm. 'We were talking about the Inca ceremony and why you want to see it.'

She seems ready to acquiesce to his suggestion. 'It's all to do with my dreams,' she says and her eyes seem to focus on something beyond his view.

'Your dreams? Are you being serious or do you joke with me?' He cannot quite catch her mood.

Her eyes move to look into his. 'I've never been more serious about anything.'

'Do you dream a lot?'

'Well, yes, I suppose I do. These strange dreams began when I received my jaguar pendant, the first pendant, from my Uncle who lived in Cuzco.'

'And what do you dream about?' Diego hopes his interest will win her confidence.

Now she is flustered and looks away again. 'I'm not sure I can explain this without it sounding ridiculous.'

'I am a good listener, Christina. You can tell me your deepest secrets and I will not tell another living soul.' He keeps his voice sincere and his expression earnest.

'Very well, Diego, I will tell you.' She takes a deep breath and then begins. 'I dream about a girl. She lives in a strange land, which at first, I didn't recognise. There are mountains and forests, strange sheep with long necks and wild animals. The people are very poor, walking barefoot and eating with their fingers.

Diego finds that, in spite of himself, he is interested and wants to know what else she recalls. 'Can you remember any of these dreams?'

'There have been several dreams where the wild cat appears, the jaguar. In one, the girl is trapped in a cave with the animal. In fact there are several like that, but the jaguar never attacks her.' Christina is thoughtful for a while and drinks her wine again.

'The cave is in a sacred mountain, I remember that. It was a hiding place for golden treasure, but it was also the jaguar's lair. That's why I find Egecati's legend of the jaguar so fascinating. It all ties in with my dreams. In fact now I have come here, I know the dreams speak of a life in Perú; my life, hundreds of years ago.'

Diego is very thoughtful but he sees she is convinced by her own conclusions. All the time he is working out how he can use this strange scenario to his own advantage. He is looking for a way into her heart. 'Maybe the spiritualist woman in Rio spoke the truth. What do you recall of this treasure?'

Christina is encouraged by his interest. 'From the dreams it seems that the treasure came from the Sun Temple at Cuzco. It was brought by Incas, and the girl's father was asked to hide it, which he did, in the mountain. I suppose that was to stop the Spaniards from finding it. I remember being very afraid of a man who always appeared on a big horse. He chased me, trying to capture me. Sometimes I got away but in another dream he caught me.'

Diego realises she really thinks this dream person was herself. He doesn't know whether to laugh or cry but manages to keep his façade of interest. 'What was he like, this man on the horse?'

'Well, he was dressed like a lord and I do believe he may have been one of the conquistadors.'

Now Diego can't help laughing out loud. 'Oh goodness, a wicked Spaniard disturbing your dreams; my ancestors have a lot to answer for.'

Christina seems anxious to tell him more. 'I know it all sounds quite ridiculous, but since we arrived in Perú everything is so familiar. I know I have been here before. I felt it today at Machu Picchu.' She is once more staring off into space locked in her own thoughts.

Whilst Diego is anxious to hear more, he is also very keen to get closer to Christina, away from prying eyes. As they have finished their supper he suggests they go outside and walk by the river in the moonlight. She wears her wrap and he takes her hand leading her outside and towards the banks of the Urubamba. She is a little unsteady on her feet, perhaps from the wine, but they walk, arms linked, and the night sky is a star-studded blanket of indigo blue laid across the tops of the mountains and falling all around them.

She looks up. 'This is why I'm so sure I'm right. These beautiful stars, the snow-capped mountains, and the raging river, all these feature constantly in my dreams. I cannot be mistaken.'

'Ah, you must tell me all about it. You can trust me implicitly to be your confidant.' Diego wants to know everything about her dreams, especially concerning the Inca treasure.

47

Dangerous Liaison

I don't know why I'm telling Diego all this. I feel I am baring my soul to him, but he is probably the only one who will listen to me. We have the same wild romantic streak, the same passion for adventure, although I mustn't lose sight of his devious nature. It is obvious he is in love with me so perhaps I can persuade him to tell me more about himself. If he is lying, sooner or later the truth will be revealed.

This walk in the moonlight is intimate and will test my resolve. 'Tell me what happened to your cousin Roberto.' His hand flinches in mine. I must not react so I continue speaking. 'Our meeting was just a fleeting moment but I am so sad to know he is dead.'

We stop and he turns to face me. Deep shadow under his fedora hides his face so I can't read his expression. He takes hold of my other hand and stands very close, as close as when we danced together.

'Roberto must have made a big impression for you to remember him so clearly after seven years, Christina.'

'I suppose he did,' I answer. 'It was a memorable time in my life, just before my mother and brother died of influenza.'

'Oh, the little boy with the limp.' I think he speaks without thinking.

'Yes, my brother Tom.' It is all said so quickly but I realise the implication. 'How did you know that?'

We begin to walk again and he tries to brush it aside. 'You must have told me before, or maybe Roberto told me. I don't know how I knew but it is not important.'

But of course it *is* important. Only Roberto himself could have described Tom so aptly and I have never spoken about my brother to Diego. My heart is beating fast for I feel on the brink of a dangerous discovery. I repeat my question. 'How did Roberto die?'

We stop again and he starts to speak rapidly, as if he wants to get this out of the way. 'Two years ago, we left Spain together by boat. Roberto was always gambling and he got into a fight with another passenger. It was dark and during the fight Roberto fell overboard. By the time a boat was launched to search for him, he had gone, lost under the waves of the Atlantic.'

'Oh, how dreadful.' I am truly horrified by this account and shiver thinking about it. Diego must sense my mood and puts his arm around my shoulder. His magnetism is very strong and I want to believe him. If he hadn't spoken of Tom I would just accept his explanation. Instead it has only added to my confusion about his real identity. I am fearful but summon all my courage for I cannot let this go, so I say, 'I'm not sure that I believe you.' I hear the sharp intake of breath and feel him stiffen in an animal-like defence. He is so close, fiercely grasping both my arms.

'What do you mean, you don't believe me?'

There is power and strength in his hands that would be impossible to overcome, but I am compelled to continue. 'I think that *you* are Roberto.'

My words seem to echo in the night air, floating across the river and bouncing back from the far bank. I can't see his features clearly but I can feel his body language as he reacts. It's as if he's been attacked by an unseen assailant. He seems to sag and momentarily turns away. But instantly he turns back and wraps me tightly in his arms. His mouth finds mine and he kisses me passionately, pressing close to me and moulding me into the contours of his body. I am breathless, afraid and exhilarated all at once.

He holds me locked in the caress of a wild bear and eventually he speaks. 'So, we both have secrets, like kindred spirits. Now we will have to make promises that will bind us together forever.'

'What do you mean, Diego, no ...Roberto?'

'Precisely, my darling. I cannot allow you to know this or to tell anyone else my secret. It is, after all, a matter of life and death – for me and now for you.'

'What are you saying? I don't understand.' I am like a tightly budded flower. I know he has the power to make me bloom or to grind me under his heel.

'It is quite simple, my darling, you have nothing to fear.' His voice is smooth and persuasive. His hands stroke my arms where his fingers gripped me just a moment ago. 'A fortune awaits us: gold, silver and precious stones, and I have over a million dollars at my disposal with which to obtain these riches.'

His hands move to my face and he traces his fingers across my cheeks, gently massaging behind my ears and through my hair; a soothing gesture which stimulates my emotions. 'You know I love you and we can share this fortune, Christina. You and I can be lovers with riches beyond our wildest dreams.' His arm slips around my waist and he pulls me towards him. I am hypnotised and have no strength or will to resist. His kiss is soft and then it is passionate. I cannot think clearly to put even two words together let alone protest.

Is he really Roberto? His eyes light up with renewed enthusiasm, emboldened I am sure, by my silence. 'Imagine, Christina, my mine, my mountain, could be the same Yaguar Mountain where the Inca's treasure was hidden. It could still be there! Waiting for you, waiting for us to find it! Didn't the old woman tell you so? Didn't you see this in your dreams?'

My head nods and my heart says, yes, yes, yes! I know he is crazy. I know he is dangerous. I know he is Roberto, and because of this I know I love him. I cannot help myself for I have always loved him. Caution, good sense, upbringing and commitment have flown away. I am powerless, in the grip of a deep emotional longing to be with this man, whatever the consequences. It is like another dream but I know this time it is real and I will go with him.

We turn away from the fast flowing river and the dreamy night sky returning to the guest house. On the way he tells me what we will do. I am to pack my smallest bag and be ready to leave at first light. We will go with Egecati to see the Inti Raymi ceremony, just the three of us. He assures me that Grace and Martin will not be awake at that hour; besides it was arranged for us to go so they will not be alarmed. The only change in the arrangement is that I will not return. I will travel on with Roberto and Egecati to find the Yaguar Mountain.

Roberto! I have no words to say how happy I am now that I know it is him and he is alive. All my doubts surrounding this man have vanished. My confidence in him allows me to tell him about the manuscript Uncle Peter was translating: Tlalli's testament, including the account of Manco Inca's treasure entombed in the Yaguar Mountain.

'But it might not be the same mountain,' I caution. 'Egecati says the old names were used locally and could have been reused many times for other mountains.'

He laughs, 'Christina, you are forgetting something else you were told. The spirit of the jaguar will guide you! That is why we must go together on this journey. It is our destiny!'

Now I see it. Oh, so clearly! My whole life has been a preparation for this moment. No matter how outrageous my actions, or however much I may be condemned by others, I must follow the Spirit of the Jaguar.

When we say goodnight on the landing outside my bedroom door he whispers, 'There is just one thing I ask of you, Christina.' At this moment, I would agree to almost anything. 'To the rest of the world I must remain Diego Alvarez. No one must ever know I am Roberto. Promise me you will keep my secret.'

I do not hesitate. 'Of course, I will never tell.' I believe I understand the need for this. All his documents would be void if his real name were revealed. Yet in my heart I know that is not the only reason. The words of the spiritualist woman flash into my mind. *He has blood on his hands.* I push the thought away. I don't want to think about anything that will degrade the man or this moment. For I am drunk on euphoria and want it to last, to buoy me up for what is yet to come.

48

The Casket

1539, Vilcabamba, Perú

Tlalli and Paullu continued to climb the hills surrounding the city until they were clear of the most used paths. Tlalli constantly looked to the river to keep the casket in view.

'We should split up. I can stay near the river following the casket and you go ahead with the llama. See if you can discover Manco's whereabouts.' She was determined to follow her plan so they shared out their food supply and Tlalli tied her bundle on her back.

'Follow the casket but stay under cover,' cautioned Paullu. 'I will see what I can discover. You must try and reach the place where the Urubamba and the Vilcabamba rivers come together. Manco will probably have made for the area around Vitcos, where the jungle will slow his pursuers down. That's no more than two or three days from here.' Paullu held her close. 'Take care, my love.' He kissed her then he let her go.

'I will wait for you where the rivers meet, Paullu. If I miss you there I will go on to Vitcos,' said Tlalli. She watched Paullu hurry away taking the high track.

Tlalli picked her way down to where the river flowed away from Ollantaytambo towards the west. She hid in deep cover, above the bank of the river, keeping the casket in sight, not following too close. Now she could see that the casket was in fact a small bamboo boat; a coracle like the ones used by fishermen. There was no sign of the terrible men who set it adrift and she didn't want to alert them to her presence. But when the casket became entangled in tree roots on the other side of the river, two men suddenly appeared from the bushes, and pushed it back out into the flow of the current; so she knew they still followed the casket.

Tlalli waited a long time before resuming her vigil. The Canari posed a greater threat than the Spaniards. These natives knew the landscape and could easily track her down. That night, hidden up in the branches of a tree, Tlalli undid her bundle and curled the blanket round her shoulders. She chewed the chunk of bread she had shared with Paullu and, when she felt it was safe, she climbed down and scooped water from the river drinking from her hand.

The moon rose, shedding a pale eerie light on the surface of the water. The casket had once more become snagged near the bank, this time on her side of the river. So far no one had come to send it on its way. She had an idea. One that might discourage the Canari followers from tracking the casket, but she knew she would have to be quick before they appeared again.

She had no time to think, for once the idea had taken root she knew she must follow her instinct. She quickly wrapped her belongings in the thin blanket and waded down into the cold water. Holding the bundle above her head she edged noiselessly along through the shallows to where the casket had caught up some distance from the bank. The men would have to wade out to release it from under the tree's branches.

As she reached the casket she grasped the bamboo sides and lifted her head peering inside. It rocked up and down, but there was indeed a body, dumped without ceremony and left uncovered. Tlalli tossed her bundle inside and mustering all her strength heaved her body up over the side and rolled into the little boat.

She lay flat and listened. She could hear the lap of the water sloshing against the sides and her own heavy breathing but nothing else. Low branches trailing in the water from a huge acacia tree had trapped the boat preventing it from moving. The presence of the Coya's body overwhelmed her senses. The smell of death filled her nostrils. In the moon's light she could see the bloodied wounds inflicted on the Coya's body but her face was unscathed and she still looked beautiful. There was little dignity in this terrible ending for Cora Ocllo. Fighting back her tears Tlalli pulled out her thin blanket and covered her mistress's remains to keep the flies away.

She needed to free the trapped boat, and was bracing herself to sit up, when she heard voices from the direction of the river bank. Tlalli flung herself flat down in the boat, partly over the body of her former mistress. Her wildly beating heart sounded so loud in her ears she felt sure the men would hear her from the river bank. There came a thud on the side of the boat and it rocked as a pole began pushing it. It came again, long poles pushing and shoving at the little vessel, and the voices of the men on the bank seemed closer as they waded in close and fought to push the casket back into the river. Tlalli lay still, clasping her jaguar talisman and wishing she was still hidden on the bank. The little boat twisted to and fro with agitated motion and then it began to move out into the river. Once it was free of the tree branches and floating again, Tlalli felt brave enough to put the rest of her plan into action.

She trembled as she forced herself upright, and began waving her arms over her head. Cries of dismay came from the men on the shore; shouts, wails and shrieks of alarm. Tlalli looked back at their shadows moving in the moon's light, emitting frightened cries and pointing towards the casket. While she continued to wave her arms she let out a howl, which she hoped they would think came from the ghost of the Coya. Her likeness to Cora Ocllo seemed to have convinced the startled, superstitious tribesmen that the spirit of the Coya had come to bewitch them. Soon the little boat floated too far away for her to see the men or hear their anguished cries. Tlalli's heart beat fast, but she felt nothing but relief. The plan seemed to have worked and she fervently hoped the superstitious Canari men would now be too afraid to follow the casket.

49

Two Rivers

Tlalli steered the little bamboo casket as best she could with her hands, trying to keep to the centre of the river and avoid the numerous rocks and minor rapids. She felt re-energised for she had achieved something good in her vendetta against the Spanish. Once again the jaguar goddess Izella seemed to be by her side.

As the moon paled in the sky, dawn broke and she lost the cover of darkness. The river left the open hills behind as the landscape changed. She travelled on and on through endless landscapes. At times the river wound through dark jungle and forests where she caught glimpses of giant otters and river dolphins.

When the altitude changed again, the land opened up once more into rolling hills and valleys with the rugged mountains seemingly on all sides. Wide rapids appeared, when she had to beach the boat and drag it down the steep rocky sides and then slip it back into the fast flowing current, using long sticks to guide it back to a safer passage. Towards evening, as the light began to fade, she passed the point of exhaustion from lack of food and she just wanted to lie down and sleep.

The river grew wider and Tlalli could see the approach of the confluence with the Vilcabamba River. She looked for any sign of Paullu. If he waited there he would call to her, for the boat would be visible from the shore, but she heard nothing and he didn't appear.

Disappointed, she steered away from the Urubamba into the Vilcabamba, travelling west. The forest grew thicker, the trees more numerous on both banks. In places they almost touched, arching over the water creating cool dark tunnels. The familiar sounds of jungle life filled the air and she steered the boat into the side where it was flat and muddy. Tiredness overcame her and worry over not finding Paullu. She lay down next to the body of her former mistress and slept.

Early morning bird calls awakened her with a start. Her thoughts were a whirl of confusion until she remembered everything that had happened. She rubbed her eyes to wake up. All her senses returned to full alert. Had she been followed by the fearsome Canari who had murdered Cora Ocllo? Where was Paullu? She needed food and fresh water so she jumped out into the mud and hauled the casket nearer the shore scrambling onto the river bank.

This area was not far from her homeland although she had rarely ventured to this low level where the river ran deep in the dark canyons of the Vilcabamba. Her family had lived at a higher altitude. The four quarters of their world came together in this place, one on top of another. At the top were the high mountain peaks sometimes capped with snow; beneath these were the foothills and farming terraces, where the local tribes lived and the cloud forests which provided them with plants and game, flourished. Below this, the steep canyons, carved out by the fast flowing rivers, were filled with the dark humid jungle.

Tlalli searched around for what she needed. She gathered some more stout sticks that she could use to steer the boat and some berries she knew would be good to eat. She found fresh water collecting in big broad leaves under the trees and drank as much as she could. Then she returned to where she had left the little boat.

She knew immediately something had changed for the boat had moved from where she had left it. She watched, almost paralysed, as it moved, invisibly pulled towards the water. Her hands automatically grasped at her talisman as her eyes clamped on the shape of a huge crocodile dragging the boat into the river.

Tlalli gasped aloud, shouting with fear and anger at the beast. 'No! You shall not have her!' She squelched on to the mud and grasped hold of the back of the boat, trying to pull against the strength of the crocodile's jaws. As if from nowhere Tlalli felt a rush of air go straight past her and she heard a mighty roar. A streak of gold and black brushed so close she was knocked off her feet into the mud. In a second she was up scrambling back to the safety of the bank. But in the shallows of the muddy river a terrible battle had begun between the crocodile and a jaguar!

Both animals fought with a speed and agility Tlalli could barely follow. She saw them move out into the water as the jaguar leapt on top of the thrashing crocodile, fixing its strong jaws into the back of the reptile's head.

'No! She cried aloud, seeing the crocodile open its huge mouth trying to grasp hold of any part of the jaguar it could, thrashing and twisting to dislodge the cat from its back. Tlalli put her hands over her face in despair. Then, daring to look through her finger, she saw the jaguar's quick movements as it clamped its claws tight, holding the crocodile fast. The jaguar sank its sharp teeth through the reptile's thick skin and crushed right through to the bone with its powerful jaws, severing the creature's spinal cord.

Tlalli's mind whirled in a daze of disbelief. The crocodile's body was being dragged onto the far bank of the river by the victor. But could this be her jaguar? No, it was far too big; a full-grown male. Would it turn on her and attack? While it was still engrossed with the kill she slipped from the bank and retrieved the casket. The smell of death from the Coya's corpse filled the air. Maybe both animals had been drawn to the casket because of this. She dragged the casket through the mud away from the scene of death and pushed it back into the flow of the river, heaving herself on board. Using the sticks she punted the little boat away from the scene. She was still trembling from what she had just witnessed knowing there could have been a different outcome ending in her own death. Instinctively her hand found her talisman, and she remembered Paullu now wore the other: Izella and the male jaguar god Toquri. Had Paullu's faith now awakened him also?

The appearance of the male jaguar had certainly saved her life, but it had also reopened the yearning in her heart to return to her home and discover if the jaguars still lived in the mountain. First she had to fulfil her obligation to Cora Ocllo and return her remains to Manco Inca. To be sure of completing her task she had to find Paullu. She struggled to keep the casket moving forward to the deeper currents, while constantly scanning the banks, afraid of missing the meeting place and her chance of finding him. She travelled on for several hours, and as darkness fell, once more she punted the casket towards the bank on the south side of the river. The ancient Inca settlement of Vitcos was near this part of the river. Paullu had named this as a possible retreat for Manco, provided the Spanish had not reached it already.

Tlalli secured the boat using vines and branches and set off again to find food. The forest reached right down to the water's edge. Night had crept upon her quickly, making it too dark to find anything. She returned to the boat empty-handed and dejected. She sensed danger all around her. Wild animals and venomous snakes and spiders inhabited these parts. If the Spanish soldiers, or worse still Canari warriors, had reached this far she would not be able to defend herself.

There came a sharp cracking sound nearby instantly alerting her to danger. With no time to release the boat and reach the safety of the river, she quickly hid behind a large tree, holding her breath. Three shadows moved towards the river from the forest, their feet snapping twigs in the thick undergrowth.

'It is too dark to find anything now,' said a voice. 'We will come back at first light.' Tlalli chilled at the unfamiliar tone.

'Wait, I am sure I saw her on the river just before dark. I know she will wait somewhere near here.'

Tlalli felt the surging joy of recognition and relief. 'Paullu, Paullu!' she called out and she ran towards the dark shape of the man who had spoken and threw herself into his arms. A third voice gave a deep throaty laugh which she also recognised. 'Father, is that you?'

'Yes, my child, I am here also.'

Tlalli moved towards him and they embraced. But her joy was quickly tempered. The third man, whom she did not know, now spoke. 'We must hurry from this place for the Spanish spies are everywhere looking for our Lord Inca.'

Tlalli said, 'I have brought the Coya's body. We must take her to him now.'

'Paullu has told us of this terrible act by the invaders and the wretched Canari enemies,' said Kusi. 'You have been very brave, Tlalli, to bring her body so far. Come, we will return to Vitcos and take the Coya to her family.'

The men hoisted the casket onto their shoulders and led the way back through the dark forest. Tlalli followed behind Paullu holding on to his tunic. In spite of being so very weary she walked lightly, overjoyed by their reunion, and with her dear father. As they drew near to Vitcos her fears resurfaced; what would happen to her when she again came before Manco, the Sapa Inca?

50

Keep Her Close

June 1931, Vilcabamba, Perú

He lies awake searching his mind. In the end it was so easy, almost too easy. Christina fell so easily into his trap. He muses that women are such strange unpredictable creatures. It had only happened when she discovered he was Roberto. He would never have guessed this would be the key to unlocking her heart; a discovery made quite by accident.

He hadn't wanted anyone to know his dark secret, his real identity. Such knowledge could be very dangerous, but it has worked to his advantage. Now he must keep her close and be sure his past is never revealed. That will be a pleasure. Keeping her close is exactly what he has wanted since the moment he first saw her on the airship. Now she has remembered their encounter on the ferry boat several years ago. The impressionable child had kept his youthful image in her heart and this has driven her straight to him. Luck has always been his lady; luck and his magnetic personality.

He wanted to bring her to his bed last night but that would have ruined his plans. It is a matter of deep regret that it has been necessary to deny himself the exquisite pleasure of making love to her. But the time for chastity is nearly over. He needs her to break off the engagement with Sam Watson and to stay with him forever. For this to be accomplished he must not make one wrong move.

He contemplates her wealth. With her father's fortune and now her uncle's properties and investments she is exceedingly rich. All he has are the deeds to several mines of unknown value. But now, because of his intelligent scheming, he has amassed over half a million US dollars in cash and there is a lot more to be had. Once he can persuade Christina to stay with him and leave her old life behind her, they can go anywhere in the world and they will be rich, rich, rich!

Diego gives up trying to sleep and relights the oil lamp, casting strange shadows around the room. He still has most of the money he acquired in Rio and Lima, plus the additional large sum from the bank in Cuzco. He wraps this in his spare clothing, packing it at the bottom of his bag. He repacks all his belongings on top and dresses in his riding habit. He must look the part and maintain his debonair appearance. His other luggage is still at the hotel in Cuzco. It will be no great loss if he is not able to collect it. His documents and the money are all that matter now.

He slips quietly down the staircase and goes outside. It is still dark but traces of light in the east show the dawn is not far off. He goes round the stone built house to the stables. The Indian guide Egecati is lying across the doorway his hat tipped over his eyes. He stands up as Diego approaches and addresses him in Spanish. 'Good morning, Senor. You are awake early.'

'We will start early today. There will only be myself and Senorita Freeman going on this trip. So please get the horses ready for us.'

The Indian raises his brows slightly but says nothing. Diego is confident the man knows his place and will ignore anything he may witness. Chambi of course, would be different, but Diego hopes he will not wake up until long after they are gone and Lady Grace will not be in a position to go anywhere thanks to her little accident yesterday. Lady luck was with him again when that happened.

Diego returns to the house and goes to the kitchen. The owner's wife is there preparing fruit and vegetables and making bread for the day ahead. Diego asks for provisions to be packed for their journey and an early breakfast for two. She bangs about in her kitchen but he knows his orders will be followed. These people are so pliable and can be bought for a few soles.

He is about to go back upstairs when he sees Christina coming down. She carries a travel bag and is dressed in her safari style suit and wears a small brimmed hat. He thinks she looks divine and he rushes to take the bag from her. 'Oh, does this mean you are ready to go with me. You have not changed your mind?'

'No, I have not changed my mind. In fact my mind is quite set against Sam now. I feel he has treated me quite shabbily.' Her face is a mix of hurt and anger but then she beams a beautiful smile at him. 'Besides, Roberto, I know now that you are my true love and always have been.' She comes close to him and kisses his cheek.

He is flattered but also a little alarmed and looks around checking they have not been overheard. 'You are so very sweet, my dear, but please, we must be discreet, at least until we are able to be quite alone. Please, I beg you, call me Diego. That way we will not have to make explanations to others. Let it remain our little secret.'

He returns her kiss but on her lips and reminds himself how very important this secret is. Roberto is a wanted man. Of course, even as Diego he is not without stain; there is the question of embezzlement in several countries and the theft of a rare Perúvian artefact in Rio. He had paid the jeweller three hundred American dollars to turn a blind eye, but nevertheless it was still theft.

He brushes these thoughts aside, for they are thousands of miles from where these crimes occurred, and he takes her hand, 'Now we will have some breakfast and start on our journey.' They move into the little dining room and the manager's wife serves them with fruit and corn-bread.

'Have you told Lady Grace anything of our conversation, my dear?' Diego is anxious about her companion's reaction to Christina's change of plan.

'She is still asleep so I have left her a note. But she knew we were going today.' Christina seems almost matter-of-fact about their imminent departure. 'I said not to worry if we are away overnight as we don't know how far we will travel to see the ceremony.' She smiles at him. 'That is all I said.'

Diego tries to remain calm. 'Good,' he says, 'no point in her raising the alarm when we don't return.'

Christina looks quite determined. 'There is no reason for her to raise the alarm at all. I'm fully entitled to change my mind about anything if I want to.' She sighs. 'She is of course entitled to an explanation, as is Sam.'

'Of course, of course.' Diego is more delighted with every word she utters.

'I will telephone or telegraph her when we arrive at our destination, wherever that may be.'

Diego says nothing. He does not imagine there will be any telephones or telegraph stations where they are going. By then, Christina will be totally smitten and he will be able to control their future, so it is best he says nothing to make her apprehensive. He thinks perhaps Ecuador or Mexico may offer him refuge from prosecution, so the sooner they begin their journey, the better.

51

Manco Inca

1539 Vitcos, Vilcabamba, Perú

The journey through the forest in the dark seemed endless. The stranger, who knew the area well, led the way to the temporary court set up for Manco Inca among the ruined Inca buildings, burned by the Spanish in the earlier battle. Inca guards surrounding the hill-top settlement allowed the Coya's escorts to enter.

Kusi led them into the chamber where Manco Inca sat on a low stool. They laid the casket at his feet and retreated to allow him privacy with his Coya's remains. Tlalli closed her eyes listening to Manco's cries of grief and despair. She knew that he and Cora Ocllo had been inseparable since childhood, for they were also brother and sister. Her own grief for Ispaca still cut deeply.

Manco and Cora Ocllo's Royal Inca blood had dictated they would marry, thereby assuring the purity of their bloodline. Cora Ocllo had died when only nineteen years old, but she had given birth to Manco's sons, three young boys who were safe in their father's court. Tlalli clenched her hands in despair witnessing Manco's pain at the loss of his young Coya.

Eventually Manco called for the embalmers to take his Coya away and prepare her for an Inca funeral. Kusi then brought Tlalli and Paullu for an audience with the Inca. Tlalli knelt behind Paullu for she feared she would have to return to the court to serve as a holy Aclla.

The Inca asked what had happened at Ollantaytambo and how his Coya had died. Paullu related their story without dwelling on Cora Ocllo's harrowing ordeal at the hands of the Spaniards and the Canari warriors.

'As we left the city we saw the casket being floated into the river,' said Paullu. 'It seemed this was meant to be a trap to find you, my lord Inca, so Tlalli wanted to follow the casket while I sought your whereabouts to warn you.' He turned, revealing her presence to the Inca.

The Manco looked at Tlalli. 'Are you the same Tlalli Manari brought before my court and renamed Inguill by the Coya?'

Tlalli kept her eyes fixed on the ground as she replied in a hoarse whisper. 'Yes, my lord Inca.'

'And how did you escape being captured by the spies sent to follow the casket, and be able to bring my beloved to me?' The Inca did not seem angry only curious.

'I climbed into the casket with my lady Coya.' Tlalli shuddered as she spoke directly to this god-like man. 'I think the men saw me in the casket and thought I was the Coya's spirit for they seemed very frightened and ran away.' Silence fell on the court and Tlalli feared she had angered the Inca in some way. Then he began to laugh, softly at first, and then quite loudly. All the men assembled in the court joined in and laughed with him.

'Well done, Tlalli Manari. Yes, you do resemble the Coya,' said Manco. 'Your action has probably saved us all.' He instructed her to look at him and Tlalli saw that he was smiling. 'Now, we must see that you are suitably rewarded, Tlalli Manari. What can I give you?'

Tlalli felt stunned and didn't know how to respond. She looked towards her father for guidance. Kusi took Tlalli to one side. 'Ask for your freedom, daughter.' Tlalli's spirits rose. She had lived in fear of being returned to the Inca's service and losing any possibility of a life outside the court. If this offered her a chance of freedom, she must take it.

Tlalli knelt before the Inca once again and steadied her nerves by looking at the floor. 'All I ask is that I may be released from my duty to the court and allowed to return to my home as a free woman.' For the second time her words met silence and she again feared the Inca's displeasure. Eventually he spoke, addressing the whole court.

'It is seven years since these strangers came to our land. During this time I have been guilty of making bad judgements.' He looked around at mutterings of dissension. 'Oh, yes, even me. I trusted these men with their serpent tongues, not once, but many times. I was the leader of a great nation, an empire, entrusted to me by my forefathers.' Manco looked down. His voice grew sad and his voice broke with emotion. 'And now it is all but gone and my dearest Cora Ocllo, my sister, my Coya and mother of my children, has been murdered by these wretched people.

'I have no need of any more Acllas. There are sufficient women still in this court to meet our needs. I give you your freedom, Tlalli Manari. You have earned it with your selfless devotion to the Coya. Now tell me, what will you do with your freedom?'

Tlalli's joy brimmed over and she wanted the Inca to know what was in her heart. 'I will return to the land of my tribe, Lord Inca. Our people have been abused and enslaved by the Spanish for too long. I want to inspire them to fight back. We must recover our homes and our old way of life. I will spread the word that the tribes must work against the Spanish not with them.'

Tlalli felt this was the right time to tell the court about the rebels. 'My lord Inca, we have already begun this work.' She held out her hand to Paullu and he joined her, kneeling before Manco. 'I have long been inspired by dreams and visions of the ancient jaguar gods, Toquri and Izella. Since we left Calca, Paullu and I travelled with other, like minded folk, all true to you, Lord Inca. We found the ancient Sacred City built by

229

your forefather, Patchahuti. A ruined citadel on a mountain top near Ollantaytambo.'

Manco's eyes lit up with interest but he said nothing so she continued. 'From there we began our rebel movement and call it 'The Spirit of the Jaguar.' We have been responsible for many acts of rebellion against the enemy. We have killed many Spanish enemies, on the roads and in homes they built on land stolen from your people. We have set many slaves free and taken them into our movement. The work is being continued by them, even as we speak.' The whole court had fallen silent, waiting to know the Inca's reaction and wanting to hear more.

'Now we want to return to our own villages in what was once the Willkapampa and continue the work we have begun.'

She looked up and found Manco Inca was smiling and nodding his head. 'Well said, Tlalli Manari. You are an inspiration to us all. I had heard of the Jaguar warriors in the mountains but did not know if it was true.' He waved his arms around encompassing everyone in the court. 'I have decided I will move this court back into the jungle, to the old city of Willkapampa. I will take my three dear sons, and we will defend ourselves there against the Spanish aggressors.' He turned his face to Tlalli again. 'Go, Tlalli, and may your words encourage my people to continue with the rebellion. Your spirit is true, and may the Jaguar gods guide you and keep you safe.'

Tlalli rose and walked backwards out of the court. Paullu and Kusi followed her. Once beyond the hearing of the court, Tlalli and Paullu clung to each other; Paullu was ecstatic. 'You are a free woman, dear Tlalli.' He turned to Kusi. 'Sir, I have long loved your daughter and ask your permission for us to marry.'

Kusi's weather-beaten face looked resigned. 'Here I was, thinking I had got my daughter back, only to have her snatched from me once again!' Then his features erupted into a broad grin and deep rumbling laughter. 'And now I have a rebel daughter also. I always knew you were a special child and now I recognise this was your destiny.' Kusi embraced Paullu also. 'I salute you both. You are an inspiration to us all.'

Tlalli embraced her father once more. 'We will go home first, father, and see what remains of our village,' said Tlalli as they walked down to where they could eat and rest for the night.

Kusi became serious once more. 'Home, yes indeed, if it still remains and is free of Spaniards. Perhaps some of our family are still there. I will stay with Manco for now. Perhaps we could still mobilise more warriors to help the Inca make a last stand.'

Tlalli held her father's hands. 'Yes, father. You must stay and protect the Inca. But Paullu and I want to help our people to recover their land and to find our old way of life.'

'You are wise, Tlalli, but I'm not sure that will ever be possible.' Kusi suddenly looked very old and tired. 'Go with Paullu. Marry with my blessing. I will join you when I can.'

Tlalli and Paullu left Kusi to make his own plans with the Inca. 'What else do you want to do when we return home?' said Paullu.

Tlalli knew immediately. 'I want to go to Mount Yaguar and find the sacred jaguar family again.' And her eyes shone with love and hope.

'And the Inca's gold?' asked Paullu.

She did not answer him, but in her heart she knew the priceless treasures would always remain in the mountain, protected by the Spirit of the Jaguars.

52

Inti Raymi

June 1931, Vilcabamba, Perú

Egecati walks in front leading an old grey mule which sags and sways under a heavy load. Diego is astride the black stallion. I ride Juana having grown quite attached to this trustworthy little mare. Our guide sets a brisk pace as we follow the trail from Aguas Calientes, still within sight and sound of the Urubamba River.

I am determined not to feel guilty about my actions. I haven't disclosed to Roberto that Grace is still officially my guardian, but she has always allowed me to make my own decisions. I can't bear to think Sam has not been truthful with me about Rosita. If that is the case, I will have just cause to break off our engagement. Surely that will justify my transferring my affections to another man?

Today is fine, no clouds cloak the rising sun. Roberto keeps beside me where the trail allows. The ponies kick up the dust as we pass round the foothills of Machu Picchu. It gets hotter and I am thankful when we reach a village called Santa Teresa. We stop to rest beside a pool in the shade of tall trees and allow the ponies to drink and graze.

I fall into thinking about what I have learned from reading Tlalli's testament. Her life became so challenging, physically fighting with her rebel band against the Spanish. Her actions following the execution of the Coya show she was so brave and devoted to her cause. I feel very humble knowing I am not at all like her. I want to be, but at this moment I feel swept along in an emotional wind towards an unknown destination. I hope the spirits of her gods will lead me and keep me safe – perhaps from my own impetuousness.

Egecati and Roberto discuss our route then we strikes off on a new path taking a different direction. This is also an old Inca trail but it is not as broad as the one we have left and in places it disappears altogether. We have also left the river behind and seem to be entering a landscape of narrow valleys and high mountains, totally devoid of human habitation. My back aches and my blouse is damp with perspiration and it is not yet noon.

Egecati stops by a rocky outcrop on a hillside which affords a little shade. 'Thank goodness,' I say slipping from the saddle. 'How much further, Egecati?'

He hands out fruits from the mule's saddlebag. 'A little way to go,' he replies. 'We will be guided to the ceremony by scouts, so do not be alarmed when they come for us.'

Roberto asks him, 'Why would we be alarmed if they are expecting us?' Egecati just shrugs his shoulders and does not answer his question. We travel on for what seems like miles, crossing wide valleys and high ridges. I look back and realise we have climbed much higher, where it is cooler, and we are closer to the mountains.

As we cross another valley Egecati stops and points ahead. On the ridge which marks the top of the rise three men have appeared. They are a chilling sight; silent and carrying spears. Egecati gives them a sign and we continue slowly up towards them. Now I can see they are dressed in deep red and white costumes with feathers and beads plaited into their hair. Faces and arms are painted with patterns. It is how I imagined the mountain Indians would dress for ceremonial occasions. But Roberto is alarmed and shouts to Egecati to ask why they are armed.

Egecati says, 'They are the lookouts and have to be prepared for trouble. I did warn you, Senor.'

Roberto rides close to me. He pulls back his jacket revealing he carries a small revolver in a breast holster. 'Don't worry, Christina,' he says, 'I will look after you.'

'I'm sure you won't need that,' I say, but now I am worried that his hot Spanish temperament might lead us into trouble.

Egecati converses with the men and they lead us along the top of the high ridge. We have left the grassy savannahs and the path is all granite outcrops twisting and turning towards the mountain heights. The men lead us through a narrow passage, a gorge, where the sides brush close to our feet and the granite walls tower over our heads. It is like the neck of a bottle and when we emerge we look down the mountainside to a flat area like an amphitheatre.

This place has been carved and hewn by men with steps cut into the rock leading down to an arena. In the centre is what I can only describe as a throne made of huge flat stones. The surrounding granite has been carved smooth to form straight walls at the back and sides. Beside the throne is a pit in which burns a fire. The fourth side is open and faces south towards the sun.

The arena is full of people. There must be fifty men all dressed similarly to the scouts who brought us here. They have led us to the side where we can sit and look down. The ceremony is apparently in progress as Indians are chanting and raising their arms towards the sun which is now high in the sky. The men process around the arena and one man is carried in a litter by attendants. He is splendidly dressed in gold garments and on his head is a tall head-dress with a woven tapestry circlet, plume feathers and strings of beads. He holds a golden mask on a long stick handle in front of his face. He steps from the litter to the stone throne.

I have witnessed a similar scene in my dreams. I feel elated, almost delirious, recalling the magic of this spectacle through Tlalli's eyes. The man on the throne is the Sapa Inca, their King. He directs the mask towards the sun and it reflects sunbeams towards the people bowing down before him. To them, the Sapa Inca is the manifestation of the Sun God Inti, and he is shining his light on his people. Who could not be enthralled and spellbound by this act of faith? These Indians, who live in Perú today, are re-enacting this ancient festival to keep their old religion alive and I applaud their courage.

During the afternoon the chanting continues, becoming softer and quieter until it ceases completely. Now food and drink is brought out. Some is consumed and some is thrown into the fire as a sacrifice to Inti. There doesn't appear to be any representation of the ancestors here. Perhaps there are none left to display

Roberto whispers to me, 'I hope they don't want to make human sacrifices.' I stare at him but his eyes are mocking and I guess he is trying to joke with me.

Egecati hears him and shakes his head. 'Inti does not require blood of man, but if you betray them, these men will not hesitate to kill you.'

I feel I must put an end to this before there can be any trouble over our visit. 'Here is the money, Egecati,' I say, handing him the amount requested in a pouch. 'Please thank these people for allowing our visit and tell them we will not betray them to the police.'

Egecati takes the pouch and goes down to the Indians in the arena. He speaks with the man on the throne who looks up and hails us to come to him. I am surprised when he shakes my hand and Roberto's also. It is difficult to realise these people are not part of an ancient tribe, but modern Perúvians. Egecati interprets as the man thanks me for the money and wishes us a good journey.

Roberto says, 'Ask this fellow if he knows the location of the Yaguar Mountain.' Egecati speaks to them, but not in Spanish; he converses in the local language which is Quechua. A debate begins between some of the Indians but eventually amidst arm waving and pointing they seem to agree and give Egecati an answer. We take our leave of these people and are given food from their feast, bottles of drink and coca leaves. I am relieved for it shows they accept our word not to cause them trouble.

They take us back through the pass and up onto the high ridge. The escorts give us more directions, pointing up into the mountain range ahead of us. As we resume our journey Egecati tells us we are in the heart of the old Vilcabamba which became the Incas' retreat from the Spanish after their failed rebellion.

The task of finding one mountain in this vast range where there seem to be hundreds of peaks looks daunting. I remember the brothers' quest to find the golden mountain in The Legend of the Jaguar, both from my dreams and through Egecati's retelling, and how their dream ended in disaster. Now we are the treasure-seekers and I shudder, thinking what we might find.

53

The Homecoming

1539 Vitcos, Vilcabamba, Perú

After all the days of fear and hunger Tlalli slept well. As the dawn broke over the mountain pass and the old fortress of Vitcos, daylight filtered down through the forest illuminating the river below. She awoke, remembering that her duty to the Coya had come to an end. She had been made a free woman and could now marry Paullu, the only man she had ever loved. She had wanted this for so long, and yet she was restless. She could feel the call to fulfil a destiny far beyond being a wife and mother; there were other promises she must keep. She hoped she could do both, and not have to choose between them.

As Tlalli and Paullu made ready to leave, the Inca's court once again prepared to move. Reports of more enemy sightings close by had hardened Manco's decision to return to the old city of Willkapampa. Tlalli knew this place offered better defence for the beleaguered Inca and his remaining followers; it was deeper in the jungle and less accessible by the Spanish soldiers on horseback.

Kusi bade goodbye to his daughter for he would stay and continue to uphold the Inca's defences. 'Take good care of my daughter, Paullu,' he said. 'It is my greatest wish that you should marry and continue the Manari line for our tribe. I do not know what lies ahead for me.' Tlalli could see the sadness in her father's eyes yet she knew he would always put duty first. 'I was born a warrior and must continue this fight against the usurpers.'

Paullu removed Ispaca's jaguar talisman and offered it to Kusi. But the old man shook his head. 'You are my son now, Paullu. You and Tlalli will need the protection of the Jaguar gods. Wear it always and may you both be protected. Ispaca would have wanted you to have it.'

Tlalli's fought back her tears but she understood Kusi's reasons for staying with the Inca. Neither spoke. They embraced fiercely and then parted. Her thoughts were of her brother killed by the Spaniards. She knew her father would not rest until his son's death had been fully avenged and in her heart neither would she.

They took what provisions they could carry and set off on foot. With the enemy close by, the journey would be fraught with danger. The greatest threat came from the Canari tribesmen. Paullu guided them away from the river and jungle areas, up through the mist-covered cloud forests and towards the high plateau, so disliked by the jungle warriors. It took all day and they stopped frequently, listening and waiting, before moving on again. Only when the hilltop at last levelled out did they feel safe. Paullu had grown up with the high pastures. He could spot a llama a mile away and his keen eyes scanned the area as they moved on.

He set a fast pace, staying below the skyline to minimise their visibility. Tlalli struggled, sometimes running to keep up. As they journeyed, thoughts of home chafed at her, for she knew their lives could never be as in the past. As the birds fly, their village was not very far, but to reach it they would have to go across country, up mountain trails, down and across ravines and rivers. Old Inca roads cut into the mountain sides but they avoided these as the most likely route for Spanish or native auxiliary troops on the move.

Towards the end of the first day Paullu found a rocky outcrop on a high hillside. 'We can stop here for the night,' he said, 'but we can't risk a fire.' It was a sheltered spot and they could camp in the cover of overhanging rocks and have a clear view of the valley below. On the far side, the foothills of another mountain rose. Further on more mountains appeared, their peaks vying for space in the sky like jostling giants.

Paullu shaded his eyes against the setting sun. 'There is a road on the other side of this valley,' he said. Tlalli's eyes searched the far hillside. They both saw the movement at the same time. The unmistakable flutter of flying pennants displayed from Spanish lances and the glint of metal from their armour came into view in a long snaking line. They were a long way off and travelling in the opposite direction but neither of them moved a muscle until they could no longer see the troop.

'It is good Manco and Kusi have moved from Vitcos,' said Paullu.

'I hope they will be safe wherever they are.' Tlalli touched her talisman and thought of her father.

They spent a restless night in the shelter of the rocks and continued on at first light. As they drew closer to what had been their homeland Paullu followed familiar trails past isolated homesteads. They found stone houses cut into hillsides, where farmers had once raised a few head of llama and grown crops to feed their families; most either burned out or deserted. He sought out the stone hut where he had left his parents and sister, but it was abandoned.

'This is a bad omen,' he said and his brow furrowed.

'We mustn't give up hope,' said Tlalli squeezing his hand. 'They could have returned to the village.'

'Perhaps,' he replied, without enthusiasm. They continued on. As they passed what had once been familiar landmarks, it seemed nowhere had escaped the onslaught of the invaders. Some roadside tambos showed visible signs of destruction and burning; others had been left empty and exposed to the elements. As the sun began to sink in the west they neared the end of their journey. The fate of their own village lay heavily between them.

They topped a high ridge leading to their valley. Tlalli gripped hold of Paullu's hand as she sensed all her expectations seep away. Fear made it hard to keep going. In the distance was the peak of Mount Yaguar; solid and indestructible. But even this could not raise her spirits and as the daylight slipped away they looked in vain for signs of life. Not a flicker of light showed. They entered the valley, listening and watching for sign of friend or foe.

They came down the hillside to where the settlement should have been. Stone rubble lay strewn around where walls had collapsed; their homes had been razed to the ground. The Spanish soldiers had destroyed everything and the whole area seemed deserted. Tlalli stumbled to where she thought her home had been. The ground was scorched and the remnants of the walls blackened. Broken pots and vessels littered the area; nothing she could recognize remained. As she fought back angry tears they moved on to view the rest of the settlement. Paullu's last hope that his family had returned to the village now seemed futile, for there was no village.

'What about the families we left at Calca?' Tlalli said, trying to find something to give her hope. 'Father said my mother was going to find her way home with the other women from the camp in the Yucay valley.' As she spoke, she wondered if the women and children ever did come back, and if so, would it have been before or after the village had been sacked?

Their long-awaited homecoming had become a harrowing pilgrimage. Silently, not daring to voice hope or despair to each other, they continued down the valley to the terraces where weeds and creepers grew. Further down the hillside the forest began, thin at first with stunted trees, then thicker as the ground dropped steadily towards the gorge where the great river flowed.

Paullu broke the silence. 'It is too late now to look for any signs of life.' He put his arm on her shoulder and Tlalli drew comfort from his presence. 'We will be safer here,' he said and he began to make a clearing within the forest.

The gnarled trees looked menacing, stunted and tightly packed together. The branches were covered with moss, dripping with water droplets from the low mists and the scene was dark and sombre. Snakes like bushmasters and corals inhabited the area and Paullu beat the ground with a stick before they settled on a place to sleep. They were too tired and dejected to make a fire and chewed a little bread and drank the last of the water they had carried. They lay close together and soon fell into a restless sleep.

Tlalli felt Paullu stir. She opened her eyes. Darkness still hung over them but cracks of light broke through the sky. Paullu put his finger to his lips and Tlalli listened hard. A twig snapped nearby and then another. The soft murmur of voices filtered through the undergrowth and Paullu drew out his knife. The sounds became clearer until they recognised them as people walking through the forest. The daylight grew stronger and Tlalli and Paullu stayed still as the trees and waited. Along the trail a little way off they saw a native man and then another. A group of them were walking in single file; men, women and children.

Tlalli recognized her mother and immediately called out. 'Mother, Mother! It's me, Tlalli!' The group stopped abruptly and everyone began to talk and run at once.

As they came together Tlalli recognized more people: her younger sisters and baby brother, now grown big and looking just like Ispaca. Caution was forgotten as they laughed and shouted with joy. Paullu found his sister and learned that his parents, as he feared, had both died. Tlalli excitedly passed from one person to the next, exchanging news and grasping hands in renewed friendships. Her Uncle Tutsi had joined them only one day ago and Tlalli's news that Kusi lived, fighting with Manco Inca, lifted the tribe's spirits.

'We will rebuild our homes,' said Tutsi. 'Then we will not have to live in fear in the forest.'

'This tribe is fortunate,' said Paullu, 'for we have the skills of mountain people and forest Indians; we will survive the wretched Spanish invaders.'

'A plague on them all,' said Neneti and she shook her fist, 'for they have all but destroyed our land and our people.'

Tlalli felt that now she was back with her family it would be easy for her to return to a life of obscurity, to disappear into the mountains and pretend she was just another village girl. But she had been charged with a mission by the jaguar gods, and now by the Inca in granting her freedom. Thoughts of the jaguar gods filled her with the same courage and resolve she had felt when guiding the rebels at the Sacred City. She lifted up her arms and raised her voice over everyone's joyful greetings.

'Listen! Please listen to me, my friends and family. Paullu and I have travelled through much of our homeland over the last few years. From Cuzco to Ollantaytambo, and down into the Antisuyo as far as Vitcos and Willkapampa City. Apart from this last stronghold, where the Inca still has his rebel court, our entire country has been taken over by the Spanish invaders and our people have been robbed, murdered and enslaved.' The small crowd around them had fallen silent waiting to hear what she would say.

'Paullu and I have already guided a rebel movement from the mountains and we want to continue this work. If we organise ourselves and plan our missions, we can continue to fight against the invaders.' She had the attention of all the remaining Manari tribe, her own people.

'Manco Inca, with loyal captains like my father Kusi, is now determined to hold out against them. The battle for Cuzco was lost but the rebellion must continue.' She looked around her. This would be much harder than it had been at the Sacred City. Here she was surrounded by her own kith and kin, women, children, old people and few men of fighting age. She drew on every bit of courage she could find. She climbed up on a high rock and raised her arms up to the sky.

'We are still free and have not been captured or enslaved and we must do everything in our power to remain so. We must harass and outwit this vile enemy in any way we can. Also we are charged by the Inca to spread the word to others to do the same.'

Tlalli realised everyone had fallen silent listening to her and that this was a turning point in her life; she had to become a leader for her people. She continued addressing the crowd. 'Many Spanish have now been granted land and given Indians to work for them as slaves. We must seek out these usurpers and murder them just as they have murdered our people. We must turn the enslaved natives against their masters.' The people continued listening to Tlalli. She was well aware they were not used to a woman speaking like this, but she was her father's daughter and was prepared to take her leading role.

'When Spanish men travel on our Inca roads they must be ambushed and killed by the local tribes.' Paullu and I have already done these things. We have to make them fear us!' She turned around and raised her voice in a rallying call. 'Burn their homes! Kill their horses! Give them a taste of what our people have endured since they first arrived in our land. You must not be afraid, for right is on our side and our gods will endure over their god.'

Paullu stood beside Tlalli. Now he continued the rallying words. 'We will divide into small groups and send out spies. Spanish horses are useless in the high mountains and in the low jungles. Main routes must be blocked so the enemy will be forced onto trails where we can pick them off, one by one. There are many ways in which we can defeat our enemy, using stealth and cunning.'

Tlalli took Paullu's hand and smiled as she spoke again. 'We also have good news for you. Manco Inca has released me from my oath as an Aclla and granted me my freedom. In return, I have vowed to spread the word about continuing the rebellion as a secret movement.'

Paullu spoke up, 'Friends, Kusi has agreed to our marriage, at last.' He turned to Tutsi. 'Your brother asks that you perform this ceremony for him, Uncle.'

Tutsi laughed with everyone else. 'A wedding will lift our spirits, and I hope you will keep my young niece in order, for she has returned to us with the courage of a warrior and the heart of a jaguar.'

54

Inca Treasure

Roberto has been happy to humour Christina in her wish to view the Inca ceremony. But for him it was a means of getting her away from Lady Grace and Martin Chambi. Their concerns for her safety and her reputation are in direct opposition to his desire to get his hands on her money and, of course, her beautiful ravishing body; all of which he is sure will soon be his.

Now he is excited by another source of fortune which has presented itself, something he had not expected. The lost treasure of Manco Inca, which has been a recurring legend in these parts for many years, may also now be within his grasp. He has long doubted that his family's mine, which his maps show is at the Yaguar Mountain site, would be a profitable venture. He had lied about the prospects to his backers and investors, but now by a turn of fate, there may be gold in his mountain after all.

Dearest Christina has unwittingly put him on to this quest. Since they became closer, dare he think almost lovers, he has gained her trust, to the point where she has opened up her heart to him and revealed secrets from her dreams; secrets about Inca treasure hidden long ago in a mountain called Yaguar. Ordinarily of course, he wouldn't think of acting on the impulse of a mere dream, but it now appears there is written evidence that treasure was indeed hidden at this location. She has told him about the translation made by her uncle from old Spanish parchments written over three hundred years ago, a document she actually has with her, supposedly a true account of this same treasure secreted in this very mountain!

Roberto can feel the blood of the Spanish conquistadors coursing through his veins. The lust for gold and wealth is very strong and he is determined not to miss out on his chance to enrich himself even further. But this terrain is very difficult and he is entirely dependent on his Indian guide even to find the mountain, never mind the treasure. They seem to be following a little used trail, with evidence here and there of abandoned ruined hovels, dry stone walls and occasional piles of stones on the hillsides.

Egecati tells them, 'We are getting close. I think these ruins suggest this was once a settlement. We should stop here for the night.'

Christina seems relieved and dismounts from her pony. 'I am ready to drop but where can we sleep?'

Egecati climbs up the hillside to where there is an old stone ruin and Diego follows him. 'So long as there is a comfortable place for the Senorita to sleep, Egecati,' he says.

They return to tell Christina the ruins can be made habitable for her. Egecati has anticipated their needs and unloads the mule. He has blankets, an oil lamp and even an old tinder-box. They picket the ponies and the mule so they can graze and Egecati collects scrub and soon has a fire going. They share the food and drink and Roberto slips an extra ingredient into Christina's cup, just to ensure she has a restful sleep. When their provisions are gone they will have to return to Santa Teresa which is many miles behind them.

The Andean night creeps in with its deep purple sky studded with millions of stars. Egecati has rolled in his blanket near the ponies and appears to be sleeping. Roberto sits next to Christina sharing their body heat under the blankets for the temperature has dropped considerably. The last embers of the fire still glow and as Christina seems to drift in and out of sleep, his mind drifts back to Spain and his last night at home in Toledo, the night he murdered his friend Antonio. He loves contemplating his own wicked past; it is his guilty pleasure.

He recalls the argument and the insults they traded in the casino's private room. Antonio had drawn his knife first and bloodied him with a shoulder wound. But his knife had found Antonio's heart and he was dead within a minute. He smiles now, remembering how he slowly withdrew the blade from Antonio's chest, wiped the blood on the dead man's shirt and then replaced the knife in the sheath hidden under his jacket. He had lifted his former friend up over his shoulder and carried him out of the back entrance into the darkness of the alley.

He'd run like the wind to his friends at the Cantina hoping to establish his alibi with Maria, his flamenco whore. But the body was discovered within minutes and he'd been forced to flee, to escape arrest and death by firing squad. Roberto Chavez was then a wanted man.

His father had ordered him to accompany his cousin Diego on the boat from Cadiz the following day. Diego's journey to South America was to locate and re-open the families' mines, using the deeds brought back to Spain by their grandfather. He was forced to leave Spain with the cousin he hated; more so for keeping him like a dog in the ship's hold, being very sea-sick for the first few days and nights. Oh, how he hated his cousin for that.

He remembers exploring his confinement for possible escape and found none. He still had his bag with precious few clothes and possessions, but also, concealed in the bottom, was the knife; the very one he'd used to murder Antonio. Once he had recovered his strength from the dreadful sea-sickness, he'd waited until Diego had come to check on him at night, bringing a meagre ration of bread and water, Roberto had been waiting in the dark.

Recalling this key event from his past heightens his passions and reminds him he is invincible. Diego had called out, 'Hey, where are you?' as Roberto hid behind some barrels. Diego had come further into the hold peering into the darkness. Roberto crept silently from his hiding place and thrust the knife into his cousin's back. He could still feel the glorious sensation as the blade penetrated into soft flesh then ground against bone. As he forced the struggling man to the floor, he pulled the knife out and slit his throat. The memory still has the power to thrill him.

Diego died very quickly, just as Antonio had done. He'd stood there, in the dark, taking big gulps of air, trembling with fear and exhaustion. Then a feeling of pure elation had spread from his feet, through his body, exploding in his head. It all happened so quickly and exactly as he'd planned. He had meant to kill Diego.

He'd gone up on deck, determined that this time he wouldn't be caught. He'd easily found Diego's cabin, for it was marked on the keys. They were sufficiently alike that he'd been able to take over his cousin's identity. As Diego Alvarez, he had access to the money entrusted to Diego by Don Rodriguez Chavez, *his* father, and the deeds of the South American mines. Roberto, the fugitive from Spanish justice, could be declared lost at sea.

He'd carried the body up to the stern in the dead of night, and without being seen, he tipped Diego over into the sea. Within a minute the bobbing corpse was out of sight. If it were ever washed up on a foreign beach, it would tally with the report he'd made back to his father, Don Rodriguez, saying that his son Roberto, had disappeared from the ship before they reached South America. From that moment Roberto had become his cousin, Diego Alvarez. Roberto Chavez was dead. That was a bitter pill to swallow and his only regret.

Christina stirs, still awake and he strokes her face with his fingers. 'I did not intend you to suffer such deprivations, my darling,' he says, 'but this country's so wild, and distances are much further than I imagined.' He is thrilled that she knows he is Roberto; to her, he can be his true self. Her eyes are open and shining; her face seems to glow in the fading firelight.

'Oh no, don't be sorry,' she whispers. 'This is a wonderful adventure. I came because I wanted to. It feels so good to do what I want instead of always bowing to convention.'

'Does that include running away with a Spanish adventurer?'

She looks coy. 'We haven't run away; this trip was planned. It's just that the others didn't come with us.'

He laughs. 'Tell me again about the story of the Yaguar Mountain, the story from your dreams.' She snuggles into his arms, trusting, almost childlike. Now he will have his greatest prize – the princess of his dreams. He has nearly won her over but it is essential she gives herself to him freely.

She tells him again about the Perúvian girl she calls Tlalli and the treasure hidden in the mountain. 'Since I received my pendant I've had many dreams about Tlalli. It is like meeting a friend in my sleep, a sort of kindred spirit. I only realised it was a true story when I received photographs and documents after my Uncle Peter died.'

'And now you have this new documentary evidence also.' Roberto knows the issue is sensitive and that he must keep her trust.

'The dreams were all rather hazy but the translation from the written story makes it all much clearer.' Christina squeezes his hand. 'It's so exciting! It would be wonderful to find some real proof. Although in a sense, we already have.' She puts her hand to her neck and pulls out the two jaguar pendants. 'I'm sure these are the talismans Tlalli's father gave to her and her brother.'

Roberto cannot see them clearly in the dark but he runs his fingers over them entwining his hand with hers. 'Well,' he whispers, 'they do say we have all lived before, so perhaps I was with you in this past life. Perhaps I was your lover.' He laughs, throwing his head back. 'Or maybe I was the wicked Spanish conquistador and carried you off on my black horse! Or was it a white stallion?'

He looks again at her beautiful face. She is sleepy from the draught he gave her. She is pliable – suggestable – just as he had hoped. His mood changes from humorous to intense and he moves closer pulling her into a frenzied embrace. 'Oh, Christina, I do believe we were always meant to be together.' He kisses her lips, moving them apart with his own, seeking to explore her mouth. His hands begin to caress her, stroking those special places to increase her desire. His breathing becomes rapid. Has the time to take her come? There is one more thing he can say.

'My darling, I love you so much. I am afraid I have to make a confession and beg your forgiveness.'

She is immediately alert but asks, 'What is troubling you?'

'I wanted to protect you and not cause you more anxiety.' He brushes her hair back with his hand and bends his head to kiss her neck then lifts his eyes to look into hers. 'I wasn't honest with you about Sam.'

He feels her stiffen and he continues to massage her head and neck with soothing strokes.

'He has not been true to you, as I led you to believe. I have witnessed his infidelity with his servant, Rosita.'

'Oh, no, no!' she cries.

She is upset, that is obvious. But he hopes this will work to his advantage.

'He is not worthy of your love. A love which is sadly misplaced.' He waits while her mind apparently deals with his revelations. This waiting is exquisite torture as he resists the desire to ravage her.

She doesn't say a word; no recriminations against him or Sam. After a few minutes she seems to relax as if she has made a decision and she responds to his attentions. Christina begins to return his kisses and he feels her passions rise with his own. He smiles to himself. He has waited patiently for this moment and now she is his.

55

Spirit of Izella

1539 Mount Yaguar, Vilcabamba, Perú

In spite of her rallying words, Tlalli was well aware the remaining members of her Manari tribe feared the Spaniards would return. Now the people placed their trust in Tlalli, Paullu and Tutsi to keep them safe. They continued to sleep in the forest, the tribe's spiritual home.

In his brother's absence, Tutsi took responsibility for the tribe and his immediate family. He told everyone to prepare for Tlalli and Paullu's wedding. The villagers were amused, for they knew the young couple had lived as man and wife for a long time. Tlalli and Paullu wanted to continue the resistance movement with the help of their own families. It was a huge task, but first they agreed to allow their families to organise their wedding.

'We will celebrate seven days from now,' said Tutsi. 'In accordance with our traditions, we will keep you two apart until then.' Everyone laughed as Neneti led Tlalli away. The women joked about how they would create a wedding gown from feathers, flowers and ferns. Tlalli gave into her mother's schemes; it was good to hear Neneti laugh after the sorrow she had endured.

The next day Paullu went away on a hunting trip. Venison for the feast and rounding up llamas and alpacas for new herds were his priority. But they were also going to search the surrounding countryside to find more recruits to the rebel movement.

'We will only be gone two or three days, my love,' he told her. 'Then at last we will truly be man and wife.' They kissed a fond farewell and Tlalli thought she would burst from the happiness within her.

Tutsi and some of the other men went with Paullu, and as she watched him top the ridge and turn and wave, she missed him already. They had agreed that she would prepare the tribe for the resistance work ahead and turn their campsite into a fortress against the invaders, should they return.

Tlalli called all the women and children to her. She wanted to inspire them but as she looked around the group, her own tribe, she felt a mix of love, pity and compassion. Girls her own age looked so much older, worn down by years moving from place to place, losing fathers, husbands, brothers, never having enough food to eat or feed to their children. Her mother Neneti was among the oldest; all the older villagers had died. Many seemed to have lost their purpose for living; they had given up.

What could she say to them to change anything? She remembered her own happy childhood and nights round the campfire, the music and the storytelling. It all seemed so long ago, and of course it was long ago, before the wretched Spanish arrived; before the war, before she became a rebel.

Had the young children in this group ever experienced anything like that in their young lives? She thought not, so perhaps she needed to remedy that first. Before turning them into fighters they had to experience a way of life worth fighting for.

'Come,' she said, 'we must find a good place in the forest to make a better camp and to set a fire for cooking.' They all looked puzzled but Tlalli took control. 'Follow me and as we walk we must collect dry wood for burning.' At first, the children were excited and noisy. She held up her hand. 'No, that will not do.' She lowered her voice and bent down. 'We must go quietly. True Indians walk through the jungle silently. You children have missed out on your fathers' teaching, so I will teach you now.' She held a finger to her lips. 'We creep through the forest like a deer or an agouti.'

'Or a snake,' said a boy of about five years.

'Or a jaguar!' said an older boy, and all the children gasped and held tightly to their mothers' hands.

'Yes,' said Tlalli in a whisper. 'All animals move very quietly and you must learn to do the same. Then you will learn to be the hunters, not the hunted.' They moved on, one behind the other, much quieter now. Tlalli was pleased. She made up her mind to give the tribe back its traditional ways as she had been taught.

She led them further away from the worn tracks surrounding their old home, deeper into the forest. Everywhere the sounds of birds and animals followed them. Some of the women and children seemed quite afraid. They had been used to the open hills around their village and were mostly of Mountain Indian descent. For Tlalli, the forest was her home, a place of safety.

She stopped and called everyone to her. 'Here is a good place to stop. See, it is a hollow surrounded by trees and bushes. 'If we light a fire here the smoke will disappear into the branches and not be seen.' She pointed around the back of the hollow where the ground rose up. 'That will give shelter and make a good lookout point.' Everyone was given a job to do, even the little ones to collect more wood.

Tlalli used every opportunity to teach the children how to look for animal signs, listen to the sounds of the forest and learn the calls of different animals and birds. The mothers collected berries and leaves and showed the children which were good to eat or make into drink. Tlalli showed them how to make fire using the Indian bow drill. She remembered how she had lit the cave in the mountain with her burning torch and found the Inca's treasure. This reminded her sharply that she had another mission to complete as soon as possible; she must return to Mount Yaguar.

Soon they had a small fire smouldering away. Tlalli felt she had achieved a lot by bringing them here. They crowded round the fire and she asked them, 'Who knows the story of the Legend of the Jaguar?' One or two of the mothers laughed and said they remembered the story from childhood, but none of the children had heard it. The old storyteller from Tlalli's childhood was long gone. Over the last few years there had been no time for storytelling with fathers away fighting and families hiding from Spanish invaders.

'Well then, I shall tell you myself.' As she began the story she knew so well, her heart swelled with pride in her people's heritage and history: their creator god Viracocha, the sun god Inti, and the moon goddess Mama Quilla, and all the sacred mountains, forests and animals that had provided them with food, water and homes for thousands of years. The children were enthralled when she told how the two brothers met with the jaguar god Toquri and how they eventually learned that family was their most treasured possession. The importance of the legend was immeasurable to keep the cultural identity of these children and for them to remember this for their future.

While Tlalli talked with the children, her mother and other women cooked a soup on the fire from the bounty they had collected in the forest. By evening they had collected ferns and branches and made hides and sleeping places. The children were settled down to sleep and Tlalli, Neneti and the other women took turns keeping watch through the night.

Tlalli wanted to complete her own pilgrimage back to Mount Yaguar. She longed to discover if the family of jaguars were still living in the mountain. For her, this was a spiritual mission, to reignite the Spirit of the Jaguar and strengthen her resolve to keep the pledges she had made to the tribe. She was fairly sure she could complete her mission in one day, so the following day she set off early, when the other women were going into the forest to gather plants and berries.

She took the old trail which led to the disused mineshaft as the quickest way. On the ground around the entrance and just inside the tunnel there were hoof prints in the soft soil. She realised only Spaniards' horses could have left the marks, which were no more than a few days old. That was disturbing so close to the settlement. It was clear that all efforts to reopen the collapsed tunnel had been abandoned. She hoped the Spaniards had also now given up on finding Manco's lost treasure in the mountain.

As she emerged back out into the sunlight she stopped to listen to the familiar sounds of bird calls, grasses and trees humming with insect life, as the breezes moved through the valley. She put her ear to the ground, alert for the drum of horses' hooves, but heard none. The area seemed safe for now and she broke into a run. At first she followed the marked trail, then branched off to circle around the mountain foothills.

She stopped to get her breath back and scan the terrain. She had already moved a good way up from the level of the trail and was now trekking even higher. The entrance she had discovered all those years ago, that led into the mountain, was a long way away. Now she was at the place where she had once seen the mother jaguar with her cub up on the escarpment. She stood still and shaded her eyes. Her heart nearly stopped beating as she caught a brief glimpse of a golden movement in the very same place. It was a long way up, and she could no longer see it, but was sure she had not been mistaken. There had to be a reason why the jaguars went that way, as well as using the cave entrance on the far side of the mountain.

As the sun gained height in the morning sky she began to climb higher, over the rocks and granite outcrops, to where she thought she had seen the jaguar. Tlalli had no idea where this might lead her. She had never climbed the mountain from this side and was putting all her faith in the animals, praying they would guide her. Another hour of scrambling for handholds and dragging her legs up the steep slopes brought her up on to a ledge.

She looked up and realised she had probably climbed all this way for nothing. Above her was a sheer, flat wall of granite. The only route open was to follow the ledge and she edged along sideways, hoping it would not end in a sheer drop. Just as it seemed she had come to a dead end, she discovered the rock behind her spilt open, making it possible to scramble though a gap and up onto the next level, away from the steep and dangerous ledge.

At this height, the air was cooler and the wind stronger. She didn't think anyone from the tribe had ever climbed to this part of the mountain. From below it had seemed impossible but the jaguar's appearance had shown her the way. Now she wanted to search for the shaft she had seen from inside the mountain. It was a long time ago, but she remembered scrambling down the passageway between the jaguar's cave and the one where the treasure lay, and finding the overhead shaft where daylight filtered down into the mountain. Acting entirely on instinct, she was sure this would be the jaguar's second way in and out of the mountain. An animal as wise as a jaguar would never allow itself to be trapped without an escape route.

Now she was out of the immediate danger posed by the narrow ledge, she rested for a few minutes. Fleetingly she thought she should perhaps turn for home now; instead she fell into thinking about the legend which had first ignited her love of the wild cat, how Egecati had climbed up the mountain to the jaguar god Toquri, and the rocks had opened up behind him, revealing the canyon. So perhaps, if the legend was true, it was close to this spot. She moved on again climbing even higher, working towards a rocky outcrop jutting up from the sheer granite slope. Pulling herself onto the rocks she looked over the top. There was a crevice, a narrow chasm. Was this the place she had been seeking?

Her heart was beating very fast and she knew she was near to her beloved jaguars. She wanted to draw on the strength of their spirit and absorb their wisdom. According to the legend, the jaguar god Toquri and his goddess Izella could change their shape from feline to human and then back to feline. Tlalli closed her eyes and remembered the time, when she was very young, that this had seemed to happen to her. Even now, she could not be sure if it had been a dream, but she concentrated on all the memories she had stored in her head and on her still vivid recollection of that day.

She felt herself drifting through space, lifting out of her body and looking down on the girl crouched asleep on the mountainside. It seemed as if she had just been born, although simultaneously she felt as old as time itself. She floated back down on to the mountain, alighting near the chasm, next to the slumbering girl she knew was herself. As she approached the entrance to the shaft she looked down. Her feet had transformed into feline paws and her body moved silently, long and sleek. She gleamed with golden fur, shining with the distinctive, beautiful black rosette markings of an adult jaguar. She opened her mouth and uttered a long, low roar and her heart soared with the joy of this miracle.

She entered the mountain, bounding down the shaft with feline agility, in a way no human could ever have done. But she was not concerned with such thoughts, she was a spirit with a task to fulfil and her name was Izella. She stopped by the trickling pool to fulfil her animal needs, lapping the cool water from the mountain spring which had served her ancestors for thousands of years. These tunnels no longer glittered with golden ore but the pupils of her eyes had dilated to catch the almost non-existent light. She moved lithely down the passage with imprinted instinct and inherited knowledge towards her lair.

The cave was exactly as she had left it. Izella's leaving had been but two hours ago; Tlalli's was several years since. No matter, they were one being now; feline and human, one spirit. The Inca's treasure was still intact, partly covered by rotting sacks, but just as she remembered it. She moved on further into the cave and was rewarded by the sweet mewing of two jaguar cubs, only five days old. She lay beside them, their mewling mouths sucked and sighed. She sang her song, a loving lullaby, in the safety of this ancient place. Only the movement of the earth's surface had ever threatened this sacred hideout, cutting off the entrance made by man, but not those used by the jaguars. Tlalli, in her feline form, had been allowed entrance for she was under their protection.

When she had fed her cubs she cleaned them with soft licking until they fell asleep. She stirred, head up, ears gyrating. As Izella, she would have to go back now to the top of the shaft, to release Tlalli from her human sleep. They would then go their separate ways, wiser in the knowledge they had a joint mission to accomplish, both filled with the Spirit of the Jaguar.

56

Lone Rebel

Tlalli awoke cold and stiff. The sun had moved beyond the middle of the sky, sinking to the west. For a moment she felt confusion, wondering how she came to be on this barren mountainside, shielded only by a few boulders. Her eyes focused on the entrance to the shaft and all her thoughts tumbled together as she remembered everything: her journey, the climb, finding this inaccessible place But most of all she remembered entering the mountain in the form of a jaguar.

Had it been a dream? If so it was the most fantastic, lifelike dream she had ever experienced. Her belief in the jaguar gods and the power of their spirit convinced her it must have really happened and she would hold the memory deep inside her forever. It confirmed her belief that the spirit of the sacred jaguars ran in her blood. She could use it and fulfil her destiny to lift her people out of the tyranny brought by the Spanish invaders. If it took her a lifetime, if it took an eternity, she had to do this, she had to succeed.

Now, she must find her way back down the mountain. She needed to reach the campsite in the forest before any marauding Spaniards came back to the area, especially the vengeful Gonzalo Pizarro; she had no greater enemy than him. She felt sure it must be him who had been to the mine recently and that he still lusted after Manco Inca's lost treasure.

She picked her way down to the narrow ledge. It was much more terrifying going down than climbing up. She didn't look down and filled her mind with the animal instincts of the jaguars, following in their mythical footsteps.

When Tlalli at last reached the gently sloping foothills she began to run, keeping away from the skyline, seeking the lower paths. She moved away from the trail to cut through the forest, taking the quickest and safest route. Her enemies were not far away and at all costs she must reach the tribe before them. The villagers would have to move again, go deeper into the forest to escape the men she felt sure must be close by.

Sharp thorns ripped her clothing and tore at her arms and legs. She took great gulps of air into her lungs and her breath came in short rasps as she fought her way through thickets and boggy swamps. Biting insects stung her skin and her feet protested, sore and weary. It seemed to take forever, but eventually she recognized the lie of the land, their temporary camp in the forest's margins.

As Tlalli found the trail she had taken yesterday to the new campsite she crept cautiously through the bushes. Had any Spaniards reached there before her? She peered through the branches to where she could see the women grinding seeds with stones and cooking over an open fire while children played nearby. There did not appear to be any alarm amongst them. Tlalli stepped out from the bushes and ran into the hollow. As they saw her the women began to call out. She held up her hand to silence them, begging them to be quiet.

'Where have you been?' said her mother in a bewildered tone. 'You have been gone a whole day. I thought you had been captured again.'

'No, but the Spaniards have been back to the mine,' Tlalli explained breathlessly. 'We must move our camp for they are very close. Have Paullu and Uncle Tutsi returned?'

'No,' her mother replied, 'we are still without our protectors.'

Tlalli spoke hurriedly. 'I fear Gonzalo Pizarro will come here again,' she said to her mother.

'Why does he keep seeking you out, daughter?'

'He thinks I can lead him to the Inca's treasure.'

'But it is sealed in the mountain,' said Neneti.

'And so it must remain, Mother. Now help me, we need to move everyone into hiding.' She looked around realizing how vulnerable this little group of villagers were. In the absence of the men, she would have to take charge to protect everyone.

The women had gathered round listening to her and Neneti. Tlalli spoke urgently raising her voice a little. 'You must gather your children and hide, for the bad Spaniard is nearby.'

Full of confusion and fear the women called their little ones to them and ran off into the forest. Tlalli began helping her mother, calling her younger brothers and sisters, when a shout rent the air. She looked up and saw Gonzalo Pizarro riding on his huge black stallion, galloping at a fast pace towards them.

'Run!' she shouted. 'Hide wherever you can!' She pushed her mother away for she would have to stand her ground to protect the others. Pizarro seemed to be alone. As he reached the clearing, reining his horse to a halt, she pulled a long wooden pole out from the campfire. She would fight to the death rather than be taken by this deadly enemy again.

She held the burning pole as she had seen warriors do, ready to swing at the horse's head should he approach. Pizarro began to shout at her, his anger raised to a point of fury. 'Heathen woman! Infidel! Snake! Vile creature!'

Let him vent his anger with words, she thought, as she carefully watched his movements. He drew his sword and pointed it towards her, gathering his reins to charge, as she knew he would. She kept the campfire between them and as he passed to one side she leaped the other way turning to face him once more.

He wheeled round on the big animal and prepared to charge again, holding his sword as if it were a lance. Once more the fire was between them as he charged towards her. Again she leapt the opposite way, swinging her pole down on the side of the horse's head. The unexpected blow sent the animal towards the flames and the horse reared in fear. Gonzalo was unseated and toppled from his saddle, sprawling on the ground, losing his sword.

Tlalli did not have time to be afraid and she leapt forward, knocking the sword out of his reach with the pole, sending it hurtling into the bushes. Once more she faced him across the fire, but with his horse behind him, she watched helpless as he regained his feet and caught the animal. He had no sword but mounted the horse, once more ready to resume their skirmish. This time he did not charge; bringing the horse close to the fire, he began to circle round it.

Tlalli was unprepared for this change in tactics as he closed the gap between them. Soon he was close enough to reach her and he kicked out at her arm, knocking the pole from her grasp. Fear coursed through her veins. How could she defeat this fearsome adversary with no means of defence? All she could do was run and hope to reach the safety of the trees. In that instance of indecision a flash of gold leapt from the bushes onto the horse's flanks. The horse screamed in terror and once again reared on its hind legs, unseating the Spaniard.

Tlalli's heart went from despair to joy. She took her chance and ran for the safety of the trees, climbing up to the branches as Ispaca had taught her when they were children. Beneath her, a scene of carnage unfolded as a big male jaguar attacked the horse. Was this the same animal that had saved her once before from the jaws of the crocodile? The answer was as clear as her experience on the mountain had been earlier that day. This jaguar possessed the spirit of the god Toquri, come to defend her. In her heart she knew this to be so. But the battle had not ended, not yet.

Gonzalo Pizarro had fallen more heavily this time and was still lying stunned on the ground. The horse lay dying, for the jaguar had sliced through its throat with its massive jaws. Tlalli stared transfixed, wondering if it would attack the man. Gonzalo regained his senses and struggled to his feet. The jaguar faced him, crouched ready to spring, ears back, barring its deadly fanged teeth, raising its huge paw and emitting a deep throaty roar. Just as the Spaniard seemed at the mercy of this fierce wild animal, the sound of hoof beats came from the direction of the trail.

Tlalli's heart thudded as she saw three more Spaniards ride towards the clearing. The jaguar heard them also and in an instant he melted away and disappeared, back into the forest, as if he had never been there. Even from her lookout in the tree, Tlalli could not see him now. She held her breath hoping the Spaniards could not see her either.

From the way they greeted Pizarro it seemed they had been looking for him and had followed his trail. They stripped the dead horse of its saddle and leathers and made ready to leave. Pizarro remembered his sword and scoured the bushes until he found it. He shouted to his rescuers and she caught the words she knew meant, 'Manari's daughter'; he had not forgotten her.

Her hopes of escape disappeared with the realisation they could find the others: her mother, the women and the children. As the Spaniards began searching, she knew she could not let that happen. She called out, 'I am here. I am coming down!' At the sound of her voice they turned and surrounded her as she reached the ground.

'So, you would think to kill my horse with sorcery, witch!' Gonzalo thundered. 'Now I have you at my mercy.'

She could guess at the meaning of his words and waited for the blow from his sword that would end her life.

He yelled at her. 'Death will be your fate when I say the word!' He shouted orders to his men and they trussed her up with rope and slung her over the neck of one of the horses, her head dangling down. Gonzalo Pizarro came up close and spat on her. 'You are my prisoner now. I will have the Inca's treasure and you will take me to it.' He punched her head with a fierce blow and she reeled with the pain, knowing there would be more of that for her, much more. She had fleeting thoughts of Paullu coming to her rescue, but he was miles away hunting for their wedding feast; a wedding that now would never take place.

'Come, Gonzalo,' said one of the Spaniards. 'We must ride to join the army marching north. We must go now.'

'Then you must go on without me,' shouted Gonzalo. 'I intend to have this gold hoard while I have this woman at my mercy.' He wheeled the horse round in a circle. 'You go on and I will join you a richer man.' The other Spaniards seemed to hesitate and they conferred with each other. The lure of gold and treasure proved strong.

'We will come with you, Gonzalo,' called one. 'Your mission may be dangerous.'

He laughed as he began to ride on. 'When are they not? I thrive on danger.' The others fell in behind him.

57

Return to Mount Yaguar

June 1931, Vilcabamba, Perú
My dreams are inhabited by many ghosts, but prime among these is the image of the man Tlalli feared, whom I also came to fear though the dream. Now her testament has confirmed this was the Spanish conquistador Gonzalo Pizarro. Re-reading my journal entries last year of my encounter with the Spanish student on the ferry journey from Calais in 1924, it was his features that fascinated me and imprinted on my childhood fantasies: Roberto Chavez.

Last night I experienced this man's love. My last thought before sleep engulfed me was I had at last found my true love. Sleep overcame me and I fell into another dream. In this dream Tlalli had another confrontation with the conquistador. I feel her revulsion of the man and her fear over what will happen if she opposes him. I hear her pleas to the jaguar gods to help her defeat him.

I awake, confused and with a heavy thumping in my head and a lump of misery in my heart. I am cold and stiff and regret coming on this 'adventure'. More than that, I feel an even deeper sense of shame that I succumbed to his deceit and allowed Roberto to make love to me. Poor sleep and bad dreams have sapped all the exhilaration I felt yesterday. I had been so thrilled to discover Diego was in fact Roberto. I truly believed everything he said. Now that knowledge is sullied by the warning in my dream, as if the scales have fallen from my eyes. I'm sure he gave me something to make me put aside my morals so easily. Yet I am entirely in his hands and at his mercy. I must find a way out of this dilemma for I have created it myself.

I begin to look at everything with different eyes. I feel a strong connection to these ancient ruins nestled in the mountains. Could these be the remains of Tlalli's childhood home, the village where she grew up? I feel sure that if I descend from this place, cross the trail and continue walking down, I will eventually find myself in her cloud forest. I smell a campfire smouldering into life, so wrapping the blanket around me I leave my makeshift night shelter, moving to where Egecati is preparing an equally makeshift breakfast.

He smiles. 'Coffee, Senorita,' and he passes me a tin mug containing a hot liquid which doesn't taste much like coffee but warms me.

'Thank you, Egecati. Where is Senor Alvarez?'

'He is spying out the trail for a route to his Yaguar Mountain.' As he says this I see Roberto coming down from the ridge behind us.

He calls out, 'Ah, Christina!' He comes up to us looking flushed and excited. 'I think our quest is nearly over. I have consulted the map I had with me for the Yaguar mine and I'm sure I have located the site.'

'How far away is it?' I say and I am stirred to remember this is what I really came to Perú for; to find Tlalli's mountain, the source of her strength and the home of the sacred jaguars. If she is guiding me, how can I desert her?

'One hour on our ponies, I promise you, Christina.'

I give a little nod to show I accept this and then I walk away from him. I am trying to pretend last night didn't happen and I follow the route that was in my mind earlier, crossing our trail and going further down the hillside. I find a little pool of rainwater and in the cover of the bushes I splash cold water over my face. This wakes me up and sharpens my brain into being decisive. I will go on to the mountain and then insist on returning to the guest house. I will use concern over Grace's condition to cover my change of heart. At least I will have Egecati's presence to keep Roberto from pressurising me to stay.

Roberto? Diego? Who is this man? Whoever he turns out to be I know now he is devious and can't imagine how I let myself be deceived. I can empathise with Tlalli now, for the conquistador was her enemy and he also lusted for the gold treasure and for her. I linger for a while, enjoying the solitude and honing my plan. I think of the words I will use to gain the advantage against Roberto's wily tongue. I return to the campsite determined to end this crazy situation.

I know immediately something is wrong. 'Where is Egecati?' I say, and can hear how alarmed my voice sounds. I can see the mule is packed and ready for our onward journey but our guide is nowhere to be seen.

'I have sent him back down the trail to obtain more supplies for us.' He says this casually, as if it is of no account.

Now I am very alarmed and quite mystified as I mentally calculate how long ago he left and how long it will be until he can return. I scan the trail but there is no sign of him. 'Why did you not consult with me? How can we continue without him?'

His reply is disarming. 'Why, Christina, my darling, what has happened to your spirit of adventure? I know the way and I will look after you.' His calm reassurances sound hollow. He takes a wad of paper from his inside pocket and opens it out, coming close he shows me an old map. It marks the site of the Yaguar mine. 'You see, Christina, this old map has proved quite accurate.'

I look up and can see the drawing shows an exact replication of the mountain tops closest to us. He points to the map again. 'This is Yaguar

Mountain,' he says, 'so we have no need of a guide. Besides, my dear, he will be back by tomorrow and will soon follow our trail.'

'I would have returned with him had I known.' I say this as a protest although I know it is useless.

He laughs. 'No, Christina, I don't think you would. We are too close to your own quest for you to abandon me. You want to know if this is the Yaguar Mountain of your dreams as much as I do.' He helps me to mount Juana and the mule is tied behind his black stallion. 'Egecati will travel very swiftly without us. He is probably halfway to Santa Teresa already.' Flicking his reins Roberto turns his stallion and sets off in the lead and I have no option but to follow. Even if we become lost, I trust, I pray, Egecati will find us.

The mountain looms before us like a giant stone colossus. It is higher and more forbidding than Machu Picchu. Roberto's one hour has become four, and for the last two we have been scaling the foothills. Green has turned to grey and the early warmth of the day evaporates as we climb higher.

'Roberto!' I call out. 'We must stop. I can go no further.' As I say this I slide off Juana's saddle. I can barely stand and lean on my pony for support, groping in the saddlebag for my water bottle.

In an instant he is beside me. 'Of course, my dear, you must rest. How thoughtless of me not to stop before.' He busies himself picketing the ponies and spreading a blanket for me. All our fruit is gone but he finds some dry biscuits for us to chew and we wash them down with water. I take in our surroundings and know I have been here before.

He is scrutinising my face. 'Do you recognise anything, Christina?'

I jump at his words. 'No, of course not,' I reply, 'how could I?'

He leans close. 'Oh, but you have dreamed of this mountain. You know this is where the Inca treasure was hidden.'

'Well perhaps my imagination wove those stories to fill my lonely life.'

'Perhaps.' He gives a roguish grin. 'But your little friend, Tlalli, when she was old, she told her grandson, and he told the chronicler, and he wrote it down.'

My mind flies to make the connection and take in what he is driving at. I jump up and rush to my saddlebag rummaging inside. 'It's gone! My manuscript, it's gone!' I turn to him and stare accusingly.

'Guilty!' he says holding up his hands and then he laughs. 'Oh, Christina, I am sorry. I just wanted to read it for myself. After all, I am now the owner of this fabled Yaguar Mountain.'

I must keep my dignity although my anger is intense. 'Please, Roberto, give it back to me.'

'Of course, my darling, but first we must find the entrance into the tunnels. I'm not going anywhere without you so your manuscript is quite

258

safe.' He walks a little way away and I know he is manipulating me. We are on a narrow path with cliff-like walls above us. The grey slopes below drop thousands of feet into a gorge. The trail has petered out and I realise the ponies will not be able to carry us any further.

I cannot imagine how we will find an entrance. It is four hundred years since Tlalli came to this place. Earthquakes since then could have closed all her entrances. Perhaps they never existed, and the whole thing is a fable, a story that has taken on a life of its own.

I can see Roberto scanning all the ridges and crevices looking for a way up. I shade my eyes and look up also. On the highest slope to my right I see a movement. Is it a bird stretching its wings? I squint and steady my gaze. It is the briefest glimpse but I freeze. A cat, I'm sure it was a cat, the shape and colour of...a jaguar?

I bite my tongue not to call out. It is gone now and I look to Roberto. Did he see it also? He is grinning at me, a look of triumph. He points to the exact spot. 'That is the way we must go,' he says. My spirits drop, perhaps a thousand feet, and I wish I was anywhere on earth except where I am. Roberto takes one of the saddlebags. Inside he puts food, our water bottles and two electric torches with spare batteries, and loops it across his shoulders.

I feel a hollow void inside me, and am sure history is now repeating itself; only our identities are changed. He comes to me and takes hold of my hand, leading me in the climb, and I do not resist. It is as if I have to do this although there is no sane reason why I should. I am not a prisoner, but there is nowhere I can flee to, and I feel invisible ropes pulling at me from the past.

58

Revenge of the Jaguars

June 1931, Mount Yaguar, Vilcabamba, Perú
As we make our ascent he keeps close behind me and guides me where to wedge my feet and to find the hand-holds to help me climb. I am glad of my slacks and walking boots and my body finds a rhythm that holds my wild thoughts in check. I lose track of time and only know we have come a long way up.

Our ascent is broken by a flat ledge. As we haul our scrabbling feet onto this, I see this slim perch curves off to the right and turns out of sight. It is very narrow and we follow it round, one behind the other. I dare not look down and as the part that was hidden comes into view the ledge stops abruptly, replaced by a wall of granite. A deep vertical crack in the granite seems to lead right into the mountain.

Perhaps this was the first entrance Tlalli used, although if it is, time has eroded its constricted entrance as we are both able to squeeze through the passage. I recall Tlalli found it difficult to enter, even when she was quite young, and the Spaniard could not enter at all. We have to crawl in places and in others go sideways, but eventually we reach a wider space. Without the torches I would not have come this far as the passage is dark and very claustrophobic. Even now I find myself gasping and wanting to turn back to the light and fresh air.

At the end of this passage we have to go down almost flat to the rock and squeeze through a low gap. Roberto shines a torch ahead, a luxury Tlalli did not have. She groped through the gap not knowing what lay beyond. I sniff the air; musty and acidic. Is that a jaguar smell? I don't know but I don't think the cat is here. I stay crouched on the hard granite floor but Roberto stands up and flicks the light from the torch all around.

'Well, this is a cave,' he says, 'but there is no treasure here.' He sounds disappointed and I wonder if I can convince him there's no point in looking further.

'After four hundred years I'm sure treasure hunters would have been here and taken anything of value.' I say this hoping it is true but uncertain what is in his mind.

'Oh, Christina, I'm not about to give up so easily.' He crouches down beside me, shining the torch in my face, making me flinch. He strokes his hand across my cheek and down my throat. I stiffen, I can't tell if the gesture is loving or sinister. 'I have read your Tlalli's story most carefully.

It's a pity your uncle did not complete the translation, for I'm sure it would tell us a lot more.'

The original documents are still locked away in Uncle Peter's house but I'm not going to say anything that will encourage Roberto in this foolhardy quest to find hidden Inca treasure. 'Perhaps we should wait and go back to Cuzco.' I cast around for words that will stop this madness. 'We could come back better informed and with your mining equipment. With more men we could make a proper search. Please, let's do that; this is crazy.' I don't want to be afraid of Roberto for he holds my life in his hands. If he truly loves me surely I must trust him to look after me?

He laughs loudly, throwing back his head in that way I remember so well. Was it the student on the boat who I now know was him? Or is my memory jostled by an older adversary, another man from another life? He stands again and goes to the back of this cave leaving me in darkness. I see the light from the torch flicking on the rough granite walls.

His voice comes to me like a hollow echo. 'There is a passage leading down.' He comes back to where I'm still sitting on the hard cold stone. 'Come, my darling, we must follow in Tlalli's footsteps, down into the heart of this mountain.'

My heart lurches. 'Oh, no, I don't think that is wise,' I say, desperate to stop him. 'Suppose our torch runs out. Suppose we cannot get back.' He takes hold of my arm and pulls me up; his hold on me is very firm.

'I have spare batteries.' His tone is clipped and determined. 'We will be quite safe. You must trust in the story Tlalli has left for you. She meant you to follow her.'

I could almost believe this is true, I want to believe in his judgement. He pulls me across the cave floor to the other side then shines the light down a tunnel and I see the slope that we must follow. The tunnel is round and as we enter the opening we cannot stand up straight. I can hear water dripping from the roof and the way is strewn with stones, wet and slippery under foot. He is ahead of me but I have to follow else be left alone in the darkness. I steady myself bracing my hands against the damp, cold walls. My skin pricks as I feel the full impact of this strange world. Fear grips me by the throat and I cry out, 'Roberto, please, we must go back!'

He turns to me but ignores my plea. 'No, Christina, look there are steps here. It will be easier now.' He shines the torch ahead and I see the granite is cut into wide steps leading down. The tunnel is steeper and the steps are worn and broken, strewn with pebbles that roll and skitter down ahead of us as we kick them loose. The tunnel twists and turns and I sense we are descending deep inside this mountain.

In spite of the danger, Roberto seems to hurry, as if he cannot wait to discover what lies ahead. I try to keep up with him and the light from his torch. I am stiff with the fear of this place and my breath comes in frantic gasps as I urge my feet to hurry on. The steps end and the passage widens. The light from the torch grows dim. Roberto curses in Spanish. He takes a second torch from his bag.

'Hold this, Christina, shine it on my hands.' He changes the battery in the first torch. 'Now we must hurry and complete our mission before our lights run out. Turn that one off,' he says. I do as he says but he doesn't take it back and I feel a little thrill of triumph as I push it into my jacket pocket.

He struts off again like a creature possessed, down the passage which is now more level, though the way is still littered with rocks and stones which we have to avoid stumbling into. There are more twists and turns and then unexpectedly the tunnel grows light and I look up. Far above a shaft of daylight seeps through an opening in the rock-face. The drop is almost vertical and as Roberto flashes his torch around the sides, I see bats flit across the surface. They hide in the crevices and cling to the rocks.

I know exactly where we are, but don't say anything. My knowledge comes from my last dream, not from the manuscript. I touch my two jaguar pendants. They are warm and seem to vibrate as if they would speak to me. So much from my dreams lies in my subconscious. Being here drags the images and emotions up to the surface.

'Impossible to climb,' he says. 'Perhaps a ventilation shaft or maybe a natural chasm.' He looks at me. 'What do you think, Christina?'

'I expect you are right,' I answer, 'one or the other.' I am wary what I say. An image from my dream rises unbidden. The treasure cave was nearby, but that was also the mother jaguar's den, where she had her cubs. It was a place of safety for her.

I hear rumbling as if the mountain trembles. We both freeze, waiting, listening. The air in the tunnel seems to sigh like a creature's breath then everything is silent again.

'Come, my darling,' he says and puts my arm in his. 'No more delay. This must be the way.' But I don't move. I have so many questions about this man crushing in on me and feeding my fear. 'Please, Roberto,' I say, 'if you took on your cousin's identity, what happened to the real Diego Alvarez?'

He laughs again and I flinch. 'I wondered how long it would take you to work that out, my dearest.' He holds both my hands. 'He was the one lost at sea, not me, not Roberto Chavez.'

'But how did he die?'

His voice is cold as ice. 'He treated me like a cur, locking me in a dark hold on the boat. He ignored my pleas for light, water, food. He deserved the end he surely intended for me. A knife in his back and a watery grave.'

I pull my hands away. 'You killed him?'

'Of course I killed him. Just as I had killed a man in Spain, whose death had forced me to flee the country of my birth.' He wags his finger in my face. 'I swear both deaths were in self-defence. Roberto Chavez was entitled to defend his reputation and his life. At last I can free myself of these dead men on my back. Now come!'

He grins at me and I see only evil; he's like a snake shedding its old skin in the hope of being renewed. I feel myself almost dragged along further down the tunnel, leaving the shaft and the daylight behind us. At the next turn I hear the trickle of water. Roberto shines his torch up and water is running down the rock-face splashing into a perfect rock-pool in the wall. Another image comes to me. A jaguar drinks beside me. There is an understanding between us – the jaguar and me. No, it wasn't me, it was Tlalli. Roberto drops the bag from his shoulder and we quench our thirst together. I scoop up water in my hand. It has a metallic taste but is fresh and clear.

I remember there are more questions I must have answers to. My trust in him is almost gone. How can I love a man who has committed cold-blooded murder?

'Roberto, tell me, I thought you came to Perú to open your mine in this very mountain. Isn't that why you have so much money from your investors?' Again, he makes that deep throaty laugh, throwing back his head. I see the conquistador, taking the very same stance and my mind fills with dread.

He flicks the torch around the tunnel. 'See for yourself, Christina. There is no gold left in this mountain, or any of the other mines I where I hold the deeds. My surveys were fabrications. But they served their purpose: over a million dollars! A fortune for us to feast on. Together with your own fortunes, we will be so rich, my darling, no one will be able to touch us.' He seems to almost dance with glee.

'Come!' he says, 'There are more riches to find but we must hurry.' He turns and struts off further down the passage and I'm compelled follow. I count my paces from the pool. I have reached thirty when he shouts out to me.

'Another cave, come Christina, quickly.' I hurry to him and together we enter the cave. He shines his torch around and I can hear my heart thumping. There are no jaguars here but what there is astounds me, even though I knew this was the place. Splashes of gold reflect in the torchlight. Roberto rushes forward to touch the pieces. Old sackcloth which had once covered them disintegrates or is already turned to dust.

Roberto is like a madman. 'Gold! Gold! The Inca's gold!' he moves from piece to piece: carved plates, statues, ornaments, amulets, necklaces, cups and bowls. There must be hundreds of separate pieces. He dances back to me. 'I'm rich! Christina, look, I'm rich!' He rushes back to the treasure and begins collecting pieces in his arms.

'Roberto, we can't possibly remove anything now,' I say, 'besides, this place is sacred. The treasure should stay here.' But he isn't listening to me. He is gasping over a large golden disc he has found.

'Look, Christina. This piece alone will be worth a fortune, a king's ransom!' He staggers over to where I still hover near to the entrance. I know what this object is. It is the Inca's great *Punchao*. It came from the Sun Temple in Cuzco. I think of the irony that it was hidden so it didn't become part of the ransom demanded by the Spanish for the life of the Sapa Inca. He pushes the golden disc into my hands and shines the torch on it. It is beautifully moulded in a representation of the sun god Inti. It is magnificent but very heavy.

'Take it back to where the daylight entered the passage, Christina, while I gather more pieces together,' he says. I want to protest but I know he will not listen to me. Every instinct tells me this is wrong. He is like a madman, greedy for the gold, just as the conquistador had been. I carry the *Punchao* back into the passage. It is immediately dark so I stop and take the torch from my pocket. I switch it on and rest it on the golden disc. It lights up like a death mask and a chill passes through me. I go as far as the rock pool and stop, knowing I am nearly there. Rumbling seems to come again from deep inside the mountain. The sound is like a roar and I feel the ground tremble.

I shout out in alarm. 'Roberto!' but he doesn't answer. I leave the *Punchao* by the rock pool and taking the torch I hurry back down the passage calling out to him. 'We must go!' I say, 'leave the gold, we have to get out!'

As I try to run the passage is shaking and I lurch banging into first one side, then I'm thrown across to the other, tearing my hands and face on the rough stone walls. I hear a terrible high pitched scream in my ears, and then I hear a deep roar as the rocks around me pitch and slide. The mountain seems full of hundreds of big cats calling in distress.

I gasp and sob but cannot find the cave entrance and don't know how much further it is down the passage. 'Roberto! Where are you?' I am on my knees, I try to stand but everything is moving. The walls seem to lurch towards me and rocks fall all around. I feel a heavy blow to the side of my head and the ground comes up to meet me. As I fall, though I have not thought of him all day, I think of Sam, and I know Roberto lied to me.

59

Spirit of the Jaguar

1539 Mount Yaguar, Vilcabamba, Perú

All Tlalli could feel was the incessant jogging of the horse and the digging pinch of the rider's knees in her back. She could barely breathe, for her hands and feet had been tied together under the horse's girth.

'Hey, Gonzalo!' One of his companions shouted. 'Be careful, friend, this woman bites.'

'So does my whip!' he replied. As he rode on he lashed Tlalli across her back. She felt the sting as the leather thong bit into her skin but the dread in her heart was sharper fearing what he planned to do. She didn't have long to wait as he began to rant as he galloped along the trail. 'I will have the Inca's treasure, woman.' He lashed out with his whip as if to reinforce his order. 'This time, you will not escape me, Tlalli Manari!'

The whip's thongs with cruel knotted ends lashed into her back. She must endure the pain. This would be her greatest test and she must not fail. Her mission, her people, the sacred jaguars, all depended on her holding fast to her vows.

Night had come and they stopped. The horses were picketed but the men left her, still trussed to the animal. The Spaniards shared a meagre supply of food and a leather bottle of wine but Tlalli received nothing. When they had satisfied their appetites Tlalli was taken down from the horse and brought before Gonzalo. His face glowed purple from the wine and the heat of the campfire, but she also saw a cruel burning lust in his eyes. She remembered the first time she saw this man with his cruel lustful eyes. She had been little more than a child and had hidden behind her father for protection. Now she was a grown woman and totally at his mercy.

That night Tlalli suffered unspeakable acts of violation and humiliation. When Pizarro had his fill she was turned over to his men for more sport. She wished desperately that she would die at their hands as they took turns abusing her. Tlalli's body burned from cuts and bruises but she knew they would not kill her tonight. Pizarro still needed her to satisfy his greed and find the gold, but after that yes, they would kill her.

When they tired of her, she felt their kicks and heard their drunken laughter. She lay on the bare earth, so weak she wished she would die in the night. She had been humiliated and damaged beyond repair, her body violated. Beyond tears, she felt only utter despair; as worthless as the dirt on which she lay, hardly conscious, her breathing shallow. But eventually she fell into troubled sleep, and with sleep came a dream.

The jaguar goddess Izella appeared to her once more. She didn't speak but drew close to the sleeping girl. With her big soft tongue she washed Tlalli's near lifeless body as if she were a new-born cub. She cleansed her wounds and with each stroke transferred her power, renewing Tlalli's faith and restoring her courage.

Just before the dawn she awoke, remembering the horrors of the night. Slowly, the threads of her dream returned. She could still feel the warmth and comfort of the big cat. Little by little she understood; Izella had healed her and renewed her strength and resolve. She must not fail, her mission must continue. She had been given the strength to fight on, even if just for one more day.

But she was only a girl, a human girl. How could she thwart this vile wicked man? Ten times stronger than her, and armed with sword, dagger and whip, she had little in her favour. What did she have to fight with? A voice sang within her; 'Spirit of the Jaguar, Spirit of the Jaguar'. If her faith was being tested, it would hold fast. She had witnessed the Spirit, she had become the Jaguar. She would do whatever it took to defeat this man and she would trust in the Spirit to show her how.

At first light they resumed the journey. Once again she was tethered to Pizarro's horse. He mounted up, soon venting his anger with his tongue and his whip. They continued, taking the route she had used the previous day, round the foothills of Mount Yaguar.

He reined the horse to a stop and grasping her hair he yanked her head up. They were almost back at the point where she had begun her climb the previous day. 'Show me the way to go, woman. Lead me to the treasure.' He pulled her head up even more and she thought her neck would surely snap but she gritted her teeth against the pain. To mislead him she would have to be cunning, for he was already familiar with the trails around the mountain.

She looked towards the back trail, the one leading to the dark side of Mount Yaguar.

'Ha, I have been that way and the entrance is too small. You think to trick me again and disappear into a hole I cannot enter.' She felt the heavy thrust of a blow from the handle of his whip beat down on her back. She cried out in pain and thought she would break in two.

How could she survive and keep her tormentors away from the trail? She only knew one other way into the mountain, the way she had found yesterday, quite by chance. But even she could not enter down the shaft in human form, so neither could the Spaniard. But to take him so close to the entrance and the treasure was too great a risk. She remembered the two jaguar cubs in the treasure cave. Once she showed him the entrance he might kill her and then, with the other men, use ropes to climb into the shaft. No, the risk was too great. There had to be another way to mislead him. Show me Izella, show me!

She felt the ropes tying her to the horse loosen. As the bonds fell away she tumbled to the ground too weak to stand. His hands were on her before she could think of running, although she doubted she had the strength. One of his companions began pointing and jabbering in Spanish. They all looked up to where he indicated and there, on the high ridge, was a jaguar. Tlalli's spirits plunged for she wished the Spaniards had not seen it. Was Izella warning them to stay away? Or did Toquri want to lead them into a trap? She waited, fearful of the Spaniard's reaction.

Gonzalo shook his fist. 'There is the animal that killed my horse. Now he will die.' He instructed one Spaniard to guard their horses, and taking all the ropes they had, they prepared to climb. Tlalli felt more pain as a rope was tied to one of her ankles and Gonzalo pushed her on, ahead of them. She didn't want to take them up the way she had gone before, but she knew there was no other route and besides, they had seen the jaguar and knew where they were headed.

Hampered by their armour and weapons the Spaniards climbed clumsily, while in spite of the tether she could scale the steep ridge and find the footholds more easily. But the climb became harder as she gasped for breath and trembled with exhaustion. If Gonzalo fell she would go with him for they were roped together. She tried to lead them away from the obvious route but there was no other way and she was forced to continue up. After several hours hard climbing they eventually reached the ledge where the Spaniard had glimpsed the jaguar.

They spread out on the ledge. She felt a terrible sense of betraying her beloved jaguars. She remembered the two little cubs who even now slept on in the heart of this great mountain, oblivious to the threat creeping ever closer to them. She gritted her teeth drawing on her little remaining strength. I will go no further. If they push me off the ledge, if they kill me! I will not show them the entrance.

The Spaniard who had originally seen the jaguar had now traversed to the far end of the ledge and he shouted out. He had found the gap that led only one way - up to the top of the high granite ridge. One by one the Spaniards disappeared through the gap. As Gonzalo went into the gap he hauled on the rope, almost dragging her through.

The men continued to climb even though she was not now leading them. There seemed to be no way she could stop them from finding the shaft entrance. She looked up and realised the man now leading the climb had reached the place where the entrance lay hidden. In a few minutes they had all reached the same spot and Gonzalo pulled her roughly towards the shaft.

'Is this your secret entrance, witch?' he shouted angrily.

Tlalli shook her head violently. She didn't want him to find the treasure but worse than that, they would find the cubs. One by one the Spaniards peered down the shaft. One threw a stone into the void and they listened as it bounced off the sides and rattled to the bottom. As Tlalli had already known, none of these men could enter as it was too steep and narrow.

Gonzalo shouted again. 'You will go down and bring me gold, Tlalli Manari.' She pretended not to understand him. 'Oori, oori!' he repeated.

She shook her head again. He pulled her to him and began tying the rope around her waist. He twisted it around her shoulders with the knots at the back, impossible for her to untie. She was dragged by two men to the head of the shaft and lowered in. She grabbed at the rope and felt her feet and legs scrape on the hard granite. It was nearly midday and the sun shone brightly, but as she dropped down into the mountain, now as a captive, a dark fear took hold and she found it difficult to breathe, difficult to think. How can I overcome these men and keep my promises?

Her feet touched the bottom of the shaft and she looked up. She could see the daylight and the heads of the men looking down, but she knew they could not see her. She tried to wriggle out of the rope cage Gonzalo had tied round her. If she could only release the ropes she would be free. She could hide down here for days. She had water and they could not reach her. Then she remembered the tribe in the forest; he would take his revenge on them. But what could she do? She felt a pull on the rope and heard Gonzalo shout from the top of the shaft. Even down here she was his prisoner and her options were very limited.

From memory she found her way to the pool of water and quenched her thirst. As she scooped the water and drank from her hand she became aware of another sound close by. She listened, it was the steady lap of a cat's tongue quenching its thirst also, but she wasn't afraid.

She sensed the animal move closer, and she reached out, feeling soft fur under her hand. Instinct told her this was the mother cat and she trusted Tlalli. She stroked the animal's head rubbing behind her ears. 'I will not let these strangers hurt you or your cubs,' she whispered, 'but you must help me.' The jaguar nuzzled her hand. 'Can you bite through this rope? She pulled the rope around her waist towards the cat's head.

The cat immediately began to gnaw at the rope. Tlalli remembered long ago in the forest, the first time she had become a jaguar and rescued the cub caught in the hunter's trap, tethered by a rope. She had severed the rope with her sharp animal teeth. Was this the same cat, the one she called Izella? Does she remember me and link me with her rescue? As she thought she continued to talk to the jaguar and reassure her, and the cat continued to shred the rope with her teeth. Tlalli felt fear and joy, amazed how gentle this fierce wild animal could be. As the last thread of rope fell away she slipped out from her bonds only just in time. She still had the rope in her hand when she felt it tug and the Spaniard's impatient voice bellowed down the shaft.

'Where are you, girl? Where is my gold?'

She shouted back that it was dark and he must wait. She didn't know if he understood her words but she let go of the rope so he would soon know that she had freed herself. The jaguar began to move away. In the dark tunnel Tlalli could see nothing. Grasping the jaguar's tail she followed. Gonzalo's voice came in an angry bellow, echoing down to her. She looked back towards the shaft. Both the light and the voice faded as she followed the jaguar into the darkness.

They had reached the treasure cave where the cubs lay. Her eyes were growing accustomed to the darkness. The walls of the tunnel were not completely black. Tiny veins of colour ran through the rock face; white, sapphire, emerald, ruby, silver and gold. They lifted the black to a navigable gloom. As they entered the cave the jaguar gave a low roar. She let go of the animal's tail and it moved further into the cave, towards her cubs, mewing and excited by their mother's return. Tlalli tried to look around the cave for the Inca's treasure left there so long ago.

Even in this low light, the pieces exposed by the rotted sacking, glittered. Tlalli had resolved not to hand anything over to the Spaniards waiting above. Even if she died in here she would not betray the rebel movement she had begun. Yet she had to consider what the Spaniards might do to even the score. Thinking about the danger to her family, her resolve began to waver. Her eyes fell on the sacred Punchao and she remembered how the Inca used it during the Inti Raymi ceremony. She felt for her jaguar talisman and with her heart beating wildly she prayed to Izella for guidance. Gradually her panic receded and she felt calmer. When she opened her eyes she knew what she must do.

60

Ghosts and Dreams

June 1931, Mount Yaguar, Vilcabamba, Perú

When I wake, I feel the hard cold surface beneath me and excruciating pain in every part of my body. My mouth is dry and when I try to open my eyes, the lids are stuck together. I have no idea where I am or how I got here. My thoughts revolve around something I have just witnessed. Was it real or a dream or a vision? I can't recall what, but it was something terrible.

I flex my fingers; they are stiff and cold and I slowly turn onto my back to rub my hands and arms, then my legs. Blood returns, stinging my limbs like freezing water. It is a painful process but not as painful as the dull ache in my head. I put my hand where it hurts. There is a wound; sore to touch but the blood is dried. So I must have I been lying here some time. There is also a large swelling above my temple, throbbing in time with my pulse. Who am I? I search my mind for clues but find only confusion, conflicting images which run together and tell me all and nothing.

My thirst is overwhelming. I must find water but it is so dark I am afraid to move. An image from the vision, or dream, reaches out to me. A pool filled with fresh clear water, here, in this place. I know I have to find it. I am too weak to stand and will have to crawl. But which way to go? I will try the way I am facing first. As I scrabble about on my hands and knees, I touch loose stones, grit and rocks in my path. I remember these fell on me and that I am in a tunnel. The tunnel shook and threw me to the ground. Yes, that is what happened, but why was I here?

My name is Tlalli. I was forced to come here by someone. He wanted me to show him where treasure lay hidden in the mountain. I must do everything in my power to stop him finding this golden hoard. It is under the protection of the jaguar gods and must remain so. I am amazed that I remember all this but who are the jaguar gods?

My hand flies to my neck. Two chains, two pendants. My fingers trace their shape. In the dark I cannot tell them apart, but I can picture them in my head. One has eyes that bulge and a fierce mouth with fangs and barred teeth; the other is serene, with oval eyes half closed and a gentle mouth. A god and his goddess, and this place is their spiritual home. I am inside a mountain and I believe I have survived an earthquake.

My hands come up against a wall of rubble that blocks the tunnel. Was this near to the cave holding the treasure? I am confused again. When I left this cave it was still open but I took something with me. A big golden disc:

the *Punchao*. But I wasn't alone, there was a jaguar with me, in the cave, in the mountain. The jaguar had chewed through the ropes that bound me. Was that me? No, Tlalli. I am not Tlalli, she is in my dreams. She lived four hundred years ago. The question remains, who am I and why am I here?

Water. I am searching for the pool. I turn my body round and go back in the opposite direction. I can stand now but must walk very carefully for the ground is littered with debris. I count my steps though I don't know why. At ten I stop to rest. This must be near to where I lay unconscious. I sink to the floor and run my hand across the ground. I touch something that is not a rock. Long and round, it is a torch. I find the switch and push it. The tunnel lights up and I am amazed. I remember the torch, I was holding it when I fell. Somehow it must have turned off so still has power.

'Thank you, Izella,' I say, and then wonder why I spoke that name. There are two people in my head, but Tlalli's voice is the stronger. It is she who thanks the jaguar goddess.

Now I have light I shine it back the way I have just come. I can see the wall of rubble blocking the passage and can only guess beyond that lays the cave with the treasure. Was the Spaniard in there? No, my enemies were at the top of the shaft. They had lowered me down, tied to a rope, to bring the treasure to them. My mind is in a fog again. Water. I must find water.

I turn away and begin up the passage again. It is easier now I have the torch and I count from ten to thirty. I know this is where I was, when? How many days ago? I can hear the drip, drip of water and shine the torch up and round. There! The water seeps from the rocks and drips into the pool. This part of the passage is exactly as it was, untouched by the tremors. I crouch beside the pool and immerse my hands and face. I drink straight from the surface, sucking the water into my mouth, gasping and drinking much too fast. I dip my aching head right into the water and feel a cool relief.

I sit back gasping; the water is sacred, I will be healed. I will survive. I pick up the torch and it catches a flash of gold on the ground by my feet. The Inca's *Punchao*. The shining image of the sun god Inti.

I scoop more water from the pool, drinking a little at a time. I shuffle back leaning against the granite and close my eyes. I must remember, sort dream from reality, for they are interwoven. A man's image floats behind my eyelids. I study it as his features come into focus. I know him quite well: Diego – no, Roberto! He was with me in this tunnel, but where is he now? I breathe deeply and drink again. I must clear my thoughts, I must remember.

I decide to walk further on. This torch will not last long and I must conserve the battery. Around the next bend I feel a change in the air, fresher, I look up. Through a high, narrow opening, I can see the night sky and stars. It is too far up to climb unless I had a rope. The dream image resurfaces. I was lowered down on the rope by the Spaniards. No, Tlalli was lowered down on the rope. So who am I? I look down at my hands, my clothing, although it is torn and filthy. A jacket with belt and pockets, slacks, soft boots. I see myself in a mirror when I bought them. I am with a friend and we are dressed alike. We are laughing – she is Grace.

Grace, Diego or Roberto. There is someone else I must remember then I will know who I am. I look up again at the stars. The sky is lightening, washing out the stars. Sam! How could I have forgotten? We are in love, we are engaged. My name is Christina Freeman.

I sink to the ground with such relief and bless that my memory has returned. I close my eyes and realise there are still many questions I must answer. Why was I inside this mountain with Roberto? Another image returns. I am standing in the entrance to a cave holding the *Punchao*. I am watching Roberto collecting together dozens of gold pieces. He is gabbling like a mad man, shrieking out, 'Gold, Gold! I am rich. I have found a King's ransom!' I leave him and come back to this shaft, carrying the *Punchao*.

That's when the tremors began and the mountain shook. It roared like an animal and as I tried to get back to him, rocks rained down on me and I was thrown to the ground. How long did I lie there before I came round? How incredible that I wasn't crushed by the falling rocks. Did the spirit of the jaguar protect me? And what of Roberto? Could he still be alive on the other side of the rock fall? I remember hearing a terrible scream. Was that him? I know I will have to try to find him. I will wait until full daylight. Now I must rest again for I am so very tired.

I open my eyes and the sun is shining above me. Its light reaches down and warms me and I think it must be midday. I remember the dawn was breaking when I fell asleep. I go back to the pool to drink, so thankful that I remember who I am. I also remember that Roberto is the other side of the rock fall and I don't know if he is dead or alive. Other thoughts crowd in and I remember why we came here together.

I feel a deep sense of shame knowing I deliberately came with Roberto leaving Grace and someone else behind. It wasn't Sam, he had already left me after we had argued. The other man was Martin Chambi. Dear Mr Chambi, who had been such a friend to me and to my Uncle Peter. I remember so many things now I feel my head will explode. I have been a fool, a headstrong stupid fool. Why, oh why, did I allow myself to be seduced by Roberto?

There was someone else. We visited the Inti Raymi ceremony in a hidden valley. We were taken there by the Indian guide, Egecati. Yes, of course, he was with us all the way. Until Roberto sent him back for supplies. At least, that is what he told me. So perhaps Egecati will return and come to find us. I can only hope that he does.

First, I must try to discover if Roberto survived the earthquake. I don't want to go back down the dark passage but I must. I know now he is a rogue, but I had thought I loved him when I discovered he was Roberto. My teenage fantasies had coloured my memory and led me to make a bad decision. Now I may pay for that with my life.

I use the torch sparingly and count my footsteps, remembering it was thirty to the treasure cave. My legs are week as rotten sticks but I must steel myself and not give way to despair. The wall of rubble stops me at twenty-eight; only two paces from the cave. I kick the wall with the sole of my boot. Nothing moves, it is packed solid. What had been the top of the tunnel has collapsed, and this could still be a very dangerous place.

I shout out, 'Roberto!' and listen to my voice echo round the tunnels. I yell louder, 'Roberto!' I strain my ears for the smallest sound and wait. All is silent. What else can I do? I pick up a heavy lump of rock and bang it as hard as I can on the wall near to where I guess lies the cave entrance. I bang the rock again and call out his name. There is no answering call. I see the torch begin to dim. Afraid for my own safety I snatch it up and hurry back to the pool and the daylight. This is the only place where I feel safe – at least for now. I cannot guess how Roberto's end might have been but I am sure he is dead. I have to believe that for the alternative is unthinkable.

As it is, I am trapped alive, but for how long? I suddenly feel very hungry so drink from the pool. At least that should keep my hunger a little subdued. I risk the torch to look around and suddenly see something square covered with rock dust. It is Roberto's bag! I remember he left it there before going into the treasure cave. I grab it greedily and rummage inside. There are two biscuits and a torch battery, but that is all; I don't know which is the greater treasure. I nibble one of the biscuits and reluctantly put the other back in the bag. But the battery will be a great help.

I have one more thing I must do. Find the way back up the steps to the first cave where we entered the mountain. The thought terrifies me but I grit my teeth; I must do all I can to help myself, for help from outside may never come, or come too late. From the shaft, I know it is still day, but I don't know how many hours are left. I am torn between leaving the pool which is my lifeline and finding a possible way out. I take the latter, thinking I can come back here if I have to.

I know the way and pass under the shaft and on along the tunnel again leaving the daylight behind. I travel about fifty paces, sliding my feet forward carefully, not to stumble into rocks or stones. I have changed the battery in the torch and flick it back on and see the steps are about ten feet away. I am trembling from fear and cold but I must do this. I shuffle ten more paces then risk the torch again. I shine it up and know there will be no escape for me this way. The tunnel is blocked by another rock fall. I don't know if I am scared because this means my rescuers can't reach me, or relieved I will not have to climb the steps in the dark and risk if I could escape that way. Now I know the shaft and the pool are my only option, even if I die here.

I drink from the pool and then return to the shaft. I witness the passing of day into the night once more. I have eaten the last biscuit and everything is hopeless. This area is so remote and Egecati has not returned. If help does come, it will be too late. I can't even cry.

I lay on my back and watch the indigo sky. Stars appear; the brightest first followed by millions of others. In clusters and swirls they fill my window. I think how utterly beautiful they are and that this may be the last view I have in my life.

My hand moves to my neck and I seek out the Izella pendant, holding it with one hand, caressing the jaguar head with the other. If I am to pray for my soul, it is fitting that I pray to the gods of this sacred place. As I fall asleep I despair, for I still don't know how Tlalli's story ended.

61

The Punchao

1539 Mount Yaguar, Vilcabamba, Perú

This sacred Punchao was special. It had been made for the exclusive use of the reigning Inca in the capital city of Cuzco. Tlalli's father had hidden it here and she had found it against the wall of the cave, half-visible where the old sacking fell away. She lifted it up. Its weight tested her strength. She ran her fingers over the intricate pattern on the surface. It mirrored the face of the shining sun, the outer edge set with a circle of flames. It was a face mask, with apertures for the eyes of the Inca. The years incarcerated in the cave had not diminished its brilliance.

She held the outer edges and carried the Punchao from the cave back up the passageway. She could see the daylight from the shaft and continued saying her prayers to Izella and now also to the sun god Inti. Her actions were being driven by spiritual forces and she didn't know how they could work to her advantage; that was in the hands of the gods.

The rope still hung down and she could hear the Spaniards' loud voices shouting from the entrance. The noonday sun was immediately above the shaft just as she had hoped. Tlalli called out to the Spaniards to ensure they were looking down the shaft. She lifted the Punchao up in front of her face and tilted it towards the sun. Through the apertures she could see the reflected rays of the sun beam upwards, just as the Inca would have beamed the sun's light on to his people. From the top she heard shouts of dismay as the men were blinded by the strong beam of light. In that very moment, a miracle took place.

A hail of stones fell on the Spaniards from above them and she heard the blood-curdling cries of her rebels in battle, the animal cries they used to frighten foes on their raids. More stones pelted the men above her and she drew back as the missiles rattled down the shaft. Her spirits soared and she felt blood surging through her veins. She opened her mouth to shout the rebel cry and uttered a deep roar. Her body transformed as it had before. Her hands became huge paws and her shape feline. Her body grew strong; the advantage she needed to join the battle above.

She leapt up the shaft, finding the animal footholds to push upwards, a pattern learned over hundreds of years. She burst to the surface with a roar of rage, snapping and snarling at the terrified Spaniards. The rebels drove down on them, hurling stones and boulders on the enemies.

'Kill the beast!' screamed Gonzalo. Tlalli had him in her sights and charged straight for him, butting him head-on and knocking him to the ground. As he fell, dropping his sword it caught her a glancing blow, grazing the skin on her neck. She heard a voice shouting from above.

'The Spirit of the Jaguar has come to our aid. Rebels follow me!' Even in her animal form Tlalli knew the voice as Paullu's. The rebels poured down from the top of the mountain yelling and shouting. The Spaniards began to retreat down towards the ledge.

Tlalli had Gonzalo under her paw. He had lost his sword and it would have been easy for her to bite through his neck and kill him. The rebels had nearly reached the place and were howling, ready to chase their enemies off the mountain. She could see Paullu striding towards her and knew she had to disappear again. She would not taint the jaguar with Gonzalo's blood; she would leave his fate to the rebels.

She leapt back down the shaft, elated that the spirit had worked within her and brought Paullu to her rescue. She went to the pool and as she quenched her animal thirst she felt herself changing back into human form. As this miracle took place she watched the strangest apparition. Before her eyes a figure came from the gloom. She could almost see the shape change from human to animal, just as she changed from animal to human. A trickle of blood oozed from the jaguar's neck, trickling down her golden fur. Now Tlalli understood completely. This animal came in flesh and blood, but also possessed the spirit of the sacred jaguar goddess Izella, who had once been a girl called Tlalli. She had been chosen to continue as part of this sacred pact.

Tlalli lifted up the Punchao and followed the jaguar back to the treasure cave. The mother cat returned to her cubs and Tlalli placed the sacred treasure back where she had found it. She spoke to the Jaguar:

'I leave this treasure under your protection, Izella, for you are the Spirit of the Jaguar. I will go back to my world and fight for my people. I will be true to my vow until the end of my days.' The jaguar lifted her head and gave a loud roar and then she lay down with her cubs. Tlalli turned away and stumbled back along the passage.

She could see Paullu at the shaft head. He was calling, 'Tlalli! Tlalli, are you down there?'

'I'm here, Paullu. Is Pizarro dead?'

'Oh, thanks be to Inti, you are alive,' shouted Paullu. 'The rebels are chasing the Spaniards back down the mountain. We have already captured their horses and killed the guard, so they will not get away. Now I must get you out. I'm guessing you can't climb out as the jaguar did. Oh, that was incredible!'

Tlalli allowed herself a smile, but she would not tell, not even Paullu.

The rope used by the Spaniards to lower her down still hung at the bottom. 'Can you secure the rope and pull me up?'

'I have it tight, Tlalli. Test your weight on it.'

She put her feet into the knotted loop in the end of the rope and Paullu began to pull her up. Her body swung, scraping on the rough granite sides, but she felt no pain, only a delirious happiness, as she rose up towards Paullu - her soulmate, the man she loved.

Perhaps one day she would tell her story, how she truly became the Jaguar Girl, filled with the Spirit of the Jaguar.

62

The Spirit Lives

June 1931, Mount Yaguar, Vilcabamba, Perú
When I wake I can barely open my eyes. They feel crusty and gritty. What little vision I have is blurred. I try to stand but am too weak. Daylight filters through my blinkered eyelids and I realise this is probably the third, maybe fourth day, since I entered the mountain with Roberto; I must not think of him for that is too painful.

I can't give in; surely help will come soon. I crawl to the pool and drink, then I dunk my head under the water and come up gasping for breath. At least I am more awake now and can see better. My eyes focus on the *Punchao,* lying where I left it. It's as if a light switches on in my head and I remember the dream I have just experienced. It showed me how Tlalli was rescued from this very place. The jaguar goddess, the *Punchao,* and the man she was going to marry, all played a part in her rescue. A fleeting sense of joy for her is quickly replaced by the despair that enveloped me yesterday. How can knowing Tlalli's story possibly help me now?

My change in mood shakes my confidence that help could be near. I sink back to the ground beneath the shaft. I watch bats returning to their roosts and envy their wings. A sound reaches out to me. A call, a strong roar. At the top of the shaft I see the outline of a cat – a jaguar - displaying its head and shoulders. It stands proud and regal. It lifts its head and calls again. I am mesmerised. Does it call to me or another of its kind? Is it real, or a trick of the light?

I have to shade my eyes, for the sun has reached my window on the sky. Another cat's head appears on the other side; a mirror of the first. They seem to speak to each other in low growls. I wait to see if they will attempt to climb down the chasm for I had seen this in my dream of Tlalli. They came here for the water, and the mother cat had cubs hidden in the treasure cave. That was when Tlalli lived, not now.

I blink against the sun and when I look again they have gone. But they did tell me something; jaguars still live on and in this mountain. Their spirit still protects the Inca's treasure. It was an earthquake that prevented the conquistadors from taking it then, and an earthquake has prevented another Spaniard from taking it now. I remember Tlalli's vow that the treasure represented the freedom and sacred beliefs of her people. It must remain hidden, protected by the jaguar gods until such time as her people, the Incas and all the tribes of their empire, are free again.

I crawl onto my knees and lift up my hands to the sky and croak out loud with a husky voice: 'To all the gods of the world; to the sun god, Inti; to the jaguar gods, Izella and Toquri; and any other gods who will listen to me. If you will grant me release from this sacred place which has become my prison, I promise to work tirelessly for the freedom of Tlalli's people, to fulfil her mission under The Spirit of the Jaguar!'

Then I am beset with doubts. Tlalli's rescue came about through her deep faith in the jaguar gods. She had proved her worth by working with her rebel movement. She deserved to be saved. What have I done to be worthy of the gods' benevolence?

My answer comes from the mountain itself. A rumble, deep in its heart, travels up to the surface. I feel the rocks vibrate. The sensation travels through my body setting me trembling. I hold my breath but it has ceased. Only the whining howl of the wind through the tunnels remains. I am left in the bitter wind of regret that I did not heed the wise words of the legend – without family-love a man or a woman is nothing. I didn't value my own family when I had them. Now I have rejected Sam and the chance to making a new family with him. I am worthless and will surely forfeit my life for my bad decisions. The wind howls again and I am reminded there are forces here I cannot control. I could be swept away in an instant, crushed, as surely as Roberto has been. Perhaps that will be my fate for I deserve nothing more. Thirst drives me back to the pool, though I wonder why I drink to prolong my life. I am sure now I will die in this place, either from hunger or crushed in another earthquake. There will be no escape.

I pick up the *Punchao* and return to the shaft where I can see the sky and watch the sun at its highest arc. I run my hand over the intricate design on the plate. I know it is not a plate but a mask, twice the circumference of the Sapa Inca's face. He would hold this golden mask, covering his face, during Inca ceremonies. When the sun's rays caught the golden disc, the light would be reflected on to his people. They would bow down, convinced the Inca was not a mortal man, but the manifestation of the sun god Inti.

The dream has shown me Tlalli used this very *Punchao* during her ordeal. She shone the reflected light up onto the faces of her Spanish tormentors as they peered into the chasm. This startled them and allowed Paullu and the rebels enough time to get close to the enemy for the final battle on the mountainside. But what use is it to me when there is no one to see the reflection?

I can hear a distant sound like throbbing and feel sure the mountain is preparing for my demise. When I hold my hand to the rocks, I feel it through my skin, so faint I could almost think I had imagined it. But my ears don't deceive me and the sound is getting louder. Now there are two distinct and different sounds. The mountain rumbles and the throbbing is

… above me. I look up and think it is a vision. I cannot believe what I see. The *Graf Zeppelin*!

My thoughts begin to jumble with how, why, and who, but I push them away, gaping up into the sky. The throbbing is from the engines and I can see the propellers whirling. Has it come to rescue me, or is this a fluke, a giant coincidence in its travels round the globe? I wave and shout, then realise the futility of that and immediately know what I must do. I raise the Punchao over my head, feeling its weight test my remaining strength to the limit. I tilt it to and fro praying I can catch the sunlight and send a beam of light, a message to this glorious airship, my only hope of life.

The airship passes over and disappears from my view. I throw the *Punchao* to the ground and yell. 'No! No, don't leave me. Don't go!' I stamp and scream then huddle sobbing on the ground. I am making such a din, I don't at first hear the engines throbbing again. When I do, I look up to see the ship is again above me. I grab the *Punchao* and repeat moving the disc to and fro. This time I look through the eye apertures and can see the beams touch the silver skin on the *Graf.*

'Please, please see me,' I croak. 'In the name of the sacred jaguar gods, rescue me!' The muscles in my arms are burning but I continue to move the disc. I hear a change in the engine's note. The airship appears to be stationary, hovering in the sky. I can hardly believe I am seeing this but I know that unless I continue to send the beams they cannot see me.

The mountain is rumbling and now it roars. I can feel movement through the rocks and fear my rescuers have come too late. Then comes the most wonderful sight of all. A rope ladder begins to descend from the airship, just as Eckener had described its use for the arctic. It is played out quickly and twists and dances in the air. The *Graf* seems to grow larger as it drops down. I can see a figure on the ladder, coming towards me.

Gasps of hysterical laughter escape from my throat, then screams of fear as the mountain begins moving under my feet. The shaft is breaking up and splitting apart. My view of the airship directly overhead is gone as palls of dust and grit billow, turning the chasm into a cauldron. I again catch sight of the figure on the ladder, as this lifeline lowers down into the void.

'Christina!' he shouts and I am overwhelmed hearing Sam's voice.

I babble and croak an incoherent reply.

'Here it comes, my darling,' he calls. 'Have courage, I will soon have you out.'

A hail of stones and grit forces me to close my eyes as it rains down. I reach out blind and by some miracle the rope ladder comes within my grasp, I swallow the madness bubbling within me and take a firm hold, willing my aching arms not to fail me. I begin to climb and am horrified as the bottom of the chasm seems to rise with me, as if to overtake my ascent.

Simultaneously, the rocky sides fall away, opening out like the petals of a flower. I look up and through the hail of dust, I see Sam on the ladder above me, frantically waving his arm in a circle. I come out through the top and am lifted away from the mountain, up towards the *Graf*. The airship is moving up and we swing below as if we are trapeze artists. I do not even feel the ropes cutting into my palms as the ladder is hauled safely into the airship. As we rise the last few feet I fall into the gondola and am immediately lifted from the floor by Sam.

'Oh, my darling Christina. I thought I had lost you.' I cling to him for a moment then I push my way back to the open hatch to look down, ignoring questions raining down on me. I hear Grace, Martin, Sam and others, but my eyes are fixed on the mountain below. The chasm is gone. Palls of smoke and clouds of dust still rise into the sky.

The airship circles round and I see two big cats moving purposefully down the mountainside towards the lower slopes, the gorge, and the safety of the jungle. They are jaguars and I know them well. They are Toquri and Izella. The legend has turned full circle, their work is done. The Inca's treasure is forever sealed in the mountain. But the work of Tlalli's rebel movement, the Spirit of the Jaguar, that begins again now. A promise I will keep.

The End

Author's Postscript - Telling the Truth

When I set out to write this book, I began on Christina's story. I wanted to pay tribute to the passenger airship, the *Graf Zeppelin* and its creator, Hugo Eckener. Between 1928 and 1937 this airship made numerous trips to America, particularly to Brazil. Hugo Eckener was its captain during the airship's round-the-world flight of 1929 when Lady Grace Drummond-Hay, Karl Henry von Wiegand and Bill Leeds were all among its passengers. The *Graf Zeppelin* also went to the North Pole during 1931. The possibility of the airship hovering over the Andes, in the way it had over the arctic ice, provided a unique fictional rescue opportunity for Christina years before helicopters were invented.

Grace and Karl were indeed lovers and their early relationship has been documented as I have describe it. Later, they embarked on a permanent liaison and went to live abroad. During the Second World War they were in the Philippines when the islands fell to the Japanese. They were interned in a prison camp and suffered considerable hardship. After VJ day in 1945, they returned to New York. Grace was very ill and died in 1946 at the age of only 51. In my fictional story, it would have been Grace and Karl who alerted Dr Eckener to engage in the mountain rescue operation.

The Perúvian photographer, Martin Chambi, is another real person now residing in my fiction. I came across his work and story looking for photographs of Perú in the 1930s. I obtained more information about Martin, his work and his influence on Perú during that era from Paul Yule, who had produced a documentary film entitled *Martin Chambi and the Heirs of the Incas*. I was able to obtain a copy of this unique film which helped me to include Martin as a character. He was an extraordinary photographer of great talent in the early twentieth century. He was also a leading figure in the revolutionary, artistic and social movements that swept South America in the 1930s. His magnificent photographs of Perú were the visual epitome of the *Indigenista* quest to rediscover the native culture of the Andes, a theme I was particularly keen to highlight. His actual studio in Cuzco opened at a date later than told in this story; such are the needs of fiction.

South America in the early 1930s has its own story to tell. A vast continent, with its Amerindian and post-Columbian social history, was being opened up and exploited by foreigners hungry for its natural resources. Sam's venture into charter flights was typical of the new entrepreneurs flocking to the continent. I was very fortunate to strike up correspondence with Andy Riddle of *Footprints Travel Guides*. Their company has been producing travel guides since the early twentieth century. I was even more fortunate when he agreed to lend me a copy of *The South American Handbook for 1930* from their archives. The book was a revelation, as travel guides at that time were produced for business travellers rather than for tourists; perfect for my little group of business voyagers to lay their respective plans to make their fortunes.

All the rest of my research involved the history of the Inca Empire: the ancient pre-conquest history, the story of the Spanish conquest, its impact on the people and the country at that time and the subsequent post-conquest history. It has been a complex and fascinating journey. Tlalli and her family are fiction, but their circumstances are not. The background history of the Inca nation, their leaders, and the crushing of their dynasty and empire by the invading Spanish is well documented. I studied it from the perspective of many chroniclers and more modern historians and explorers.

Tlalli's tribe represent the indigenous people who were living within the Inca Empire. Before the Spanish conquest, they had already been subjected to ethnic cleansing by the Incas, who moved whole tribes from one part of the empire to another, thus controlling warring factions and more importantly, ensuring the whole nation had the manpower and resources to feed itself and remain loyal to the Inca rule.

When the Spanish arrived, this slender balance of power was overturned. Some tribes sided with the Spanish against the Incas, but others remained loyal, dependent on the subsistence they eked from a harsh environment and the protection of their rulers. We know that rebel factions emerged during this period of history, but most individual stories of rebel leaders have been lost. Tlalli represents these brave warriors, male and female, who lived and died to protect their beliefs, their heritage and of course, their very lives.

I have tried to incorporate some lesser known facts into my story. Like the rebel nation ruled by Manco Inca, and then his sons, in the heart of the Vilcabamba. This continued for over forty years after the execution of Atahualpa and the fall of Cuzco. And the amazing story of the Acllas, known better as the *Virgins of the Sun,* whose lives were similar to nuns, but dedicated to the service of the sun god Inti. Also the cruel execution ordered by Francisco Pizarro, of Manco's Coya, Cora Ocllo, and the floating of her open coffin down the Urubamba River to flush Manco out of hiding.

The leading conquistadors, the four Pizarro brothers are also part of this history; real men who were utterly ruthless in their pursuit of gold and glory, both for Spain and themselves. It was hard to resist the temptation to have Tlalli kill Gonzalo Pizarro in the final battle on the mountain. But true history had to prevail. He was executed in 1546 by a new Viceroy, sent by the King of Spain, to outlaw the excesses of the original conquistadors and their maltreatment of the native Perúvians.

When the Spanish first arrived on the continent the Incas threw their gold and silver treasures into lakes and rivers, and hid them in caves and underground tombs, all to thwart the greed of the conquistadors. In the centuries since the Spanish conquest, tales of Eldorado and its golden cities have fuelled the expectations of explorers and treasure-hunters to criss-cross South America in search of lost cities and hidden treasure. Financial fraud as practiced by the character Diego Alvarez, aka Roberto Chavez, is an extension of this greed for wealth, to be amassed by fair means or foul.

The Legend of the Jaguar features in both parts of the story. The jaguar appears consistently in the art and history of many South American countries as a sacred being and as a god in many forms. There is much evidence that the jaguar was once worshipped in ancient South America thousands of years before the Incas. Also, that shape-shifters took on animal forms either through the imagination of an audience during religious worship, or by hallucinatory inducement. I searched for many months for any reference to a named jaguar god in Amerindian history. Unfortunately, few actual names or stories appear to have survived. So my legend and my jaguar gods are fiction. But I would like to think I have presented their story in the spirit of all such legends from across the world. The moral here is, without family love and loyalty, the richest man in the world is a pauper.

You can follow my blog at www.susan-pope.co.uk

As a bonus read, the full text of *The Legend of the Jaguar* begins on the following page.

A Folk Tale

The Legend of the Jaguar

Tawantinsuyu. Many, many years ago.

When the world began the great creator god, Viracocha, rose up from the sacred Lake Titicaca and created the sun, the moon and the stars and they became his children. His son he called Inti, the golden light of day. His daughter he called Mama Quilla, the moon of the night.

Viracocha called his world Tawantinsuyu, a harsh but beautiful land divided into four quarters. In the first quarter, the long coast of the west faced a great ocean and the beginning of his world. In the second quarter lay endless deserts of sand. In the third quarter many mountains of great height, capped with snow, reached up into the clouds. In the fourth quarter, lush green forests grew around the mountains and on to the end of Viracocha's world. Where the four quarters converged he said, 'This is the navel of the world, my sacred city. I name it Cuzco.'

Viracocha's children all became gods: gods of the sun the moon and the stars, and of the mountains, the animals, and the features of the land. The children of the gods divided into tribes and the people of the tribes multiplied. Their descendants filled the land with many more people. The people lived in all the four corners of Tawantinsuyu. They built towns and cities and farmed the land and fished the ocean and the lakes. They laboured and prospered. Some were rich and some were poor. The rich people governed the land and looked after the poor people who farmed and laboured. Although in time their legends and rituals changed and they had many gods, they all worshipped Inti, the sun god. In Cuzco the sons of rich men were expected to go out into the four quarters of the world and make their fortune before they took a wife.

So it was that one day two brothers left their home and went to seek their fortunes. They were the sons of Temotzin, called Egecati, meaning wind serpent, and his younger brother Huayna, which means youthful. The two brothers could not agree how to make their fortunes, so they went to find a wise old man who lived in the desert and ask for his advice. They travelled for many days and found the old man sitting cross-legged on the burning sand, staring across the desert.

'Are you the wise old man?' asked Huayna.

'Why do you ask?' said the old man.

Egecati said, 'It does not seem wise to me to sit all day in the hot, arid desert. Are you not afraid you will die of thirst?'

The old man laughed. 'Come, sit next to me.' Huayna and Egecati sat down on the hot sand next to the old man. 'Fix your eyes on the horizon and tell me what you see.'

The two brothers stared across the desert and after a while Huayna said, 'I can see a lake full of blue water!'

'Yes,' said Egecati, 'it is shimmering in the distance.'

The old man nodded. 'I am never thirsty or hungry in the desert,' he said. 'I just think about what I would like and it appears before me.'

Huayna asked the old man, 'If I think about fish or wild animals or precious stones will I see them?'

'Of course,' said the old man 'If you desire something enough you will see it, but you may have to go into the other quarters of the world to find your heart's desire.'

Huayna asked him again, 'If I want to find lots of fish and the beautiful pink mulla shells to make into jewellery where should I go?'

'You must go to the coast and in the ocean you will find these things are plentiful,' answered the old man.

Then Huayna asked him, 'If I want fruit and nuts, and the meat and skins of wild animals where should I go?'

'You must go into the forests and you will find these things are plentiful,' answered the old man.

Egecati eyes glinted with greed. He wanted to find greater wealth than shells or wild animal skins so he asked the old man, 'If I seek gold and silver and precious stones where will these be found, old man?'

'Ah,' said the wise man, 'you will find these in the mountains. You must look for a place where the river flows and sparkles with gold and that will lead to the golden mountain.'

'But there are many mountains and many rivers,' said Egecati. 'How will I know where to look?'

The old man answered. 'You must look for the golden jaguar for he is god of the sacred mountain and he guards the gold. His name is Toquri, but he will set you a task. If you complete the task Toquri will give you gold, but it will not be easy.'

The brothers thanked the wise old man for his counsel and left him in the desert. They walked to the foothills of the mountains and climbed to the first peak. They looked to the north and could see hundreds of mountains reaching as far as they could see. Then they looked to the south and again saw hundreds more mountains reaching to the end of the world.

Huayna despaired, 'The fish and the shells in the ocean would have been plentiful and the wild animals and plants in the forest would have been in great numbers. We could have made our fortunes more easily with them.'

But Egecati was gripped with a fever for the greater riches of gold. 'We have only to find the jaguar on the mountain to make ourselves very rich,' he said to his brother.

'You are forgetting, we will have to perform a task set by the jaguar before he will give us any gold,' said Huayna.

Egecati smiled. 'And you are forgetting, brother we came prepared to kill wild animals in the forest, and what is a jaguar but a wild animal.'

Huayna had a gentle nature but he was afraid of Egecati and so he followed his brother as they searched the mountains for the jaguar. They walked for many days, up and down the mountain passes. They examined the rivers flowing through the gorges beneath the steep precipices and scaled great heights and plumbed great depths, crossing rapids and panning in the waters looking for traces of gold. They camped on the river banks and sat on the mountain sides wrapped in their warm blankets. After many weeks even Egecati seemed ready to give up the search, for the jaguar could not be found on any of the mountains.

As they broke camp on the very day they had agreed to try their luck at the coast, Huayna sat and stared at the mountain above them. As he stared he saw a shimmering movement high up on the rocks near the mountain's peak, just as the wise old man had said. Huayna shaded his eyes and looked again. He saw the golden jaguar. He called out to his brother and the jaguar saw them and stared back down. The golden jaguar guarded the place where a spring gushed from the rocks and fed into the river. The two brothers began to climb up the rock-face.

Egecati said, 'Do not fear, my brother, for I have my sling and a pocket full of hard round stones.'

'You forget, brother. This jaguar is a god and his name is Toquri. He is god of the mountain. I would rather speak with him and find out what it is we must do,' said Huayna. 'If we anger a god we are the ones who will finish up dead and our bones will be picked clean by the condors.'

'Very well,' said Egecati, 'we will see what the jaguar says, but if he tries to kill us I will use my sling and knife and you must do the same.'

Huayna did not answer his brother and kept his own counsel. It was a difficult climb and the jaguar had the advantage as he was above them. But the jaguar did not attack and allowed them to come within a few yards of his territory.

He crouched on the top of a great flat rock and looked down on the two brothers. Then he gave a mighty roar that echoed across the mountains. 'Why have you come to Yaguar, my sacred mountain?' said the jaguar.

Egecati thought to humour the jaguar, for he did not believe he could be a god but flesh and blood like any other wild animal. 'Oh, jaguar, we have come to seek the gold and precious stones in this mountain. We wish to make our fortunes before we each take a wife.'

Now they were close to the jaguar they could see his coat was pure gold and decorated with beautiful patterns of black shapes and spots.

The jaguar roared again and said, 'I am Toquri, god of the mountain. What will you give me in return for my gold?'

Huayna believed the jaguar truly was a god and he answered. 'What do you desire, Oh, great god Toquri?'

And the jaguar said to Huayna, 'You must go to the sacred lake where all life began and find a wife. Bring me your firstborn child and I will give you half the gold in the mountain.'

Huayna felt very sad at the jaguar's words, but he said he would do as the jaguar had commanded.

Egecati asked. 'What do you want of me, jaguar?'

The jaguar gave a fierce growl and said to Egecati, 'I should kill you now for you are a non-believer and wish me harm. But I will give you the same task as your brother. Go to the sacred lake, find a wife and bring me your first born child and I will give you the other half of all the gold in the mountain.'

When Egecati realised the jaguar could read his mind he felt very afraid and thought better of his plan to kill him. 'I will do as you say, Oh, great god Toquri, and return with my first born child.' Egecati soon overcame his fear. He smiled to himself for he thought the task would be easy. Once he was married he would have lots of children so giving one to the jaguar would not cause him any grief.

And so the two brothers travelled to the great sacred Lake Titicaca, famed for its beautiful maidens descended from the moon goddess, Mama Quilla. Egecati and Huayna stood on the shore and watched the fishermen take their reed boats out across the waters of the lake.

'Where are you going?' asked Egecati.

The fishermen replied, 'We are going to the Island of the Sun and the Island of the Moon. The fish are plentiful there and the maidens are all virgins.'

'We have come to find wives,' said Huayna to the fishermen. 'Will you take us there?'

One fisherman said, 'What will you pay?'

The brothers felt in their pockets. 'I have a sling and six round stones,' said Egecati.

'And I have a knife made from wood and silver,' said Huayna.

The fisherman looked at their offerings and accepted them. 'I will take you to the Island of the Moon. That's where the maidens who are the daughters of Mama Quilla live.' So the two brothers clambered aboard the little boat.

The surface of the lake was still like a mirror, as clear and blue as the sky. The snow-capped mountains in the distance reflected in the water and the fish in the lake seemed to swim over the mountains. The sun shone down and it was very warm.

Even so, Huayna still looked sad, as he had since the jaguar set their tasks. 'Cheer up, brother,' said Egecati. 'Inti is smiling on us today for he knows we will soon be rich men.' Huayna nodded, but he kept his thoughts to himself and did not voice his fears over completing the jaguar's task.

They reached the Island of the Moon and saw many maidens punting their little reed boats to and fro the shoreline and through the reed-beds out onto the lake. The girls were pretty and wore brightly coloured clothes and straw hats with brims to keep the sun from their eyes. They smiled, too shy to speak to the brothers.

Huayna watched a girl with big black eyes and rosy cheeks. She stood in her reed boat with her punt and her figure was like the branches of the willow, bending up and down. As she came to the shore Huayna ran to help her pull up her boat and tie it fast. 'What is your name?' he asked her.

She smiled at him as she pulled her line of fish from the boat and hung it on a stick. 'I am called Centehua,' she said. 'It means "only one"'. She laughed and began to walk away.

Huayna ran after her. 'And are you the only one? Your parents' only child?' he asked.

She laughed again. 'I was when they named me, but now they have four more daughters.' This time Huayna laughed also. He thought her very beautiful and very funny and that she would make a good wife.

'My name is Huayna and I have come here to seek a wife. I think you are the only one for me. Will you marry me, Centehua?'

'She laughed again and said, 'You must come and speak with my family for I have no dowry to give a husband.'

Huayna had already fallen in love with Centehua and did not care about a dowry, so he went with her to see her mother and father.

Her father said to Huayna, 'We are a big family and Centehua catches many fish for us to eat and sell. She has no dowry but she is worth her own weight in gold. What would you trade to have her for your wife?'

Huayna thought hard about what he should offer and he said. 'If you will allow us to marry now, I will stay here and give you my labour until our first child is born. Then we will have to leave and return to my home in Cuzco.' He did not say anything about his promise to the jaguar or the gold he would receive. Centehua's father was very pleased with the bargain for he could tell Huayna was a strong young man and would help him greatly, and maybe they would stay.

Meanwhile, Egecati also found a girl to make him a good wife. She was called Nelli, which means truth. She was a big strong girl and Egecati thought she would give him many children and also work hard as a wife. He made the same bargain with Nelli's father, as his brother had made with Centehua's father, but Egecati had no intention of labouring for his wife's family. All he wanted was for Nelli to give him a child as soon as possible and return to the mountain to claim his gold from the jaguar.

The two brothers married their brides by the lake and the families covered them with many flowers and there was much singing and dancing to the music of panpipes and drums. When the bridal feast ended Huayna went to live with Centehua in her parents' house. They were a happy family and made Huayna very welcome.

Egecati wanted a house of his own and asked Nelli's father to find one for them. He said that when their first child was born he would inherit a fortune and would repay Nelli's father in gold. In fact, he received many favours from his father-in-law, using the same promise.

The two brides soon both fell with child. Huayna worked very hard for his keep and for his wife's keep also, and never complained. However, his brother Egecati never lifted a finger and let his wife continue fishing even when she grew too big with child to punt her boat. He lived off his father-in-law with the promise of gold in return. So they continued like this throughout the rainy season.

In the spring, within a few days of each other, the young wives each gave birth to their first child. Centehua had a son. Huayna was ecstatic with joy and when he held his son in his arms he knew he could never give the child away, not for all the gold in the world. They called the baby Nahuati, which means four waters, for the lake had brought him his wife and his son.

Nelli had a daughter, whom she named Tlalli meaning earth. Egecati could not hide his disappointment for he had also wanted a son. Not for himself, but he felt the jaguar would look more favourably on a boy. He went to see his brother. 'Now at last we can return to the mountain and claim our gold,' he declared. Egecati rubbed his hands together and Huayna could see the light of greed glinting in his brother's eyes.

Huayna said, 'We should wait until our wives are fully recovered from giving birth before we travel so far. We will have to scale the mountain. With the babies that will be very difficult.' He was trying to delay the journey for he did not want to go.

Egecati laughed, 'With the baby on her back Nelli will climb like a monkey. You should have thought about that when you chose a pretty little weakling for a bride.'

Huayna did not answer him for he was afraid what his brother would do if he refused to return to the mountain. So he went home and prepared Centehua and his baby Nahuati for the journey. One thing the brothers did agree on was that they would not tell their wives where they were going or what would happen when they arrived.

A few days later they set out with their families. Nelli and Centehua were surprised when they did not go to Cuzco so Egecati told them, 'We cannot return to our homes until we have made our fortunes. We know a place where gold is to be found and that is where we are going.'

They travelled for many days back to the mountain where they had seen the golden jaguar. When they arrived they made camp and waited. The next morning Huayna sat at the foot of the mountain and stared up towards the peak. Just as on the first occasion, the golden jaguar appeared on the ledge. When Egecati saw the jaguar he became very excited. He said to Nelli, 'Give me the child for she is promised to the jaguar in return for gold and riches from the mountain.' Poor Nelli protested and tried to run off with her baby but Egecati went after her and hauled her back to the camp and took the child from her.

Centehua became very upset when she saw this happen and she turned to Huayna and said, 'Please don't give our son to the jaguar. We have no need of gold or riches.'

'Do not fear,' Huayna told his wife. 'This jaguar is sacred. He is called Toquri, and is god of the mountain. He promised us riches if we returned with our wives and first born children. Give me the child to take to the jaguar. But I promise you I will not let any harm come to Nahuati.' Because Centehua loved Huayna very much, she believed him, and gave him the child.

The two brothers put on their wives' back-pouches with the babies in them and climbed up the mountain. They could hear Nelli sobbing and crying while Centehua remained calm and tried to comfort her sister-in-law.

When the men climbed up to the ridge they found the jaguar on the big flat stone. He lay in a crouching position, flicking his tail and watching them with his huge amber eyes. He gave out his mighty roar and then spoke to Huayna first. 'Have you brought me your firstborn child?'

Huayna said, 'Oh, jaguar, great god Toquri, I have done as you asked and returned with my firstborn child. But I must tell you that I love my wife and child dearly and I will not part with my son, not for all the gold in your mountain.'

Toquri gave out a great roar and the mountain shook. Huayna held Nahuati close to his chest and knelt on the ground to protect the child from harm. Toquri said to him, 'You are wise, for family is the greatest treasure a man can have. Go and live in peace with your wife and child. You will be rich in spirit and I will always protect you.'

Then Toquri turned to Egecati and said, 'Have you brought me your firstborn child?'

'Oh yes, great god Toquri, here is my daughter, Tlalli, and I claim my gold.' Even up here on the mountainside, Nelli's cries could be heard calling for her daughter. Yet Egecati ignored these and laid the baby at the feet of the jaguar.

Toquri looked at Egecati with eyes of fire. 'Very well, you have made your choice,' he said. 'The child belongs to me now and you can take half the gold in this mountain but not a grain more. If you disobey me, the child will die. Keep to our bargain and she will become a goddess, a legend of the mountains.'

So the brothers parted. Huayna took his family back to Cuzco and they lived poorly but very happily. Egecati stayed at the Yaguar Mountain and made poor Nelli work with him as they mined the gold. After one year they had taken half the gold from the mountain. Egecati hoped that if Nelli had another baby the jaguar would let him have the rest of the gold in the mountain. But poor Nelli did not conceive another child. She was very unhappy with her life and wished she had not married Egecati. So with half the gold from the mountain they went to live in Cuzco.

The gold brought them many things. They had a beautiful house on the main square, fine clothes, and servants. 'There Nelli,' said her husband, 'you do not have to work hard now so perhaps we will have more children.'

Nelli shook her head. 'I will not have another child, for you will take it from me and give it to the jaguar.'

Huayna and Centehua often came to visit them. By now they had three children and when they came to the beautiful big house they filled it with laughter and happy voices. Nelli was always pleased to see them but Egecati scowled at his brother's joy. He was beginning to understand the words the jaguar had spoken to Huayna when he refused to hand over his son.

He wailed at Nelli, 'Why can you not produce lots of children? We would be both rich and happy with our own family.'

But Nelli still grieved for the child they left on the mountain and because she remained barren Egecati reluctantly agreed that he may have been wrong to want riches in place of his only child. 'Very well, Nelli', he said, 'I will go back to the mountain and speak with the jaguar again.'

He went alone and climbed up the mountain to speak to the jaguar. He found him, just as before, on the big flat stone which was his throne. 'Why have you returned to my mountain, man?' said the jaguar.

'Oh, great god Toquri,' Egecati said, 'I made the wrong choice. My brother refused your gold and kept his wife and child. Now he has many children and they are all very happy, even though they are poor.'

'That is good,' said Toquri, 'They live under my protection and are all my children.'

Egecati said, 'But I gave up my child and took the gold instead. My wife is unhappy and we have no children and now I am unhappy too.'

The jaguar smiled. 'But you are very rich,' said Toquri. 'Is that not what you wanted?'

Egecati thought about all his possessions; his fine clothes and grand house, his servants and all his wealth. 'Yes, I am very rich but that means nothing now for I do not have a family. If you would return my child to me that will make my wife happy and we will have more children. Then in time, I could give you another child, my youngest perhaps.'

Toquri gave a great roar of rage. 'You have not learned your lesson, man. You still covet riches above the love of a child.' He rose from the stone lashing his tail and his eyes turned from golden amber to fiery red. 'You made your choice and it cannot be undone. I will show you your daughter. Look up to the top of my mountain.'

Egecati looked up and there on the high rocks was a beautiful young jaguar. As she moved she glowed as if made of molten gold. The jaguar spoke again. 'Your daughter Tlalli is now Izella, the jaguar goddess, and she is my wife.'

Egecati looked again and the golden female jaguar had three little cubs beside her on the mountain.

'They are *my* family now and I will protect them, for I am the great god Toquri, god of the mountain and god of all jaguars and I am a son of Inti, the sun god.'

But Toquri was not a vengeful god. He took pity on Egecati for he could see he was genuinely unhappy. 'Go back to your home and give away all your riches. When you have done this your wife will give you a son and you will be forgiven.'

So Egecati returned to his grand house in Cuzco and told Nelli what had become of their daughter. When he told her that the jaguar had said they were to give all their wealth away and would then have a family, she replied, 'Let us do as he commands, having children will be better than living in this grand empty house.'

So they began to give away their gold ornaments and statues, and all their beautiful jewellery and fine clothes. Nelli dismissed their servants and sent them off with gold and bales of fine yarn from the fleece of the wild vicunas. Nelli and Egecati left the grand house and moved into a little hovel at the bottom of the town. Egecati was not happy with this for he was a proud man, but he needed to test the jaguar's prediction that now this was done Nelli would fall with child.

Sure enough, the following spring Nelli gave him a son. By the end of the hot season she had produced a second child, a daughter. The boy was called Chimalli for shield, and the girl was named Itotia, which means dance. Nelli was now very happy and the children brought love and sunshine into their lives.

However, Egecati still hungered after the riches he had given away. He did not like being poor and having to work for a living. He knew that the jaguar had only given him half the gold in the mountain and he lusted after the riches he knew were still there. He waited until Nelli was to give birth again and decided this child would be given to the jaguar. He consoled himself with the knowledge that their first born child, Tlalli, was now the jaguar goddess, Izella, and wife to Toquri.

So while Nelli was still confined after the birth of her new baby daughter called Necahual, which means survivor, Egecati wrapped the new born baby in a blanket and stole out during the night. He travelled back to the mountain to find the jaguar once more. Little Necahual cried and would not take the llama milk Egecati had brought with him. When he reached the mountain he climbed up to the flat stone on the ridge. He waited all day but the jaguar did not appear. He called out, 'Oh, great god Toquri, I have brought you my youngest child and I claim the other half of the gold in your mountain. Speak to me, oh, Toquri.'

There came a mighty crack of thunder and lightning flashed around the mountain peak. The ground began to shake and Egecati clung to the rocks to prevent him toppling off the mountainside. The rocks began to smoke and crack, and a huge fissure opened up in front of him. It led down into the heart of the mountain. A voice came from within.

'Oh, man! Why have you returned to my mountain?'

Egecati could not see anything but he knew it was the voice of the jaguar. He summoned all his courage and spoke. 'I have come to claim the gold and brought you my youngest child.' As he said this he looked down at little Necahual. She was sleeping peacefully and looked so beautiful.

The jaguar's voice boomed out from the rocks. 'Give me the child.'

Egecati was beginning to regret coming but his lust for the gold was stronger. 'Shall I leave her on the stone, oh jaguar?'

There came a deep rumbling from within the mountain. 'Climb down into my cavern and bring her to me.'

Egecati's resolve began to waiver. 'Will she die?'

'Do you care if she lives or dies so long as you have your gold?' asked the rumbling voice of Toquri.

Egecati began the steep descent into the cavern and he called out, 'Do you want her for another wife, another goddess?'

'What does it matter to you what becomes of her?' said Toquri, and the mountain again trembled and shook. Egecati feared that he would fall and drop his precious baby. He reached the heart of the mountain and saw gold glittering in the rocky walls of the cavern. Toquri appeared in the form of a man, sitting on a golden throne dressed in golden robes. The sight of so much gold re-ignited Egecati's greed for the precious metal.

Toquri said, 'I have no need of another wife, my family is complete.' Behind the throne stood a beautiful woman and three little children and they were clothed in gold.

'So now, man, you have a choice: your child or gold. Which is it to be?'

Egecati was torn between love for his family and his greed for riches. He was also used to having what he wanted so he said to Toquri, 'Really, I would like both,' adding quickly, 'for you have both a family and much gold, oh, Toquri, god of the mountain.' He knew he had perhaps been too bold and he held his breath waiting for Toquri to answer him.

Toquri began to laugh, his laughter grew loud and filled the cavern, and then it became a great roar and he changed his form back to that of a jaguar. At the same time, the woman and the three children all turned back into feline form. The jaguar's roar filled the mountain and Egecati shook with fear.

The jaguar came right up to him, within inches of his face, and he feared both he and little Necahual would be eaten alive. Toquri spoke with a voice of thunder. 'You wish to keep the child *and* take the gold?'

In a very frightened voice and quaking with terror Egecati stammered, 'Yes...oh, Toquri.'

Toquri lashed his tail and said, 'Very well, man, you have made your choice and this cannot be undone! Place the child on my throne.' So Egecati did as the jaguar commanded and lay little Necahual on the golden throne.

Another mighty crack of thunder and lightning flashed within the mountain. Smoke rose from the bowels of the earth and Egecati fell to his knees and covered his head with his arms.

A silence fell, almost as chilling as the storm that had preceded it. The smoke began to clear and Egecati could now make out the shape of the cavern. No longer did it glitter with gold veins running through the granite, and Toquri's golden throne had vanished; so had the jaguar and his family. All Egecati could see was the coloured blanket in which he had wrapped Necahual. He crawled to where it lay in a crumpled heap on the floor of the cavern and carefully pulled back the folds.

He gasped, and called out in despair. 'My child, my baby! Oh, what have I done to you?' For within the blanket lay little Necahual, and although she was perfect in every detail, she was made of pure gold.

Egecati slumped over, a broken man. He could not take his golden child back to Cuzco and have her melted down for riches, and he could not have her returned to him as a living, breathing child. Neither could he go home and face his wife and two other children. His greed had robbed him of everything in his life and he realised too late that he really loved them. So he began to wander throughout the mountains and he became known as a shaman or wise man.

You may see him still, for he is the guardian of the sacred site called Mount Yaguar. He will tell travellers he is anything but wise, and entreats all people to listen to the voices of their gods and follow their commandments. He will say that after Viracocha the creator and Inti the sun god, the wisest god is Toquri and that he takes the form of a jaguar.

He will show you the sacred mountain and the stone statue nearby which is in the shape of a crouching jaguar. He calls this a *huacas,* a natural shrine. Egecati will also tell how Toquri commanded an earthquake to seal the mountain called Yaguar, to keep away all gold-seekers. Any people who come and take gold from this mountain, will be cursed, and lose everything they hold dear. For the Yaguar Mountain is protected by the Spirit of the Jaguar, the god Toquri, his goddess Izella, and all their descendants, forever.

The End

Lightning Source UK Ltd.
Milton Keynes UK
UKOW05f1809230617
303960UK00002B/49/P